Ghost Country

Also by Chris Petit

Robinson
The Psalm Killer
Back from the Dead
The Hard Shoulder
The Human Pool
The Passenger
The Butchers of Berlin
Pale Horse Riding
Mister Wolf

Ghost Country

CHRIS PETIT

SIMON & SCHUSTER

London · New York · Sydney · Toronto · New Delhi

First published in Great Britain by Simon & Schuster UK Ltd, 2022

1 3 5 7 9 10 8 6 4 2

Simon & Schuster UK Ltd
1st Floor
222 Gray's Inn Road
London WC1X 8HB

Simon & Schuster Australia, Sydney
Simon & Schuster India, New Delhi

www.simonandschuster.co.uk
www.simonandschuster.com.au
www.simonandschuster.co.in

A CIP catalogue record for this book
is available from the British Library

Hardback ISBN: 978-1-4711-8876-3
Trade Paperback ISBN: 978-1-4711-8877-0
eBook ISBN: 978-1-4711-8878-7
Audio ISBN: 978-1-3985-1383-9

Typeset in Hoefler by M Rules
Printed and bound by CPI Group (UK) Ltd, Croydon, CR0 4YY

The Wild Bunch is simply what
happens when killers go to Mexico.

SAM PECKINPAH

I

'There is no such thing as remission, only undiagnosed illness,' her father told Charlotte Waites as they sat eating a late Christmas lunch. She stared at the array of pills in front of him. His recent health scare had turned out to be a false alarm but the battery of medication remained formidable.

They were in the old dining room, rarely used these days, with the silver service.

'This is where your grandmother used to entertain her lawnmowers for tea.'

It was a story he often told, how when still merely eccentric she treated the several machines she owned to her hospitality rather than the man who mowed.

Charlotte remembered another Christmas meal in the same room when she was a child. It was the only time she had seen her grandmother tipsy, on sherry, after which she spent the meal singing music hall songs to herself in a low birdlike trill. Towards the end of her life, her grandmother had ended up in the care home over the road after she had taken to wandering around local shops in a state of undress.

Charlotte had been fifteen the last time she saw her, one wet summer afternoon, in the home's day room, her chair apart from the other residents, who sat slumped in front of a television watching a film – from what she could hear Charlotte guessed *Planet of the Apes* – until one rose, staggered forward and changed channels, causing an uproar that brought staff running. The film was returned to and the residents resumed their comatose state.

Her grandmother ignored the disturbance. She had hunted in her younger days, riding sidesaddle, with the straightest back in the county. Now she sat vacant. A paperback lay on her lap. Charlotte asked what she was reading. *The Belstone Fox*, her grandmother said, passing it over with a sly smile. She hadn't put her teeth in. The dog-eared copy was so splayed it reminded Charlotte of an accordion. Inside she found a quarter of a partly eaten ham sandwich, covered in a green mould, squashed flat between the pages. She shut the book, and made a show of reading the cover, fearing her grandmother's madness awaited her.

Her father had lived in the house since retiring. It was a plain construction, dating from the early 1950s when there were still post-war building restrictions. Set well back from a road of dreary bungalows and houses, it stood in an acre of walled garden whose size was out of all proportion to the modest three-bedroom house. What Charlotte remembered as an enchanted space kept by her grandmother – mowing, weeding, pruning and even scything – had been allowed to run wild. Only the lawn immediately behind the house was occasionally mown by her father in summer. The rest was a jungle of holly thickets, towering brambles and invasive conifers planted by her grandmother, which obscured the view of the Malvern Hills beyond.

Charlotte had driven down empty motorways that morning and would stay for Boxing Day, before going on to Cheltenham for work. Cheltenham was forty minutes away, her father said; she was welcome to stay on and commute. Thanks all the same, she replied, trying to sound grateful, but she was booked in to a Premier Inn that was paid for.

The holiday was spent observing rituals to which neither subscribed: tree, presents and even a stocking for her, for fuck's sake – at thirty-two! – using the same old pillowcase with her childhood Pentel drawing of a Santa. This annual get-together, which more resembled a hangover of Christmas past than any present celebration, was all rather strange to Charlotte because her father was not nostalgic or sentimental. There wasn't a photograph to be seen in the house of her mother, dead ten years, or of herself, and her father's passage through life seemed to have gone unrecorded. This struck her as odd because he made a point of being seen as outgoing and charming, taking time to chat with local shopkeepers and so on. Over the years she had grown resistant to his charm, perhaps because she had refused to cultivate such a quality herself, mistrusting it as a male trope. She took more after her mother, reserved and sometimes sullen. She had worked hard to free herself of her mother's influence, being professional, competent and even ambitious, but she knew that withdrawal was her fallback position.

Once, during the protracted conflict of the last years of her parents' marriage, her mother had hissed to her while standing at the kitchen sink, 'He has a wank magazine in his sock drawer!'

Charlotte remembered being more surprised by her mother's language than the observation. The exclamation invited no response and there was nothing she could think of or wanted to say.

Although still eligible, and not so old, her father seemed to have made no effort to find anyone else after her mother died, so Charlotte presumed he maintained a regime of self-maintenance via the sock drawer (which she had never looked in, despite being tempted).

Her father had been in military intelligence, about which he was vague, apart from occasional mention of the Warsaw Pact and Northern Ireland. Charlotte suspected her own recruitment to the Home Office had had something to do with him. She had been approached after a couple of years of drifting through jobs following university, without ever considering such a career.

She still had trouble thinking of herself as a grown-up around her father.

She watched his stiff farewell wave in the rearview mirror as she drove away on the morning of 27 December. She crossed the river at Upton and took the motorway to Cheltenham. She was glad to have got Christmas over. She didn't even turn on the radio for company, brooding instead about work, its atmosphere of bullying and constant cuts. Hopkins had been brought in to steer what was known as the Leadership Team. The woman wasn't much older than her; had been friendly at first, but soon showed herself to be fast, intolerant, and expert at covering her back. There was her irritating cock of the head to signal disbelief and her talent for derailing any argument by correcting irrelevant details. Charlotte didn't know why Hopkins was picking on her. No one had before and she was ill-equipped to deal with it. She had been slow to realise that Hopkins was a refinement of the classic bully, clever enough to avoid accusation while selecting juniors to be the target of others' aggression, sacrificial figures in waiting.

The Home Office was not an employer to offer much hope or instil confidence, and under Hopkins office politics had become aggressively polite and deadly. Their jobs were in doubt. DAD, the Department of Analysis and Data, had been created before Charlotte's time, to liaise with

European security services in response to a technological revolution that still very few understood. Since leaving Europe it had fallen out of fashion, failed to compete and was underfunded as a result.

Before Hopkins, the office's reputation was for casual internal security. Thanks to her reforms, Charlotte had found herself in trouble after breaching a new rule requiring any computer left unattended, even during a coffee or toilet break, to be logged off. Nobody bothered because of the time it took to log on again. Hopkins's response to this was to make secret checks, using technicians pretending to be researchers. It was because of a summons by Hopkins that Charlotte had left her desk in the first place. As no one else was reported, she wondered if she had been called in because Hopkins wanted to catch her out.

The incident became connected in Charlotte's mind with the point of the meeting and whether that too wasn't as random as it had appeared. Hopkins had told her to check an intel flag that would not normally have required a face-to-face. According to Hopkins, it was because she was still getting to know her staff. A regular complaint of hers was to ask what anyone actually did.

The intel flag Hopkins wanted her to check mentioned a plan to assassinate a leading British politician. The source was a Russian site known for hacking, in this case emails and material belonging to a Dublin-based freelance journalist by the name of Brindley.

Charlotte rang him. Elderly, with a boozer's voice, both defensive and embarrassed because he had been foolish and responded to a phishing email. He insisted the assassination rumour had been inserted. He said he was old enough to know not to send inflammatory material that could be read by the huge network of security checking machines. Smart enough to know that, Charlotte thought, but mug enough to fall for a phishing email.

Other tainted material, according to Brindley, included mention of a Russian oligarch and his involvement in African sex trafficking and child prostitution. Brindley claimed he had never heard of the man.

She ran checks on the oligarch, a UK resident with a London address, who appeared to spend most of his time at another home in Liechtenstein. Her enquiries revealed that the London house was empty while being renovated. She checked the local residents' register and noted that a near neighbour was Secretary of State Michael McCavity. She ran his and the names of other prominent politicians through GCHQ's Tempora system, applied the appropriate trigger words and drew a blank, apart from one mention of McCavity on a Muslim hate site, calling him 'a mad dog deserving to be put down'.

Checking far-right and Islamic extremist platforms produced no sign of any intended attack.

The accusations of financial and sexual skulduggery against the Russian had been picked up by other sites. One noted the man's close association with Conservative MPs with no mention of the secretary of state. When Charlotte checked further on the internal Home Office system, she found full access to the Russian's file blocked. She concluded he fell into the category of yet another suppressed political report on Russian connections to the Conservative Party and left it at that as he wasn't the point of the enquiry.

By then she had decided Hopkins had probably set her the task as part of some secret internal assessment. There was talk of redundancies. She concluded that the intel flag was standard disinformation, reported it as such, and told Hopkins she had taken it as far as she could and the matter of the oligarch should be further investigated by someone with a higher clearance than herself. Because of the proximity of the minister's address, she recommended that his security team be advised of the situation. And that was that, however much she sensed Hopkins's disapproval at her lack of what were called 'decision-making skills'.

Given the couple of crap jobs she had been assigned over Christmas, Charlotte decided she had failed the test, whatever it had been, and was quickly becoming surplus to requirements within the department.

Situated on a ring road in Cheltenham, GCHQ's once futuristic design resembled a large, grounded flying saucer. In that deprecating English manner it was known as the Doughnut. The huge site reminded Charlotte of a planeless airport whose perimeter was given over to parking for five thousand cars. She was always struck by how this huge manifestation of the secret state stood in contrast to the staid Regency town. She could never quite see the point of Cheltenham.

Her next three days were spent in windowless basements, monitoring a recruiting exercise involving bright young technicians playing cyber war games. Only the numbered shirts of the examinees – most of them little more than school kids – indicated that an attack on a nuclear power station or a financial institution, which then escalated to include transport and utilities, might not be real. The tense atmosphere, the banks of monitors and subdued high-tech surroundings stood in contrast to the ramshackle set-up of Charlotte's London office, scarred by cutbacks, massive arse-covering and no sense of collective responsibility. General demoralisation had allowed a ruthless, buccaneering spirit to flourish at the top, which Charlotte had seen previously in the financial sector, only because it had been her misfortune to have briefly gone out with an investment banker.

Boyfriends she had never quite got the hang of. They had been selected from a small pool, usually work-related. What she thought interested her about someone usually turned out not to be the case. She was currently living with 'Clive', whom she found it hard to think of without the quotation marks. 'Living with' was rather overstating it. She shared his Barbican flat, which belonged to his parents, in exchange for paying rent and sex. For her, among the advantages of the relationship – Clive was quite eligible – were far better accommodation than the over-expensive shared rentals she was used to, whose standard of living was little better than when she had been a student. She in return was dutiful, tidied up after herself and cooked most of the meals because she was the better cook.

Part of her time in Cheltenham was spent having to listen to expensive consultants advise on how to make GCHQ recruitment more attractive. For all their flip charts and designer clothes, they offered the usual rehash of more social media, more neuro-diverse candidates to improve teamwork; more gamers, freaks and geeks; more summer schools; more black, Asian and minority ethnic backgrounds – none of which addressed why anyone would want to work there rather than be in London, or why they would sign on for a government department that could not compete with civilian salaries.

Charlotte's Premier Inn was down the wrong end of the high street. Looking for somewhere to eat, she soon found herself in a stretch that reflected the town's collapse. Several Polish stores were boarded up. The sweet shop had ceased trading. Cheltenham Kebabs-Burgers she didn't trust. The

Oriental Food Store was still in business but closed, as was the halal butchers. The one pub looked an unwelcoming dive. The one tea room was shut. Two Chinese takeaways in a row seemed to cancel each other out, as there were no takers in either.

She gave up and made do with a snack from the hotel vending machine.

After three days of dull work and two dreary Premier Inn nights, rather than drive to Birmingham and an identical hotel room for her job the next day, Charlotte turned off back to her father's, which was more or less on the way. She had meant to phone, thinking if he was out she would drive on. She was setting a sort of test, she realised, by surprising him to see if he really was pleased to see her.

Instead, she managed only to mess up his plans. She saw this immediately upon his opening the door and saying he had been expecting someone else.

Anyone she knew, she asked, thinking it must be a woman. Just a chum from army days, he told her. Charlotte knew most of them by name but not this one, who sounded Greek. She made polite noises, saying she didn't want to be in the way; she had just stopped off as she was passing. Her father over-insisted that she stay.

The friend turned up soon afterwards with an overnight case, after taking the short walk down from the station, which suggested he had visited before. He was good-looking in a Mediterranean way, maybe twenty-five years younger than her father, who was in his late seventies. Charlotte sensed the man was thrown by her presence. They ate an awkward supper of cold ham and salad, which she prepared and tidied away. Her father and his guest made polite conversation. Charlotte suspected she was in the way and shooed them off to the pub, watched television for an hour and went to bed early, unsettled by her intrusion. She supposed her father had wanted to talk shop but was inhibited by her presence. The friend, introduced as Dimitrios, puzzled her. Her father's regiment could not have been more English and friends throughout his life were drawn from the same class and background. Being nosy, she had asked how they had met and was told through NATO. The man's English was faultless. He said he was stopping off on his way up north.

She was woken by someone getting up in the night and heard the toilet flush. After that she lay awake fretting about work. Once fast-tracked, she was not any more it seemed. It was too late to call Clive, who was with his mother whose short-term memory was shot, confining her to endless repetition that Clive, in one of his funnier moments, said was like being in a Beckett play.

Charlotte left before the others were up and drove for an hour down the motorway to Birmingham International Airport, where she conducted two days of internal security reviews. More meetings in airless spaces among men of questionable personal hygiene; grey faces, beige carpets, plastic cups, watery coffee, no biscuits (budget cuts). The exercise was to test Border Force's internal security by sending Home Office staff posing as terrorists through immigration channels to see if they were picked up. They nabbed one and missed three. More meetings, more excuses. They were short-staffed because of illness and the holiday season. If morale was low in the Home Office it was rock bottom in Border Force. Charlotte listened to complaints that staff dispirited by pay freezes were being put under intolerable strain with longer hours, mounting caseloads and unrealistic targets. Most recruits quit within months, which left them relying on temporary staff with minimal training. The overall mood was dismal. She sighed at the thought of writing her report. Hopkins, a can-doer, was intolerant of bad news.

It was dark and starting to rain as Charlotte set out for London. The motorway was full of returning holiday traffic. Lorries were chucking up spray that reduced her visibility, which was already hampered by defective wipers. Her Astra was part of the office pool, unloved and poorly serviced. It smelt of something unpleasant and unidentifiable.

The rain fell harder. Charlotte didn't trust the car at more than fifty-five. She tucked into the inside lane, keeping her distance from the muck thrown up by the vehicle in front, which only left a space for the lorry behind to overtake and force her to repeat the process.

The squeak of the old wipers became like a mantra, leaving her in danger of drifting off. She stopped at the next service station. It was crowded and she sat and watched the people go about their distracted post-Christmas business with a look of those who could not quite believe what they had signed up for. Nothing had ever really returned to normal after the events of the last few years, though everyone tried to pretend it had. The tabloids were full of threats of imminent new waves of virus, stoking fears about border control and more lockdowns.

Motorway service stations did little to lift anyone's spirits, even if Watford Gap's choice was better than it once was. For all that, it still came down to the same old dreary cellophane-wrapped sandwiches, plastic bottles of water and too much confectionery at the check-out desks. The frustrated dads, the put-upon mums and their sullen kids made Charlotte wonder about the point of families. A classic portrait sat at the next table in silent communication with their mobile phones. Our island story.

It was the last day of the year. Everything continued to be sold off, regardless of the official optimism promoted by the government and media. No vision of the future was being offered, only a backward charge into a mythical past. At Charlotte's work the fallout was silent and invisible. Staff would abruptly disappear, followed by terse memos announcing their long-term illness; it was never quite clear whether these were real or just soft firings.

Charlotte filled up on the way out at the forecourt, paying well above the regular rate. She resisted the enticements of the Wild Bean coffee machine as she waited in a long line of customers, most of whom were there just to buy snacks and fizzy drinks rather than pay for petrol. Our island fucking story.

A hungover New Year's morning. What was the point of housework, Charlotte wondered while tidying the flat, when it all just got dirty again? Her mother had dedicated herself to it in exchange for no pleasure or reward from what Charlotte could see. But she could say the same of herself. She was just as much of a slave to a system. Her and Clive's jobs took up too much of their time. Clive worked for what he called a deadly dull think tank barely capable of stringing two ideas together and it wasn't worth talking about. He in turn asked little about her work and tried to sound reasonable when she banged on about Hopkins.

What was depressingly known as 'downtime' was spent recovering. There was always a backlog of work. You were never really allowed to be out of reach; staff were expected always to be on call.

That New Year's Eve they had gone out and drunk too much, watched fireworks on the river, gone to bed and had sex. The next morning they lay in and bickered over whose turn it was to make breakfast. It wasn't a row, but it wasn't far off one.

Clive had little to say about his Christmas, stuck with his mother repeating the same conversation every two minutes. It was good to be home, he said.

The apartment was rather grand, on the eighteenth floor of a Barbican tower with fine views to the north. For Charlotte the main advantage was a ten-minute walk to Upper Thames Street and work. Before that she had been condemned to fifty minutes on the District Line.

Clive was reasonably good-looking and could be amusing when he put his mind to it but, as with a lot of men who had been packed off to boarding school at an early age, there was an emotional hole (perhaps doughnut-shaped). Her own background had involved a useless progressive school in north London where, until she pulled herself together, her education consisted of smoking weed and running around with a gang of brash girls who called themselves the Jew Crew. Through hanging out with them she became acquainted with the cold draft of anti-Semitism. She was asked sometimes if she was Jewish herself. She denied it, always feeling uncomfortable without knowing why. The answer she eventually came to give – 'What if I was?' – left her equally unsatisfied. She adapted that to 'What if I were?' This was picked up by a pedant in the Foreign Office – a young man with a smooth complexion and a touching habit of blushing – who drolly observed, 'Use of subjunctive noted.'

New year, new broom. She had a week's washing and asked Clive if he had any. He dumped a pile on the floor. She automatically checked the pockets before loading and in the front of his jeans found a pair of knickers; not hers: a pink thong, fringed with black lace.

Her first reaction was to laugh. She was aware of Clive calling her. Her phone was ringing. She wondered what to do with the offending thong, stuffed it back where she had found it, and went and answered her phone, thinking about what to say to Clive. It was a short call. She hung up and went to get her coat.

'I'm needed at work,' she said. 'There's been a shooting.'

2

The call had come from Hopkins, tersely ordering Charlotte to attend a meeting at an address that turned out to be another dreary government building in Westminster, old enough to have swirly carpet.

She went in a daze, passing through the Barbican station turnstile, staring at the 'Mind the Gap' sign on the platform while waiting for a train (four minutes on the board; more like seven). Only as she swiped her card at the exit did the implications of what she had been told hit her. The secretary of state had been shot, after her report had said that wouldn't happen.

In the building's lobby she signed the visitors' book, noting on the page above her a senior military officer, the Met, counter-terrorism, as well as what she suspected were the intelligence services masquerading under obscure acronyms. Such a meeting would not normally involve her clearance level. It suggested what she had suspected, that she was there to account for herself.

A tinny lift took her up three floors to a conference room with people standing around drinking what was probably stewed coffee (cups and saucers), looking both subdued and put out at being dragged in on a bank holiday. She observed the preening alpha males and the shrinking cocks, then spotted the tall figure of Parker, the pariah of her department, standing on his own. His psoriasis looked worse than ever, hands purple and scaly, face and scalp covered with blotchy, cratered deposits of dry skin with angry red haloes. It was said he spent all his free time at the cinema watching old films, comfortable only in the dark.

Charlotte was worried that Hopkins had brought him as her backup. He was one of the information diggers and had been marginally involved in the Russian angle of the intel flag. She had referred to him about the oligarch because of his reputation as the best researcher. Everyone tended to avoid him, which was easily done as he worked alone in a hutch in the basement. He hadn't said much to her other than that he knew of her as the one who hadn't logged off.

There had been a later brief exchange when Parker raised the matter of the intel flag's authenticity and even wondered whether it was one of those exercises designed to keep everyone on their toes.

She'd asked what he meant.

'It's not impossible that someone this end hacked the Russian site and inserted the doctored emails as reverse mischief. But I wouldn't worry as that's not part of your brief.'

She couldn't decide whether Parker was sympathetic. Everything about the man was guarded. The office gossip was fanciful and malicious: that he lived on a diet of champagne, whelks and pork scratchings; that he drank a litre of olive oil a day for his skin; that he was a virgin in the market for a mail-order bride.

She went over. He was probably around her age but he behaved as though he were older, perhaps as a way of coping with his affliction.

'Hello, Beatrice,' he said.

Charlotte supposed he must have her muddled with someone else. Parker was blushing. She didn't know what to make of that other than to feel uncomfortable. She asked what was going on. Parker said he didn't know; it wasn't as though the secretary of state was on anyone's hit list. He added that he had been shot while out jogging. His tone implied that even the idea of jogging was absurd and sufficient motive for shooting the man. Charlotte wondered if Parker might be more mischievous than he let on.

'Happy New Year,' he said, suggesting it was anything but, and asked if she'd had plans for the day. Nothing she could think of, she replied, relieved at not spending it confronting or avoiding Clive. Parker said he was meant to attend a rare screening that afternoon at the National Film Theatre of Lars von Trier's *The Kingdom*, a Danish television miniseries from the 1990s set in a hospital. She only half-listened, dreading that her mistake would be exposed.

The meeting convened. They were told their minutes would be passed on to COBRA, which was sitting. Charlotte counted twenty-five around the long table: nearly all white men, mostly of an age, education and look; a few women; some of both sexes from minorities, and one or two drones, such as herself, struggling down the corridors of institutional power.

A senior woman from the Met established what was known. A shooting had occurred, which, given the target, indicated a political assassination or an act of terrorism. The facts to date were a single shot fired from a probably silenced rifle, at a distance, suggesting a professional marksman using a vantage point as yet unidentified. The shooting had occurred at 8.23am in Earl's Court. McCavity had left his house and was shot while exercising with his security guards, then he was taken to Cromwell Road Hospital where he remained in a critical state.

Charlotte broke out in a cold sweat: what if the shot

turned out to have been fired from the Russian's house? She thought she might keel over.

The woman from the Met asked for the opinions of others.

The Home and Foreign Offices said the situation wasn't yet clear in terms of demarcation of responsibility. Both referred to 'the target', which then became just 'target'. Charlotte, breathless and dizzy, had trouble following, apart from suspecting that no one really knew what they were talking about.

Parliamentary and Diplomatic Protection, which provided residential security for high-profile ministers, was keeping very quiet, other than to say it had followed procedure.

The senior bores led – 'Let us not be hasty in jumping to conclusions.' No one was claiming responsibility for the shooting yet.

Charlotte was sitting next to Parker, aware of others staring at him. She wondered how he shaved, asking herself only because he seemed an unlikely candidate for aftershave; perhaps the astringent helped his skin. The seat on his other side was empty, the only one in the room. Parker had an old-fashioned reporter's pad in which he occasionally wrote, using a Bic biro with a chewed end. He wrote in tiny capitals. The table surface around him was soon covered with a fine coating of powdery skin.

Most of the others were already on their mobiles busy texting and looking stuff up.

An officer from Counter Terrorism gave a brisk lecture on professional snipers, saying they usually worked in pairs, which raised the question of whether the shooter had used an accomplice. Operational essentials were preparatory scouting and a planned escape route, therefore it should be ascertained whether anyone unusual had been seen in the area prior to the shooting.

The door opened and a tall, silver-headed mandarin wandered in and looked around the room with amused contempt. His tag was stuffed in his top pocket, making it impossible to tell where he was from. Charlotte thought: Older, wiser and senior, probably from one of the snobbier departments, possibly the Foreign Office. His suit was a chalk-stripe that looked like it had been around for years, definitely not off-the-peg, which was the point; made to last and its wearing a small act of vanity, as if to say: See, I haven't had to have the waist let out. The man had kept his hair, which he wore brushed back. It was getting long over the ears and due a cut. The tie she didn't recognise – diagonal stripes representing whatever club, regiment or old school he belonged to. Double cuffs on the shirt, with links. The shoes she couldn't see. A man of his age and class would consider brogues too casual and even vulgar for the office. Charlotte knew all this only because her father had been a stickler for sartorial correctness, until he had retired and, as he put it, gone native. She had since seen him in jogging pants and denim, and – the horror – wearing Crocs, all of which he would have sneered at before.

The new arrival sat down in the empty chair next to Parker. Single vent in his jacket, Charlotte noted. Another of her father's judgements was never trust a man with double vents. She noticed manicured hands and wondered if it was an acceptable part of a gentleman's grooming or a bit of a giveaway. His opaque pale eyes reminded her of children's gobstoppers. He looked like he had been lethal in his day, one of those known as being good at games, including the bedding department.

Parker was occasionally making a strange snuffling noise.

He couldn't care less what he wore, Charlotte could see, beyond it being a symphony of brown – shabby corduroy jacket, shiny at the elbows; shapeless cardigan; baggy trousers and ancient Hush Puppies, with parts of the suede rubbed to black. Parker's affliction and scruffiness would be an affront to the man next to him, to whom correct appearance was an indication of breeding and superiority. It remained a highly coded world. In her Premier Inn she had watched an old television show from before she was born, which she had found at the higher end of the channel ladder, where the cheap stuff and old dross were, after wasting twenty minutes of her life watching a shopping programme. The drama was set in the Inns of Court. Charlotte found it mildly entertaining and a bit depressing, with stalwart actors – most of them probably dead – and a far greater sense of class gradation than was apparent now. The depressing part was showing how the world had changed beyond recognition but at the same time hardly at all, with many of the old assumptions still evident in the room in which she sat.

Parker looked like he thought all meetings were a waste of time. It took twenty minutes to conclude what anyone with common sense would have arrived at in five: databases of known terrorists and trained marksmen to be scoured, shooting club members' lists to be gone over. Islamist terrorists were discounted. Charlotte broke into a sweat again, thinking of the hate site calling for the secretary of state to be put down like a mad dog. In the mangled drawl of another counter-terrorist expert, such a shooting was considered too specific as Islamists tended to blow things up, smash into them or run amok. Someone mentioned the Christchurch and Norway massacres, which provoked mild panic in case this was the start of a spree.

The elephant in the room was the Russians but no one seemed keen to bring that up. In the way of such meetings, procedure was less about tactical response than departmental defence, about not appearing insufficiently forewarned or playing into the hands of rivals: the old bureaucratic two-step.

A dark-skinned man's mobile burbled. Its ringtone – Cockney Rebel's 'Make Me Smile' – temporarily undid the gravity of the situation.

'It's the hospital,' he said, and announced he was a doctor. He left the room to take the call.

Parker was writing in his notepad. Seeing Charlotte looking, he turned away, so she was surprised when he slid the pad towards her. The fine snow of dandruff covering the table's shiny surface lay disturbed where he had moved it.

She read: 'Only a matter of time before school kids on the rampage mow down classmates, and shooters shoot up malls.'

Charlotte didn't know why Parker was showing her. Paranoia left her wondering whether he was trying to catch her out, or if he was reading the event differently from everyone else. He had a reputation for lateral thinking.

Her response was to shrug, neither agreeing nor disagreeing.

Parker retrieved the pad and wrote again. Charlotte looked past Parker at the chalk-stripe man, sitting ramrod straight, apparently unaware of their exchange.

Parker's next note read: 'The red-tops will drum up a state of Mexican-style grief, to distract from the real agenda – demands for ramped-up security.'

Charlotte didn't know what to make of that either. If Parker was a subversive why should he trust her with his views? But he had a point. Increased security would be a financial lifeline for Hopkins if the department could be reorganised to meet such needs. The woman was probably already assessing the situation for what might be gained.

Charlotte slid the pad back, grateful for the distraction from the inevitable moment when Hopkins would ask her to share her thoughts with the meeting.

Having finished his call, the doctor returned. The chalk-stripe man used the moment to help himself to Parker's pad. He had noticed after all. Charlotte studied his face as he read. It remained impassive. He returned the pad without comment but Charlotte thought she detected a glint of hard amusement.

The doctor put on a good-news face. The patient was, against all odds, hanging on. The bullet had travelled the length of the left side of the brain. Its trajectory was cause for optimism. Surviving such a trauma depended on the brain areas penetrated, the velocity of the bullet and whether it had exited. Someone suffering injury to both sides of the brain would stand no chance. That the patient had been capable of responding to those addressing him after his injury indicated he was still capable of understanding and processing language, which boded well for his recovery.

Charlotte wondered if the news let her halfway off the hook.

The doctor droned on, making the most of his moment, spared being the purveyor of bad news.

Charlotte googled: What chance of surviving getting shot in the head.

An even stranger feeling of unreality descended. The doctor's summary was a virtual crib of what she was reading. Expert or not, he seemed to be taking the same short cuts as everyone else by looking stuff up.

The doctor was interrupted by a call for the woman from

the Met; her ringtone was a more sombre old-fashioned telephone jangle.

It was police at the scene, she announced, nodding briskly as she listened, holding her hand up to show the news was important. She rang off and said that the probable location of the sniper's nest was a house undergoing renovation, not being worked on that morning because of the holiday. It was said to belong to a Russian.

Charlotte thought she might be physically sick and swallowed hard, dimly aware of Hopkins saying, 'We might have something on that. Ms Waites here can explain.'

She sensed the chalk-stripe man inspecting her as she desperately composed her thoughts, until the woman from the Met prompted, 'Well?'

When at last Charlotte spoke up she was grateful that the words came out in more or less the right order. The intel flag. The hacked emails. The Russian site. Disinformation. Apart from a coincidence of geography, there was nothing to suggest any connection between the Russian and the target, or the credibility of any such assassination plan.

'Until now,' someone said.

'How seriously was this taken at the time?' someone else asked.

Hopkins chipped in to say that correct procedure had been followed. Charlotte was thankful she was not being altogether dumped in it.

She was left to field questions. The mood was curious and hostile.

Yes, she had spoken to the Irish journalist and his story stood up.

Yes, she had checked out the Russian. No, she hadn't talked to him as he was not available, being abroad.

She was asked if she had gone to the address.

She listened to herself explain how she had checked out the site, posing as HMRC, investigating possible financial irregularities relating to jobs done without paying VAT.

And what had she found?

Just a house in the early stages of renovation with no expense spared.

Nothing irregular?

Nothing apart from the absence of a project manager, who was off sick that day.

And the workers?

Mainly Ukrainians.

She was asked if she spoke Ukrainian.

She said some could speak English and they had told her where they were from.

Had they appeared suspicious in any way?

The implication was one might have been the shooter. Charlotte was tempted to say they hadn't looked like secret agents but restricted herself to answering in the negative.

One of the bores wanted to know if the Ukrainians were working in accordance with building regs, and so forth.

Charlotte wondered at the point of the question, under the circumstances.

She said the building had been properly boarded, with the usual displays announcing they were caring contractors, and they'd all had luminous jackets and hard hats – she had been given a set to wear herself and ended up feeling like she was in *Grand Designs*.

Nothing appeared out of the ordinary, she insisted.

Including the books?

She had in fact been referred to a management company, which was able to show payments were invoiced. She had wondered about that because the Russians had a habit of using casual labour, but apparently not in this case.

She was asked what this had to do with the original intel flag. The question implied she had been wasting time.

Feeling more confident, she countered that had irregularities been found she would have reported them to HMRC.

The next question returned to Brindley, the Irish journalist. Was Ms Waites aware the man was a friend of the IRA?

She was spared answering because someone else interrupted to ask if she had verified the Russian insertions.

She lied and said she had referred the emails to 'an expert' – she was thinking of Parker though she hadn't discussed it with him – to scrutinise for inconsistencies of language and style, and this expert had pinpointed the two sections the journalist claimed he hadn't written: the business of the Russian and the possible political assassination.

Had the target been named?

Only as a senior politician.

Had she identified who it might be?

She thought of the Muslim hate site and wasn't sure how to answer.

She was saved by the interjection of a man asking in disbelief, 'We're not saying it's IRA?'

Attention shifted from her to dismiss any such idea. IRA turf wars these days were reduced to local vigilante action, usually against drug dealers.

Charlotte sensed she had just about got away with it. She had done nothing wrong in the first place, she told herself. She had answered each question carefully without making a fool of herself, thinking as she did how they all spent their lives staring at screens and were rendered comatose by the sheer volume of information being flung at them.

Attention turned to whether the Russians would be stupid enough to draw attention to themselves by using such a clearly connected location for the sniper. The man asking answered himself, saying, 'Unless they want to discredit the homeowner.'

A man next to him piped up. 'That said, the Russians tend to be more surreptitious. Poison and so forth.'

A third suggested they wait and see. In the meantime, some digging on the house owner needed to be done.

Someone else asked, 'Is there any documentation on this?'

Charlotte answered that she had submitted a report. She did not mention that she had been denied full access to the oligarch's file.

Hopkins butted in to say she had copies and started passing them around.

When handed hers, Charlotte looked at what she had written and saw that Hopkins had dropped her in it after all. The report was and yet was not hers. Unlike the journalist's emails, nothing had been added but there were omissions. Mention of the Muslim website looked as though it hadn't been followed up. The recommendation of a referral to the minister's security detachment was no longer there. In the light of events, it read like a sloppy piece of work.

Charlotte blurted out that it must be a mistake – it was not her report and had to be the work of whomever it had been referred on to.

The woman from the Met said, 'There's no mention of any referral,' and looked to Hopkins, who confirmed that its contents were as she had received them. Hopkins was so sure of herself that Charlotte couldn't decide whether she was lying because she'd had the report doctored or was covering her back by dropping Charlotte in the shit.

What Hopkins said next astonished Charlotte even more: that she probably should not have entrusted Ms Waites with the job because she had been found in breach of office regulations and was exhibiting signs of stress; the first Charlotte had heard.

'That was my mistake,' conceded Hopkins, before offering a half-hearted endorsement of Charlotte's abilities, however clear it was that she had no faith in them.

Hopkins spoke briskly, pointing out that the internet was full of false leads. She had the figures at her fingertips, down to the high percentage of such cases that turned out to be a waste of time. She concluded that nothing significant enough to follow up had emerged from Ms Waites's findings, implying that, however insufficient they were, there were no glaring omissions. Her tone made it clear that this was not the end of the matter. Charlotte suspected she would be subjected to an endless post-mortem. Her immediate concern was that someone would leak the story to the press with her name attached, setting her up to take the blame. She wondered if Hopkins would ask her to resign.

With the meeting adjourned, everyone looked busy. Tight huddles consulted. Charlotte was aware of glancing looks. She couldn't wait to get out. She didn't know what to do. Parker seemed to be avoiding her. Hopkins would leave her dangling.

The chalk-stripe man stood surveying the room with an air of superior knowledge. Parker stared at the floor as he moved aside to let Charlotte past. She squeezed by the chalk-stripe man, keeping her head down, staring at his tie.

He said, 'It won't tell you much.' She looked up. 'The tie,' he said, his gaze fixed on her. 'I Zingari cricket club. Amateur.'

The eyes were unblinking. He seemed to enjoy her humiliation. Charlotte wasn't sure how she would get through the rest of the day. She was angry at the thought of Clive and the knickers she'd found. She was aware of the chalk-stripe man addressing her but she was distracted by seeing Parker leave with Hopkins, so missed the first part and tuned in only as he said, 'At least you didn't roll over. Fought your corner. Like your father.'

Flustered, Charlotte wondered how on earth the man knew her father.

Before she could say anything he strolled off, hands in pockets, leaving her standing alone in a state of acute anxiety in a nearly empty room. Mind the gap, she thought.

3

As Charlotte passed through St James's Park station she caught a glimpse of herself on a monitor, looking apprehensive. She took the Tube to London Bridge and went to the office. Senior staff had rooms with views of the river. Hers, shared with eighteen others, looked out on to a narrow canyon of grubby light and the flank wall of the building next door.

The office was too old to accommodate the necessary technology for their department and required a lot of improvised ducting. Their allocated square footage reduced them to the working equivalent of battery hens. There was something uniquely dispiriting about that many adults sitting in cubby holes under unflattering lights, staring at computers.

She logged on and scrolled through her sent emails until she came to the attachment she had mailed to Hopkins. She opened it, started to read and saw it was not her report but that morning's doctored version.

She sat back, asking herself could she really have been so careless?

She looked to check the folder that contained her drafts and final copy. But the folder wasn't on the desktop where it should be.

She searched all her other folders, in case she had accidentally moved it; she hadn't. She tried everything she could think of, refusing to accept that her computer had been tampered with. Because it was her computer she figured the fault was somehow hers. There must be something she had overlooked. Then she remembered her reflex habit of emailing important documents to herself as a backup. What she had sent Hopkins should still be lying unopened in her own inbox.

Except it wasn't.

She started to panic. Computers did what they were told. Hers now appeared hostile.

She checked the rest of her sent box. She couldn't locate any of her emails dealing with the intel flag, including a couple to the journalist Brindley. She checked her trash to see if everything had somehow ended up there. It hadn't.

Apart from her doctored report, there was no evidence of any of her work or contacts for the file.

Fuck, she thought. The cleaners had been in.

Hopkins arrived looking purposeful and immediately summoned her. Charlotte went fearing the worst.

Without bothering to look up, Hopkins said, 'You are to report to Moffat. He is waiting for you at the RAC in Pall Mall.'

Charlotte asked who Moffat was.

'He asked for you so I presumed you would know.'

It was phrased as a question when it wasn't, accompanied by that annoying cock of the head.

'Moffat?' repeated Charlotte stupidly.

'This morning's meeting. The man next to Parker.'

The chalk-stripe man. I Zingari. Knew her father. Did Hopkins know that? What if Moffat were calling her in over Hopkins's head? She wouldn't be happy about that.

There was more. Hopkins appeared nervous. From having the upper hand, she now seemed to be cast in the role of messenger, and wary of Charlotte. She told her to go home and pack for an overnight stay.

'Overnight?' Charlotte said, surprised.

Hopkins replied, 'Is there an echo in the room?'

Charlotte went up to the roof and called Clive, dreading that he might be at home. He wasn't, he said. She wondered how much she really knew about him. He never introduced her to his colleagues but then neither did she. The Thames below her was sluggish and brown, the sky overcast. It was cold. She should have brought her coat.

She told him she would be away for the night and, curious to know if she might catch him out, said, 'I found a pair of knickers in your pocket.'

He managed a baffled laugh and said, 'I am sure I don't know what you mean.'

'In your black jeans for washing. A thong.'

He tried to make a joke of it. 'Not my mother's then.'

Charlotte hung up, thinking had she been there she probably would have hit him. Perhaps Clive was a better liar than she thought.

Before she left the roof she called her father and asked about Moffat.

'Moffat?' he asked, making a point of remembering, then said they were acquainted at best. 'That said, better avoided. They were all shits in SIS.'

SIS. MI6. Charlotte thought it typical of him to use the less familiar term, just as it was typical that he showed no curiosity. She told him anyway how Moffat was asking for her. She said everyone was running around in circles after the shooting, desperate to avoid blame.

Her father didn't sound very bothered. He asked what the weather was like. She waited for him to say goodbye, so was surprised when he announced that she should be careful of Moffat.

'In what way?'

'He had a habit of dropping people in it.'

Why me? she thought. Had Moffat chosen her because of her name?

She went home and chucked some things in a bag but didn't take her laptop because she hadn't been told to and she wasn't feeling co-operative. She put the washing on, making a point of removing the thong from Clive's pocket before chucking it in with the rest, then texted him to hang the clothes to dry.

Thinking of a taxi, she saw she was short of cash. She stopped off at the NatWest by the station. Both ATMs were out of order, which left her no choice but the Tube.

Barbican to Green Park was normally twenty minutes. Because of the reduced holiday timetable it took forty. A good service was announced on all lines except hers.

The RAC looked much like the rest of Pall Mall, built in the establishment's favoured style of solid and imposing with little of distinction or merit.

The receptionist told Charlotte she was expected and directed her to a tea room where the decor was fussy, with loads of painted gold. Moffat was now dressed in a hacking jacket, cravat and chukka boots, looking as though he had just been riding in Green Park. A New & Lingwood shopping bag lay beside his chair.

Moffat said he had taken the liberty of ordering tea, which promptly arrived after she sat down.

'Let me be mother,' he said. 'Milk in first?'

Charlotte wasn't falling for that and said whichever. She wondered whether the occasion was going to be spent jumping etiquette hurdles.

The cucumber sandwiches looked harmless enough.

'Tuck in,' said Moffat. 'You look like you could do with feeding up.'

Charlotte saw she was expected to be on her best behaviour and was almost too eager to make up for what had been seen as her mistake.

Moffat said, 'I want you to trawl through our distinguished minister's back catalogue. See if you can come up with any angle on who might have wanted to shoot him.'

Charlotte tugged at her skirt, aware of Moffat inspecting her legs.

'From the obvious to the far-fetched,' he went on.

'Far-fetched?'

'Say that fellow in Norway mentioned in the meeting, who mowed down all those people on that island.'

'Breivik.'

'That's the one.'

Charlotte suspected Moffat cultivated deflection as a way of checking how up-to-speed she was. But were they really looking for a psycho-killer?

Moffat continued. 'Breivik produced a 1500-page manifesto. Saw himself as a Knight Templar on a crusade against the infidel. In it he made approving mention of the secretary of state for their shared views. Are you familiar?'

She wasn't.

'They both believed that liberalism, immigration and multiculturalism have allowed radical Islamism to undermine and take over western civilisation.'

He made it sound inevitable.

Why me? thought Charlotte again.

Moffat answered her unspoken question. 'I am told you have sound instincts, do good research, and your department is not overtaxed.'

She was surprised by his assessment. It couldn't have come from Hopkins.

'I am rather under a cloud at the moment,' Charlotte volunteered, hoping she might yet extricate herself from whatever it was that Moffat wanted.

'Of course. But you are familiar with the run-in, so you are up to speed. There's the coincidence of my knowing your father. Unfashionable these days, I dare say, but such connections still count. "People like us", as they say. I want you to look for the footprint, look for the backstory, use your female intuition.'

Patronising, she thought.

'Everything you need is upstairs – computer and all the rest. Free wi-fi. A south-facing single with views of Big Ben and Parliament. Quite comfortable.'

The last thing Moffat said was: 'Go away, immerse yourself and meet me here tomorrow at twelve. Avoid conspiracy theories if you can.'

Easier said than done; the internet was bursting with them but nothing yet on the shooting.

A trawl of YouTube showed McCavity's public manner to be almost aggressively polite and schoolmasterish. He liked to point out that an interviewer had got a minor fact wrong, which let him sidestep any accusation. It was a trick Charlotte recognised from Hopkins.

He was a friendly face on breakfast TV, pally on the sofa, with orthodontist's teeth and expensively cut hair. What seemed to distinguish him from most of his colleagues was the cultivation of a public image that moved seamlessly between politics and broadcast entertainment where he was competitive to a fault while suggesting he was still able to laugh at himself. The humour seemed acquired rather than natural.

Public displays had included a successful stint on *Celebrity MasterChef,* which had led to a short-lived restaurant column for the *Evening Standard*, which he announced he was giving up after a few weeks because he was 'getting a bit of a tum'. On a *Who Wants To Be a Millionaire?* celebrity special he had got a football question, a subject on which he professed to be proudly ignorant. Having already previously asked the audience, he phoned a friend ('You are probably surprised I have any') who didn't know, then went fifty-fifty and guessed wrong.

Charlotte was intrigued by these performances, all but forgotten steps towards creating the impression of a willing participant. He'd had a teary moment on *Who Do You Think You Are?* as he shared how his parents had died in a car crash on the A1, in the days before seatbelts became law. As an orphaned only child, aged six, he had been taken in and raised by what sounded like a coven of Protestant maiden aunts in the Northern Irish town of Portadown. He described himself as a proud 'redbrick boy': grammar school; University of Manchester (Philosophy, Politics and Economics). Inspired by his school motto, 'With courage and courtesy', he had aspired to a life in politics and 'helping people'.

Charlotte wasn't sure how much of this show of dedication she believed, any more than she bought the man's explanation for remaining unmarried for so long because he enjoyed the company of women too much to settle for one.

She found one incident of reprobate behaviour, dating back a dozen years, when he had been arrested for being drunk and disorderly after he was found staggering alone on Clapham Common at 3am, in shirtsleeves, with the temperature below zero. The contrition was handled with aplomb: a wry apology for 'bad-boy behaviour', excused by the explanation that he had gone to a private party where his drink had been spiked by unnamed political enemies in the hope of provoking an incident. If the story was improbable, the delivery was convincing, with its hint of chicanery.

Charlotte wondered if the man was in the closet. More clicks. A recent photograph showed him opening a village charity fete in his constituency. A woman was standing next to him, both of them grinning; identified as his wife.

He had been married six months. Click. Big spread in *Hello!* magazine and more grinning. So he was not above exploiting himself. The bride had her own following as a combative radio talk-show host. Charlotte vaguely recognised her – plump and comely, a peroxide blonde, Welsh lilt, strident views. Another forgettable celebrity, she thought sourly. Two kids from a previous marriage, with whom she lived in a large house in north London where her new husband now spent half his week. The woman's hair, Charlotte read – thanks to the Mail Online's 'Marriage of Styles' – had been kept that way since her stint in some minor indie band. Charlotte checked: one hit had made the Top Twenty, just. Yesterday's anarchy had calcified into fog-horn views, espousing patriotic values, which she maintained had been there all along.

The size of McCavity's own house in Earl's Court and the ubiquitous Range Rover indicated rather more than the combined income of a Parliamentary salary and occasional journalism; there was no £250,000 a year column. She googled to ask if any financial irregularity was attached to the name. Like many, he had been caught out in the MPs' expenses scandal years ago, claiming several thousand pounds' worth of furnishings, but it wasn't as though he had used taxpayers' money to have a castle moat dug, as one had. Further clicks led her to an article on vested interests, with alleged high-profit investments in a drugs company while a junior health minister. According to the story, the company had lobbied him to oppose the legalisation of cannabis medication because it was developing its own pharmaceutical version, which could be patented, whereas the natural stuff could not, and the company wasn't keen on competition. He had pushed hard against any prescription of the natural variety, forcing the medical profession to close ranks.

The story hadn't been picked up from what Charlotte could see. McCavity got a kind press on the whole because he had made a point of remaining a friend of the tabloids, having served in what he called their trenches, before moving on to edit Sunday broadsheets. Charlotte remembered her father complaining how these had been taken downmarket and a profession that had once pursued real stories became trivialised.

The man's political views were more extreme than Charlotte was expecting, given the cultivated manner. What he stood for focused more on what he was against. As Moffat had noted, he had talked up the Islamic threat following the London 2005 bombings in newspaper columns attacking 'Muslim terror enabled by democratic appeasement'.

The same fault had been applied to Northern Ireland in older articles. He denounced the 1998 Good Friday Agreement, saying that the IRA should never have been negotiated with, but smashed and eradicated.

It was easy to glide over such hardline views because they were expressed in mushy prose, modulated to appear reasonable where another writer might have turned such material into populist rants. Even so, she noted recurring tropes: alarmism; identification of an evil enemy; criticism of liberal elites; intolerance of alternatives. Yet it was all done in a way that was curiously forgettable; deliberately, perhaps, because the man seemed to understand that in a world of content overload any position was liable to revision. Charlotte suspected what actually mattered were the moves no one saw, seeking the levers of power rather than any display of it.

She supposed, given his views on the IRA, she was bound to ask whether there might be a connection to the shooting, involving long memories of harboured revenge, but that morning's meeting had declared it a spent force.

She switched tack, surfing in pursuit of the Norwegian shooter Breivik, mentioned by Moffat. As was the way with such meandering paths, she found herself hunting down McCavity's apparent endorsement of a woman described as 'an anti-Islam hate preacher'. She didn't know what to expect so was surprised when the woman in question turned out to be quite a famous and beautiful darling of the American media. She was even more surprised by her history of fraud and fabrication, available at a couple of clicks, and her apparent defence of Breivik, who had cited her with approval. Other sources maintained she was misquoted. The woman's imaginative biography had done her no harm. She had married a British historian who was a face on telly. She seemed to Charlotte in many ways typical of the age: a photogenic saleswoman with a hard message and an unapologetic knack for reinvention. But, as with what was available on McCavity, it was hard to distinguish between fact, gossip and spite. Browser beware, Charlotte told herself as she pressed on.

Several more clicks took her down a vertiginous slide into a murky world of uncensored hate that was like finding a secret diary purporting to tell the real truth lurking beneath the surface of decorum and civilisation. Most of it was reminiscent of her skimming of Breivik's turgid manifesto, a cut-and-paste of second-hand opinion: 'faux liberals' and something called the 'anti-new atheist brigade', whatever that was, versus 'anti-Muslim neocon warmongers' and 'pro-Zionists known to whitewash Zionist crimes'. Another site declared: 'Scratch an Islamophile even a little bit, uncover a raving anti-Semite.' Charlotte couldn't decide if McCavity was a digestible version of such ravings, repackaged for *Daily Mail* readers.

She moved on and wasted more time on a hobby of her father's: the 1963 assassination of President John F. Kennedy. She looked it up to re-familiarise herself with the most famous so-called lone-gun shooting of all.

That morning's gunman had also used a rifle from a high distance, except the shooter remained at large whereas Lee Harvey Oswald had been arrested shortly after. The official verdict that Oswald acted alone had been questioned endlessly since, leaving unresolved whether it was a coup d'état. Oswald hadn't been given the chance to tell his side, being gunned down two days later while being transferred under police escort, shot by a Dallas night-club owner with Mafia connections, in a killing watched by millions on nationwide television. The deaths of the alleged perpetrator and his victim had both been caught on camera, with none of the questions answered.

Charlotte suspected the truth about Kennedy's death had been deliberately obscured by all the crap placed around it. Her father had studied the case for years, to no end other than to drive himself half-crazy. His only conclusion was that conspiracy theories were an inevitable consequence of the lapsed state, in which doubt replaced faith. Charlotte hadn't understood what he meant by that but staring at the screen she had her own small epiphany – how thanks to social media everything could be shown to be a conspiracy. She suspected Twitter feeds were already developing their own theories about that morning's shooting, and if some authority were responsible it would be inserting its own disinformation. The obvious difference between Kennedy and the current shooting was that one was an obvious target and the other was not.

She did six hours straight: zig-zagging and regrouping. An interesting strand emerged, drawing attention to McCavity's possibly crucial role in masterminding the Brexit Leave campaign from behind the scenes, while a couple of clowns were sent out to front the show. A few journalists had pointed out, to largely deaf ears, that it had amounted to a political coup, through the manipulation of law and social media. Charlotte suspected that McCavity's avoidance of Twitter was because he was smart enough to know how it could be manipulated. He was interesting in that respect: even the arch fogeys in the party tweeted all the time.

There were rumours that he wasn't happy with his later elevation to a Cabinet full of duds and yes men. Charlotte found an off-the-record remark attributed to him, saying this wasn't all disadvantage because it left him to get on with the proper job of dismantling the old for a better new. That job involved reconstructive surgery on the 'castrated British bulldog', which through the development of hi-tech would emerge with 'balls bigger than ever'.

McCavity's pronouncements about 'our great heritage' were parroted by the right-wing press while a few independent voices claimed he was selling them down the river – the United Kingdom, or what was left of it, would become a hi-tech brothel for rent, with the economic collapse of other sectors blamed on 'enemies'. One *Guardian* opinion piece declared it wasn't a conspiracy as such, more an internal revolution within the establishment led by a core of zealots, largely unaccountable and hard to identify, of which the secretary of state was fingered as a possible leading player.

Charlotte watched a clip of the man being asked whether the Leave campaign had used illegal funds. He denied it. Charlotte thought: He touches his tie when he lies. It wasn't even a giveaway, more a sign for those in the know, as though the lies should be seen just as little entertainments.

While not usually short of words, in another interview, when asked about Vote Leave abandoning its appeal against the Electoral Commission's finding of financial illegality, he remained silent, the tie untouched.

A few clicks later Charlotte was reading how the questionable funds had been paid to a Canadian firm, fronting for a British one – Cambridge Analytica, since defunct, usefully summarised as an IT service management company and political consultant – which combined misappropriation of digital assets, data mining, data brokerage, and data analysis with strategic communication during the electoral processes. As one does, thought Charlotte.

'Move fast and break things' was a war cry of the Silicon Valley crowd that she remembered as one of those smart, meaningless slogans. The exhortation struck her when she found herself returning to Cambridge Analytica. It had a history of political manipulation in Third World countries and was cultivated by Donald Trump's then political strategist, Steve Bannon, who was a fast mover and broke things. Charlotte's image of the man went little further than a volatile, right-wing loudmouth, but such men were always mad at something. They were all angry. Charlotte wasn't sure whom she meant by 'all' or whether anger had played a part in the shooting. But Trump's man had identified the rage of the unheard as the key to political change and understood how social media could be used to channel that. With the Leave campaign, technicians had taken it to the dark side. Breivik to Brexit didn't strike her as such a stretch in that it was possible a mind as disturbed as Breivik's could have been applied to the further reaches of institutional psychopathic thinking.

It was a risky business for the establishment to pose as anti-establishment and could always explode in one's face. Charlotte wondered if it had. Was the shooting perhaps a result of what US intelligence called blowback – the unintended consequence of a covert operation that rebounded on its operators?

Midnight passed, each click leading to another. Charlotte dived into the murky world of think tanks – that sphere of invisible influences where McCavity turned out to be a terrific joiner: founder member of a charity-registered neoconservative one; adviser to another, described by enemies as 'top hate enablers'; founder member of a third, operating under the guise of democratic principles but held by opponents to be deeply Islamophobic and a supporter of the war on terror. One of these institutions, while he was its chair, had produced a report whose anti-Islam agenda was exposed, along with pro-Israel funders. According to another site, as under-secretary for education, McCavity had been behind banning school workshops on Palestinian literature. More clicks. Much of the material was questionable yet it was difficult not to get sucked in. The enormous beast of information had an answer to almost everything. She wasn't sure where it had got her other than to realise that before the internet it would have taken weeks to assemble what she had, involving a snail's trail of telephone calls, leads, false leads, legwork, interviews, digging, talking to someone who knew a man, and so on.

Charlotte was starting to think anyone could have done it. Perhaps, as with the Kennedy shooting, they could stretch the conspiracy to show that everyone had been involved – CIA, Mafia, the vice president, oil billionaires and the entire military-industrial complex.

Let's not forget the Russians, she thought, as she pursued another think tank whose members inevitably included the secretary of state, with a mission to create global pathways from poverty to prosperity. The institute's founder had made his fortune in Russia and was suspected of intelligence links to Moscow.

Which took Charlotte back to where she had come in: a leaked email with an insert about a Russian living in London – a man of murky background, a friend of the Conservatives, and possibly protected. And said Russian owned a house used by the shooter.

Charlotte found nothing to suggest that the target had sufficient enemies at home for anyone to eliminate him. The strongest angle seemed to lie in geopolitics and the Middle East. McCavity subscribed to the idea of an Islamic crusade to destroy the West, aided and abetted by the usual suspects: the left, political correctness, the elite, academics and the media; all guilty. Several clicks later Charlotte was trawling through the dark, apocalyptic world of far-right Islamophobic conspiracy theories where everything spiralled, looped and made a mad kind of sense.

Enough, she thought, when she found herself reading about a French racist novel from the 1970s, in which France capitulated to an unarmed invasion of starving, sex-crazed Indian refugees.

Start at home, she told herself, after making coffee. The shooting had occurred in the man's neighbourhood not at Ben Gurion Airport.

She read for two hours, not taking notes, and at the end thought she might have something. The aspect of the man's career which most nagged her was his tenure as under-secretary of education when almost certainly false secret Islamist documents revealing a conspiracy to radicalise Birmingham schools had been leaked to the media. They referred to a Muslim Trojan horse and the press, disregarding their questionable authenticity, had run with the story enough for the education authorities to crack down on threatened schools with dawn raids, aggressive inspections and the appointment of an anti-terrorist expert to supervise.

But whose Trojan horse? Charlotte agreed with the sceptics that the reference was more typical of anti-Muslim groups. Breivik had adopted the term in his manifesto. Right-wing politicians and white supremacists shared the view that the Muslim horse was now inside the citadel. Charlotte could find nothing pointing to those behind the fabrication but if McCavity had been one of Brexit's masterminds, working largely offstage – and he had attracted little attention during the campaign – had he been doing the same earlier? The answer still came as a shock. An idle enquiry showed that while still in newspapers he had shared bylines with the journalists who had broken the Trojan horse story. It didn't prove anything but the connection was there.

Charlotte asked herself whether there might be any link between the Birmingham schools affair and the shooter. She found herself looking up army bases in the Midlands region and came up with the Mercian Regiment, whose first and second battalions had served in Iraq and Afghanistan.

She wrote: 'Had a serving soldier, say Muslim, come back and developed a grudge?'

Breivik had been an obsessive gamer, spending months

immersed, and she added: 'What if the shooter were a product of military discipline *and* violent internet fantasies?'

So many of these games were about slaughter. The risk to the player was inconsequential because even after losing lives you came back. It was about adrenalin and reward, solitary and group fantasies, peer pressure, and always the screen. Ninety-nine per cent of the time it stayed in the room.

Charlotte found herself pitched into Breivik's world. A disturbed kid in the way a lot from split families were, but not so different. His self-proclaimed metrosexual life in middle-class Oslo seemed almost more reassuringly real than Clive's infidelity, which Charlotte found impossible to process as something that might actually be happening to her. What disturbed her most was how shallow and boring Breivik's world was, yet how logical the progression was towards killing.

When she at last made a list for Moffat she had:

1) Muslim terrorist operation, despite the uncharacteristic method.
2) Hired gun, an ex-soldier, either acting alone or for a third party, even an outside chance of the IRA.
3) A politicised psycho.
4) A combination of all the above.

But everything faltered against the question of motive, which took her back to some form of revenge.

Of the target, she summarised: 'The mild public facade softens a hard political line, which seems less about conviction than power. A Cardinal type, slinky, mendacious and Machiavellian. Makes a public show of trying to be liked. The man's smirk says: "I may be square but I have one over on you." Values defiantly traditional. A declared Christian.'

The man was clearly adept at not being called out, given some of the practices he had endorsed, including creationism being taught in schools. His lack of accountability fascinated Charlotte. She could see he was good at revision, with his fussy corrections when challenged, qualifying what he was once supposed to have said by announcing that a proper fact check would reveal he hadn't in fact said that at all. She suspected that his stated positions had nothing to do with any real political belief and everything to do with calculation.

It was 5.25am. Charlotte stared at her reflection in the window and wondered to what brief Moffat was operating. She hadn't known what to expect. McCavity seemed shadowy, even shadowless, a sinister, almost comic turn with a geopolitical profile and a high cringe factor, which was perhaps a calculated distraction – as was the unfailing politeness – from what could be got away with in plain sight. His views, so reasonably held, were translated by public forums into hysteria that exploited emotional insecurity. Here his main agent was the tabloids, cranking up the dial in pursuit of the sensational to compensate for their declining circulations.

Charlotte's abiding impression was of insecure white men obsessed with infiltration by darker foreign bodies.

4

At noon, Moffat was waiting for Charlotte in the lobby, back to his formal best, his manner curt. He took her to a private, windowless meeting room and said, 'Tell me what you have.'

Charlotte summarised her findings. Moffat steepled his hands and asked, 'Are you talking about a man?'

'Not a woman.'

'Is your man a hunter?'

'I beg your pardon?'

'Men stalk. Maybe he considered the target worth hunting.'

She remembered that McCavity was pro-blood sports, for badger culling and was a very shy green, with a dire voting record on environmental issues. It had not occurred to her that the foxy minister might be a deserving target for an eco-extremist.

'What's your best theory?' asked Moffat.

She told him and he nodded. 'Yes, a Muslim ex-soldier with a grudge. Or?'

'A Muslim family with a son or brother in the armed services—'

'—recruited by radical extremists,' Moffat finished for her.

It occurred to her that she was being steered.

Perhaps sensing as much, Moffat said, 'The government is keen not to stir up racial tension.' He snorted. 'They haven't got the police for it.'

He gave her a mobile number and said, 'Do more work. Give me some names. There can't be that many former Muslim soldiers. Should be easy enough to narrow them down, draw up a shortlist. Keep it between us for the moment.'

'And if I am asked?' She was thinking of Hopkins.

'I am sure you'll think of something.'

Moffat showed his friskier side before they left, saying, 'The best unofficial theory is that McCavity was the author of his own near demise; did you come across that on the internet?'

She hadn't. Moffat seemed amused.

'The shooting was meant as a publicity stunt, to distract from this or that, or to draw attention to something else. Except the shooter hadn't missed as he was supposed to.'

Charlotte was in no hurry to go to work so she took the bus. The first two were full. Twenty minutes later two came at once.

London looked old and sick under a yellow sky. The man in front of her was reading the previous day's *Daily Mail*. Another quote from Prince William: 'Ten years to save the world.' The *Mail* should carry a health warning, Charlotte thought.

The rest of the deck was either reading the free rag or on mobiles, apart from one middle-aged woman talking to herself in a foreign tongue Charlotte didn't recognise. The new year was a day-and-a-half old. A minister had been shot, and as for her and Clive, perhaps she should pack her bags, except she had nowhere to go. A stringy bicycle guerrilla swept past on an ostentatiously scruffy, gearless bike and gave the door of a stationary car a sharp kick as he sped through a red light. Charlotte gazed down at people glued to their screens and the drunken-like lurch of texting walkers. She could just about remember when the English used to have a reputation for restraint. Her father had once told her people never used to cry on TV; now they did all the time. Hopkins, meanwhile, encouraged a snitching culture, seen as part of a new openness. At school it had been known as telling tales, and you were told not to, especially by the bullies. Somewhere in Charlotte's mind snitching connected with open-plan offices and human resources and workplace insecurity.

She put in an official request to the Mercian Regiment for a record of serving soldiers for the last ten years.

Hopkins made a point of not asking about Moffat when she told Charlotte to go over all the CCTV footage of the area where the shooting had occurred, working backwards for the last sixty days.

'Don't they have machines that do that?' Charlotte asked.

'Nothing as good as a proper pair of eyes.'

She was being sent to sit in a cupboard until told she could come out.

'Parker will assist you,' said Hopkins, leaving her wondering again if Parker was Hopkins's spy. She didn't know what she thought of the prospect of enforced isolation in the man's company, other than to buy him a new aftershave.

She arrived home to find Clive deep in laborious preparation. Was cooking dinner a sign of a guilty conscience? Thai curry, he said. Usually he came up with a variation of school dinners: shepherd's pie, sometimes steak and kidney, with Jus-Rol pastry. Clive had chilled wine. Charlotte fancied a beer. She knew the wine was a Waitrose offer because she had seen it on the shelves.

Long story short, she thought after his explanation, which involved going to a stag party where a strippergram had mistaken him for the bridegroom so the knickers had ended up in his pocket, to general hilarity.

Clive lied well. Enough eye contact and sense of incredulity at the unlikeliness of his story. His invite for the wedding stood on a mantelpiece, as evidence. The stag do was a last-minute affair, after Charlotte had already left for her trip to Cheltenham and Birmingham. He hadn't mentioned it because he was rather embarrassed by such occasions and had gone only because his mother was being especially difficult and he was grateful for the excuse. He had come up on the train and returned to his mother's the next day.

Clive was having an affair, Charlotte was sure of that.

The Mercian Regiment replied with a list of former and serving soldiers. Charlotte would have to go through it at home, a prospect about as attractive as grinding through the CCTV footage in a windowless basement room. Banks of monitors filled the space. The equipment was old. With practice, she grew more adept at shuttling images back and forth. She had been told to look for faces. The cameras made suspects of everyone, down to the kids and their Slavic-looking childminders. Sometimes a technician called to ask for further grabs for face recognition and Charlotte would end up staring at the screen, wondering what was so special about that particular face.

Parker looked in from time to time, then came and sat with her more. He didn't say much and sat behind her so she couldn't see him.

He drank endless cups of tea, which Charlotte got into the habit of fetching, sensing that he was uncomfortable passing through the office upstairs on the way to the vending machine, and because it gave her a break from the horrible room.

Vehicles were being cross-checked with the DVLA by others. She was nevertheless asked to note patterns of movement outside the ordinary. On one of the screens a postal van was doing its rounds, and as she worked Parker told her about an old short story in which the murderer posed as a postman because everyone takes the postman for granted.

Charlotte noticed for the first time that Parker had a pleasant way of speaking: a modulated baritone, a handsome voice.

He volunteered that he had just started watching *Breaking Bad*, having missed it at the time. He asked if she had seen it. She'd heard of it of course, she said, adding that she didn't watch much television. Actually, that wasn't true. She watched any old junk, but she didn't bother with serial dramas, even the ones everyone had gone on about.

'Is that the one about the chemistry teacher with cancer who starts dealing drugs?' she asked, in an effort to keep the conversation going.

'Crystal meth, which he makes with the help of a drop-out pupil.'

'Is it any good?'

'Series two is supposed to be better than series one in which everything becomes more emotionally fraught as everyone grows more sullen, hysterical and unsympathetic.'

'Sounds just the ticket.'

'Of an evening and a moderately disgusting Tesco microwave dinner,' said Parker.

She got around to telling him about Moffat, after deciding she wasn't going to give anything away about herself, and described the visit to the RAC and her resulting investigation.

'What was that about?' she asked when she had finished, more rhetorically than in expectation of an answer.

Parker was silent for a long time, assessing, before saying, 'An ex-soldier, quite probable. Trained sniper, probable. A Muslim, possible. Many people don't know we have quite a lot serving. But where did he get the rifle?'

Charlotte didn't know.

Parker said, 'Curiously, no forensic information has been released about what type of rifle or ballistics were used.'

'Is that important?'

'I would be interested to know.'

In the evenings she carried on compiling a shortlist of soldiers' names from over three thousand, segregating the obvious Muslim ones, then checking their army skills. A motor mechanic or a cook was not going to be a trained sniper. Nor would an officer, she learned. She was looking for an infantry soldier.

She thought about indoctrination and brainwashing. Breivik had brainwashed himself, but he could just as easily have been manipulated by others. The idea persisted: a nut but a controlled nut. Rather than a gun-for-hire or a motivated shooter – Moffat's hunter perhaps – maybe she should be looking for someone malleable on the extreme political fringes who had been recruited and put in place.

Charlotte wondered how resistant she would be if someone manipulated her.

She took to sleeping on the sofa, using working late as an excuse. Clive didn't protest and she suspected this new distancing suited them both.

Late at night she blitzed flat rental sites and ended up dispirited by how few she could afford, and how most of them she wouldn't be seen dead in.

The news on McCavity fell strangely silent, other than to report his condition as still critical. Charlotte found it hard to say how urgently anyone was taking the shooting. It was as though they hoped it would go away of its own accord.

Mindful of Parker's story of the invisible postman, Charlotte checked footage of regular deliveries that were part of the neighbourhood. The DHL truck made its daily rounds at around the same time; a plumber's Transit van stood parked outside a house for a couple of days. She watched the workers arrive at the Russian house, observed by a distant camera. They came with their lunchboxes and left with their lunchboxes. Some days a dozen came and on others as many as twenty. Was the shooter among them?

The site was secured at night but Parker said anyone with the right skills could come and go out of sight of the camera. No cars pulled up. No surreptitious activity. Once Charlotte detected a peripheral movement that turned out to be a cat running across the road. She wondered whether to post it on YouTube.

Parker agreed that the house's renovation made it an obvious choice as it wasn't being worked on over the holidays. He thought its location was the determining factor, rather than the owner's nationality. The area was full of houses bought by Russians. He would have been surprised if the owner had turned out not to be Russian.

'Or an Arab.'

Charlotte couldn't tell if Parker was stating a fact or he didn't like Arabs.

To break the sequential monotony she went back several weeks, to see if anything was different. Random seemed just as valid as systematic. She watched days of drizzle, thinking how even screen weather could affect one's mood. The timecode made it feel like it was her own life she was reviewing.

Clive, after professing concern for his mother, announced he was taking himself off for the weekend. She wondered after he was gone whether he expected her not to be there when he got back. Fuck him, she thought, just tell her rather than leave her guessing.

She went to Waitrose before it closed and bought an expensive bottle of red and drank half of it while staring at the darkened city eighteen storeys below. She entertained herself with a brief fantasy of braining Clive with a heavy object then making his body disappear – she could work out the details later – and carrying on living there alone, which would suit her just fine.

She reluctantly set to work and at last whittled the regimental list down to half-a-dozen, all ex-servicemen. Without knowing why, she found herself texting Parker to ask what she should do next. She had names, she said, but no note of present whereabouts or professions.

Parker texted straight back and said it would be easier to talk. She rang him. He answered awkwardly. She suspected he didn't get many calls. He surprised her by asking if anything was the matter.

'Not really. I'm just at a bit of a dead end.'

She was thinking of Clive but she could hardly talk about that. She could hear a television in the background, which stopped when Parker paused it.

He told her that in terms of wanting to know where someone lived or worked the Department of Work and Pensions could be accessed 'out of hours'.

Was he offering to help, off the record?

'If you have a mobile number you can track his location but it depends on whether your man has been covering his tracks,' he went on. 'He may be using burner phones, may have dropped out or may not even have a phone. Or he may be protected and undercover.'

Charlotte had never heard Parker volunteer so much.

'I would use horses to get out of the country,' he said.

'Horses!'

'They get specially flown out for big continental race

meetings. The shooting happened at 8.20am. The man could have been out in hours.'

'Do you think that's what happened?'

'No, I already checked.'

Charlotte couldn't tell how serious he was. She asked what he was watching. More *Breaking Bad*.

'Season two is better than season one. Hank's doing what you're doing.'

'What's that?'

'Checking CCTV footage.'

'Hard to make a drama of that. Who's Hank?'

'Albuquerque DEA, leading the investigation into the big local meth cook, unaware that it's his brother-in-law. That's Walter, the main character.'

'What's going on?'

'Hank's reviewing footage of a warehouse break-in without realising he is watching Walter and his sidekick Jesse.'

Charlotte asked if he was working at the office tomorrow. She was thinking of going in even though it was the weekend.

'Are you asking for help?'

It was a strangely direct question from someone as withheld as Parker.

That was what she had meant.

'Not in the office,' he said.

'You can always come here. I'm on my own.' What was she thinking?

She told him where she was and he said it was only ten minutes away. He was in a big residential block in the same street as the office. She guessed he probably chose to live there to avoid public transport. The National Film Theatre was only a short walk away.

Charlotte said, 'I could give you lunch,' again wondering

what she was doing, hoping he would decline, but he said that was very kind of her.

She hung up, wondering when Parker had last had a social invitation.

She drank the rest of the wine and decided to sleep on the sofa, not wanting to use Clive's bed even when he was away. She thought of her parents' marriage and how that had devoured itself over time.

On the way back from the bathroom she passed Clive's desk and opened it without intending to – everything was shipshape, as she would have expected; Clive was a neat man. He had a little Letts diary for the previous year, the sort of Christmas present once given by an elderly relative to a schoolchild. It still was by the look of it, from someone who didn't realise no one used diaries any more.

She flipped through it. The pages were blank until the last where Clive had neatly written down all his passwords. His Apple one was Mommaswamp973. Fuck me, she thought. What sort of mind comes up with that?

Unable to sleep, she googled: Easy way to access someone's location remotely via their mobile phone.

After some browsing, a site told her: It is in a way like a private detective, minus all the money wasted and the chances of you being creepy.

Which was exactly what she was being.

Seeing Parker's face upon opening her front door, Charlotte regretted her invitation. She made polite noises, saying she didn't know if he was vegetarian so she had bought a quiche and potato salad.

'And apple pie to follow, with creme fraiche.'

She had resisted returning to the mobile tracking sites. She had, however, rung Clive and got no answer.

Parker had a method of making himself unobtrusive and a restless way of conversing, which left her feeling less bad about not looking at him. He had made an effort to appear more presentable, wearing a pale leather jacket, which didn't show his dandruff, and a knitted cap he preferred not to take off as his skin was particularly bad that day.

'Is it difficult?' she asked tactlessly.

He said some days he found it impossible not to lacerate himself, but as he had never known anything else he couldn't really say; it just was.

As she brought the food through Parker was inspecting the bookshelves. It was not an impressive collection. Charlotte excused the selection, saying the books belonged to Clive's parents, and asked Parker if he read.

'All the time, when I'm not watching stuff.'

She asked what sort of books.

'Thrillers mainly. And you?'

'I used to, now hardly at all.'

They ate. Parker's manners were impeccable without being forced. The quiche was passable. Charlotte had gone to Waitrose early enough to have chilled a Sancerre. She asked why he read thrillers.

'There's a film from the 1970s, *Three Days of the Condor*, about a conspiracy, where someone asks why a book that hasn't sold in its original language exists in several foreign translations. That got me started. The question was asked by Robert Redford, who was working for a backwater CIA research unit. While he's out buying breakfast everyone gets shot.'

'The whole office?'

'By a team of assassins. The film uses the trick of the postman. The receptionist buzzes him in and is dead before she can finish her cigarette. I don't remember whether the film ever answered the question about the translated books but I have a theory that several best-selling authors were underwritten by CIA.'

Charlotte said it sounded like the more far-fetched stuff she had found while digging for Moffat.

Parker said, 'Seriously, CIA has a huge history of cultural control – US radio stations abroad, literary magazines, museums and art, so why not books? If you have a bestseller that conforms to a line the Agency wants to push it makes sense. Tom Clancy's first novel, about hunting a Russian submarine, was a huge hit. If it was an investment on the part of the Agency it was very good one.'

'Were they sharing material or dictating what he wrote?'

'No, it was picked up by a small specialist press and may have come to the attention of someone like the Redford character in *Condor*, who was basically hired to read and analyse books. Being a Cold War thriller, the attraction of Clancy's book to the Agency might have been as simple as promoting a story about facing up to current realities and a new mood that was both hawkish and more accommodating. Reagan was President and not known to read yet was photographed with a copy and quoted as saying it was unputdownable, probably because he had never picked it up in the first place, except for the photo op.'

By paying attention to what Parker was saying, Charlotte found she became less disturbed by his presence.

'And with your work?'

'Intelligence is a bit like fiction – it's about making stuff up, so the truth becomes endlessly revisable. Something like who killed JFK will probably never be solved because even if it were – and for all we know, it already has been – it would be trumped by another version that has already been programmed into the cover-up. The JFK case remains the paradigm of the lie.'

'Who do you think shot Kennedy?'

'I rather find myself returning to the lone gun theory. The Warren Commission concluded there was nothing to say Oswald hadn't acted alone, and it cited an old thriller to support its argument, in which a man attempts to assassinate an unnamed head of state, clearly Hitler, by shooting him from a distance. Only he is stopped before he can.'

'And his reason?'

'Apparently for the thrill of the hunt and the sport of having the man in his sights, though it turns out there is a specific motive, which I won't spoil.'

'And in our case?' she asked.

'Everyone wants to know who did it – that's why people read Agatha Christie – but the important question is why. I can remember most of Christie's murderers, but I would be pushed to recall their motive. In this case, if you know why McCavity was shot, then you would have a pretty good idea of who did it. As well as motive there is method. The gun used is an anomaly.'

'How do you know?'

Parker said he was able to draw on a loose affiliation of like-minded souls, some official, some not.

'But in this instance I called the forensics lab in Lambeth Road, spoke to a contact and she faxed the sheet. Sometimes we're old-fashioned that way.'

Charlotte offered coffee. Parker said he didn't drink it and asked for tea.

When they were settled again he said, 'The method suggests a proper operation, though the weapon used was not a professional hunter's rifle. According to UK gun laws, one rifle you are allowed to buy is a .22 Rimfire.'

'Rimfire?'

'The cartridge came from one. It's easily identified because the hammer strikes the edge. Most bullets have a percussion cap in the centre. It makes the Rimfire much less powerful, and asks questions about the shooter.'

'In what way?'

'A Rimfire can kill a deer, perhaps even a bear, but it's not a weapon for precision shooting, unless the shooter had no choice.'

Charlotte realised it would have made much more sense for Moffat to have used Parker rather than her.

'And afterwards,' she asked, 'what would he have done with it?'

'He was in an empty building, plenty of places to dump it. The forensic report is based on the spent bullet, but if the rifle is found it won't show much. There'd be no fingerprints. The gun itself will tell you rather less than its type. Now let's look at your list.'

Parker's speed on the computer made Charlotte look like a novice.

She had six names, all former soldiers from the Mercian Regiment's two battalions. From knowing next to nothing about them, the six subjects started to take shape as Parker jumped from site to site.

Charlotte made him cups of tea. He seemed oblivious to her presence. The teas grew cold as he became more immersed, once stopping to ask for pen and paper on which he made notes in his tiny capitals.

It was getting dark when Parker said, 'You can probably cross off Lance Corporal Khan. He's in gainful employment in his family's motor repairs business in Stafford. Medically discharged after losing a foot in Afghanistan. Sergeant Sadiq seems to have left the country after the army; last known address Baden-Baden. And Corporal Akmal is dead, killed in a head-on collision on the A46 outside Evesham. Which leaves Hassan, Ebrahim and Halim.'

Charlotte turned on lights, tidied up and stacked the dishwasher while Parker carried on. He called through to her, 'Ebrahim appears to be a respected community figure in his local area. Interestingly, he attended Park View, one of the schools which was central to the row about a Muslim extremist takeover.'

Charlotte asked, 'How do you know this?'

'Mr Ebrahim is very active on Facebook.'

She joined him and saw Ebrahim's profile on the screen.

'Ebrahim is older,' Parker went on. 'Over fifty. Married, three kids. Regular worshipper. Runs a family business. Textiles. Nothing political. Still lives in Alum Rock where he grew up. Do you have Facebook?'

'Used to. Well, I still do but never use it.'

A few minutes was all it took before her page was on the screen.

Parker recited, 'Account holder since 2007, inactive since 2011. Probably for the best. Twitter?'

'No.'

'Snapchat? Instagram?'

'No and no.'

'People give far too much away about themselves. Internet banking?'

'Lloyds.'

'Want to know your balance?'

She couldn't tell if he was serious.

Parker said, 'It's all pretty much an open book. Hassan, like Ebrahim, went to the same school at Park View, but some years later. Since leaving the army he is listed as living near Pershore.'

Charlotte knew it, a town not far from her father.

'Drew unemployment benefit until last year. No subsequent record of work. A couple of minor infringements, one for driving a car without an MOT and a recent speeding ticket in a built-up area, in Smethwick, which is the last recorded mention I can find.'

Charlotte suspected that for Parker the thrill was the ease with which he could open up people's lives, perhaps in compensation for his affliction: watching while unwatched.

He said, 'Corporal Halim I found by chance on a BBC Midlands site about the Mercians in Afghanistan.'

Parker showed her a photograph of a harmless-looking fellow and asked for the bathroom.

'Read what it says,' he said, and left the room.

Charlotte sat. Parker had brought his own brush with which he regularly dusted the keyboard. She had watched him use it only a couple of minutes before. Even so, the keys were already covered with a fine powder of skin particles. She was aware of the toilet flushing and the sound of running water as she read.

Halim spoke of the terror of being in an ambush, then how in a subsequent skirmish he had thrown his rifle down and started walking towards the Taliban. His commanding officer ordered his platoon sergeant to shoot him dead if he got within 200 yards of them. Had he been captured he would have been tortured for information he had on tactical techniques and the locations of patrol bases. As it was, he was rescued, left the army and fell into drug use.

Parker returned. Charlotte stood for him to resume his seat and carry on.

He said, 'Halim seems to have worked for Amazon in Daventry between November and March last year, according to the DWP's PAYE system. Before that he was employed by FedEx at Birmingham Airport. So a van driver, I guess. Current whereabouts unknown. That's the best I can do. Three names you can give Moffat. Nothing conclusive but they all received advanced weapons training. Halim won several shooting cups – the army is keen on its competitions.'

He stood and said he was off to a screening. Charlotte asked what.

'*The Conversation*.'

Charlotte didn't know it.

'Paranoid conspiracy, about a professional eavesdropper with the line, "There is no moment between human beings that I cannot record." '

She watched the trailer after Parker was gone, a creepy world of hidden microphones with Gene Hackman capable of bugging anybody, anywhere, any time, until the bugger gets bugged and is told, 'We prepare a full dossier on everyone.'

Charlotte called Moffat. There was no answer or voicemail. She texted to say she had prepared a list, then went to Waitrose for another bottle of wine.

She watched crap on television. She considered calling Clive until it struck her that he might not be with his mother after all.

By nine Moffat hadn't answered. Charlotte sat staring at the television until the football came on and she went to bed.

She was woken after midnight by the ping of her phone. It was Moffat. His text told her to send her findings to a complicated email address; nothing so obvious as 'gov.uk'.

She got up and sent the file, wondering what she looked like to anyone watching: an anxious woman in jogging pants and an old T-shirt, fiddling with her hair, perhaps with the same fearful look as the woman in *The Conversation* trailer, who says to her companion, 'Do you see him, the man with the hearing aid? He's been following us.'

5

As it was mindless work, Charlotte spent her Sunday in the office logging more footage. Upstairs, while fetching coffee, she ran into Hopkins who seemed surprised, as if she had forgotten about her. In contrast to her usual aggressive smartness, Hopkins was casually dressed in a purple tracksuit, with her hair pulled back in a ponytail. She asked how Charlotte was getting on with Parker. Charlotte's first thought was that Parker must have already reported the previous afternoon's meeting.

'We get along fine,' Charlotte said.

'And what is Moffat interested in?' Hopkins asked, archly.

'An ex-soldier with a history of active service, trained as a sniper, possibly Muslim,' she conceded, thinking Hopkins probably knew already.

'What do you think?'

'It's a line we ought to pursue,' said Charlotte stiffly.

'Please be so good as to share your findings.' Charlotte hesitated. Hopkins prompted. 'We shan't get anywhere unless we co-operate.'

'I am sure Moffat would be willing,' Charlotte said, implying it was for Hopkins and not her to ask.

Hopkins smelt of sweat and perfume. Charlotte wondered if she had been out running. She noted expensive trainers.

'We won't bother Moffat. Send over whatever you have.'

Seeing that Charlotte was undecided, Hopkins added, 'I am in a position to make that other stuff go away in terms of your record. Let's be sensible.'

Charlotte wanted to protest that her computer had been tampered with. Instead she said, 'I will put it on a stick.'

'Bring it tomorrow. Don't forget.'

Charlotte was left thinking she needed to talk to Moffat. She rang and got no answer. Moffat looked the sort to take the weekend off. Did it really matter whether she showed her findings to Hopkins, even if Moffat had told her to keep it between them? She told herself not to be naive. Hopkins wasn't to be trusted any more than Moffat. She texted Moffat, asking to speak. She had no idea what she would say.

She was thinking of leaving after an afternoon of fruitless viewing but she didn't want to go home. Clive would be back at some point and she would no doubt have to face his accusing presence. Like a lot of men he did that rather well, implying it was somehow all her fault, as a result of past omissions: had she sucked his dick, for a start, then this wouldn't have happened.

She worked on. The day she was looking at was three weeks before the shooting. A Tuesday. Average weather. A telephone engineer was working on a junction box in a road running at a right angle to the one with the Russian house. A BT van was parked across the street. The engineer was a tall man, around thirty-five, with a dark complexion. Charlotte watched him go to the van and on the way back she saw his face more clearly. She froze the screen and thought: I know you.

She wound it back and watched again. Was it the walk? She enlarged the face. It started to blur. She reset it at the best resolution. It remained vague but she was sure she had seen him before; not recently. She watched the sequence over, thinking she didn't know any telephone engineers. She noted the date and time: 10 December, 09.35.

He worked on the box, stopping twice to smoke. Instead of throwing the butts away he bent down to stub them out before dropping them down a drain. She remembered the man she was trying to think of as smoking too.

With his work completed at 11.03 he packed up and left. Charlotte made a note of the van's number. She already suspected that BT's worksheets would not show any of its engineers in the area that morning. As it was a Sunday she couldn't check.

Procedure required that she forward images of the man for facial recognition, yet she didn't.

She looked again at his face. The image just wasn't clear enough. Then it came back to her. She knew the man only too well and prayed she was wrong.

She sat for a long time, thinking she could pretend she hadn't accessed the footage, knowing there was probably an invisible hard drive somewhere recording everything she logged.

It hadn't even been a fling and now she was confronted by the unwelcome memory of a reckless sexual encounter.

He had been unusual, being from Belfast with a Pakistani father and a Roman Catholic mother. Not many of those, he had told her, describing himself as a 'half-breed'. They'd had casual, drunken, urgent sex.

She tried and failed to see herself telling Hopkins that.

Other than that one encounter, Charlotte knew almost nothing about him, but it left her with a spoor that others could trace.

*

On her walk home she passed the Two Brewers in Whitecross Street. From the corner outside she could see the tower where she lived. She counted up the storeys. The eighteenth floor was dark.

She loitered in the pub over an overpriced gin and tonic, which was served without flourish: a quick squirt of the optic measure, half a bottle of Schweppes plonked in, a scoopful of already melting ice and a thin twist of pale lemon. She thought about the engineer's careful habit of stubbing out his cigarette ends and dropping them down a drain.

Her phone pinged: Clive texting to say he was driving back in the morning as his mother was not good. Charlotte revised his schedule to have him banged up in a hotel with a woman on the Saturday with a quick dash for a Sunday overnight with his mother.

Her phone pinged again. This time it was Moffat texting to say he would ring her tomorrow.

More waiting.

She considered calling Parker but didn't want to appear needy; then she relented and texted:

– If I have someone's Apple ID can I access phone location? I'm not very technical.

Parker answered straight away.

– *Number?*

Charlotte texted Clive's number.

Parker's answer came back within minutes, saying the mobile was currently near Colchester. So Clive was at his mother's after all. Benefit of the doubt, she thought. Just.

She texted Parker again, saying:

– I have a problem.

This time she got no answer until much later when she was woken by the ping of her phone. It was 1.35am. A one-word text from Parker:

– *Problem?*

She texted back:

– Recognised someone from CCTV I once worked with.

– *Why a problem?*

– Personal history. Don't know if I need to say.

– *What does he do?*

– Intel then, don't know now.

– *Circumstance of sighting?*

– As telephone engineer in vicinity. 10 Dec.

Parker didn't text back. Charlotte felt lonely and apprehensive. Then after ten minutes he did.

– *What's guy's name?*

– Only remember as John.

– *Need more! Circs of meet?*

– Big security exercise out near Heathrow, two days.

– *Date?*

– Summer maybe two years ago.

At least she had a note of that on her computer calendar and forwarded it, adding:

– From Belfast. Father Pakistani, mother local RC.

– *Rare bird. Will get back.*

He didn't. Charlotte felt she was pushing her luck and left him to it.

She looked back over the texts. Strangely intimate, this messaging in the night. With anyone else she would have taken it as a sign of possible first moves.

She and Parker were sitting in the viewing room. It was Monday morning, 9.25am. Parker had said nothing about what he had found. Charlotte couldn't tell if he had got cold feet or was biding his time.

She asked how *The Conversation* had been.

'Interesting. Its real author is the editor, who was also

responsible for the sound montage. Fascinating man. Translated Malaparte in his spare time.'

'Malaparte?'

'Italian author, war correspondent and diplomat. He even made a couple of films. He was fascist then he wasn't. His work was banned by the Vatican. He built an extraordinary brutalist house on Capri that was used in Godard's film *Contempt* with Brigitte Bardot. He wrote two books on the war, one of which, *The Skin*, about the American liberation of Naples in 1944, was made into a film by Liliana Cavani. Hard to see but there was a rare screening last year. Great work from Marcello Mastroianni.'

Parker looked at Charlotte to see if she at least knew who he was.

'*La Dolce Vita*?' he prompted.

Charlotte had woken in desperate straits, waiting on Clive's return and for Moffat to call. She had managed to escape before Clive turned up, with his no doubt rehearsed act of 'this is me coming home from looking after my mother'. Then there was what to do about Hopkins. Charlotte's corner was starting to get very crowded. It hadn't mattered at the time that she'd had sex with a man when she probably shouldn't have, but when the same man turned up in an area where three weeks later a minister was shot, following an intel flag on which she had failed to draw the right conclusions ... it left her looking very questionable.

With Parker remaining silent, she decided to continue as normal. She made a brief trip upstairs to fetch him a tea and when she got back he said she had received a text. She was expecting Moffat but saw it was from Parker, sent two minutes before. She read:

– Show me footage of engineer.

She looked at him and he put a finger to his lips. Charlotte wondered if he was overreacting to *The Conversation*'s paranoia. Indulge him, she thought, as she texted back.

– Hopkins asking for names I gave Moffat. Not sure what to do.

She watched him type a reply.

– Did you agree?

– Said would put on stick.

– Did you?

– Yes but haven't given yet.

With all the other distractions, she had forgotten to bring it, after lying awake worrying.

She showed Parker the footage, after which he texted:

– Forget Hopkins, she probably has Moffat's names. Already being run with.

'By Moffat?' Charlotte asked, thrown by the speed at which everything was moving. Parker silenced her with a warning look.

He texted again and Charlotte read:

– Get sandwich for lunch and meet outside 58 Upper Thames Street, set back on left by hotel that spans road. 12.45.

She texted back, feeling ridiculous.

– Can I get you anything?

– Tuna mayo brown.

He added as an afterthought:

– Not Pret.

It was a bright day for a change, with the usual tailback of traffic down Upper Thames Street and a smog of exhaust. Before leaving, Parker had told her that the junction with Southwark Bridge had featured in a 1960s' spy film, involving an agent being shot in his car while waiting for the lights to change. In that casual encyclopaedic way of his, he said the idea had been taken from a silent movie that had done it much better.

Parker was waiting outside the block, wearing his woollen hat and sunglasses that covered most of his face.

'Tuna mayo not Pret,' she said, handing him his sandwich.

He gestured that they should go inside and swiped the lock. The reception area more resembled a hotel than an apartment block. Parker led the way to the lift. Charlotte clutched her sandwich, thinking how conversations in lifts always sounded forced. She remembered at school being with kids she hadn't wanted to be seen with and she felt the same about Parker, knowing that the problem was her awkwardness rather than him. He opened his sandwich and inspected it as the lift stopped and she followed him down a long windowless corridor. His door was halfway down on the left with impressive deadlocks. She stepped after him into a tiny hall. There was a kitchen on the right. Charlotte's first impression was that it was like being inside Parker's head. The place was full of so much wiring and stacked electronic equipment that it should have been a mess but everything was orderly and pristine.

The main room was dominated by a huge TV with a lounger opposite. The rest was given over to a network of conduits, and tables and shelves stacked to the ceiling with more machines. Through slatted Venetian blinds she could see the river and Southwark Bridge and lunchtime strollers on the river path.

They ate their sandwiches, perched awkwardly on a couple of stools. After their texting bouts, which had acquired a fluency of their own – ask question, get answer – Charlotte found conversation difficult.

Parker ate slowly then used sanitiser and offered it to her. She accepted out of politeness. When he pointed out she had stray food on her chin she caught herself doing that delayed double take of embarrassment that irritated her when anyone else did it.

Parker said, 'Your man's name is Cross, John. He changed it by deed poll before joining the army. Aged thirty-seven. Birth name Sandhu, first name Joseph, known as Joe. Not an easy path when you're surrounded by Irish bigots. His mother, Mary Rose O'Grady, Roman Catholic, was ostracised by her community for marrying a "darkie". Her husband was an accountant and worked in local government.'

'How do you know this?'

'Working backwards. Cross was listed as a participant in the official report on the Heathrow operation, which is easy enough to access. You're in it too.'

Parker seemed reluctant about volunteering that.

'As for the rest, Mary Rosc O'Grady had a sister who was an active local feminist until she died of cancer. She published an internet pamphlet on race and difference in Belfast, in admonition of local intolerance, using the example of her brother-in-law, who was dead by then. If you search Cross under his original name it comes up as cited in the pamphlet. The sister writes about the boy's difficult childhood, bullying at school where he was known as Curry Face. Did well academically. A few brushes with the law. A faked ID. Muslim graffiti which must have terrified the locals.'

Charlotte remembered how Breivik had fancied himself as a tagger and travelled to Denmark to buy his spray paints.

'Are you thinking Cross is a suspect?'

The name sounded unfamiliar as it left her lips. She remembered the one thing they hadn't done was kiss.

Parker said, 'Unlike the names on Moffat's list, he is directly connected to the scene of crime, and he has the training. He joined the Royal Irish Regiment, aged eighteen, nominally as a Roman Catholic, through his mother, when the rest of the regiment was almost exclusively Protestant. In Helmand he was caught in a long siege of brutal sustained action involving fifty men who were cut off. Look at this.'

It was grainy footage on one of a bank of several tiny monitors, showing a dusty landscape and camouflaged soldiers with helmets and rifles taking turns to fire over a low wall while two more operated a mortar, followed by the distant crump of its explosion.

'Too early to have been shot on an iPhone,' Parker said. 'I would say a camcorder.'

In between shooting, the soldiers rested against the wall, feet splayed. One took his helmet off to wipe his brow and drank from a canteen. The camera zoomed in and he obliged with a thumbs up.

'John Cross,' Charlotte said. It was like watching time collapse.

'Are there any overlaps between him and the three other names?' she asked.

'No, but your theory concerning a Muslim ex-soldier is starting to be floated in social media. Someone seems to be thinking along the same lines.'

'Names?'

'No names as yet.'

Was Hopkins running with this? Had Moffat been using her all along? And what was Parker's role? Or hers?

Parker said, 'Moving on, there are veterans' correspondence sites. Some offer real support but many are just interlopers pretending to have seen active service. Cross seems to have acquired his own legend, if he is the JC referred to.'

Parker reached for a notepad in which he had written and read aloud, ' "JC could walk on water." "Dead eye."

"Professional loner." There is some discussion about whether JC was the sniper who went out by himself at night to hunt Taliban. The story is taken up by others. According to some, JC was reported dead, but a rumour persisted that he had either volunteered or been coerced into fighting for the Taliban and became one of its deadliest snipers. This draws quite a lot of flak. "Bollocks." "You were never there, whatever you say." "Who makes this stuff up?" One late interjection states JC was an arsehole and "he was always one of them anyway", presumably a reference to his racial background. There is a mention on another veterans' site that one of the Taliban's deadliest snipers was a British soldier who defected and Cross's name comes up.'

Parker put the pad aside.

'But if that was him it doesn't explain how he progressed to UK counter-terrorist operations, or was seen masquerading as a telephone engineer.'

'It's him, no doubt about it. There must be a record of his service following Afghanistan.'

'There isn't.' Parker looked at his watch. 'You should get back to work while I carry on looking.'

In the office, Charlotte found a note from Hopkins, telling her she had the names she needed, adding that it would have helped if Charlotte had provided them.

Either way, it confirmed what Parker had said. She felt outmanoeuvred, not that she was sure of her position other than to suspect she was being used. Were Moffat and Hopkins working together after all? Or had Hopkins acquired the names from another party, which left Charlotte questioning whether Parker should be trusted either.

Charlotte went back to the time of the shooting and the twenty minutes after. She didn't expect to find anything.

Any reconnoitre of an escape route would have noted to avoid cameras. That New Year's morning was mostly empty, given the holiday. Light traffic. Few on the streets. She watched a couple the worse for wear, returning from an all-nighter.

Her phone rang. No caller ID. It was Moffat, but there were no preliminaries. 'Meet me in Postman's Park at five o'clock,' he said as soon as she answered, expecting her to recognise his voice. 'Do you know where that is?'

She did, as it turned out, just not by name; a small space off Aldersgate, which she often walked past. Moffat hung up without saying goodbye.

Charlotte returned her attention to the frozen screen: a traffic junction and background detail so commonplace she would have missed it otherwise – a passing cyclist, glimpsed between cars pulling away from the lights. Her first thought was: New Year's resolution – exercise more. The man had on a helmet and wraparound glasses. He was wearing Lycra. Her second thought was: So that's how you got away, on a fucking bicycle. She was sure it was Cross.

Charlotte arrived early at Postman's Park to find Moffat already waiting with a dog on a lead.

'Lakeland terrier,' he said. 'Given to bolting, hence the leash.'

He made it sound like he might be referring to Charlotte.

Moffat went on. 'I didn't, from what I remember, ask you to share your findings.'

'Who told you I did?'

'That woman Hopkins, who else?'

Charlotte denied sharing and said she thought she had been hacked.

'Who did the hacking, and to what end?'

She said her office computer had been tampered with,

which was why she had used her own for his work, but now that must have been hacked too.

'You didn't think to say?'

'I've only just realised.'

She was thinking of Parker though it crossed her mind that Moffat could have leaked the names himself because he wanted that angle pursued.

The dog took a shit. Moffat produced a black plastic sack and scooped it up. She walked with him to the bin and watched him dump the bag.

Moffat asked, 'Do you like dogs?'

She said she'd never had one.

'Not what I asked. This belonged to my wife. A wilful creature.'

Charlotte couldn't tell if he meant the dog or the wife. She sensed the woman was dead.

'Married?' Moffat asked.

Charlotte found herself telling him about Clive because she was nervous about what Moffat might be getting her into. She knew nothing of what he did or why he was using her. She asked if he had children.

'Not now. Do you know about chuck or keep? With regard to the boyfriend.'

She said she didn't.

'Useful when it comes to getting rid of. Used to do it with my boy when he was little.'

So there had been a child.

'When it comes to sorting give marks out of ten. Five and under goes. What's your fellow?'

'About a three,' she said without thinking.

'That's a clear chuck.'

'I've come up with a man from Belfast,' she said.

'We're not talking about your private life now.'

They were but she wasn't going to mention that.

'He fits the profile. And he was in the area of the shooting on 10 December.'

'Tell me what you know.'

She did, apart from the sex.

Moffat asked, 'I presume you checked he doesn't work for BT.'

'I checked.'

'Who else knows?'

'Only Parker.'

'Parker?'

'The one with the skin condition sitting next to you in the big meeting.'

'Terrible affliction. Had a boy at school with the same. Teased mercilessly. How long have you known about this Belfast man?'

'Since yesterday.'

'Done anything about it?'

'I wasn't sure whether to tell you first.'

'You just said you told Parker,' Moffat said, exasperated. 'Who else knows? And what are you talking about anyway? That Hopkins had your computer hacked as part of some massive arse-covering exercise?'

Charlotte said she had no proof. Again she was thinking of Parker.

'Keep me informed. Anything you have. Use the email address I gave you.'

She watched him stroll off in the direction of St Paul's.

Charlotte walked the short distance back across the Barbican walkway to the flat. Her mind remained on Moffat, then moved on to Cross, of whom she had never expected to think about again.

She walked in the front door, contemplating a hot bath and taking advantage of a brief respite before Clive got back from work, usually around seven, only to be confronted by two strangers.

'Excuse me?' she asked, as in: Who the fuck are you?

The couple regarded her as though she was the intruder.

They turned out to be Clive's father and his second wife. It was the first Charlotte had heard of any visit, and they had no idea who she was, so where was bloody Clive when he was needed?

She tried calling him, thinking how the father was nothing like his son. Clive pampered himself with skin conditioners and moisturisers. The father was weather-beaten and wearing sandals in January. The wife with wild white hair looked like a mad old hippie.

Clive didn't answer. Charlotte opted for a swift retreat to the pub and told the ghastly couple she had to go straight out again.

She always found waiting for the lift a psychological impediment to leaving the building. The doors at last opened and as she moved forward out stepped Clive.

He appeared flustered as he ushered her back inside the flat where he proceeded to act like a demented master of ceremonies, ignoring her, explaining nothing of their relationship, and asking his father pointless questions about their journey. Charlotte wondered what the odd couple made of the bedding on the sofa, which spoke plainly of domestic breakdown.

'Are we going out to dinner?' the father eventually asked after further banalities that had excluded Charlotte.

The invitation clearly didn't extend to her. She cheerfully announced she had a work panic on, thankful to be spared the ordeal.

At last they left. She passed the evening drained of energy, unable even to run a bath, reduced to playing double-pack solitaire on her computer, without a single game coming out.

Clive returned alone. His father and the wife were staying at the Thistle Hotel, he said. Charlotte could see it from where she was standing, just up the road. They were travelling in the morning to Cornwall for a short walking holiday.

The words 'We need to talk,' formed and died in Charlotte's mouth. Instead she asked if anything was the matter. Clive made a little speech apologising for the muddle.

'I should have told you, but I've got a bit of thing at work.'

His excuse was he thought he was being passed over for promotion.

'Join the club,' Charlotte said.

'My father's talking about moving back here. For good,' Clive said, sounding evasive.

'When?'

'Quite soon.'

She wondered if it were even true. She supposed it was Clive's way of getting around to chucking her. She refused to give him the satisfaction of drawing her into an argument. She looked around, depressed at the thought of what she could afford in terms of anywhere else to live. Whatever the shortcomings of her relationship with Clive, she had been willing to overlook them in exchange for a standard of living that was unimaginable compared to previous lodgings.

The next morning at 10am Hopkins summoned Charlotte to a meeting in an overheated windowless room where they were joined by Parker at Hopkins's request. Charlotte found it hard to concentrate.

'You're saying you recognise this man?'

It was Hopkins asking.

She repeated that she knew Cross from a security exercise.

Hopkins looked at her notes. 'And these three ex-soldiers, is there any connection to Cross during his time in the military?'

'None that is obvious.'

'I suggest you dig deeper.'

Charlotte half-listened as Parker summarised Cross's career while she wondered how much longer before she would have to move. Part of her was tempted to hang on as long as possible to spite Clive.

'Cross seems to have had US connections,' Parker said, 'but no one is sure what these were or his whereabouts after being assigned to special duties in Afghanistan.'

Hopkins grew impatient. She wanted bullet points. 'What about now?'

'Six months after the Heathrow exercise he was sentenced at Lewes Crown Court to nine months for grievous bodily harm.'

'GBH?'

'A fight outside a pub,' Parker said.

'Really? And after prison?' Hopkins asked.

'Went to live with his mother, who had moved to Liverpool. Since then he has been deporting illegal immigrants.'

'What? For the Home Office!' Hopkins exclaimed.

'Working under his mother's maiden name of O'Grady.'

Hopkins's eyebrows shot up. 'With a criminal record and an alias? Why would they stand for that?'

'Criminal checks are only done on the security guards. He runs the company and management isn't subject to clearance. The Home Office has shelled out millions. He handles over a hundred deportations a month at two thousand quid a go.'

'Where is Mr Cross-slash-O'Grady now?'

'Before Christmas he told his mother he was going to Antigua for a holiday with a new girlfriend and he hasn't been heard of since.'

Charlotte supposed Parker must have talked to the mother.

'How long to find him?' Hopkins asked.

'It could take forty-eight hours, could take a week.'

Hopkins said, 'You have twenty-four. Now these other names, the soldiers.' She ran through them and said, 'I want more on the man from Alum Rock, the textile merchant.'

When the meeting broke up Hopkins told Charlotte to stay. She wanted a physical check made on Ebrahim under the pretext of a spot VAT inspection.

'You can drive Parker up to Birmingham. If you leave now, you'll be back by the end of the day.'

It looked like Hopkins was assigning her to chauffeuring duties. Charlotte was about to complain but Hopkins anticipated her.

'Parker doesn't drive and it would be unfair to make him take the train. Anyway, a disconcerting presence is useful.'

'You just said you wanted Cross found in twenty-four hours.'

'Parker can work in the car. Can you afford to overlook any possible link between Ebrahim and Cross?'

Charlotte noted the 'you' rather than 'we'.

As she made to leave, Hopkins said, 'As for you and Mr Cross, any more you wish to add?'

Charlotte stared back. Did the woman know?

'Nothing to add,' she said, thinking: Call her bluff.

Hopkins wasn't done. 'We will want to question you further about Mr Cross. Tomorrow morning at nine. Here.'

'We?'

Hopkins ignored the question and looked at Charlotte for a long time before adding, 'I am trying to work out how much of a coincidence it is you knowing the man.'

There were only so many degrees of separation, Charlotte said. 'There were plenty of others on the exercise. I hardly knew him.'

Hopkins cocked her head. 'Bear in mind that your file will have been read and you would be advised to be more forthcoming than you have been with me.'

The motorway felt as ancient as an old Roman road. Charlotte concentrated on driving while Parker worked on his laptop, making occasional observations, such as Cross's company not having filed accounts for the last tax year.

'Perhaps we should stop and call Cross's mother,' he said.

'Was it you who spoke to her before?'

'I told her I was HMRC calling about his outstanding tax bill.'

'Does HMRC make such calls?'

'Sometimes.'

'You seem very knowledgeable.'

'I used to be a tax inspector.'

'You're full of surprises,' said Charlotte.

'Wherever Cross went it wasn't Antigua. British Airways flies direct. No passenger under any of his names. He could have gone via Amsterdam or Paris, but again the names didn't come up. Perhaps you should speak to the mother. She may be more receptive to a woman.'

'Speak to her as whom?' asked Charlotte, and realised she already knew the answer. As herself.

They stopped off at the next service station. Charlotte bought Parker a cup of tea from the garage shop and a coffee for herself. As an afterthought she added a KitKat.

She split the KitKat and offered Parker half.

Parker had the O'Grady woman's landline. He gave Charlotte a phone from his pocket, not his usual one.

She asked how many he had. He said it depended, without saying on what.

Charlotte was about to hang up when at last the woman answered. Her voice sounded old and frail and wary of the telephone.

Charlotte made a point of being polite, established who she was speaking to and asked whether she was the mother of a friend of hers, John Cross.

The woman grew guarded and Charlotte hurried on, saying she and her son had had a bit of a thing a while ago. She realised she was repeating what Clive had said about work: 'a bit of a thing'.

'We ran into each other again and agreed to stay in touch. Stupid of me but I have managed to lose his number. He told me you were in Liverpool and he had been living with you.'

'Who are you again?' She spoke with a hard accent, chopping her vowels.

Charlotte gave her name. She could tell the woman was in two minds. Cross had probably warned her against giving his number out.

The woman said, 'Give me yours, missy, and I will pass it on, then if he wants he can call you.'

So they are in touch, Charlotte thought.

She looked at Parker who nodded. She had no idea what number she was calling from and gave her own. The woman took her time writing it down.

'Is he in Liverpool?' Charlotte asked.

'What's that to you?'

The earlier frailty was gone. She sounded tough and suspicious.

'You're not the first to be asking,' she said, and hung up.

When Charlotte called back she got an answer machine and a man's voice on the message. A tempered Belfast accent. A voice she hadn't heard since that night over two years ago.

They left the service station and drove on. Charlotte said, 'I wasn't the first to be asking.'

Parker said nothing, looked at passing traffic then went back to his computer.

'We need to talk,' Charlotte finally managed, after seventy miles of trying to get it out.

She was sure Hopkins knew about her and Cross.

'I told you in so many words and now she knows.'

'And you think I told her.'

Parker sounded resigned.

'I haven't told anyone else,' Charlotte said pointedly.

'There is, I am afraid, a straightforward explanation. You said you and Cross had history but I knew anyway. It says in your file, which Hopkins would have read too.'

'You read my file and you didn't think to tell me?'

'I didn't think it any of my business.'

'What does the file say?'

The car behind was tailgating. Charlotte pulled into the nearside lane to let it pass, which it did, with an angry blast on its horn.

'Sexual indiscretion,' Parker said.

'Excuse me?'

'Wanton recklessness,' Parker went on, sounding miserable.

Wanton recklessness? What public schoolboy had come up with that?

'We were drunk. Everyone was high after the operation. I am sure I wasn't the only one.'

Parker sighed. 'I read files, I don't make judgements.'

'What was the point of reporting it in the first place?'

'During such exercises, private as well as professional behaviour is under scrutiny. Post-op parties are not seen by off-duty participants as part of the exercise but they are monitored as such.'

So she had been reported.

The satnav took them to an industrial estate, a mixture of older red-brick buildings and new big sheds. Ebrahim's was one of the older ones.

If he was surprised by their unannounced arrival he gave no sign of it. He had an office on a mezzanine overlooking the shop floor. He had put on weight since the photograph Charlotte had seen, with a hard protruding gut, but he had kept his military bearing and was smartly turned out in a silk shirt and linen suit. Polite in a guarded way, he offered tea like a man with nothing to hide.

'Our books are in order,' he said. 'The VAT due on 7 January has been paid. We have excellent relations with HMRC, so I don't understand why you are here.'

Ebrahim, for all his courtesy, was having trouble not staring at Parker, who said, 'We carry out spot checks.'

'Presumably with a reason,' Ebrahim said. His smile suggested their trip was a waste of their time.

As Parker had the air of a man who knew his job, Charlotte deferred. She was still fuming about her file and who had reported her. Had Cross bragged in the way that men do? She couldn't see that. He was naturally secretive.

She excused herself and wandered around the shop floor. Bolts of colourful fabrics stood stacked against walls and lay on shelves. Women in headscarves sat at sewing machines whose hum filled the room. Most of the work involved fabric pleating. Charlotte was very aware of her whiteness and ignorance. There had been no Muslim girls at her school and not many she had come across in the civil service.

Back upstairs a Hispanic-looking man was showing Parker the books. Ebrahim appeared relaxed, perched on the corner of his desk.

Parker said, 'Our only point of curiosity was a test on the randomness of your figures.'

'I don't understand,' said Ebrahim.

'In most sources of data the number one occurs as the first digit around thirty per cent of the time. Larger numbers occur less frequently. Fraudsters are likely to choose numbers that do not fit the pattern.'

Ebrahim for the first time showed irritation.

'I'm sorry if they don't conform to your theory. They are what they are.'

Parker said, 'We may have to ask for a full inspection.'

'A waste of taxpayer's money.'

It had been a waste of their day too, Charlotte decided. She could not see Ebrahim as anything other than working hard to make ends meet. The Mercedes parked outside was presumably his; nothing flash and not new.

As they were leaving, Charlotte said, 'A colleague of ours passes on his regards. He said he knew you in the army.'

Ebrahim looked doubtful at this.

'John Cross?' Charlotte suggested.

Ebrahim shook his head. 'What regiment?'

An Irish one, she said.

'In Afghanistan,' she offered.

'Not in Afghanistan; we didn't serve with the Irish.'

'It must be a mistake then.'

But she left with the impression that the name had registered.

It didn't seem such a stretch that two soldiers of Muslim background should have links, any more than she had turned out to be directly connected to both Moffat and Cross.

Back in the car, Parker returned to his computer as Charlotte drove.

'We would be better off looking at Ebrahim's brother,' he eventually said.

'Why?'

'Just a hunch,' he said, and went back to his screen.

Lulled by the dull progression of the passing miles Charlotte found herself saying she was having boyfriend trouble.

It wasn't as though she were really telling Parker; it was more like thinking aloud for her own benefit. She didn't mention the knickers, only that she feared she was about to get kicked out and her lack of options.

She supposed Parker was untroubled by any such problems and his life was monastic.

'Imagine ending up stuck out in zone six,' she said.

'No friends you can stay with until you get settled?'

'Moved on, got kids. Anyway, you were saying about Ebrahim's brother.'

Parker looked relieved to change the subject.

'A tearaway in his youth. Didn't settle. Became involved in local radical politics but he doesn't turn up on any database as being active or dangerous. Still lives in Birmingham but seems not to have any contact with Ebrahim, whose Facebook mentions a lot of family but not this brother, who doesn't seem to do social media.'

'And about Cross, what are you thinking?'

'I want to stop at the next service station and check a couple of things.'

This time they sat in the main area while Parker worked on his laptop. The place was even more depressing than when Charlotte had last been there. Watford Gap. Mind the Gap.

Parker asked her to call Cross's deportation service. He said someone should still be there. She used the phone he had given her before.

A receptionist answered. Charlotte asked to speak to Mr O'Grady, saying it was the Home Office. The woman told her Mr O'Grady was no longer with them. Charlotte said she was calling about a possible breach of internal security. She was put through to a Mr Mullen, whose Geordie accent gave her trouble.

Charlotte said she was not authorised to discuss details with anyone other than Mr O'Grady, except to point out a possible weakness in the company's security. Mullen didn't sound bothered by that. From his offhand manner, Charlotte suspected the job involved nothing more than showing foreigners the door.

'No one informed us of Mr O'Grady's departure,' Charlotte said officiously. 'When was this?'

'Before Christmas.'

'Then where is he? It is your responsibility to keep us updated, or we file a formal complaint.'

'Hang on,' said Mullen.

'Belfast,' Charlotte said to Parker, after she had hung up. 'According to Mullen.'

'Give me five minutes,' Parker said.

Charlotte went to the toilet with its Dyson hand driers,

and at WH Smith she bought water and a green Aero bar she didn't really want.

She considered just getting in the car and driving off. This had nothing to do with Parker, more a sudden desire to escape her life.

When she got back he asked where she had been. He told her she had been gone twenty minutes. She supposed she must have been standing in a daze in the central concourse. Parker asked if she was all right.

'Just tired from driving.'

She was starting to resent the fact that Parker didn't drive.

'Give us a bit of that Aero,' Parker said. 'I ran a check on December passenger lists from Belfast. Ryanair has an O'Grady departing on 8 December for London Stansted. Your sighting was on 10 December.'

'Do you think he is still ours, undercover?' Charlotte said, wishing she had bought a regular Aero.

'The GBH, the change of name, the job, it's all classic stuff for establishing a legend. The next question is, if not ours then whose?'

'And why Belfast?'

Parker shrugged. 'It's his home turf, after all.'

6

The drive into London involved long tailbacks that frayed Charlotte's patience and left her snappish. Parker continued to work. She was still wondering if he had sold her out. Perhaps he had been hacking her from the start.

For supper she had to endure more of Clive's cooking. They were back to cottage pie, with Clive fussily pointing out the difference between cottage pie, with beef, and shepherd's, with lamb. He had bought a bottle of wine.

Charlotte supposed Clive would make a pompous speech about it being time to review their options. He would deny any affair. Clive didn't like rows.

They small-talked their way through the meal. Charlotte asked if work was still a problem. He waggled his hand while he chewed his food.

'Seems to have blown over,' he said, finishing his mouthful.

'Why do you never talk about it? Is it classified?'

'No, boring.'

'Boring work, or boring to talk about?'

'Most of my days are spent dealing with monkeys.'

For a moment she thought he was about to tell her he had been in scientific research all along. All she knew was he worked with political lobbyists, 'doing this and that'. On the few occasions she had asked he said it was barely tolerable and he didn't expect her to have to put up with it too.

'What kind of monkeys? Good pie, by the way.'

It wasn't particularly.

'Thanks. Press monkeys. We tell them what to write, which they repeat, for which they get paid.'

'Give me an example,' Charlotte said.

'Quite a lot about climate change.'

'For or against?'

'We've been doing stuff with the GWPF.'

He had to spell that out for her. 'The Global Warming Policy Foundation. A lot of the scientific thinking behind global warming is flawed.'

'What's the point?'

Clive gave her a rare smile.

'Deregulation, union reforms and business tax cuts; what else?'

So Clive was realigning himself to suit an emerging political landscape and seeking fresh opportunities. Charlotte suspected he was much more ambitious than he let on and not talking about his work was a form of condescension.

'About my father,' he said. 'You should know.'

'Is he all right?' she asked, thinking he might be ill.

'He and Naomi will be staying here.'

Clive hadn't mentioned the wife's name before. He said they would be there several days before going back to France and would move back permanently after that.

Charlotte looked at her bedding on the sofa and asked, 'Is this your excuse for dumping me?'

'Not at all,' Clive protested. 'Just while they are here, you can stay in Golden Lane in the guest rooms there.'

Golden Lane was the adjacent estate, built by the same architects, more downmarket than the Barbican. She didn't know about any guest rooms. They were for friends and relatives of residents of both estates, Clive said.

'Quite basic. Just while they're here. It's a drag. They rather sprang it on me. I've booked you one and paid for it.'

'Are we having "that conversation"?' Charlotte insisted.

'Hardly. I am just trying to arrange things.'

She looked at him, waiting for him to explain, but he just smirked, which set her off.

'Shall I save you the awkwardness of saying you don't want me around and jump forward to the bit where I tell you to fuck off?'

Clive recoiled, as though riding a punch, then laughed.

She stood and swore at him some more, before storming out, grabbing her coat, bag and phone, with no idea of where she was going.

She stood shaking in the lift, watching the descending floor numbers, marched past the desk porter, ignoring his goodnight and went out into the cold. She passed the cinema bar full of ridiculous hipsters, entered the tunnel and took a right up Golden Lane, then down Old Street, looping back to Smithfield, then south to St Paul's and its adjacent shopping centre, both floodlit.

The next thing she knew, she was sitting on the deserted embankment with a screw-top bottle of red wine, which she must have bought in the Tesco by the Tube station though she had no memory of doing so. She was typing Clive's password to access his iCloud. He had even written neat answers to his security questions in the Letts diary.

First there was a strange sensation of reading her own texts, all boring and practical.

– What do you want for supper?

– Took dry cleaning in.

There was nothing much personal other than a few 'missing yous', all in contrast to the frantic touchy-feely chain of texts she discovered between Clive and someone called Bekka.

– Hot for you.

That was him.

– Cumming now, thinking of you.

That was her. Texting while masturbating was a new one on Charlotte.

– Looking forward to more dick-tation.

Her again. Charlotte didn't know whether to laugh or cry, thinking: At least now I know.

She walked down the embankment to Blackfriars and back again until she was opposite Parker's block, sitting on the high, broad wall overlooking the river. The tide was in. Black water slapped against the ramparts. Charlotte typed and then deleted vitriol intended for Clive until she gave up, exhausted. She had no idea how long she had been sitting there. She decided to finish the wine and find a hotel. The Ibis in Southwark seemed likeliest. It was after eleven already. Hours had passed without her realising. She worked out which apartment was Parker's. Its light was on. Should she text him? She didn't; it was her business not his. She got down from the wall and walked towards Upper Thames Street.

As she reached the road she was aware of a tall figure on her left. It was Parker. She supposed he must have been watching her from his window. He hung back, not saying anything. She quickened her pace.

Parker called out to ask if she was all right.

She shouted over her shoulder that she was minding her own business and suggested he do the same.

She kept walking. He called out after her again.

'I was worried. You seemed so on edge all day.'

'That doesn't give you the right to stalk me!'

'I could see from upstairs that you were upset.'

She had been spying on Clive and now Parker was spying on her.

She stopped, turned and composed herself, thanked him sarcastically for his concern and said she was old enough to look after herself. Parker looked unsure about that. He started to tell her he had found out more about Cross.

'Save it for work,' she said, and walked on, thinking: Fuck the lot of you.

This time he didn't follow. As she turned on to Southwark Bridge she saw him still loitering where she'd left him, watching her.

She called the Ibis and was relieved to find it had a night desk and a free room. At 9am she had her meeting with Hopkins, who would no doubt notice she was wearing the same outfit. She couldn't decide whether Parker was being protective in a clumsy way or operating in a fantasy world, as in one of his films.

Charlotte bought toothpaste and a brush and used the office lavatory to make herself presentable. Hopkins, as Charlotte had suspected, clocked her still wearing yesterday's clothes. She was sitting with a man Charlotte was immediately wary of. His deathly pallor and unblinking stare gave him a messianic air. He also looked like someone who was used to getting answers. She sat down nervously, wondering who he was.

'This is Mr Roberts,' said Hopkins.

They both had coffees. There was a third cup, which Roberts pushed towards her.

Hopkins started by saying, 'We want to know about John Cross, whom as well as knowing personally, you identified from CCTV footage taken on 3 December last year.'

'It was the tenth,' Charlotte corrected. She suspected the mistake was to see if she spotted it. Roberts made a note of that. He had a fussy, precise manner. His parchment-like skin reminded her of tallow candles. She was in no doubt that he was a hostile presence.

Roberts placed his pen down and said, 'This is not a formal interview. It is not necessary to know for whom I work. Ms Hopkins's authority is sufficient for our purposes. We are also talking to others of Mr Cross's acquaintance.'

He made the last word sound unsavoury. The voice was a surprise – thin, high and pinched. Charlotte supposed him about forty. Despite his spectral appearance, he looked aggressively fit.

Roberts went on. 'We urgently need to assemble as complete a picture as possible. Feel free to say whatever comes to mind. What was your impression of Mr Cross?'

'Competent and professional.'

'Whatever comes to mind,' Roberts prompted.

'Competent and professional,' Charlotte repeated. 'He knew his job when others didn't.'

It had been a big state-of-the-art anti-terrorist exercise to foil an imminent strike on Heathrow Airport and a race against the clock that had threatened to get out of hand with the overenthusiastic interrogation of 'suspects'. The operation had been distinguished by a lot of blind-eyeing, with a few screaming fits thrown in.

'Go on,' said Roberts.

Charlotte shrugged. 'It was a boys' exercise and women were treated as excess baggage.'

She was aware of Roberts studying her.

'Is what comes to mind,' she added, holding his gaze.

'How so?'

'If you were a woman and queried anything you were seen as indecisive.'

Roberts looked bored as though the answer confirmed her shortcomings.

The questions were routine at first. Hopkins remained silent. Charlotte had time to study Roberts. His appearance combined a military manner and expensive designer kit: en brosse haircut; a turtleneck – cashmere if she wasn't mistaken; olive leather jacket with plenty of useful pockets; black jeans and Chelsea boots with heavy rubber soles.

Roberts started to push and the easy questions were left behind.

'There are one or two things I want to clear up,' he said. 'It notes when you were asked to comment in your post-op debriefing on Mr Cross's questionable methods you did not do so, saying, quote, "it isn't for me to comment", unquote. Do you remember saying that?'

'If that's what it says, then I suppose I did.'

'Why did you?'

'Because it wasn't my job to assess Mr Cross's performance. If he had crossed the line it was up to others to say.'

'Were you present at interrogations?'

'No.'

'Then how do you know he crossed the line?'

'Others spoke of it.'

'How?'

'In shocked terms. It was supposed to have been an exercise and Mr Cross treated it as though it weren't, and he told me so.'

'Told you what?'

'He said, "I really stuck it to the fuckers." '

The truth was she had been shocked and scared. The mood over the two days had been panicked and aggressive. When the operation looked like failing Cross had stepped in and berated them.

'Did you perhaps not say anything because you were besotted with Mr Cross?' Roberts asked.

'No!' she protested.

'Did he say anything to you after the operation?'

She couldn't see the point of denying; Roberts probably knew anyway.

'He thanked me for not saying.'

'Directly?'

'Texted.'

'Saying?'

' "I owe you", or words to that effect.'

'Which meant he must have had your number.'

Roberts looked at her inquiringly.

'He asked for it, about meeting for a drink.'

'Meaning you were interested.'

'I thought nothing of it. It would have seemed rude not to give it.'

'And did he call you?'

'As it happened, no.'

She was being made to look guilty. Roberts made her think of the Spanish Inquisition, righteous to the point of breaking someone for the sake of a confession. The man should look more like an El Greco, she decided. He was not tall, which she hadn't realised, because they were sitting. Roberts, if that was his name, was not a desk man and she suspected he had special services training. Even the surface politeness carried a warning of threat. She thought he might even know Cross; maybe she was there to be assessed as part of the detritus of the man's life because it might tell Roberts something he didn't know.

'You had sexual intercourse with Mr Cross.'

Charlotte was less embarrassed by the revelation than she had feared.

'There was nothing to say we couldn't.'

Roberts asked, 'Are you naive, Ms Waites?'

'It was a private matter.'

'Hardly, on a roof during a party.'

Hopkins sniggered at that.

The roof was where people went to smoke. Tough job, Cross had said when he found her up there, and she agreed. She still smoked in those days. A lot of pheromones, she had said.

They ended up against a parapet, behind an emergency stairway exit. At the time she'd thought of it as an opportunity for a sort of daring she secretly craved. She remembered saying, 'I'll let you fuck me but you can't put your hand around my throat.' He removed it and after that she concentrated on her own pleasure, enough to consider it worthwhile. Back downstairs, she avoided him as a way of saying she had moved on already. Lust had blinded her to the fact that he had beaten a suspect that afternoon. It left her with a feeling of grubby excitement.

'Have you ever been to Belfast?' asked Roberts.

'No,' said Charlotte, alarmed by the question, given that Cross had recently.

'How well would you say you know Mr Cross?'

'Nothing I haven't told you that you don't already know.'

'Has he been in touch with you since?'

She said no, thinking about how she had left her number with Cross's mother.

Roberts said, 'To go back to the exercise, did it occur to you that Mr Cross might have been told to overstep the mark to see what others said?'

'It hadn't, but it doesn't surprise me.'

'Meaning?'

'I probably should have realised that the exercise also contained private tests on those taking part.'

'When one thing led to another, did you ask yourself

about that too?' asked Roberts with an air of false innocence. 'How many other women were on this exercise?'

Roberts made it sound like 'sexercise'. Charlotte knew she had been played for a fool.

'Maybe five or six. I am sure you know already.'

'It was seven. A high-security operation,' Roberts reminded her. 'Perhaps it only occurs to you now that Mr Cross might have been instructed to see if any of the women were susceptible to a sexual approach.'

Roberts leered. Charlotte sat back feeling crushed.

'These are the facts of life,' said Roberts. 'Professional job, no emotional involvement.'

Hopkins gave her a nasty look. 'As in can a woman who drops her knickers for a virtual stranger be trusted to keep her mouth shut?'

Charlotte wanted to ask what was so special about Hopkins's sex life. She said, 'I fail to see what my gullibility has to do with your gathering information on Mr Cross.'

She wouldn't put it past Hopkins to have included this humiliation for an extra kick.

Roberts took a folder from a briefcase and produced a photograph.

'Do you recognise him?'

It was a grainy CCTV image showing Cross leaving a Chinese takeaway.

'Excellent facial recognition work by Parker,' said Hopkins.

Whatever technology Parker was using, it was a lot faster than her shuffling through endless CCTV footage.

'Where was this taken?' Charlotte asked.

'Belfast,' said Roberts. 'As part of a police undercover operation.'

She looked at them, wondering how much they weren't telling.

'Let's dangle you there and see if Mr Cross gets in touch,' said Roberts.

Charlotte protested that she had no experience of field work.

'Eyes and ears only,' Hopkins said airily. 'We do the rest.'

Charlotte thought: I bet you will. Roberts was staring at her queerly.

Hopkins said, 'You're booked on a flight this afternoon. Parker will go with you.'

She was being given no choice. The prospect of encountering Cross again was the last thing she wanted: used once, used twice? She could imagine Roberts saying to Hopkins, 'She's the flame. Let's see if she draws the moth.'

7

Charlotte packed in a hurry. Clearing the bathroom she caught sight of herself and thought how bitter she looked. She left Clive's Letts diary open on its page of passwords. Taking one of his neat collection of Stabilo highlighters, she marked the iCloud passwords, then used one of his Lamy pens to say she was away at short notice, didn't know for how long and would pick up her stuff later. She left the top off the pen to annoy him.

She and Parker were booked on a flight from City Airport. She took the Docklands Light Railway, arrived early, drifted pointlessly through the duty-free shop and decided to call her father, who answered as always by laboriously reciting the whole telephone number. Asked why he did that, he said, as though it were perfectly obvious, that someone might be calling a wrong number.

She told him she was going to Belfast, waiting for him to ask why.

'Weren't you there?' she prompted.

It had been an army posting before she was born. As he wasn't going to volunteer anything more than to say it had been years ago, she asked instead how he was.

'Oh, you know.'

She heard her voice grow brittle as she said she was evidently calling at a bad time.

'No, not at all,' he conceded. 'I am just always rather surprised by the telephone.'

He lapsed into silence.

'Are you okay?' she asked.

He eventually said, 'I have been meaning to talk to you.'

She couldn't remember him ever offering to talk about anything. She presumed he meant his health.

'About?'

'Your mother.'

Charlotte wanted to ask why now, after all these years, but then all he said was: 'Not on the telephone.'

She spotted Parker and said she had to go, knowing her father would think she was brushing him off.

As the call was ending, he managed to come out with, 'Call me from Belfast, let me know how you're getting on. Never saw much of the city. We were stuck in fortified compounds.'

'Doing what?'

Her father gave a snort of a laugh.

'Keeping the peace.'

She hung up irritated, curious to know what he wanted to tell her.

Parker asked if she was okay.

She brushed the question aside, saying, 'I'm sorted now. What has Hopkins told you?'

'Observe, listen, sit on our hands, presumably to give her time to make up her mind about what we are supposed to be doing.'

Hopkins seemed to be packing them off with no clear plan.

'Business as usual, then,' she said, wondering what she wasn't being told.

They arrived after dark at George Best Airport. The security checking area in London had been playing piped music. She had never come across that before and asked Parker if he knew why. To enhance passenger experience, he told her. Not with Ed Sheeran, she replied. In the Belfast corridor between Customs and Arrivals it was Van Morrison's 'Spanish Rose', which put a spring in her step.

A driver was waiting with Parker's name on a card. The road from an airport into a town was always the same, thought Charlotte as she watched passing neon and the first spots of rain hit the window.

They were driven to a police barracks where they were met by an unwelcoming uniformed senior officer who shook hands with Charlotte and avoided Parker's. They weren't invited to sit.

'London is pulling rank,' he said. His accent sounded hostile. 'We don't welcome the intrusion. Is there anything you have to say? Fucked if I'm being told anything.'

Parker said, 'High-security enquiry in connection with a suspect recently surfaced here.'

'There was a time when we used to get properly briefed.'

The man's hard consonants amplified every grievance. Charlotte found herself staring at his extraordinarily long arms. His sleeves were too short, exposing hard knobbly wrists and huge, bony hands. Long arms and a chip on both shoulders, she decided as the man went on.

'As we've been told to ask no questions you're unlikely to find us helpful. So, watch away. Someone will drive you there.'

Access to the site had to be made undercover. They were taken in the back of an old Transit van, sitting on their suitcases in the dark. It was the end of rush hour and they made slow progress, stopping and starting. The smell of gasoline forced Charlotte to breathe through her mouth. After twenty minutes they drew up and the van reversed. The doors were swung open to reveal a doorway that the driver unlocked. Under cover of the van doors Charlotte and Parker sneaked into a dimly lit corridor. The driver told them to go upstairs.

There they found two shadowy operators who ignored them. The room was dark apart from a monitor screen. As Charlotte's eyes adjusted, she saw the one watching the monitor was little more than a kid, with cropped hair and the remains of acne. His colleague was middle-aged, going to seed, and had the air of a man doing a shit job.

The room stank of cigarettes. The place was a dump, with grubby lino on the floor, a threadbare rug, an old sideboard and a couple of sagging upholstered chairs, showing wear and tear. The blinds were lowered, enough to let a camera observe the nighttime street and the Chinese takeaway opposite. On the monitor, sickly yellow light spilling from the shopfront was reflected on the wet pavement. Its window ran with condensation, beyond which stood a smeared, stark waiting area with a couple of banquettes and a service counter. There were no customers.

The older man eventually said, 'You can watch from upstairs. Make sure you're not seen. Did you bring equipment?'

Parker said, 'I thought we were using yours.'

'No one tells us sweet FA. There are rooms in the back with camp beds. Did you bring sleeping bags?'

The answer was no. Clearly Hopkins had decided to make their trip as inconvenient and as uncomfortable as possible.

'No lights after dark,' the man went on. 'No wandering in and out. If you need to go anywhere, tell someone and we'll arrange a pick-up. Food you can order in. There are takeaway menus. You make a call and someone will fetch. We work eight-hour shifts, two at a time, sometimes with an observation vehicle parked in the street behind the Chinese. A lot of stuff goes out the back.'

It was stated as a fact rather than an offer to share.

The man concluded, 'Someone's supposed to be here twenty-four hours a day, which isn't always the case as we're short-staffed.'

After a day of watching, Charlotte wanted to run screaming down the street. The only thing stopping her was that outside looked even more inhospitable than indoors. Horrible sandwiches, soggy chips and permanently gloomy skies contributed to a sense of punishment. It was like watching the CCTV footage all over again, for real.

Parker lost himself in his computer while Charlotte spent the day staring through the slatted blind at the shuttered takeaway. Whatever previous action had been noted, their arrival seemed to mark a lull. Night took forever to fall. Trade was thin when the place opened.

They were given the cold shoulder by the rest of the team, four taciturn men and two slightly more friendly women, one of whom, with Mediterranean looks, at least offered them what she referred to as a brew.

Charlotte's camp bed was uncomfortable. The first night she'd had to improvise with her coat. She had brought no towel. A grubby bathroom was a deterrent to the pursuit of personal hygiene. On the first morning Parker arranged for two sleeping bags and towels to be delivered.

The days were marked by long silences. Charlotte couldn't tell what Parker was thinking. Most of the time she contemplated nothing or things she had thought about before, none of them interesting.

At night they took turns in four-hour shifts. Sometimes a team was downstairs; not always. There was one who invariably said on arrival, 'What's the gig?'

Once, fetching tea, Charlotte heard two of the men being rude about Parker's appearance. She told them it wasn't his fault, to which one replied, 'Is it contagious, is what we're thinking.'

Two of the men held farting competitions. The men all smoked. Sensing Parker's disapproval, one said, 'We can hardly go and stand out the back since we're not meant to be here.'

Charlotte hadn't brought anything to read. When she couldn't sleep she looked at Rightmove. Belfast was affordable and she wondered whether to put in for a transfer. Otherwise she played double-pack solitaire. Consistent with her mood, the games never came out and it always seemed to be raining.

That night Parker did the first shift. No one was downstairs so they used the monitor.

Nothing was happening, he said when it was Charlotte's turn. The screen could have been a photograph for all its absence of activity.

When she got cold she went upstairs to fetch her sleeping bag and decided to use the bathroom, not realising Parker was in there and hadn't locked the door.

She stood staring at him performing some strange private ritual, with his arm circling his head.

From his reflection in the basin mirror she saw that he had almost completed covering his head with a sticky brown bandage, like a mummy, leaving slits for the mouth and eyes. She apologised and turned away.

Parker didn't seem bothered.

'I have to do it every night, and my hands too, to stop lacerating myself in my sleep.'

He carried on while Charlotte watched in morbid fascination. He ended by tucking the loose end of the bandage under his wrist.

'There. The invisible man.'

His eyes, which were all that was left of his face apart from the mouth, looked amused.

At some point in the night she heard Parker moving around. Soon after he came down and sat on the floor. He had on his woollen cap. The bandages in the dark turned his face into a mask.

Charlotte said, 'Nothing's happening and it looks like nothing will.'

'I suspect quite a lot is going on, even if we can't see it.'

All they had spotted so far was the same two or three Chinese turn up in an SUV, usually by day when the place was closed. A couple of white faces put in appearances, sometimes at the same time as the Chinese.

Charlotte and Parker agreed that money laundering was probably a given. She was less sure about drugs as the IRA was known to kneecap dealers found operating in its territory.

Parker said, 'It's as grey as everything else in this town. This may just be about the IRA taking a cut of Chinese drug profits. It's as strapped for cash as everyone else.' He shrugged, adding, 'None of this is big news. It's covered by local press reports.'

'How does any of this connect to Cross?'

'Maybe he was just stopping by for a takeaway.'

'And if – when – he does show up again?'

'Perhaps Hopkins has people on the ground.'

Don't bet on it, Charlotte thought.

The bandage covering Parker's face seemed to vanish in the dark, as though he had succeeded in erasing himself, leaving her being stared at by a pair of eyes.

The room smelt of dead cigarettes. She was homesick. She didn't know why she was there. She didn't know what she was supposed to do. It was like standing on the edge of a high board looking down at a waterless pool.

Being able to sit in the observation car was considered a treat compared to being stuck in the room. The team played rock paper scissors to see who got to go. When the exotic woman won, Charlotte was surprised to be asked if she fancied a change of scene.

The car was waiting out the back. It was getting on for 10pm. The takeaway had been doing brisk trade. It was the weekend.

Someone had taken the trouble to make the car look more ordinary, with a kid's seat in the back and a 'Baby on Board' sticker in the rear window.

It was a cold night with clear black skies. Charlotte was surprised to find that Belfast had stars.

They parked down from the back of the takeaway, which had a small yard, with a high pebbledash wall and a door.

The woman was about Charlotte's age. She introduced herself as Delia. It was her last name but everyone called her that.

'Maltese, in answer to your next question, though I was born here.'

Her father had been a jazz pianist who said Belfast was the last place he would have settled had he not met Delia's mother.

Delia was lively and forthright.

'Most of the men are hopeless. They're lost without their mothers. What about your pal?'

'Keeps to himself.'

'Hard not to stare.'

They were being chatty and friendly, Charlotte thought, in the way of two women getting along, but you never could tell.

Twenty minutes had passed when she got a call from

Parker, who said a man with Cross's build had just gone in the front.

'But he's wearing a hoodie. He seems to be waiting for a takeaway and still has the hood up.'

Five minutes later Parker called again to say the man had gone through to the back.

'Confirm sighting if he comes out but do not approach.'

Delia said there were night-vision binoculars in the glove compartment. Charlotte practised focusing on the door.

Another ten minutes went by before the man slipped out the back entrance, his hood up. Surprised by his stealth, Charlotte was slow with the glasses. She had a glimpse of a face but couldn't be sure.

She called Parker to say she was unable to confirm.

Parker swore, as if he thought it was her fault.

Charlotte's reaction took her by surprise.

'I'm going to get a better look.' Before Parker could object she hung up and told Delia, 'Taking a walk.'

She grabbed the glasses, thinking if she looked like just another woman hurrying home and got ahead of him she could use them to check.

The cold turned her breath visible as she got out. She already regretted her decision and was disoriented at finding herself outside after her stale confinement.

The man was at the end of the block, about to turn into the main road. When she got there she thought she had lost him, then spotted the hoodie fifty yards ahead. He had crossed over.

Charlotte stayed on her side of the road, half-running, inventing a story for why she might be doing so. Enough people were still out for her not to draw attention. The man continued to walk purposefully. He didn't look round and she increased her pace. A bus passed and he was suddenly gone. She crossed the road and saw he must have gone down a side street.

This was far quieter and poorly lit but she saw him again as he passed under a lamp.

She knew she should go back. Instead, she put up the hood of her parka and walked on until there were only the two of them.

She followed when he turned a couple of corners, sticking to her side of the street, thinking he must be going somewhere local, which would give them an address.

He stopped suddenly, in the middle of the pavement, leaving her no choice but to carry on, or it would become obvious she was following him.

He remained there, looking as though he was checking his phone. She recklessly considered approaching him, knowing that she was defenceless and it would be madness.

The distance between them narrowed. Still he didn't move. Charlotte told herself there was nothing to say she wasn't walking home. She drew level, watching out of the corner of her eye as he was about to light a cigarette. The lighter flared, showing a glimpse of face. Still she couldn't be sure.

She quickened, moving ahead, feeling as though she were now the target. Whatever impulse had spurred her was gone. She was being foolhardy and was vulnerable. She decided he must have known he was being followed. He was a professional and she was untrained, alone on an empty street at night.

She counted fifty paces then pulled out her phone. She was frightened because she couldn't see the man. She called Parker and told him she wasn't sure where she was.

'What do you think you're doing?' Parker's voice was tight and angry.

She risked looking over her shoulder. The man was gone.

She told Parker she would find a spot where she felt less isolated and call again.

She hung up and continued, casting backward glances, until she decided it was safe to turn around.

She used a late-night convenience store as an excuse to appear normal. She bought a packet of mints, as though that had been the object of this fruitless exercise. The shop had no other customers. The proprietor was Indian. The counter had a metal grille and Charlotte pushed her money through. An ancient CCTV camera was pointed at her. She was tempted to buy a pack of cigarettes.

A bell rang as the shop door opened and there he was, standing behind her. His hood was up and he was looking down at his phone so his face remained hidden. Charlotte could see him on the surveillance monitor, showing them both standing there, in dreamlike black and white.

She had her hood up and kept her head down as she picked up her change with clumsy fingers, turning away so he didn't see her face, and walked out shakily.

She went back the same way, her stomach knotted. Apart from a few passing cars the streets remained empty. The pubs hadn't yet closed. She reached a junction she did not recognise and realised she had made the basic error of not making mental markers for her return. She refused to let Google Maps tell her where she was. He had been standing right behind her. What on earth had possessed her?

She was still trying to get her bearings when a car approached and slowed down. For a moment she thought it was Cross, then was relieved to see Delia behind the wheel.

She fell into the passenger seat, still clutching the mints. 'Polo?'

Delia said, 'Don't mind if I do.'

Charlotte's tasted nasty and sweet.

'How did you find me?' she asked.

'Parker tracked your phone.'

She didn't know whether to be annoyed. 'I feel like a fool now.'

'No harm done. I can claim the mileage.'

'Isn't this a police car?' Charlotte asked in surprise.

'We're so underfunded we're having to use our own.'

That explained the kiddie carrier.

Delia said, 'My shift has officially ended. If you want, come to my place for a drink. It's not like anyone's checking.'

Charlotte admitted she could do with one. She didn't call Parker. She wasn't in the mood for a post-mortem.

'Packet of crisps, salt and vinegar, and a can of Heineken?' Delia asked.

'Perfect,' said Charlotte, in a good mood for the first time in as long as she could remember.

Delia's domestic life exposed Charlotte to a bracing normality. A new house in a quiet area. A cat and a dog. A kid of around seven was still up watching telly. He greeted Delia affectionately and solemnly shook hands with Charlotte, saying he could go to bed now his mum was home safe. He had the manner of an adult and explained his sister was already asleep as she was only three. Delia's husband seemed boyish by comparison.

'Brian does most of the cooking,' Delia said.

'More than my ex,' said Charlotte, to test how the 'ex' sounded.

Delia and her husband seemed easy with each other in a way that Charlotte always found hard in her own relationships. Everything between them appeared not too ordered and not too messy, in contrast to the calculated silences of the past weeks with Clive.

Brian went to put the boy to bed. Delia kicked off her shoes and took Charlotte through to the living room, at home and relaxed in a way Charlotte never managed in London.

'I've just been dumped by my boyfriend,' she announced.

She wanted to appear a bit daring and self-deprecating. She made Delia laugh, telling her about hacking Clive's account and the texts.

They moved on and talked shop.

Delia said of their operation, 'So the place is being watched but it's beyond boring and no one tells us anything. How's your job?'

Charlotte said she was more or less in disgrace and being fast-tracked backwards.

'Why are you here, exactly?' Delia asked.

The question seemed pointed. Charlotte wondered if the woman was genuinely pleasant or making a point of appearing nice.

'Who's asking?'

Delia laughed and said, 'The boys told me to find out. "Chat her up," they said. "Girls talk." '

'Do we have to watch what we say to each other?' Charlotte asked carefully.

'I'm just saying, is all. I can tell them whatever you want.'

'What have you been told?'

'Just that we give you access.'

'We're curious about the man we saw coming out the back.'

'The one in the hoodie? What's so interesting about him?'

Charlotte was about to say then ducked the question and asked back, 'Maybe you know him? He's local but distinctive, being half Muslim. Army background.'

'There's tons of ex-squaddies acting as enforcers, collecting protection money and so on, for both Republican and Protestant gangs. The thing about here is not everybody knows everybody but usually someone knows somebody who does, and there's a terrific amount of gossip.'

Charlotte took another beer, saying she ought to be quick as she should get back.

Delia said, 'Here's my tip, for which you probably won't thank me, but try Lafferty. He's one of those squaddies, a psycho known as the Merc, as in mercenary, *and* because he drives a Merc. He fought Russians in the Ukraine, suffers from PTSD after seeing mates blown up in Afghanistan. Extremely volatile. He has convictions for possession of offensive weapons and for taking a flamethrower to a fellow's balls. That's how we know him.'

'A flamethrower!'

'Homemade. He's out now and claims to have found God. He teaches boys to box at a gym off Andersonstown Road.'

'Is he local?'

'A Brit, but a lot of these ex-soldiers hang out, regardless of which side they work for, so Lafferty might know your man. But don't say I didn't warn you.'

'Don't get started,' Charlotte said, sensing Parker's disapproval. Giving herself the benefit of the doubt, she told him she was almost sure it was Cross.

'Anyway, we can confirm. He went into a late-night store with CCTV.'

'You shouldn't have gone after him.'

'I know. Sorry.' She wasn't. 'Anyway, there's a man called Lafferty we should talk to.'

She told him about Delia.

'I brought you back a beer.'

It had been Delia's idea for her to take a six-pack of Heineken. Charlotte listened to the hiss as Parker pulled the tab.

She said, 'Downstairs is empty. Wasn't there meant to be a shift on tonight?'

'They left in a hurry. Something about a big raid at the docks.'

'And over the road?'

'Closed but they haven't left.'

A tiny middle-aged Chinese couple ran the place. They usually arrived and left carrying Asda bags for life.

Charlotte crossed to the window.

'They're locking up. Heads or tails, first shift?'

She lost and settled down for the four-hour haul, wrapped in her sleeping bag, staring at the unrelenting monitor.

'He's back,' Charlotte hissed. She'd had to wake Parker. 'Same hoodie. He must have a key. He didn't force anything.'

'Is he still there?'

Charlotte nodded. Parker got up and reached for his shoes. He was sleeping in his clothes.

'Stay here,' he said as he shrugged on his coat.

Charlotte insisted on going.

'My turn,' Parker said. 'I have the advantage of surprise.'

He pointed to his bandages. He would wait for Cross at the back.

'And?'

'I thought I would ask him for a light.'

'Seriously!?'

'He'll be thinking I'm a madman, wandering around like Frankenstein's monster in the night. I'll tell him they're burns from Afghanistan and we can take it from there.'

Charlotte listened to him go downstairs and went to the window. Parker texted to say he was in place. She wanted to tell him it was too risky. She was more concerned for him than she had realised.

After five minutes the front door of the takeaway cracked open and the hooded man slipped out.

Charlotte ran downstairs without thinking. She reached the street in time to hear a car start and depart, too far away for her to read the plate and too fast for her to use her phone camera.

She texted Parker, who joined her back upstairs and they drank their way through the rest of the beers.

'Getting warmer,' said Parker. 'Two sightings in one night.'

He started to remove his bandages then left them.

Charlotte was looking at the street when an explosion came from inside the takeaway. The windows shook and she instinctively ducked. Her first thought was a bomb and the IRA because Cross had taken nothing in with him.

Parker was on the phone to the emergency services. Already people were out on the street.

Charlotte had difficulty picturing the sequence. Had the bomb been hidden by Cross earlier? But he had brought nothing in then either. Had he returned to activate it? Bombs had timers, why not just pre-set it?

She was surprised by the speed with which the fire was spreading. Sirens were coming from all over. Police cars cordoned off the street and the growing crowd was ordered back in case of further explosions. The firefighters arrived and a small cheer went up when the hoses came on.

Parker used the emergency number they'd been given for Hopkins and left a message.

Charlotte pointed at the street and said the copper they had met on the first evening, who had complained about them being there, had just turned up looking thunderous.

He was addressing a constable while staring up at the window where Charlotte was. Though he couldn't see her he started beckoning. She told Parker, who said, 'Down we go, I suppose.'

Parker's presence caused a stir. Kids were out as well as adults and Charlotte heard one say in awe, 'It's the bogeyman.'

The copper – who bothered to introduce himself this time, as DCI Doyle – asked Parker, 'What the fuck's with you? And what the fuck is with this place?'

'Building on fire,' said Parker. 'Psoriasis, since you asked.'

He seemed to be enjoying himself. Charlotte supposed the bandages gave him an anonymous identity, like the Lone Ranger.

She gave Doyle the highlights.

Doyle grunted and said, 'Is this the fucker you're supposed to be watching?'

Charlotte suspected Doyle was one of those men who disliked women on principle.

'The same hooded man was previously seen waiting to buy a takeaway, then emerged out the back empty-handed.' She added facetiously, 'Unless he's friends with the staff and ate in the kitchen.' She left an insolent pause before adding, 'Sir.'

The blazing fire, the water arcs from the hoses sparkling in the flames, the flashing lights and Parker's bandages lent everything the air of a bad dream, from which Doyle appeared desperate to wake.

He started fiddling with a coin fished from his pocket.

'And this hooded man?'

'Unidentified,' said Parker. 'Your lot weren't here to ask.'

'They're intercepting a container of Chinks being smuggled by triads.'

'How come?' asked Parker.

'Anonymous tip-off,' Doyle said, as though he didn't see the point of the question.

Parker showed teeth, a disconcerting sight with the mask, and said, 'Two big hits against the Chinese in one night.'

Doyle dropped the coin he was playing with and didn't bother to pick it up. Charlotte considered the significance of what Parker had just said. After nothing, two things at once.

Parker's phone rang. It was Hopkins. Charlotte listened to his update while she watched Doyle fume. High blood pressure, she decided, wishing him a heart attack.

Parker was saying to Hopkins, 'There's nothing to stay here for, so we'll be moving to the Europa. At this time of year, with offers, it's within our overnight allowance. I checked. They do a very good breakfast.'

While Parker continued to wind Hopkins up, Charlotte's attention was drawn to a man standing at the back of the crowd. He was hard to make out at first because he wasn't tall and others were in front of him, and she had only a brief sighting before he turned away, but she was certain it was her sinister interrogator, Roberts. When she looked again he was gone.

8

The Europa appeared swanky with its marbled lobby but the reality was more like something built by a middle-European dictatorship punching above its weight. After the hideout Charlotte was not about to criticise. By the time they arrived in a minicab, for which they'd had to wait an age, there was time only for a moderate raid on the minibar, a bath, a couple of hours' sleep and a room-service breakfast before a meeting first thing at police headquarters.

Doyle she expected. He turned up with another man in plain clothes, about thirty-five, with sandy hair and an open face, who uttered not a word. Charlotte's sighting of Roberts the previous night had been correct because he was there too, wearing a suit and tie. Also present was Hopkins, who Charlotte hadn't expected but now realised she should have done. Hopkins was complaining to Roberts about the ungodly hour of her flight. Charlotte figured it must be important if she was there in person at such short notice.

The mood was hard to gauge until the meeting got underway and Doyle behaved with the resentment of a man not kept in the loop.

He summarised his end: undercover observation of a front for the IRA and the triads.

'Then the joint blows up, involving a man you're watching, not known to us and us not told why.'

He turned to Hopkins, who looked at Roberts. She eventually said, 'We're as much in the dark as you are.'

Charlotte was pushed not to laugh at that. Hopkins threw the ball back to Doyle.

'It's your patch. What's your immediate action?'

'Round up the usual suspects,' said Doyle, huffily. 'They'll be downstairs shortly.'

'Paint us a picture,' said Hopkins, leaning forward, hands clasped.

Doyle gave them a paragraph on how local drugs operations in Belfast had escalated since two rival outfits from Dublin had started muscling in.

'Dublin?' echoed Hopkins.

'Dublin. The market here's flooded. A spike in heroin overdoses. Guns on the street and fatal shootings. They've been watching too much *Narcos* and *Gomorrah*.'

Roberts asked, 'Who's responsible for the fire?'

Doyle was slow to answer.

Roberts pushed. 'Who do you think it was?'

'The IRA isn't going to piss on its own doorstep.' Doyle said it as though that much was obvious.

'What about the boys from south of the border?' asked Roberts.

'Nah. They aren't ready to make those sort of waves, which leaves a rival Chinese gang or—'

Roberts finished for him, 'Protestant paramilitaries.'

'Yes.'

'And which lot in particular would you be talking about?'

'The Ulster Volunteer Force, or a splinter thereof.'

'So is this political or criminal?' asked Hopkins brightly.

Doyle gave her a withering look and said, 'Your turn.'

Hopkins said, 'Mr Parker can enlighten you.'

Parker's summary made it all sound perfectly – even

suspiciously – straightforward, through the simple expedient of omitting any mention of Cross by name, referring to him throughout as O'Grady, who was being watched, as Doyle had already been told, as part of a high-security inquiry.

Charlotte wondered if Parker had been primed by Hopkins. When he got to the man's mixed-race background, Charlotte watched Doyle struggle with that. Hopkins asked if it was possible to be both Muslim and Roman Catholic. Parker surprised them by announcing, apparently in all seriousness, 'Perhaps in one's soul.'

He concluded, 'Seeing how Belfast has become a gangsters' paradise, perhaps O'Grady was here to take advantage, off his own bat.'

Doyle asked, 'Anything else you are not telling?'

'The Chinese took two significant hits last night,' replied Parker. 'Given Mr O'Grady's activities, was he the source of the police tip-off about the smuggling?'

Doyle looked unimpressed. He turned to Hopkins.

'Why is HMG flying you over at the taxpayer's expense to tell us about some aspiring gangster with a dodgy track record?'

The obvious answer, Charlotte could see, which no one would provide, was because hidden aspects of that record could compromise some of those sitting round the table.

Roberts said, 'I suggest we take a break.' He asked Doyle, 'Are the usual suspects in by now?'

'They should be downstairs.'

'Why don't we have a chat with them,' Roberts went on, sounding like the voice of reason, 'and see what light they can throw.'

They stood. Hopkins unhooked her coat from the back of her chair. A Belstaff, Charlotte noted; nothing so common as Barbour.

Hopkins seemed to have nothing to say to her. She dithered for a moment as though she might after all, then excused herself, saying she had calls to make. Roberts acknowledged Charlotte for the first time while remaining tight-lipped. Doyle and his companion, who was notable only for his silence, seethed.

Roberts said to Charlotte and Parker, 'You two come with me. You can watch. See if anything connects to what you know.'

The man's clamped jaw left Charlotte in no doubt that what mattered was Doyle didn't find out huge backstitching was going on.

Doyle took them down to the interview room, which had a separate booth with a two-way mirror.

Roberts said he would sit with Doyle and the policewoman working the recorder. He told Charlotte and Parker to watch from the booth.

The cubicle was airless and stuffy. They had no time to compare notes because the first suspect was being brought in.

The Irish were dealt with first. Their ages ranged from twenty to fifty. There were four of them. The youngest and the oldest Charlotte recognised as the local faces they had seen going in and out of the takeaway. They all assumed an air of resigned incomprehension. One wit said they had been doing community work to improve Irish-Chinese relations.

They all concurred with Doyle's interpretation.

The youngest lad said, 'It was the other lot.' He meant the UVF.

On O'Grady they were all agreed. Tried to make himself useful. A bit of a fantasist. Ran errands, hung around, not wanted.

'You know how it is with these fellows,' one said. 'They like to latch on.'

They all seemed deliberately vague about how long he had been around.

'Came and went.'

'Who did he work for?'

The oldest one, whose name was Connors, was being questioned now. He was a stout, ruddy man with a benign air that reminded Charlotte of children's stories about jolly farmers.

Connors was saying, 'Like I said, a hanger-on.'

He looked privately amused, as though he knew Doyle had nothing on him.

A little later, he said, 'You're pulling my leg.'

Doyle asked, 'How come?'

Charlotte sensed the two had had dealings before.

'I wasn't born yesterday,' Connors said. 'Fellow shows up wanting to get pally. We thought he was one of yours. That's how it usually goes, plus he was a bit of a darkie. We called him Phil Lynott after the singer in Thin Lizzy. Once your man came into a bar and the juke box was playing "The Boys Are Back in Town" and we had a laugh at his expense over that.'

Connors and Doyle shared the joke, which looked as though it had gone over Roberts's head.

Connors settled to his story, chatting on, reminiscing.

'The man was tight when it came to his round. With his religious persuasion he didn't drink, which put him at something of a social disadvantage. "And a Pepsi for me." ' Connors laughed and stopped abruptly. 'A tout, Mr Doyle, is what we thought, your informer. And we had a laugh at that too, at your expense. Trust the peelers to send a teetotaller.'

Not in her time, Charlotte remembered; Cross had been knocking back drinks after the exercise.

Connors sat relaxed, confident at spinning his line. He gave O'Grady no ground, writing him off as pathetic. The racial element repeated itself. The man would never have fitted on account of his skin.

The two Chinese interviewed were equally dismissive. Charlotte suspected their English was better than they let on. One was around sixty and had seen it all before. The other was half his age with a cocky air. He asked for an interpreter. Roberts got up and whispered in his ear while gripping his testicles and he behaved after that.

Both men separately repeated the same story. Neither seemed bothered, even the one who had been warned. The older one played to stereotype by calling him 'O'Glady'.

The lot of them behaved like they were comedians, Charlotte thought, as though humour was the best form of defence.

The Chinese verdict concurred that the man was little more than an errand boy. They were talking to the older one now.

'What kind of errands?' asked Roberts.

'Money collecting.'

'Extortion?'

'Charity work.'

'For you?' asked Doyle.

The man shook his head. 'Small fry. A bit of freelance here, a bit there. They take what they can get.'

'Collecting for the IRA then?'

The man shrugged.

'Wouldn't the IRA have problems with him being a darkie?' asked Doyle.

Parker rolled his eyes at Charlotte as the other man went on.

'IRA much more inclusive these days. They let us

open takeaway in their road. Everyone co-operate, everyone get on.'

He sat back giggling.

Doyle said, 'You don't seem too upset about losing your business.'

'Terrible thing but good insurance, can never be too careful. Business not so good anyway. Win-win for me.'

When questioned about an arson attack, the older Chinese man insisted that a deep fat fryer had been left on by accident, causing a gas canister to explode.

'Manager forgetful.'

Questioned about a man seen entering the building shortly before, he shook his head, as though that were enough to annul the evidence, but Charlotte could see he was surprised.

Of the others questioned, only Connors had seriously considered the point, asking Doyle, 'Are you telling me it was him seen going into the building?'

Doyle said it was why they were there.

Connors thought about that and said, 'I can see where you're coming from. He was a bitter fuck, hated everything about himself. He should have played the clown – to draw attention and deflect at the same time – but I've never met a Muslim with a sense of humour. So he grew bitter and not so stable. Produced a pistol in a bar – I would say the Red Devil from recollection, a quiet evening soon after opening. Your man walks in wearing a fucking regimental blazer – in the middle of the Falls Road! – and challenges me to a shooting match. No fucking way, I say, and he draws a bead – the few punters in are on the floor by then – and shoots out the optic measure on a gin bottle without breaking the bottle or spilling a drop. The mirror behind it he had to pay for.'

Connors looked around in disbelief. 'He held his gun sideways in that "gangsta" way, for Chrissakes! That's the kind of customer he was and I didn't like the way he banged on about being called Paki and Curry Face at school, and the army no better. "Excuse me," I said, "tell that to Oliver Cromwell and don't lecture me about racism." He boasted how he had shot a lot of men in Afghanistan. Maybe he came back with his head on crooked. Even if I didn't take him seriously, I steered clear. If you say he burned the place down I don't necessarily disagree. He was like one of those kids that goes off and sticks pins in a doll when you won't let him play with your toys.'

Parker and Charlotte were stuck with the police canteen for lunch. Roberts had told them to reconvene at 2pm. Parker worked on his laptop while eating.

Charlotte received a text, saw it was Clive and deleted it. She tried transferring money to her current account but the phone app wouldn't open. She called the bank to make the transfer but the number kept cutting out. The app still refused to work. She told Parker, who said he could lend her some cash.

Quite a lot was going wrong with everyday transactions. When she had first got a bank card going to a hole in the wall was like visiting a holy well.

Parker looked up from his laptop and said, 'Doyle puts it about that the UVF was behind the arson, but if the IRA's leery of Cross I can't see the UVF buying into him.'

Charlotte looked at her mashed potato and wondered if she had the stomach for it. People stared at Parker but she found she was getting used to that and made a point of staring back.

She decided with Parker that trust wasn't the whole issue.

She knew less than he did, and he knew less than Hopkins, who probably didn't know as much as Roberts or Moffat. She had emailed Moffat before leaving London to say she was off to Belfast. She hadn't been in touch since as nothing had happened. Then a lot had happened all at once.

Roberts and Hopkins marched into the afternoon meeting looking like they had been cooking up something. Doyle was grumpy as though he hadn't enjoyed his lunch. His silent companion had disappeared.

Roberts started on the front foot, asking Doyle why he hadn't been aware of O'Grady's activities.

'Or is he one of yours, as Mr Connors suggested, and you're protecting him?'

Doyle flashed a casual two fingers.

'We're like everyone else, buster. Cuts. Pay freezes. Falling recruitment levels. Short-staffed. Underfunded. We have informers, but nothing like in the old days. One reason the Dublin gangs have moved in is because they know we're barely coping. O'Grady did nothing to draw attention to himself – Mr Connors's story of producing a six-shooter in a bar notwithstanding, if you believe that – so there's no reason why we should know him.'

Doyle sounded fed up and defensive.

'Where's your pal who was here this morning?' Roberts asked. 'Fetch him.'

Doyle looked as though he hadn't even missed the man. He asked Charlotte to organise coffee and tea, which she did with bad grace, though she quite enjoyed scrounging the change from them for the machine. Otherwise they spent twenty minutes staring at their phones.

The silent one walked in looking now more like he had been snubbing them. When he opened his mouth he turned out to be English. Charlotte revised her opinion: not a copper; UK security.

Roberts addressed himself to the Englishman whose name was Baker and said, 'It's about the ministerial shooting.'

That had their attention. An interesting move of the goalposts, thought Charlotte.

Hopkins took over. 'Thanks to Ms Waites's work' – a nod at Charlotte – 'we are pursuing several former soldiers of Muslim background, with a history of active service, mental instability and radicalisation. The motive for shooting the minister would appear to be his robust line on fundamentalist terror and vocal support for Israel. Broadly speaking, isn't that right?'

This was asked of Charlotte, who wanted to say, 'Yes, but . . .' She nodded instead.

'As of the last twenty-four hours,' Hopkins went on, 'our scope has narrowed down to one of these men – disturbed background, exposed by his family to extremism, ex-military, active service, post-traumatic stress disorder, alcoholism, drugs. The man in question was almost certainly persuaded by radicalised cousins and his brother to carry out the shooting. Our profilers have him as a ninety per cent match. He has since gone on the run.'

Roberts turned to Baker.

'So why are we getting intelligence that tells us there might be an IRA connection to the shooting as well?'

Baker passed the question to Doyle, whose response was to laugh.

'Says who? To quote Mr Connors, someone is pulling your leg.'

Hopkins leaned forward. 'Be that as it may. O'Grady also has the correct profile in terms of race, background and service. But IRA?'

'Perhaps he has connections to the other fellow who's on the run,' Baker pointed out. 'Snipers work in pairs.'

Charlotte looked at him again and remembered he had been at the big meeting on New Year's Day.

'What links O'Grady to the shooting?' Baker asked equably, sounding like someone keen to resolve a needless problem.

Hopkins said he had been seen in the vicinity.

Baker said, 'The IRA doesn't have the planning, the will or the funds to execute anything like that.'

Doyle added, 'If what you're saying is the case, we would have heard.'

Baker stepped back in. 'A recent official assessment of paramilitary groups concluded that both sides continue to engage in violent activity, directed by local leadership and conducted without sanction, to exercise control at a community level. It also confirmed they are involved in big smuggling operations, drugs and extortion of local businesses. Your story will turn out to be disinformation. The minister is no friend of the IRA but that's not enough to take a shot at the man.'

Charlotte remembered McCavity's declared hatred of the IRA but that was years ago and she was inclined to agree with Baker.

Doyle added, 'The last thing a bunch of bigots would do is use a Muslim shooter. The IRA has always been proud of its boys standing up for themselves.'

Baker suggested a way forward, recommending Doyle assemble a team to hunt O'Grady down.

'He's your main suspect for the arson, after all.'

Hopkins looked pleased at that. 'Yes, keep any political complications out of it. Find him and we'll do the rest.'

9

Charlotte went back to the Europa, took a bath and slept for the rest of the afternoon until she was woken by Parker, who asked if she wanted to eat.

'After watching the takeaway for so long, I rather fancy Chinese. My treat.'

Charlotte, half asleep, looked at her watch. Six o'clock.

'When?' she asked.

'Now? I've something in mind for later.'

Parker was waiting in the lobby wearing his wraparound shades. The restaurant was a ten-minute walk. It didn't look very Chinese apart from chair covers with lotus blossoms.

Parker impressed her by not consulting the menu, instead asking if they had fried pig's intestines.

The waiter nodded cautiously. Seeing Charlotte's look, Parker said, 'Trust me.'

With plum sauce, he told the waiter, who wrote the order down while looking unsure.

Between them, they settled on prawns in their shell with chilli and garlic; and fried squid, with chilli and onion.

'I'm all right with that,' Charlotte said, realising she was famished.

After further discussion, Parker asked for pork and salted fish meatballs and a belly pork casserole with ginger. He ordered plain rice, tea and two beers, then turned to Charlotte to ask if that was all right.

'Beer goes better than wine with Chinese.'

'I wanted one anyway,' she said, thinking there was no point in getting off on the wrong foot.

'Maybe a Moutai later.'

'What's that?'

'A spirit known as the Chinese iron hat.'

Charlotte was wondering at the point of the meal. She now questioned everything, but Parker appeared relaxed. She asked whether he ate out much.

'Only Chinese. The Chinese have a great contempt for the *gweilo* so they don't stare and treat me like every other foreigner, more or less rudely.'

They were given utensils and Parker asked for chopsticks. Charlotte said she found them fiddly but could manage. The prawns were spicy. She enjoyed peeling the shells to reveal the pink meat. There was a finger bowl for rinsing.

Parker was in a talkative mood.

'I was looking at more veterans' sites this afternoon. Cross was sometimes known as Criss Cross, after the sighting hairs on a telescopic sight.'

It was almost as though Cross were several different men, Charlotte decided. The military sniper, the mystery operator and the hanger-on with an inferiority complex.

'As for the triads,' Parker was saying, 'they're turning over a million a year from dealing, weed mostly. Then there's laundering and smuggling and people trafficking. Try some crispy pork.'

Charlotte declined. Parker ate with gusto as he threw out ideas.

'Apropos of Cross aka O'Grady and his Home Office work, Northern Ireland has loads of convicted criminals previously deported from the UK. Should we make anything of that? And here's something. I checked a list of deportations made from Belfast since O'Grady was here.'

'Another Chinese connection?' Charlotte ventured.

'Two such gentlemen, long-term residents of a criminal persuasion, deported last November. The Chinese community generally minds its own business but this case ran on Twitter, saying the men had been removed illegally. In fact, technically not. The paperwork can be shown to be in order – stamped and authorised, by guess who?'

Charlotte gestured that it went without saying. Even so, she was surprised.

'Deportation is a protracted process. Presumably O'Grady performed this fast-track service on behalf of others or he took advantage of community fractures to play the field for himself.'

'How do you know this?'

'I can request deportation orders. It took a bit longer to establish that the deported men were triad members.'

'Did you know this during the meeting?'

Parker waggled his hand. 'Hopkins instructed that Doyle should be told as little as possible.'

'She changed her tune after lunch.'

'Her or Roberts. Anyway, the problem of finding O'Grady has been passed on to Doyle to sort, and no doubt for him to take the blame if anything goes wrong.'

Charlotte passed on another offer of pig's intestine.

Parker said, 'Don't think about what it is, concentrate on the taste. There's the plum sauce too.'

In an effort to appear game she bit into one, chewed, tasted and said, 'It's not bad actually. What do you make of Roberts?'

'Brought in for damage limitation, I'd say.'

'But it doesn't answer what Cross was doing here in the first place.'

'Go on.'

'Is he undercover or inserting himself as a player in the drugs war?'

'Don't think of the two as mutually exclusive.'

'But that wouldn't extend to shooting a politician.'

'He could have been turned or gone rogue, hence damage limitation.'

'Do you think he has been placed here?'

'You can't discount it.'

'Why Belfast? It's not exactly Beirut these days.'

'The Irish border is the short and long answer. Leaving Europe raises all the old questions about the past conflict. Maybe London wanted an assessment of any possible renewal of old rivalries. Maybe Cross came and thought, "Why take a government salary when you can make ten times that off your own bat?" It's also possible he has raised old ghosts. The current IRA are small beer, but there are big hitters from the old days, biding their time.'

'And your best summary?'

'I can't decide whether the drugs war is part of a wider picture. The coming of the Dublin gangs really is like *Gomorrah*, Doyle's right about that. The violence in Dublin got so bad that many of them decided to flee the fold. The leadership of one lot decamped to Dubai. Their foot soldiers who couldn't afford to go abroad hid here in the North. They needed to keep getting paid, so their bosses in Dubai extended operations to here from Dublin. Business as normal.'

The Dublin gangs would be Catholic, Charlotte thought, which lent all of this a ritualistic, hysterical edge.

'Why didn't they move in sooner, if it's such a lucrative market?'

'Different police force for a start and the North remains a nightmare of sectarianism, which isn't good for business.'

'So how do they work it?'

'The Dubai lot operate wholesale as the Protestants' main supplier,' Parker went on. 'It suits them to offload because on a local level everything in Belfast remains very partisan and vicious.'

'And the Dubai mob's rivals?'

'Less flashy, run their own operations, using former IRA elements, especially when it comes to sourcing firearms. As well as drugs they have a long history of cigarette smuggling and robbery, previously with the help of the Provisional IRA.'

'Which no longer exists.'

'Yes, but two of the men shot dead not so long ago in the Dublin gun battles had direct links with dissident IRA. So, always look to the past and it's self-perpetuating.'

'And in terms of the wider picture?'

'Maybe the drugs money is being used to finance future military operations if everything is going to kick off again.'

Parker poured the last of the tea.

'We know someone is moving against the Chinese. First the deportations, then the torched takeaway and the docks bust. With just one happening you'd say okay. Two maybe still coincidence. Three looks like war. The question is whether any of this would have happened without Cross in Belfast.'

'How do you get from that to the shooting?'

'Perhaps McCavity has been subsidising the government with major drug deals. God knows, the money has to come from somewhere.'

Charlotte wondered for a moment if he was being serious.

For dessert they were served quartered oranges, which came without being asked for. Charlotte tried the Moutai, a drink so overwhelming she could feel it in her sinuses.

Parker asked, 'Do you like boxing?'

'I've never given it any thought. No, probably not.'

'There's a boys' competition tonight at the gym where Lafferty works. That's why I suggested we eat early. Here's another of those connections. Lafferty has form here, a couple of short sentences. He also has a record on the main land. Disorderly conduct. Assault with a deadly weapon. Stealing cars. The connection is he and Cross served time together in Lewes Prison.'

'So they know each other?'

'Not proven, but given coincidence, it suggests Lafferty could be an accomplice. Now, here's the "but" concerning Cross torching the place. Lafferty's longest sentence was for arson, which raises the question of whether the hooded man was Cross after all.'

Parker asked for the bill. Charlotte offered to go Dutch but he refused.

She said, 'I'm not sure I want to take things further with Lafferty.'

'Any reason?'

'He once attacked a man with a homemade flame-thrower,' she said. After a pause, she added, 'Actually, the reason is you. How do I know I can trust you?'

Parker brushed the table cloth with his hands.

'Okay, I hacked your office computer because Hopkins said you were a security risk. I replaced the file, which I didn't read, because she said it contained errors. I hacked your private computer, again on Hopkins's orders.'

'Why am I not more surprised?'

'I run internal checks all the time. I don't think twice about them.'

'Are you still checking on me?'

Parker thought about that and eventually said, 'No. I believe Hopkins is the security risk.'

'Would you go that far?'

'I think she has fucked up.'

'Spell that out for me.'

'If it can be shown that the mainland shooting was carried out by a man in the employ of HMG then Hopkins will be rewriting that story as fast as she can.'

'Does that mean I should trust you?'

'You trusted me enough to order.'

Charlotte laughed. 'That's a pathetic answer.' She gathered her belongings. 'Okay, let's trust each other until we don't.'

A ten-minute taxi ride took them down the motorway to an industrial estate. The gym was a brick and corrugated-iron shed with a big mural of bare-knuckle pugilists, stripped to the waist and squaring up. Further down the wall, spray-canned in large letters: 'Unfinished Revolution' and 'IRA – Brits Out'.

Heavy double doors took them down a corridor where they could hear shouting. More doors led to the gym where a ring stood elevated under hard lights that spared no detail. Charlotte was surprised by the size of the crowd, around a hundred in for a local boys' event, and most on their feet, waving fists and yelling expletives.

In the ring two small lads who looked no older than ten were socking away at each other, supervised by a referee in a tracksuit. His age surprised Charlotte because he looked easily in his sixties but she could see he moved with agility as he instructed, pointed, separated the boys from a clinch, and admonished any flouting of the rules. Both boys looked dazed. The way their shoes squeaked on the canvas reminded Charlotte of fingernails being dragged down a blackboard.

The supporters were yelling at each other as much as cheering for the boys. Cries of 'Below the belt!' went up when one lad doubled up, which earned his opponent a talking-to from the referee, who held him by his neck. The reprimanded boy nodded blindly, looking like he wasn't taking a word in, being so wound up. The other one was being shouted at from his corner by a second who looked like he did a lot of weights. The fight resumed with the referee making the boys touch gloves. They had hardly restarted when the bell rang and both boys staggered to their corners exhausted. Charlotte watched them being sponged down, two lithe, stringy little fellows who looked like they had spent their lives scrapping. All the while, furious instructions were yelled in their ear by their seconds, at which they nodded and tried to look grown-up.

She and Parker stood at the back. Fight followed fight. Three rounds each. The competitors got older and bigger. They ducked around, bobbing and weaving, followed by flurries of punches like punctuation marks in messy sentences, which were surprisingly audible despite the din. Sometimes the fighters clung to each other like castaways on a raft. At other times they danced around, big gloves dangling, as they teased their opponent on.

How it worked and who won Charlotte could not say. No one got knocked out and bouts were decided on points. How these were allocated she had no idea. The one she always thought was doing best invariably lost. The losers jigged around before the verdict, still confident, then took on the same vanquished look, as though they were all the same loser. The winners pranced, looking like they could carry on fighting forever.

Charlotte was interested by the referee, controlling, interpreting, issuing clear instructions to the contestants, stopping a fight when necessary with reminders of the rules. She suspected he knew his job better than the boys. She also wondered about the iron-pumped second from the first fight, with his dangerous air of self-possession. He was how she imagined Lafferty – he should have been good-looking but somehow wasn't, as though the handsome kit he'd been handed out had gone wrong. It could have been him she had followed. He was the same height as Cross, bulkier, but that would not have been apparent with the top he had been wearing.

She didn't know how long he had been looking at them. He was standing on the edge, watching the spectators rather than the fights. Occasionally he patrolled in an arc, pacing quietly but always returning so that she and Parker were in his sight.

She leaned into Parker and said they were being watched.

Parker said, 'Yes, I know.'

Charlotte thought they should leave. They were outsiders in a partisan crowd.

The fights looked like they were about to end. Trestle tables were being set up in the space behind them, and plastic cups and jugs laid out.

She said they should get out, but before they could the hall's lights came on and the referee gave a speech, thanking them all for coming and saying what grand lads the boys were and asking for donations as the club had no government support.

'Well, there you go,' the man said. 'What can you expect?'

Parker wanted to hang around. Charlotte didn't and gestured towards the exit. The crowd broke up around them. The iron-pumped man was waiting at the door with a donations tin, making it clear that there was no question of not giving. Charlotte fished out a five-pound note and was happy to pay that to get out.

She avoided looking at the man, who gestured towards the tables and announced, 'There's only lemonade and orange juice.'

'So?' said Parker.

The man stared hard at him and said, 'Father Jerome would like a word.'

He didn't even glance twice at Parker's skin, which was when Charlotte realised he was looking at him like a butcher sizing up a carcass of meat. The accent was English. Charlotte was reluctant to open her mouth and reveal hers. She found it hard to say where he was from. Somewhere in the east she thought; Norfolk or Lincoln, perhaps. Parker stood back, seeming curious about what would happen next.

They hung around drinking lukewarm lemonade, saying nothing. Parker stood out on account of his height and condition and Charlotte sensed some of the crowd were talking about them. The mood was still raucous. Despite no alcohol being served there were plenty of private bottles. Charlotte recognised one the boys from the bouts, changed into street clothes that made him look ordinary, apart from the hungry stare he gave her. It was years since she had been eyed up like that.

People who had been screaming abuse at each other stood mingling, their differences forgotten. One woman said, 'Your Terry gave that Cullen lad a hell of a hiding. Knocked seven bells out of him.'

The other said, 'He should have flattened him while he had the chance. Father Jerome says he's got the full works apart from a killer punch.'

Charlotte saw Parker was listening too. Together they worked out that Father Jerome must be the referee. She watched him glad-handing the crowd, slapping shoulders and dispensing good cheer. A man next to him had a fifth of Jameson's. As Father Jerome took the bottle and raised it he caught Charlotte's eye. He was standing about ten feet away. There was a friendliness to the gaze but a calculation to the look. She was left in no doubt that she was being marked out.

No one was in a hurry to leave. The priest eventually approached them with the air of someone with a chore to perform. He made a point of shaking Parker by the hand and saying, 'Father Jerome.' Then he turned to Charlotte, not offering to shake hands, and asked, 'And you are?'

'Charlotte,' she said, 'Waites.'

The priest laughed at that, and said, 'And what for, is what we all ask.'

She presumed she was talking to a man of the cloth and 'Father' wasn't some kind of nickname. If he was a priest, she wasn't sure what to make of that because everything about his manner said he fancied her. It left her more disconcerted than flattered.

She asked if he had to wear a dog collar and realised too late that this could be taken for flirtation.

She was aware of Parker regarding her oddly.

'Did you enjoy the fights?' Father Jerome asked.

She said she had never seen anything like it, which was true.

'Ah, the Jesuit answer,' he said. 'Instructing them to use their fists teaches them discipline and it's good for their souls to do it under training, rather than running around the streets duffing each other up.'

The man had a softer accent than the locals, almost a lilt.

Charlotte found most older white men ended up all looking the same – balding, grey and overweight – but the priest was as lean as a whippet and had a full head of spiky hair. She suspected the bonhomie was cultivated. Deep furrows down his cheeks gave him a serious air in repose, which she supposed went with the vocation.

'I am a street priest,' he said. 'Hands on. The Jesuits, previously mentioned, say "give me the boy for the first seven years and he's mine for life". True, up to a point. I believe the groundwork really gets done between the ages of eleven and fifteen. That's what makes the man. Now, what brings you?'

Charlotte didn't know what to say.

The priest went on, 'Back in the day you would have been classed as war-zone tourists. Where are you staying?'

'The Europa.'

'Where all the foreign correspondents used to hang out during what was so quaintly called the Troubles. Trouble in my book is what you have with a boiler. I don't suppose they hold the Ugly Night Competition any more?'

'Excuse me?' asked Charlotte.

'All those hard-bitten, whiskey-sodden reporters held a contest to see who could pick up the ugliest woman, to be produced at breakfast so they could agree on a winner; not that you would be eligible by any stretch of the imagination.'

Charlotte couldn't tell if this horrible story was being told to offend her or if it was a strike against the British.

Parker said, 'We're looking for a man.'

'Another priest might tell you he could offer only the Lord Jesus. I am all ears.'

Charlotte wondered what Parker would come up with.

He said, 'I am a probate genealogist.'

Father Jerome said, 'What the fuck is that when it's at home?' He turned to Charlotte. 'Excuse my French. Priests can swear like anyone else.'

He seemed amused by Parker's declaration. He looked the sort who liked to see someone thinking on his feet. It seemed the two were playing with each other.

There was a sense of ironic performance to everything the priest did. Even in the boxing ring there had been a remoteness, as if to say: Here's me showing you how a man referees.

He addressed Parker. 'You were saying.'

'If a distant relative dies without making a will we trace the beneficiary.'

'Is it me you're looking for?' The question was more guarded, the bonhomie gone.

'Not to my knowledge.'

'What's the fellow's name?'

'O'Grady.'

'You'll have your work cut out for you. There are an awful lot of them. You'll have a fee, I suppose.'

'Twenty-five per cent.'

'Plus VAT?'

'Plus VAT.'

'Creaming upwards of a quarter!'

'Giving seventy-five per cent to someone who otherwise would have no idea of its existence.'

'Are you telling me your service is so bespoke it extends to turning up here out of hours?'

The priest glanced at Charlotte, as if to say he was still playing along.

Parker said, 'Not out of the question when large sums are involved. We need the money as much as anyone – quarter of a million isn't to be sneezed at.'

'Get on. Is that what they're getting?'

'That's our fee.'

Father Jerome threw back his head and gave an appreciative laugh. Looking at Charlotte he said, 'Well, run along now. It's getting on. Come back and we'll talk more, see if I can help you find your lucky man and you can cut me in on your fee.' He looked around and said, 'We need the money, God knows.'

With that he switched off and was gone to greet someone else. 'Fintan, my boy, you're looking a million dollars.'

Fintan looked about a hundred and six and on his last legs.

As Father Jerome left them the musclebound man sidled over to say, 'You should go now.'

The voice was polite. The eyes were not.

'Is that a warning?' Parker asked.

'For you to decide.'

'There's a fellow we're trying to get hold of,' said Parker amiably. 'Name of O'Grady. He's had a windfall. Come into a shedload of money.'

The man was wearing an unzipped blouson jacket. He put his hands on his hips to reveal the cross-hatched wooden handle of a pistol stuck in his waistband.

'Ah,' said Parker, who still looked like he wanted to stay, until Charlotte dragged him off by the arm.

Outside she asked, 'What was all that about?'

'That's the strangest priest I've ever seen. The other one must be Lafferty. He would have given us nothing but a hiding.'

They walked to the main road where Parker called an Uber.

Charlotte asked, 'What do you know about priests anyway?'

'Educated by them. I was called too for a while, spent a year in a seminary until I decided God and I didn't get on.'

Charlotte struggled with the image of a vocational Parker.

'And instead you became an inspector for HMRC, of all unlikely professions.'

'As they say, nothing certain in this world but death and taxes.'

10

The next morning Charlotte woke late to find a text from Parker saying he had gone to Dublin. Fine, she thought, irritated that she hadn't been asked, after their so-called heart-to-heart. She decided to laze around then perhaps go out and buy a book.

She emailed Moffat, not sure what to say. In the end she wrote that the trip had resulted in an unconfirmed sighting of the party, in the vicinity of a building that had burned down.

She also spoke to her father. He sounded out of sorts and she asked after his health.

'They have me on new meds I don't like. One possible side effect is psychosis. When I complained about that to the doctor, he laughed and said never read about the side effects or you'll get them.'

He tailed off. As so often with the man, Charlotte found yawning chasms of silence could suddenly overtake them.

'You were going to tell me about Mother the last time we spoke,' she announced, thinking to put him on the back foot for a change.

'Was I?' He sounded as though he had forgotten.

'Is memory loss another side effect?'

It came out sounding nastier than she'd intended. She was reminded of her mother's frequent exasperation towards her as a child, and felt as though she were now directing that towards her father. She changed the subject and reminded him that she was in Belfast. Like him, she said she hadn't seen much of the place.

He interrupted to announce in a matter-of-fact way, 'I was unfaithful to your mother many, many times.'

She should have been more surprised. It sounded like one of those confessions that had hovered on the edge of their conversations for years.

She was also puzzled. Adultery was the banal secret of many marriages, but 'many, many times' spoke of more than the odd fling. Her father had been away a lot. There had been non-family postings. Yet she found it hard to see him bothering with the complexities of an extra-marital relationship. She supposed a lot of paid sex.

She would have been less surprised if he had said that it was her mother who was adulterous. Now her father, who had always declared, 'Never let the sun go down on an argument,' seemed to be trying to tell her his personality had been a front all along. Like *Reader's Digest*, she thought sourly: a man of edited highlights. But why tell her now? She presumed the medication was playing its part.

'Did you ever love each other?' she asked, trying to sound grown-up, knowing she was wrong to ask because she had no interest in raking over the ashes of her parents' marriage.

She listened to him struggle and fail to answer.

'Have you ever loved anyone?' she asked, thinking this persistence would lead only to trouble.

After another long silence he said, 'Yes.'

'Who?'

He wouldn't say.

Her next question was pointless as she already knew the answer.

'Did you love me?'

She sensed him wrestling with the question but he sighed and said nothing.

Something snapped and she hung up, thinking it was one of those conversations she shouldn't have had. She had known the answer without having to ask.

She sat there numb until her room phone rang.

It was reception to say Mr Parker was downstairs for her. Odd, she thought. He was meant to be gone for the day, and he could have called her. She supposed he was using reception because she had been on the phone. Even so. She called his number. There was no answer so she went down to see what was going on.

It was not Parker waiting as she stepped out of the lift. For a moment Charlotte didn't recognise him, smartly turned out in chinos and an expensive-looking overcoat. He took a step back and stood with his hands folded over his crotch.

'Mr Lafferty, I presume,' she said, trying to make light of it, wondering how he'd known where to find her. Of course – they had given their names to Father Jerome, and where they were staying.

Lafferty said, 'Father Jerome wants to see you.'

Charlotte considered telling him, 'I'm not going anywhere with you,' but in the end went for: 'Perhaps later. I have appointments.'

He could tell she was a poor liar. She wondered if he still had the gun stuck in his waistband and what that said about Father Jerome.

Lafferty gripped her elbow and said, 'Come quietly.'

Charlotte tried to shake herself loose. Lafferty gripped harder.

She said, 'I have to get my coat.'

'You won't need it. You will be returned safe.'

She thought of screaming but part of her felt as she had out on the street following the man who might even have been Lafferty: a recklessness bordering on exhilaration.

She said, 'If you let go of my arm.'

He did and they crossed the lobby looking like any other couple.

Outside, a uniformed doorman stepped forward and held open the passenger door of a silver Mercedes parked on the forecourt. Charlotte got in as Lafferty gave the man a ten-pound note.

The interior was spotless. Air freshener hanging from the driving mirror was in the shape of a red rose. Lafferty's movements were precise as he put on thin black leather gloves and prepared with the thoroughness of someone about to take a driving test, adjusting the mirror, hands on the wheel at ten to two. The gloves had holes cut in them that showed the knuckles. Charlotte made a point of studying them to stop herself from thinking about what might really be going on.

Music came on with the engine, something orchestral. She felt she ought to know it. Lafferty looked as though he loved his car more than anything. He drove carefully, checking in the mirror and sticking to the limit. They passed a speed-check sign that clocked them at 29 mph and gave a smiley face.

The music changed. She asked what the track was although she had resolved not to say anything. It was brassy and macho, quite sexy and camp.

Lafferty recited robotically, '"Ain't No Doubt" by Jimmy Nail. Before that Ennio Morricone, "Once Upon a Time in America".'

He didn't look the type to like this stuff. It seemed more as though the car had programmed itself.

They were on the motorway. Charlotte supposed he was taking her to the gym, until they drove past the turn-off.

They left at the next exit. There was no point in asking as Lafferty looked in no mood to answer. After a mile or so he pulled into a lay-by and told her to get out. He put on dark glasses. His tone was reasonable.

She looked at a featureless field with a pylon and asked why she had to get out.

'You have to go in the boot,' he said, as though that was obvious.

She sat thinking: And if I don't?

'Or I leave you here,' he said.

Which might be the better choice, except she had no bag, money or phone.

They got out. Lafferty had sprung the boot's lock from inside. Charlotte noticed a blanket and a pillow and wondered if it was a common form of transportation with Lafferty. He told her to wait until there was no traffic before getting in.

She did as she was told, thinking at least it wouldn't be as freezing as standing there. She lay with her knees bent. Lafferty arranged the blanket over her, then shut the lid, leaving her in the dark.

She could hear the music and sometimes the click of the indicator when they turned. The track changed: a bossa nova duet, warm and languid. She was shivering, from cold or fear she was not sure. She reasoned that if Lafferty had meant her harm he would have knocked her about already.

They drove for another twenty minutes. Charlotte tried to think about other things and kept returning to Belfast and how her father had once been there too.

She sensed they were driving down lanes now, not roads. Once they stopped and Lafferty blew the horn, which sounded surprisingly tinny for such a solid car. Charlotte presumed they had arrived but nothing happened. The car was surrounded by the noise of lazy shuffling and then a cow lowed. They were waiting for a herd to pass. She could hear wet breathing and the animals' hooves.

They drove slowly on, the surface becoming more rutted, throwing her around, until sometime later they stopped and the boot opened. Charlotte clambered out to find herself in a remote, muddy farmyard with a tumble-down whitewashed house under a ragged slate sky. Pools of urine and splattered cow shit lay on an apron of furrowed concrete. The air was heavy with the smell of silage. A sharp wind blew, making her shiver even more.

Charlotte took in these details rather than think about why she might be there.

'Ah, there you are!'

It was Father Jerome, coming out of the front door. He was wearing the same tracksuit, had on green gumboots and was carrying a second pair.

'Put these on. Save your shoes. They'll get ruined even in the short distance.'

Charlotte felt like she was trapped in a bad dream as he offered his arm to help her balance while she took off her shoes.

'Come inside. There's a kettle on.'

Father Jerome she couldn't figure out. Either he wasn't a priest or he was a very revolutionary one with an armed guard and a hideaway.

The unreal mood persisted. She was taken into a large, warm kitchen with a range and a big pine table with rustic chairs. Books lay everywhere. Charlotte saw a copy of Margaret Drabble's *The Middle Ground*, with a cracked spine, face-up on the table. It seemed unlikely reading for the man.

She was told to make herself comfortable. Father Jerome offered tea and chatted on in a friendly way. He quite liked Drabble, he said, though not as much as Muriel Spark.

'*The Driver's Seat*, do you know that one? Quite chilling. They made a terrible film of it, which featured Andy Warhol of all people. Do you know it?'

Why should I, she thought; Parker would.

'There's another whose title escapes me where they all turn out to be dead.'

For a moment the man's friendliness was gone and Charlotte realised there was nothing inconsequential to anything he said. She was in a place so remote she could disappear and no one would know.

The mood of friendly tutorial resumed. While his circumstances might be those of someone on the run, he talked like a conscionable man of the church as he bemoaned its declining influence after so many sex scandals and priests caught with their hands up altar boys' cassocks.

'It's such a discredited profession, if you can call it that; no one pays it a blind bit of attention. Did you see *Fleabag*?'

It took Charlotte a moment to understand that he was talking about the TV show.

'The hot priest was terrific publicity for us, played by a Dublin boy,' Father Jerome went on. 'We are flesh and blood, after all. At least it took us seriously, unlike *Father Ted* where we were portrayed as idiots, drunkards and buffoons. Look at Graham Norton now. In those days he couldn't get more than a bit part as Father Noel Furlong. One of the fellows that wrote the show got his comeuppance a while ago after a row with a transgender woman, so there you go. Any thoughts on LGBT rights?'

Charlotte wasn't getting drawn into that and said, 'It must be difficult for you.'

'A nightmare. The Church preaches universal love then places restrictions on what kind of love. As for LGBTQIA+, that's a lot of weight for one acronym to carry. Now, let's discuss why you are here.'

'Not of my own accord.'

'Maybe not, but you were last night, and you're a Brit, for a start. I would say that's enough to be going on with.'

Charlotte decided bluff was her only choice and said, 'We're here about a man with unpaid taxes, going back several years. He moved from Liverpool after failing to show up for a court appearance.'

She almost believed herself.

'HMRC?'

Charlotte nodded.

Father Jerome closed his eyes and recited, 'And the Pharisees said to his disciples, "Why does your teacher eat with tax collectors and sinners?"' He looked at her and said, 'Wouldn't that be handled by the Belfast office?'

'In the first instance, but they are short-staffed.'

'Who isn't? Even the drug dealers say the same.'

The man's mask slipped for a moment.

Charlotte ploughed on, less confident. 'He changed his name and we were told of a possible association with your driver.'

'Who told?'

'The Belfast police. They had been watching our man in connection with local criminal activities, of which we were unaware. We are concerned only with his tax.'

'Then why was that clown last night banging on about genealogy?'

'He can't help it. His appearance makes him that way. It's a defence mechanism, a bit like Tourette's.'

'So, what now?'

'If we can't locate the man we will have to go home.'

'I suggest you do that.'

Charlotte suspected Father Jerome knew exactly to whom she was referring.

He said, 'You'd better not start investigating me, I haven't paid a tax bill in years.'

'You would be exempt as a member of the clergy.'

She hoped she was right. He laughed in a way that said he appreciated her joke and signalled a break for more tea. Charlotte suspected he was not done with her.

'What did you make of that show about the female assassin, written by the woman that did *Fleabag*?' he asked as the kettle boiled.

Charlotte remembered watching a couple of episodes during one of its many repeats. The man's every question was starting to sound loaded.

'The woman took most of the credit when in fact it was based on books by a man who had previously written one about fishing,' he went on. 'In that he incidentally also touched on one of the most remarkable deaths to have happened in these parts.'

Father Jerome warmed the teapot and put it down, turning to her.

'Captain Nairac. Does the name mean anything?'

'It's familiar, but I can't say why.'

She had the sensation of being about to hold her hand to a flame.

'Before your time. His body hasn't been found to this day. He was a British soldier and intelligence officer, fancied himself as an undercover man. On the last night of his life, 14 May 1977, he went to the Three Steps Inn, deep in what the Brits called Bandit Country, trying to pass for IRA. The bar was steaming with a close-packed mass of border cowboys. Not shy about drawing attention to himself, he stood up and sang a couple of rebel songs, which led to the observation that the man had the strangest accent of anyone claiming to be from North Belfast. I once had a drink with that great actor, the dear departed T. P. McKenna, who told me he'd met the fellow who'd fed Nairac's remains into a meat grinder. T. P. was a grand story teller. Now, you're milk no sugar, is that right?'

He placed the tea gently in front of her and asked, 'Did your father not mention him?'

'T. P. McKenna?' Charlotte asked, confused.

'Nairac. He would have known him.'

'Why should he?'

Then she realised what Father Jerome meant.

'If your father is the man I'm thinking of.'

She didn't feel tripped up, more that she had been pushed flat on her face. She panicked at how the priest had so casually exposed her family history, a part of which she had no knowledge and over which she had no control, yet for which he seemed to hold her accountable.

'Now, Missy from MI5, or wherever, tell me why you are here and no more fibs.'

'The Home Office,' she finally managed.

'Is the tea all right?' Father Jerome enquired mildly, and waited for her to go on.

'We're told there might be an IRA link to the mainland shooting last month.'

'If it's not fake news these days it's hardly worth reading. About this link, do you believe it?'

'The Russians are suspected of meddling.'

'Yes, terrific meddlers. Probably thanks to them that you left Europe. Go on.'

'The man we're looking for might be able to throw light on the matter.'

'Who might that be?'

'He was seen in the vicinity of the shooting three weeks before.'

Father Jerome sat back and his mind seemed to drift until his attention was drawn to a book on the table. He picked it up.

'*On Iniquity*, by Pamela Hansford Johnson, do you know it?'

Charlotte said she didn't.

'Long before your time. She wrote it after attending the trial of that pair who tortured and killed five little kiddies and buried them on the moors.'

She remembered. Brady and Hindley. They had been in the tabloids forever afterwards.

'The book contains an interesting digression about how in 1939 when the Nazis took on the Polish government they flooded local bookstalls with pornography. I am wondering if something similar isn't happening here.'

'With pornography?'

'Drugs.'

The man's eyes, which had taken on a dreamy look, snapped into focus.

'The Brits have a long and dark history of playing sides off against each other. The current drugs war could be another of their manipulations.'

'How does that connect to the shooting?'

'There would be political advantage to showing that the IRA was behind it.'

'To what end?'

Father Jerome gestured impatiently. 'For the authorities to clean up. Draconian laws, mass arrests and so forth.' He held her eye as he continued. 'When in fact the opposite was the case.'

'I don't understand.'

'The man was shot by Protestant paramilitaries.'

Charlotte thought he must be lying. She hadn't given the Protestants a second thought in her work for Moffat.

'That doesn't make sense. The British are their ally,' she said.

'Their *only* ally and a dubious one at that. The Prods are scared witless that HMG is about to dump them into the loving arms of Dublin.'

'But why shoot McCavity? He was raised here, as one of them.'

'Unless in an upside-down world it can be demonstrated that he is a slippery chancer, an opportunist and a liar, who will U-turn on them as quick as a flash.'

Easy enough to show that to be the case, Charlotte supposed.

'Even so.'

Father Jerome grew irritated. 'Don't you get it?'

'Get what?' she snapped back, tired of being patronised.

'Do it, then blame the IRA.'

'To what end?'

'To put an end to any talk of reunification. Northern Ireland would remain British. With me so far? You still look doubtful.'

'We were told the IRA lacked the wherewithal. The same would surely apply to the Protestants.'

'Do you still not get it? The Prods always had something the IRA never had. You just said it yourself. They had the Brits on their side.'

He gave her a withering look, sat back and cracked his knuckles.

'He was a strange lad, Nairac, a romantic. Fished and boxed and trained birds of prey at school. It was his kestrel they used in that film *Kes*, by the way. One of those quiet boys who was a natural show-off, swanning around like he was a combination of Bulldog Drummond and Lawrence of Arabia. Then there was HMG's clandestine policy of taking out the IRA by political assassination – shoot to kill, a phrase that doesn't mince words. My brother was murdered by SAS who opened fire without warning, discharging over two hundred rounds, with sixteen fired in return. My brother was unarmed, nineteen.'

There was no change in the man's tone. He could have been discussing another television show.

'Then there's your name. Common enough. I didn't think twice when you told me, didn't even put it down to coincidence. Only after did I wonder. You see, the Republicans were well informed. Half the senior IRA members were employed by the intelligence services. They had all the military's telephone directories, so they knew the names. Was your da army?'

Charlotte said nothing, thinking he knew anyway.

'There was a Waites variously assigned to 14 Intel and the Force Research Unit. A planner, a strategist. You perhaps can see where we are going with this.' He paused for effect. 'Someone would have lovingly shaped those operations, low-intensity stuff learned in colonial wars fighting rebel forces in Malaya and Kenya – long "e" in those days, "Keen-ya". It was a very dirty war.'

He counted off on his fingers. 'Counter-propaganda. Psy-ops. Deep undercover work. Torture. White noise. Political assassination. Pre-emptive strikes – crouching behind a wall to ambush some poor sods and shoot them to kingdom come. Your da would have been familiar with all this.'

Charlotte squirmed and said she'd had no idea, feeling as she did that she was betraying her father.

Father Jerome steepled his hands and said, 'What if the drugs war is part of a similar strategy?'

Charlotte thought: Moffat. He had known her father but hadn't said how. Would what the priest was saying explain why Moffat was taking an interest?

Father Jerome continued. 'But why is none of this being run with by your muckrakers in the press, who are usually quick enough to jump to the crack of the whip? Imagine the headlines: "IRA shoots Minister". Three words is what it comes down to these days – anything more and people don't take it in. Headline two: "Belfast Protestant Paramilitaries shoot Minister". Nearer the truth, but more of a mouthful. Headline three: "Belfast Protestant Paramilitaries in collusion with UK security forces shoot Minister". The whole truth but nowhere near a headline and nothing to interest Murdoch.'

He sat back and said, 'Makes sense?'

'How do you know this?'

'You no doubt have your sources and it would be naive of you to think I don't have mine. On the subject of political assassination, you do end up thinking why not shoot the lot of them.' Father Jerome threw back his head and laughed. 'But where's a straight shooter when you need one? Trust the Prods to botch the job.'

'Who was the actual shooter?'

'Now you're asking the wrong man. A mercenary most likely. Plenty of ex-army boys will pull the trigger if the price is right. Lafferty outside could have done it but he's found God, so we have cosy chats about the nature of damnation.'

He stood and cleared their mugs.

'Tell your da about our little chat while you are about it, if he's still alive.'

'Yes, but he might be dying.'

'Ah, there you go. I wish him well in hell. We nearly had him once. The tilt fuse failed to work, otherwise he would have ended up sitting with what was left of his legs in his lap.'

Charlotte stared at her hands. If they had succeeded she never would have been born.

'And what's the IRA's motive in the version that blames them?' she asked carefully.

Father Jerome sat back down like a man without a care in the world.

'McCavity is a longtime foe of the IRA, a staunch Unionist, against any notion of a united Ireland, talk of which is in the air again. He compared the Peace Agreement to Neville Chamberlain's capitulation to the Nazis in Munich in 1938. Even quite recently he restated that abandoning shoot to kill against the IRA was a fatal act of appeasement. The fellow's not exactly Airey Neave – google him if you must – but a pissed-off Mick might see McCavity as such and take it into his head to shoot the sanctimonious fucker.'

'But you've just said the IRA shooting him would blow any chance of reunification.'

'Motive hardly matters in any version put forward by the British press. It would denounce the shooting as a nihilistic act by what was left of a historically psychopathic, self-destructive organisation, cutting off its nose to spite its face.'

'Why are you telling me?'

'Go back and inform your people that this operation was set up by some crackpot part of HMG.'

He regarded her contemplating her options, and added, 'With any Protestant paramilitary operation, British Intelligence won't be far behind.'

'Which part of its intelligence are we talking about?'

'Look to old loyalties. The showboaters from MI6 side with Dublin because they have no jurisdiction in the North, which pretty much leaves MI5.'

He looked hard at her and said, 'You have two choices from what I can see. Report to your masters in the hope that they will uncover the truth, or a variation of it.'

'And the second?'

'Consider whistleblowing.'

Father Jerome laughed in an unfunny way. After that they sat in silence until he said, 'If you question what I am saying, think of your da and what went on in his day and how the Prods always had a little help from their friends, whether it was the murder of the Miami Showband – look that up too while you are about it – or setting off car bombs in Dublin in 1974.'

'Why do that?'

Father Jerome regarded her with the manner of a patient teacher.

'Over another agreement between the British and Irish governments concerning a deal regarding the North, which left the Prods howling betrayal. Their bombs sent a clear message to Dublin of "hands off", and after that the agreement fell apart. Job done. The gang responsible operated out of Portadown – McCavity's home town, by the way – and was run by Brits. It was no big secret. Many papers said so at the time. Nairac's name came up a lot in connection with the gang. The bombs killed over thirty people in the evening rush hour. The ambulance men in Talbot Street couldn't tell the living from the dead and the gutters were running with blood. There was a young girl decapitated and another two were thrown together by the explosion so you couldn't tell them apart. Tell that to your da.'

He stood to signal that he was done.

'Well, mind how you go. Just a final word of friendly advice: bear in mind what the Brits never understand is that hereabouts history is not the past. We live with it every day. Nothing is resolved. It's still a powder keg.'

'What about O'Grady?' Charlotte asked, thinking they both knew he was the reason she was there.

She was rewarded with another hard stare.

'The man is a loose cannon, leave it at that. Better avoided. Our friend will take you back. You won't hear from me again.'

Charlotte said she needed to use the toilet.

He pointed to where it was.

'You have to pull the chain a few times but it works in the end.'

She went down a short dark corridor with flagstones and heavy waterproofs hanging on racks. The corridor smelt of dog, though she had not seen one.

When she was done she sat with her head in her hands, unable to face going back out. She was thinking of her father. First there was that morning's self-confessed faithless husband and now the dark operator in murderous operations. Neither had anything to do with why she was there but she couldn't separate them. She felt drowned by everything. And who did Father Jerome think she was supposed to tell? The unholy trinity of Moffat, Hopkins and Roberts was out of the question. Strangely, she found herself thinking of her father as least untrustworthy in terms of her predicament because she was, after all, his daughter.

Charlotte sat up abruptly at a noise from outside: not the usual sounds of the countryside, but a muffled report. Two more followed, inside the house now. She knew then what they were. Silenced gunshots.

The toilet had no window. The corridor outside led only

back into the kitchen. She listened, ears straining, and heard nothing other than the wind.

A man's voice said, 'Whose shoes are these?' He sounded Middle Eastern.

She was still wearing the boots and had left her shoes on a chair.

She leaned forward and slipped the latch on the door, thinking she should pull the chain and walk out as though everything were normal and pray she could somehow talk them out of shooting her. Then she saw the door handle being slowly tested and the door opened. A man in fatigues and a balaclava stood there, gun in hand. Charlotte looked at the large silencer's black hole.

He spoke to someone she couldn't see. 'No one said anything about a woman.'

It was same foreign-sounding voice as before.

A second man, taller, also in a balaclava, appeared in the background.

'Go and wait outside,' he said to the other man. He spoke with a Belfast accent. 'I'll take care of this one.'

11

Later that afternoon, Parker was on the train back from Dublin. He had splashed out on first class (complimentary orange juice) for a less crowded carriage and fewer people staring.

He had spent the night before texting Brindley, the Dublin reporter who had been the start of the whole business by getting his account hacked. Parker wanted to know more about the Dublin gangs, about which the reporter turned out to be something of a specialist. Just when things were getting interesting in their texting, Brindley appeared to lose his nerve. Parker persisted. Brindley said he had been hacked once and had to watch what he said. Parker suspected the man was looking for an excuse to talk and offered to meet face to face. He explained about his skin, adding that Brindley wouldn't like what he saw. Brindley told him to come at noon to Madigan's on the station concourse.

Parker had been thinking of taking Charlotte but then texted to say he would be gone a few hours and she should enjoy a day off. The truth was, he preferred working alone.

Brindley turned out to be an old-fashioned newshound. What remained of his hair was tied in a ratty ponytail. Grubby collar and cuffs. A bushy beard had what looked like the remains of his breakfast still in it. Parker put him at sixty-five, getting by on freelance work, which turned out to be the case. He suspected the reason he was there was so Brindley could keep up a monologue of whining complaints. The man could have moaned for Ireland. He told how he had worked for years on the same rag, only to be let go weeks before becoming eligible for a full pension. At the same time his wife had left him, and he was stuck with an unemployable daughter, still living at home, suffering depression and on heavy medication whose side effects included a rioting libido.

Parker had to put up with this because he had no therapeutic skills when it came to conversation. He regretted coming. Madigan's wasn't worth the trip. What might once have been a functional old-fashioned bar for minding one's business could have done without its modern makeover.

When Brindley finally stopped complaining they haggled and settled on seventy-five euros. Parker had to go to a cash machine. The first one he tried was out of order.

From what Brindley went on to tell Parker, who plied him with drink, the most significant event seemed to have taken place a few years before. Less *Gomorrah*, more *Narcos*, given its Colombian connection. Colombia was supplying the Dubai-based Dublin gang with its drugs and everything had run smoothly until a shipment of cocaine bound for the Irish Republic was seized by Spanish Customs at Valencia.

Parker's summary was a lot more straightforward than Brindley's ramblings. The man was often hard to follow, with his haphazard boozy anecdotes, interrupted by frequent personal complaints, and a series of disjointed 'and thens'. He would abandon a story in the middle for another. One minute they were in Valencia, the next Parker found himself listening to an account of an old political scandal going back decades about how three IRA men had gone to Colombia to train local rebels and got themselves arrested in Bogotá .

Parker hadn't attached any importance to that until he noticed Brindley had a habit of licking his lips before he spoke and when making what might be a considered point his tongue protruded for several seconds. Parker was reminded of the tennis player Andre Agassi, who said he could work out which way Boris Becker would serve according to the direction of the tip of his tongue sticking out of his mouth. Noting Brindley's habit, Parker found him easier to read. A lot of the time there wasn't any protrusion, which he took for low-grade stuff of no real value.

He eventually managed to get them back to the Valencia bust.

Brindley said, 'The Colombians had the hump so the Dubai lot sent over a well-known fixer and go-between to Medellin to renegotiate terms. The Colombian response was to abduct the man, cover him in bubble wrap until he suffocated and dump his body outside the city where it lay undiscovered for several weeks.'

Brindley remembered the story well because he had been forced by his editor to write it up in the most sentimental terms: a gentle giant and dad of four, who wouldn't have harmed a fly, versus a ruthless foreign narco gang known as The Office.

The tongue appeared before Brindley went on to say that what hadn't been pointed out at the time was how several Dublin police drugs raids had left the gang strapped for cash and unable to pay the Colombians.

'So the bust could be seen as a blessing in disguise,' Parker offered.

Brindley's tongue protruded for several seconds.

Parker spelled out the inference. 'Are you saying the gang sabotaged the deal by tipping off Spanish Customs because it didn't have the funds?'

Brindley nodded. 'Killing the fixer was the Colombians' way of saying they knew.'

'Then who was the informer?'

Brindley claimed not to know. Parker suspected he did, even though the tongue stayed put.

'Another pint?'

Brindley was drinking what he called 'the amber nectar' – in fact draft Peroni, paid for by Parker's debit card – each pint consumed with a packet of salted crisps. Parker stuck to water and skipped the snacks.

When Brindley had his drink, Parker asked – hoping his day hadn't been wasted – what had happened to the three IRA men arrested in Bogotá.

'Did a runner, jumped bail and fled back here where there was no extradition treaty.'

It took more pints before Brindley made the connection Parker was hoping for.

'There was in fact a fourth gang member the Colombians missed,' Brindley said. 'The guy, never identified, escaped arrest. It was said that while he was there he cultivated contacts in the Medellin cartel and stayed in touch after returning home.'

Parker asked, 'Is the punchline that this same man all those years later tells the Colombians they have been double-crossed over the Valencia bust?'

'You said that, not me.' Brindley's tongue was sticking out. After that he became vague, apart from saying he'd heard the informer's name was leaked by an unknown source and the Dubai mob had put a price on his head. Two years later the man was still on the run, having successfully avoided his pursuers.

Parker wondered about Father Jerome. The man was old enough to have been in Colombia at that time. His accent put him as coming from the South.

Parker, fishing, said he had heard about a renegade priest.

There always were such stories, Brindley replied. Most were anti-clerical myths, including the one about the priest who bugged his confessional.

Parker said, 'This one's in Belfast, running a boys' club.'

'Probably so he can fiddle with them.'

Parker sensed the man was shutting down.

'A Father Jerome,' he prompted.

'Sorry, mate. Means nothing.'

Pints five and six produced only rubbish until Parker asked about the original hack and whether Brindley had heard anything since about why McCavity might have been shot. For a change, Brindley was quite straightforward.

'The word going round is McCavity was in secret talks about handing over the North to Dublin, which the Brits can't wait to be rid of.'

'Any grounds for believing that?'

'Whispers in the wind, but McCavity – that "proud" Ulster boy – was said to be stabbing his own people and heritage in the back for the sake of a political deal, so he was seen as a traitor to the cause.'

Night was falling by the time the train left. Passing through the suburbs, Parker could see vignettes of daily life in the lit-up backs of houses where people hadn't drawn their curtains. In one, a large dog ran around circles chasing its tail. He knew how it felt.

What Brindley had told him reminded him of old

episodes of *The Shield*, a fast-moving Los Angeles cop show, with everyone waiting for the arrival of something called the Armenian money train, and none of the attendant swirl of chaos, double-dealing and runaway corruption made much sense, except it did; you were just too dumb to follow.

As the train moved into the dark countryside, he reviewed what he had: a shooting in London, a torched Chinese takeaway, Dublin drugs gangs taking over Belfast, political affiliations and the Colombians perhaps pulling the strings. Parker suspected that under the surface lay hidden strata, which if stumbled across would be mistaken for accident or coincidence. Of the several overlapping narratives he hadn't a clue which – all, any or none of them – might have affected the shooting of McCavity.

Brindley had also passed on that the three IRA men who had skipped the country from Bogotá had finally been granted an amnesty after years of political ruckus. At the time the scandal had significantly damaged the reputation of Sinn Fein, which had been seeking legitimacy as a political organisation shorn of its terrorist connections. Similarly, in Colombia talks with their rebels broke down and the resolution had taken years.

Parker was thinking: The Republic and the North still had its peace agreement, though perhaps not for much longer, which led him to ask whether if you wanted to get two nations together, first you get the gangsters together. Seen that way, could the Dublin–Belfast drugs war in fact be preliminary moves towards settling the future landscape of a united Ireland?

The idea wasn't so far-fetched. In 1943, after invading Sicily, US military had taken a Mafia godfather to act as local fixer. In 1947, with the emerging Cold War, US

Intelligence hired Mafia gangs to stop communists taking control of Europe's docks. With order restored, a blind eye was turned as the Mafia reopened its pre-war heroin route from Marseilles to New York.

Parker even wondered if any underlying explanation for McCavity's shooting might involve an unholy alliance of intelligence services and the underworld. On top of that was his hunch that if Father Jerome had been the fourth man in Medellin he could fit anywhere in the picture without distorting it.

He tried Charlotte. He had called several times already and again got no answer. He supposed she was annoyed with him for having gone off without offering to take her.

When Charlotte didn't answer her door Parker persuaded a hotel housemaid who was turning down beds for the night to check the room. He made up a story about her being unwell and not answering calls. The woman knocked, waited, knocked again then used a key card.

The bed lay undisturbed. Charlotte's case was on the luggage rack. Her coat was on a hanger. Phone and bag were on the dressing table. In it were her purse and passport.

Parker took Charlotte's phone down to the lobby. Her password proved no obstacle as he had seen her use it. Her last text received was his, saying he was away for a few hours. He asked at reception and drew a blank. He hung around, checking the revolving door, hoping to see her walk in as normal. Outside the uniformed doorman in his silly top hat was bossing the forecourt.

Parker went out and described Charlotte. For all the man's slow show of remembering, he worked Parker like a taxi meter, while continuing to greet and salute.

It cost Parker ten quid; the note was expertly palmed.

The doorman remembered her leaving with a man and not wearing a coat. The man was well dressed and had a Mercedes. From the doorman's description, it sounded like Father Jerome's gun-toting thug.

Parker called Delia, the policewoman whose number was on Charlotte's phone. She picked up more or less straight away. He could hear children in the background, a girl's squeal of delight, followed by a barking dog. It sounded like he was interrupting their supper. He tried to imagine a world of childcare and couldn't get even close.

He told her how Charlotte had been seen leaving the hotel.

'Most likely with Lafferty. She has been gone most of the day and she didn't take anything with her, no phone or personal belongings.'

Delia sounded concerned. She was about to start a night shift and said, 'I'll see if anything has come in.'

Parker took up a position in a corner of the lobby and checked messages. Nothing.

Delia texted forty minutes later asking Parker if he knew who the man in the attached image was.

It was a traffic camera frame grab, clear enough to show Charlotte driving a Mercedes. The man was Cross.

Parker wondered what on earth she was doing driving around with Cross when she had last been seen with Lafferty. Had she been abducted? Or did her being at the wheel suggest they were somehow all in it together?

He called Delia, who said the Mercedes was registered as Lafferty's and it had been picked up by a tracking system capable of extracting and storing vehicle features for instant recall.

'It was logged at 2.35pm on the M1, entering at Junction 14, exiting two miles later at 13. Otherwise they must have travelled on roads without cameras. No sightings since but sooner or later the car'll resurface.'

Parker didn't share her optimism. Why was Cross suddenly in the picture?

He hung up just as Charlotte's phone rang. It was an unidentified caller. Parker answered, saying nothing.

A patrician voice demanded, 'Where are you?'

Parker explained he was answering for Charlotte.

'I'm here in Belfast at the airport. Put Ms Waites on. It's Moffat.'

'She's not here.'

'It's urgent.'

'She's missing.'

Parker heard the man's sharp intake of breath before he asked Parker's whereabouts and said he would get a taxi.

Everyone was crawling out of the woodwork. Straight afterwards, his own phone rang. It was Delia.

'They've found three bodies.'

Parker feared one of them was Charlotte.

'Three men on a farm south-west of here, discovered by a cowherd.'

'Who are they?'

'Unidentified. All shot. Local police have called in homicide.'

'Can you get me down there?'

Parker didn't know what strings Delia pulled but a patrol car with a policewoman picked him up twenty minutes later. Moffat hadn't arrived. Parker left a message at the hotel reception.

They drove in silence into black countryside.

The policewoman said, 'You must be important.'

Parker grunted and they left it at that. He refused to think about what lay ahead and prayed Charlotte was safe.

They turned off the road and bumped down a rutted track that ended in a farmyard lit up with police floodlights, which gave it the air of a film set. Scene-of-crime tape was in place. Official vehicles were parked to one side. Teams in white overalls went about their business.

Moffat called Charlotte's number as they arrived. Parker told him where he was.

Moffat said, 'I'll hire a car.'

Parker listened to the policewoman giving Moffat directions. He sensed Moffat knew already what this was about.

Parker could hear cattle. After the warmth of the car he was reluctant to get out.

A cold wind blew. It was spitting rain. He introduced himself to the officer in charge who was standing outside. With his gelled hair, tight suit and pointed tan shoes the man looked as though he would be more at home behind a desk. He regarded Parker askance and returned to scrolling on his mobile.

'Mind if I take a look?' Parker asked.

'Don't get in the way.'

What resembled a fairground tent had been set up over the first body, lit so it glowed. Parker put his head inside. The dead man was Lafferty, not even having had time to look surprised by his fate.

The forensics officer taking photographs barely glanced up to say, 'A shot to the back of the head,' like he was making mental notes rather than addressing Parker.

'Pistol probably,' he continued, 'won't know what calibre until we dig out the bullet. Neat job.'

'How long since he was shot?' asked Parker.

'Eight to ten hours,' the officer said, still without looking up.

Parker went inside. A large kitchen was crowded with

people trying not to fall over each other. A body lay on the floor and two men were taking bets on whether the deceased was Syrian or Libyan.

A third body lay thrown back in a wooden chair, arms outstretched as though in benediction, an appropriate last gesture for a priest. Father Jerome had been drilled through the forehead. His eyes were turned up towards the bullet hole, which resembled a Hindu bindi.

Parker was sure Charlotte must have been there, given Lafferty's presence outside, but he found it impossible to imagine the choreography or her moves.

The senior officer came in and spoke to the men examining the corpse on the floor. Parker drifted within earshot.

The officer said, 'From the pictures you sent through, Dublin Homicide has texted that your man is Hamid Hosseini. Iranian asylum seeker. Forty-three years old. Gangland gunman.'

Parker looked at the body, wondering why he was dead too if he was one of the shooters. The cops were saying how he had been shot twice, unlike the others. Parker guessed he must have been killed after Father Jerome and, to judge from the angles, from the corridor beyond the kitchen.

He hung around some more until a constable came in and asked if he was Parker; a man was waiting outside.

Moffat was conspicuous in a trilby and whipcord coat with a velvet collar. It was raining harder.

'No such thing as bad weather,' Moffat said. 'Only poor kit.'

Parker thought the man looked like he had been hollowed out.

They started with Lafferty. Moffat appeared surprised but said nothing. Inside, he barely glanced at Hosseini. When he came to Father Jerome he leaned forward, peering intently, as if trying to provoke the man into a posthumous dialogue.

He stood back up and walked out, telling Parker to follow.

They sat in Moffat's car. He hadn't stinted himself, hiring a Volvo XC60. Moffat said nothing. Parker watched the rain fall as the man flicked the wipers and stared at their sweep.

Moffat finally asked about Charlotte.

Parker explained how she had been seen leaving the hotel with Lafferty. He didn't really know what he thought about it. Moffat was one of those men whose presence threw everything into question.

Parker said, 'She was spotted driving Lafferty's car.'

'On her own?'

'With Cross.'

Moffat looked incredulous. 'Christ, man! When was this?'

'This afternoon at 2.30.'

'Are the filth offering a time on the shootings?'

'Filth?' Parker was barely thinking straight.

'The rozzers.'

'Eight hours or so.'

'Before our lovebirds were spotted then. Give me the options.'

Parker presumed 'lovebirds' was ironic.

'The fucking options, man!'

'It looks like they fled the scene of crime.' Parker considered. 'Or they went off before it happened, in Lafferty's Mercedes,' he added, which didn't sound much better.

'With her driving not exactly suggesting lack of willingness.' Moffat sighed, took out his phone, glanced at it and put it away again. 'Where's Hopkins in all this?'

Good question, thought Parker. He said, 'She knows Charlotte had a previous relationship with Cross.'

Moffat stared up at the car roof with a pained expression.

Finally he said, 'Is Hopkins up to stuff you don't know about, dear heart? She's a liability and a lesbian, of course.'

Parker had heard no such thing. He was more curious about why Moffat had stared at Father Jerome like a hunter inspecting a trophy.

'What about the dead priest?' he asked.

Moffat sucked his teeth. 'Name's Magee.'

'A real priest?'

'As it happens, yes. Known behind his back as Sonny Magee, after that black boxer Liston, because it was said his grandmother had dark blood.' Moffat giggled and said, 'I wonder if the priest knew she was Waites's daughter.'

'What's her father got to do with it?'

'Here for what they called the Troubles.' Moffat made it sound like a charabanc excursion. 'Magee held him responsible for the death of his brother.' This was stated with a moue of regret before adding, 'In an ambush.'

Look to the past, Parker had told Charlotte, never dreaming it would turn out to be personal.

'What was her father doing here?'

'Can't say, really. What I heard, he left rather under a cloud.'

The man wasn't going to volunteer so Parker asked, 'Did you ever meet Magee before tonight?'

'Good Lord, no! I had his picture on my wall and he probably had mine.'

Moffat nodded in the direction of the tent.

'Lafferty was one of mine.'

'Yours?'

'Don't be naive. As in running him as an agent. Unnerving man. Once said Christmas was the season for getting even.'

Why tell me, Parker wondered to himself, as Moffat said, 'What an utter balls-up.'

Parker finished his thought: . . . unless you plan to use me.

'Lafferty was watching Cross,' Moffat went on. 'The two indulged in mammoth drinking sessions. Tarts too. Cross's preference was for the Bullitt Hotel, ha-ha.'

Moffat took out a cheroot, was about to light up then saw the hire car's 'No Smoking' sign on the dashboard. He unlatched the boot and said, 'We can sit in the back. The hatch will give us cover.'

They got out and sat with the rain drumming overhead. Moffat lit up and asked, 'Want one?'

Parker shook his head.

'During one of their big piss-ups, Lafferty reported that Cross was in stitches over some lunatic plan to shoot a politician on the mainland.'

'Why tell Lafferty?'

'Loose lips, pissed as a newt. Cross wrote it off as a mad fantasy on the part of Magee, even though he was being considered for the shooter.'

'What did you think?'

'Lafferty told us later that Cross reported the operation scratched, which we took to mean it was all hot air.'

'Except it wasn't.'

'Nonetheless, Cross was bound to have told "London",' Moffat said, putting it in derisive quotes.

He flicked his cheroot aside.

'A lot of loose talk in Belfast. Always was. Just as likely "London" might have wanted it to happen.'

It was said as though such things were a matter of course.

Parker slowly asked, 'Are you saying "London" knew and did nothing?'

'In so many words.'

'Then "London" was told the operation was off when it was going ahead?'

Moffat rolled his wrist, apparently amused at Parker struggling to put it together.

'By "London" you mean Hopkins?'

Moffat said nothing.

Parker said, 'If Hopkins knew and believed the operation had been stood down—'

Moffat cut in. 'Magee of course may have wanted her to know, so a pile of steaming shit could be laid at her door.'

Moffat let that sink in and carried on, sounding almost academic. 'You remember of course that big meeting where Hopkins went out of her way to imply Waites was at fault.'

'Yes.'

'Don't you see?'

Parker didn't and asked Moffat to spell it out.

'Regardless of any apparent difference of opinion, Waites might have been doing Hopkins's bidding all along.'

It didn't square with what he knew of Charlotte, but when he said that Moffat accused him once again of being naive.

Moffat went on, assuming the air of a music-hall turn.

'Ain't it also occurred to you she's more involved with Cross than she has let on?'

'But—' Parker faltered, thrown by the man's change of manner.

'Go on, dear heart.'

'She came up with Cross on CCTV.'

Moffat gave a theatrical sigh.

'Unless she was told to look for him. If there were unanswered questions for Hopkins.'

Parker reluctantly conceded to himself that Charlotte could have been forced into a compromising role, similar to Hopkins using him to hack Charlotte.

'There are too many moving parts,' Moffat went on. 'Cross is out of order. Hopkins is out of order. The girl looks very much out of order, so I rather have a bone to pick. I trust you aren't out of order.'

Parker said he wasn't, thinking it depended on who was doing the ordering.

'Roberts says you're good at digging.'

'Roberts?'

'He will give you any backup you need.'

'I thought he worked with Hopkins.'

'Enterprising fellow. Covers the waterfront. I will have a word.'

Moffat stood and stretched, and added in an offhand way, 'I suspect Waites has been a fool for love. Find her. And Cross too. I would be interested to hear his side. And while you are at it try and bring me Hopkins's head on a plate.'

Parker thought: Fool for love? He felt his heart pinch.

Moffat appeared cheered up.

'Come, dear boy. Think of yourself as the Trojan horse inside the citadel.' He giggled. 'Think of me as Salome. Tell Hopkins that Waites is missing, last spotted with Cross, and see if that doesn't put her knickers in a twist.'

Whatever Moffat wanted from him, the courtesy didn't extend to offering a lift back. He said he had plans and Parker was left hanging around the farm waiting for a taxi, which cost him a small fortune.

He called Hopkins. If she was surprised by what he told her she hid it well. Her response was an 11pm strategy meeting, which she told Parker to attend. She left him with Doyle's and Roberts's numbers and orders to get them in.

Doyle was at home and sounded drunk. He grumbled about being called out so late.

Roberts picked up as Parker was about to hang up. Parker heard what he realised was gunfire. Roberts said he was on a shooting range. Like Hopkins and Moffat, he didn't sound surprised either and Parker was left wondering what loop they were all operating in.

In the taxi Parker checked his texts. Several were from FOE (reputed to stand for Fuck Off Everyone but never clarified). Parker knew FOE as a mole and occasional whistleblower with whom he regularly exchanged information on a favours basis. Parker assumed FOE was a man. All he knew was he was a night owl and occasionally complained about being confined to a wheelchair. Parker had no idea where he operated from, whether he was even English, but his information was always good.

FOE texted:

– What do you make of recent low-level breakdowns in UK infrastructure e.g. DWP failing to pay benefits last month after 'technical probs'?

Charlotte had complained about ATMs not working, and Parker had just experienced the same in Dublin.

Parker read FOE's follow-ups.

– Barcodes packed up in Bargain Booze, Co-op and Waitrose.

– Big internet provider crashed for several days, leaving parts of London down. Didn't make the news.

Parker texted:

– Deliberate or general incompetence? Russians?

FOE texted back:

– Interfere with everything and don't give a fuck.

Not for the first time it struck Parker that Hopkins had never asked him to do any work on the Russians. She said it wasn't where the money was. Parker knew it was exactly where the money was: London was awash with their laundering; which was not what Hopkins had meant.

Parker texted, curious to know:

– What's Russian position on Northern Ireland?

FOE texted back:

– *Anti-Union pro Republic. Blame Brits for historical genocide, compare Republican struggle to Russian Revolution and the North as Ireland's Crimea. Follows that united Ireland recommended.*

FOE texted again:

– *Plus a lot of fake allegation, probably Russian origin, most not picked up.*

– For instance?

– *IRA using Arab speakers to recruit Islamic State jihadis displaced from Syria!!!*

FOE's texts continued coming in during the meeting, which was held in the room they had used before, or one identical in its pastel anonymity. Doyle turned up bad-tempered and the worse for wear. A couple of police robots drifted in. Roberts arrived last and stank of cordite. They sat in silent mutual suspicion waiting for Hopkins, who was back in London, to come online while Parker glanced at FOE's latest round of texts.

– *IRA links to private armies in Colombia and militant Christian survivalists in US!*

– *Cheeky this, Irish Republicans supposedly aided the nerve agent poisoning of Russian ex-spy in Salisbury!*

– *And good luck if they can float this. Protestant Loyalist Unionist Party (doesn't exist) against all precedent, wants united Ireland and its leader told EU they're ready to leave the UK.*

Parker was nervous for Charlotte's sake and fed up with the macho silence, so he asked Doyle if he'd heard the rumour about the Loyalist Unionist Party.

Doyle said, 'Don't be bloody stupid! There's a DUP and a UUP, there's no LUP. Who's telling you this?'

'The Russians, probably.'

Parker was aware of Roberts smirking.

Hopkins came on Zoom, all concern, stressing that Charlotte's safety was paramount and pointing out the obvious: that she was with and possibly hostage to an armed and dangerous man. Train and bus stations and the airport would have to be watched.

Doyle interrupted to say they already were; Parker doubted it. Hopkins asked if Lafferty's car had been found. Doyle said he was on to that too. Doyle, having taken against Parker, gave him the task of checking car rentals; a waste of time in his unstated opinion.

Hopkins told them Roberts was there to liaise between London and Belfast. She insisted everything went through him, to Doyle's annoyance.

While they wasted time on the details, Parker texted FOE:

– Need help with possible links between three names.

He was thinking of Hopkins, Moffat and Roberts. The link between Moffat and Hopkins was opaque, but Roberts was known to both, so what was the connection?

'Are you with us, son?' Doyle asked.

'I was thinking about social media,' said Parker.

'For setting up a fundraiser to find Waites?'

It was said with heavy sarcasm.

'How the format makes any untruth indistinguishable from a biblical truth.'

'In relation to Waites?' Doyle asked in disbelief.

'Possibly.'

Parker saw Roberts looking interested.

Hopkins interrupted to say they needed to get on.

Parker didn't really know what he had meant. He supposed it was about how FOE's texts implied that hundreds if not thousands of fake stories were churned out every day and the bombardment was what really mattered – flattening the truth – and if one of these lies gained traction then the aim had been achieved.

Doyle looked at Parker and asked, 'Anything to add?'

Parker, to annoy, said, 'How can we know anything is what it says?'

Doyle snapped, 'Try reading what's on the fucking tin, son.'

Parker thought that quite funny. He was riling Doyle because he could see the man didn't give a toss about Charlotte.

Roberts said to Doyle, 'It's called lateral thinking.'

Parker was bound to wonder about Roberts. He had said little in the meeting. Parker suspected he was one of those institutional psychopaths who knew how to make the machine crush people.

As they left, Roberts approached and asked, 'Do you shoot?'

'Not especially,' said Parker, surprised by the question.

It sounded as though the man was implying guns would be waved around in any confrontation with Cross.

'Let's go to the range. I've something to show you.'

The range turned out to be downstairs in the basement. Roberts produced a key for a reinforced door, which took them into a low-ceilinged bunker. Parker blinked as the main lights came on to reveal a sandbank at the far end, and hanging human-shaped targets. Parker was surprised they were replicas of people he recognised, including Saddam Hussein, Jimmy Savile and Jeremy Corbyn.

Roberts behaved like a man in his element. He picked up a long, thin, fancy leather case, which he opened.

'Look at this beauty. A De Lisle carbine, one of the

quietest ever made. The .45 ACP round is also inherently subsonic, reducing another source of noise in a firearm.'

Parker took in the weapon's malevolent short barrel, the magazine in front of the trigger and the bolt above.

Roberts seemed inordinately proud of it.

'Used by special operations units in the Second World War. The only disadvantage is an effective range of 185 metres, so you have to overcome the fear factor of getting close to your target.'

Parker tried to appear impressed when he couldn't care less. He had better things to do than play with guns.

Roberts replaced the rifle in its snug case, lovingly closed it and wiped the leather with a shammy cloth.

He led the way to a locked glass-fronted cabinet.

'Let's fire some rounds,' he said.

Parker was given protective eyewear and ear mufflers and a pistol to blaze away with.

'Ever done this before?'

Parker shook his head, and thought: Don't tell me it's better than sex.

'Watch me.'

Roberts took up a crouched stance, arms straight, with a two-handed grip. Even with the mufflers, Parker was surprised by the snap of the reports. Of the targets at the end of the 25-yard range, Roberts chose Jeremy Corbyn.

'Now there's a blast from the past,' he said, drilling Jeremy through the eye.

His subsequent grouping peppered a neat pattern around the target's heart.

Roberts talked Parker through what he needed to do. Safety catch on; safety catch off. Relaxed not stiff. Squeeze not pull. Get the right hand as high up the grip as possible.

Parker had no interest in firing a gun and suspected Roberts knew that and was putting on a show of superiority and humiliation.

Nevertheless, he concentrated on the barrel being in line with his arm, to avoid the gun flicking up at the wrist when he fired. He squeezed the trigger and surprised himself when Jeremy took the shot in the shoulder. The next one went lower but wasn't a miss.

Roberts said, 'We'll make a shooter of you yet.'

Parker felt guilty for starting to enjoy himself. He wondered what it would be like being fired back at.

Roberts took up his position again. 'OODA,' he said. 'Do you know what that stands for?'

Parker said, 'I expect you're about to tell me.'

Roberts was one of those men who laughed regardless of whether something was funny. Parker suspected the controlled office demeanour was in deliberate contrast to this off-duty bonding.

Roberts lined up the target and punctuated each word with a shot. 'Observe. Orient. Decide. Act. OODA. That's how we find the girl.'

Parker surrendered himself to another sleepless night. Roberts had said to reconvene at 8am tomorrow; in his jargon, 'O-eight hundred'.

Parker took a bath and lay in the cooling water thinking how the farm shooting had the Dubai mob's fingerprints all over it, then found himself wondering if Belfast had direct flights to Dubai and whether Cross had ever gone there.

He hadn't, apparently, Parker decided after half an hour's checking. But the thought persisted that Cross might have been Dubai's man all along. Or had he just been playing all sides against the middle?

Parker checked the number of gangland killings in Belfast in the past three months. Twelve in all, including the three at the farmhouse. Five drive-by shootings and four doorstep killings were attributed to the escalating terror that had spread from the South; an 'epidemic' as one local newspaper had it. Parker, thinking back to his train ride from Dublin, again asked himself if the deaths might have a political dimension. He recalled how shooting people on their doorsteps had been a common form of sectarian execution during the Troubles. Was it still?

The deaths had received no coverage beyond local press.

Meanwhile, the international news was given over to the coming of yet another plague. No one was sure if it was a combination of previous mutations or a new deadlier strain. The world was grinding to a halt again. Parker had been keeping a watch on its progress. It had started to haunt his dreams, like a recurring bass note. Strange how people reacted, given everything that had happened already and how badly it was being handled as usual. Politicians continued to drone on with their tired wartime metaphors. Several European countries were shutting down while the UK was still making up its mind. An announcement was imminent. Parker suspected none of them had a clue as usual.

He was relieved when FOE texted, distracting him from his thoughts.

– Your man Roberts served eight years in ultra-clandestine Special Reconnaissance Regiment, including undercover ops Afghanistan and Northern Ireland.

– When Northern Ireland?

– Over ten years ago, infiltrating IRA in conjunction with MI6.

– Was Moffat in on that?

– Yup. Six's man, an old hand from the Troubles.

That meant Roberts and Moffat went back that far. Parker wondered what else Moffat wasn't telling.

FOE texted again:

– BTW Robbo has Russian wife. Big pile on Thames beyond his means if tax returns correct heh-heh. She filthy rich. UK resident for quite a while, dual passport.

A government agent and his Russian wife; Parker wondered what that gave them to talk about. His phone pinged, announcing FOE's next text.

– Roberts and your other name Hopkins connect to private security company, Ercon, does contract work for government departments, e.g. MI5.

Parker thought: Call me paranoid — another global virus, technical breakdowns, drug wars, an attempted political assassination, fake news, and a missing woman; were they all connected?

No one force controlled everything, he knew that. It was more like snooker where the same elements were in play but the variations infinite.

Parker was sure that those cross-references commonly known as coincidence were playing a part: Charlotte connected to Moffat through her father and directly to Cross, who knocked back to Moffat and Hopkins. Roberts seemed to answer to both Moffat and Hopkins, who appeared to all intents rivals.

In terms of historical substrata, variations of the elements repeated, with Father Jerome connected to both Moffat and Charlotte's father. Parker reckoned no one player would be aware of the full picture. Beyond that, he doubted if anyone else of higher authority was either.

In the sleepless hours before dawn, contemplating why

any hotel corridor reminded him of death, as he struggled not to tear off his bandages and lacerate himself in an orgy of scratching, he lay awake fearing for Charlotte.

12

Charlotte still couldn't work out how she had survived and ended up driving a dead man's car. She wasn't even sure how relieved she was. Outside, the dreariest possible afternoon was no advertisement for life.

Staring at the malevolent silencer, aware of the scream building in her, she had seen the balaclava-clad gunman hesitate, as though he recognised her. It was enough. The pause served them both because Charlotte could see the second gunman sneaking up on his companion, raising his arm to fire. She had no idea what she did to alert the man in front of her or whether he turned and fired through some sixth sense. Whichever, the bullet did its job and the second gunman sat down almost comically with his legs crossed before falling backwards, his head hitting the flagstone with an audible crack.

The man who had been about to kill her walked over to the fallen man, knelt down, yanked off the man's balaclava, steadied the head, stuck the gun behind his ear, then looking up and to one side – in a way that incongruously reminded Charlotte of how some men turned their heads away when opening a bottle of wine – he pulled the trigger. Because of the muffled shot Charlotte heard the skull shatter; she supposed hers would have sounded the same. She was acutely aware that the first bullet had been meant for her.

Perhaps part of her had known it was Cross: something

about his stance, or animal instinct, or the forgotten smell of the man; so she wasn't completely surprised when he removed his balaclava. Her first conscious reaction was how pathetic he looked in his quasi-combat gear, with his gun and its ugly phallic silencer in one hand and balaclava in the other.

She could see he had recognised her and wanted to know why she was there. The tiny, still functioning part of her brain managed to come out with, 'I'm here to take you in.'

Cross stared, eyes bulging.

Charlotte stood up on wobbly legs, saying, as brusquely as she could manage, 'I was "volunteered" because I'm supposed to know you. Sex on a roof, remember?'

Just as well to get that out of the way, she thought as she busied herself with drinking a glass of water from the sink while avoiding looking at the dead bodies. She recalled the Muriel Spark book mentioned by Father Jerome, in which all the characters turned out to be dead. Perhaps Cross had shot her after all and this was just the flickers of her dying brain.

'What's that about?' she asked, gesturing towards Father Jerome glaring sightlessly at the ceiling.

'He was one of the bad guys.'

For a moment she wanted to yell at him to grow up – but said instead, as calmly as she could manage, 'Your pal was about to shoot you.'

It was like they were trying to speak to each other underwater. Her only hope was to look like she knew what she was doing. She explained, as though it were perfectly obvious, 'I was abducted by your friend Lafferty for a history lesson from Father Jerome. Now, let's get back to Belfast and sort you with Hopkins.'

'Hopkins?'

He really didn't know, she could see.

'Moffat ring any bells?'

Cross shook his head and said, 'I need time to think.'

No surprise there, thought Charlotte.

'We needn't say anything about being here,' she offered.

Her legs continued to shake. She was giddy at finding herself still walking and talking.

'We can take Lafferty's car. I'll drive.'

Cross levelled the gun.

'You're not taking me to Belfast.'

His terms. She drew no consolation from the fact that the man appeared in more of a state of shock than she was.

'Tell me where then,' she said, picking up her shoes, hoping Lafferty's keys were in the car and not on him, and that Cross wouldn't change his mind and shoot her in the back.

After a tense, silent drive, apart from a few directions issued, they ended up an hour or so later in a mobile home in an empty caravan holiday park north of the city, overlooking the estuary. Cross told Charlotte to park the Mercedes down a side street; they would walk the rest. That took five minutes. God knows what she looked like. She was still wearing the green gumboots, carrying her shoes and was coatless. Her mind was all mixed up: forced that morning to travel in the boot of a Mercedes, she had then found herself driving the same vehicle that afternoon, and even surreptitiously enjoying the quality of its ride.

A sharp wind whipped off the water. The day had decided to give up early and it was almost dark. The caravan park appeared closed, even the porter's lodge. The place was all neat paths and identical trailers. Cross had keys for one, which he opened and pointed for her to go in.

It was poky, more camped out in than lived in. Charlotte presumed Cross used it as a bolthole. The room smelt damp. She noted a couple of beds with grubby candlewick spreads, a basic kitchen, a small table between two banquettes, with a separate space at the end for what she supposed was a washroom and toilet.

Cross seemed unsure about whether he was supposed to extend his hospitality or treat her as a prisoner, so Charlotte took charge of what he no doubt regarded as a woman's business, filling the kettle and switching it on, finding instant coffee and mugs. As she rinsed the mugs she was reminded of Father Jerome doing the same, for the last time, and stamped on the thought. She said she wouldn't mind some heating because it was freezing. Cross turned on an electric heater, went to a narrow cupboard and came back with a fleece, saying it would be big but was better than nothing. Charlotte put it on, nearly bursting into tears as she struggled to find the sleeve. The material smelt of fabric conditioner. Outside, none of the other homes had lights on. Cross carefully drew the curtains. His movements were tidy and economical. She thought him pointlessly house-proud of what was a dump, in a way that made him seem boring and fastidious. What she had ever seen in him, she had no idea. He wasn't bad-looking, but even so.

His behaviour swung wildly between hypervigilance – as if expecting the door to be kicked in at any moment – and near collapse as when he realised there was no milk in the fridge.

Charlotte pointed out she had no phone and needed to call people to tell them she was safe and that she'd found him. He said no.

He was bound to have a short fuse and she anticipated a

deadly game in terms of what he told and didn't, waiting to see what cards she held.

They sat at the tiny table with their milkless coffee in novelty mugs, trying to avoid each other's knees.

Charlotte composed herself and thought: Stick him with a fact.

'You were seen torching a Chinese takeaway.'

He looked caught out at that; he hadn't known it was being watched.

She went on, more confident. Be the snooty bitch, she told herself, take a leaf out of Hopkins's book.

'What was your job in Belfast as far as London was concerned?'

'Infiltrating the IRA to report on policy attitudes.'

'You make it sound like a White Paper.'

Hopkins would have been proud of that, but Cross wasn't the type to appreciate.

'Someone must have sent you,' she said, 'as in being answerable. Man or woman?'

'Marshall, male.'

'Not Hopkins, female?'

'I keep telling you.'

'Describe him for me.' She gave her sweetest smile. 'You see, I've never heard of Marshall.'

'Who sent you then?'

'I keep telling you, Hopkins. Now what does Marshall look like?'

When Cross was finished describing the man, she said, 'Also known as Roberts.'

A tight smile, despite her alarm that it was Roberts.

'Why was he interested in you?' she asked.

'He said for what he had in mind you wouldn't get anywhere without being from here.'

Charlotte looked at the man's clamped jaw, remembered his GBH sentence and wondered whether women were exempt from his violence.

Cross gave a crooked smile and said, 'Maybe I should have just shot you.'

'Maybe you still will,' she said, stumbling over an image of seeing herself face down on the Formica table, brains blown out. She struggled on.

'What was burning down the takeaway about?'

Cross took his time deciding.

'Getting the Chinks out.'

'Who wanted them out?'

'It's complicated.'

'We've got time.'

'It was about setting up another connection.'

'What sort of connection?'

He was back in alert mode. Charlotte noted the way his head twitched, accompanied by a rapid blinking. She tried to look in control rather than fighting panic.

'Drugs. It was a sting operation,' he eventually said.

'Organised by?'

'Marshall. The guy you call Roberts.'

'How was that supposed to work?'

'I was told to make myself useful to the IRA, take out the Chinks without letting the IRA know and introduce a new connection from Colombia.'

'When it was a British intelligence operation all along.'

Cross nodded. 'Using confiscated drugs to replace the triad connection. The bust was supposed to take place next week.'

'And the reason for it?'

'To take down Father Jerome.'

'Who was doing what?'

'Using drugs money to rearm the IRA. The weapons they'd kept since the peace agreement were pretty much beyond use.'

'Rearm?' she echoed.

'In response to the Prods doing the same, with the backing of British intelligence, so Father Jerome believed.'

Which was more or less what he had told her, which didn't mean it was true.

'Why?'

'The IRA was preparing for another war and needed to protect itself.'

'And what's your understanding?'

'That the Brits wanted to set the two sides off against each other as they had done in the past.'

'Why would they want to do that?'

'Father Jerome said the Brits needed a war to distract from how shite everything else is and falling apart.'

Charlotte stared at Cross's clenched fists. When he stood she thought for a moment he was going to hit her, but it was only to fetch a bottle of Scotch from a cupboard.

'Connors said you didn't drink on account of your faith,' Charlotte said, her voice shaky.

'Depends which half is in charge. What else did Connors say?'

'That you shot up a bar.'

'Connors is a terrible fibber.'

Cross poured two fingers in each glass, and raised his in salute. Charlotte hoped he wasn't expecting a fuck for old times' sake.

Cross asked, 'Do you trust anyone?'

The question surprised her.

'Not especially,' she answered, thinking: Least of all you.

Cross's head swivelled towards the door.

'Did you hear that?'

The man was wriggling like he had been holding everything in for too long.

'It was nothing.'

Charlotte was already woozy from the drink. Perhaps he would get her completely pissed before he killed her.

She waited until he was settled again and asked, 'Why was Father Jerome shot?'

'No one said. The sting operation was suddenly cancelled. Roberts was mad about that because a lot of work had gone into it. He just said Father Jerome had to be taken care of instead. New orders.'

'Did you ask why?'

'Roberts said someone had decided it was no longer in anyone's interest to have the IRA connection exposed.'

'So you obliged and shot the priest.'

'No loss there.'

'But you weren't supposed to have walked out of there either.'

If Cross had an answer, he wasn't giving it.

'What about the other man? Did you know him?'

'The Iranian, he was from Dublin. Roberts said it was some kind of joint operation and I was to take him even though I had said I would do the job myself.'

'When in fact he was hired to take you out as well.'

'I only thought that when he said a woman was there, and I sensed it was part of a trap. Then I recognised you.'

'Would you have shot me?'

'I was waiting to see what the other fellow did.'

Charlotte thought: Doesn't answer the question.

'Who might want you dead? Roberts?'

'No. He was really angry about having to do the job when he wanted to carry on with the sting.'

Charlotte supposed with everyone playing so fast and loose, someone was bound to tidy up at some point.

Cross said disconcertingly, 'I can read your mind, you know.'

'Excuse me?'

'I can hear your thoughts.'

'What am I thinking now?' Charlotte asked, fearing the man was unhinged.

'Probably that I'm mad.'

They both found that funny, Charlotte in a desperate way. She watched Cross's fists lift off the table.

'I don't trust London. I didn't trust Father Jerome. He said the story going round was I was agenting for the Brits.'

'Which you were. And?'

Cross's head started twitching again, accompanied by rapid blinking. This time his body started to jerk as though an electrical current were passing through it. This lasted long enough to alarm Charlotte into thinking she was witnessing some kind of seizure. He seemed unable to hear her frantic attempts to communicate and was unaware of her grabbing his arm.

Then it stopped, after about twenty seconds. He sat staring at her, the eyes coming back into focus.

Charlotte asked if he was all right now. He ignored her, stood up, shaking his head as if to clear it, then in a blur of motion, swivelled and punched his fist through a kitchen cupboard behind him.

Charlotte screamed. She wanted to hide under the table and never come out.

Cross frowned as if trying to recollect what had just happened and looked at her for help. She forced herself to run the cold tap and made him put his hand under it.

'It's more a graze than a cut,' she said meaninglessly. 'What happened just now?'

Cross said he sometimes had episodes involving flashbacks.

She wanted to ask if they were about Afghanistan, but he had clammed up again.

She was still trying to make sense of what he had told her. She suspected Cross's account was very partial. He had said very little about his relations with Father Jerome. Charlotte presumed the reason he was supposed to be dead was because someone decided he hadn't been playing straight.

Cross said, 'I want an immunity deal.'

'Unlikely if someone has already tried to have you killed.'

'There's a smoking gun,' Cross said.

What that was he wouldn't say. She wondered if he was a fantasist on top of everything. And I bet you'll still kill me, she thought.

'I'm a light sleeper,' Cross said, making it sound like a threat.

He checked the caravan door and put the key in his pocket. He made sure the windows were locked and removed the keys, then dragged the mattress off the second bed and placed it in front of the door.

'Take the other bed,' he said.

There was no toothpaste in the tiny bathroom. Charlotte used soap and her finger to clean her teeth, went to bed in her clothes and lay awake. Outside was so quiet that the world might as well have vanished. When she did manage to sleep she found herself tugged awake by breathless panic.

At one point she sensed Cross moving around. It was too dark to make anything out but her impression was of him standing for a long time at the end of her bed.

Somehow the night passed, drifting in and out of sleep,

chased by violent dreams. At six she was wide awake and panicking. She lay there trying to arrange her thoughts, hoping mental discipline would follow. She got up and had a shower under a thin trickle of lukewarm water. She rinsed her hair. She cleaned her teeth again with soap. She could still taste the previous night's Scotch.

Share, she told herself. Be useful.

She found eggs within their sell-by date, a loaf of stale bread and a tub of Flora. Cross was still asleep. She made coffee and scrambled eggs with toast. By the time she was done he was awake. She offered the coffee and food, which he took silently and ate ravenously. She had no appetite but forced hers down, despite the egg white still being runny. She had cooked better. She needed to persuade Cross to let her talk to Parker, then realised she had no idea what Parker's number was; it was on her phone.

She patiently explained to Cross about Parker, saying he was dependable – hoping that was true – and contacting him was the best start in terms of any sort of deal. Cross remained undecided. Every moment felt like he was on a hair-trigger between petulant indecision and outburst. At the same time part of him seemed to be looking to Charlotte.

It took far too long to grind him down, like in a relationship row where one party holds out for far longer than necessary.

'Shall I call him?' she asked when she at last saw him waver.

He handed her an old Nokia and said it was untraceable. Charlotte called her own number, hoping Parker had retrieved her phone. It went to voicemail. She left no message, waited and rang again. This time Parker answered.

Charlotte said, 'I don't have time to talk. Are you alone?'

Parker said he was.

'We need to meet and for you to tell no one.'

Parker asked if she was all right and she repeated that she didn't have time to talk.

'Come alone,' she said.

'Where?'

Charlotte looked at Cross. He said, 'Nando's in the Victoria Square Mall, and straightaway.'

She passed that on and asked Parker to give her his number as a backup. She gestured to Cross to find her something to write with. He came back with a biro and she wrote down Parker's number on her wrist, holding the phone awkwardly against her shoulder.

They took a bus. Despite the fleece, Charlotte was freezing. Cross refused to go in Lafferty's Mercedes in case they were looking for it. His behaviour remained contrary. Everything was a rush. He told Charlotte he didn't know Parker from Adam and didn't want to give him time to organise any welcome party. On the other hand, when their bus broke down and they had to wait for a replacement he refused to call a taxi or contact Parker, telling Charlotte he could wait.

When they finally got to the mall Cross became excessively cautious. Even though they were ages late he insisted on scouting the various entry points. He seemed to move almost invisibly. Sometimes he took Charlotte's arm and held her close. How strange normal looked, she thought.

He took them in through a goods entrance into a maze of concrete corridors, and Charlotte saw he had crossed into a parallel universe where everything bristled with potential threat.

He slipped them into the enormous domed shopping centre with vertiginous walkways. Charlotte stared at the retail bustle and told herself it was just another temple to shopping, too somnolent and crowded for anything bad to happen, but she was aware of Cross assessing everything in expectation of a trap. She couldn't imagine how any telltale signs of danger manifested themselves until she had a flash of what it might look like through his eyes with everywhere taking on the graphic quality of a computer war game.

They gave the appearance of a couple strolling arm-in-arm – when he was gripping her tightly – making her uncomfortably aware that he might be using her as a shield. Yet she felt strangely safe. She supposed that was what Cross's job as a sniper had entailed: controlled infiltration of hostile space, moving without being seen. She was struck by the insignificance of the crowd.

They passed a perfume counter where she was accosted by a young Slavic-looking saleswoman with an atomiser. She held out her wrist without thinking, watched her skin absorb the squirt of perfume and thought: Nerve gas! She laughed out loud in spite of herself. Cross asked what was so funny. She caught a whiff of his sour breath and felt his edginess transmit to her, leaving her panicked, just as he decided it was safe after all.

He said, 'Take the escalator, not the lift.'

Nando's was up a level. Beyond all the fad and fashion, property development, real estate and endless credit, Charlotte was struck by the place as a kind of hell.

The escalator was crowded, with people waiting behind them. Stepping on, she felt as she had as a child – hesitating with her foot raised over the moving stairway, as if it might swallow her, and then the pleasure of being carried forward.

They moved serenely up, despite which Charlotte found herself gripping the rail. The down escalator ran alongside, almost within touching distance, and was also crowded.

She looked up and saw a tall figure getting on at the top – Parker. He had on his woollen hat but not his wraparound shades, leaving his face exposed. Charlotte turned to Cross and found him transfixed by a look of horror. His head was twitching, the eyes starting to go. The next thing she knew, he was dragging her up the escalator, shoving shoppers aside. Behind her, she caught a glimpse of Parker gesturing as he moved away from her. She looked around for others who might be watching them. She saw Parker reach the bottom, turn and take the escalator back up. Cross remained in distress and Charlotte knew she was looking at a man in a state of blind panic.

She steered him into a big department store, thinking their best chance was to do what everyone else was doing: shop. She was surprised the store was still there; she'd thought the chain had gone bust. She marched through to the women's section. Most product was heavily discounted. She found a padded coat, nasty but practical, tried it on for size, took it to the till and watched the barcode being swiped by the cashier, who took Cross's money, peeled off from a roll of notes.

She pulled on the coat and asked if he was all right when he clearly wasn't. She was sure others were there besides Parker. She kept imagining Roberts everywhere. Only now did she see that Parker was unlikely to have had a free hand, and she had been naive.

Cross, alert again, told her to walk in front of him and follow signs for the emergency exit, then made her go up one floor, using the fire stairs, then through the kiddies' department and out by the opposite emergency exit. He waited, gun in hand, to see if anyone followed. When no one did he told her to go down the stairs until she reached the car park.

There, Cross took his time, checking, loitering among

parked vehicles. Charlotte found his alertness contagious and told herself she was over-imagining everything. She saw nothing out of the ordinary, only a few people collecting or leaving their cars.

Cross was behind her when he grabbed her around the throat and she felt the barrel of his gun pressed against her head, a move which left her as useless as a puppet with its strings cut. She thought he must be freaking out again until she saw Roberts standing some distance off, apparently alone, palms upturned and looking for all the world like a man who wanted to talk.

Cross's action made any discussion redundant. He walked them backwards, in what to Charlotte felt like a clumsy dance step, towards the exit she couldn't see. Roberts stood obediently still. She drew some hope from his composure, which said no one was about to do anything stupid.

Away in the distance, Parker came through a door by the ticket machine and stopped when he saw Roberts immobile. Charlotte wondered how Parker had found them, then realised he and Roberts must be in radio communication.

Cross had been right to mistrust the situation.

His breath was hot in her ear. Whatever was going on in his head, she doubted if he was seeing it through her eyes, still being in whatever state of dread had blindsided him on the escalator.

She couldn't tell if Roberts had others standing back and was signalling them not to come forward. She hoped he was trying to extricate her, which was why he was doing nothing to provoke. Otherwise, she had no doubt Cross would not hesitate to shoot.

A couple of children ran into the car park screaming, breaking the spell. Cross and Charlotte were by then parallel to the exit ramp. A big SUV was approaching. Charlotte half-expected Cross to hijack it, given his mood. She saw Roberts shrug and turn away with a half salute. Cross let go of her and lowered the pistol.

When they hurried out past the automatic barriers and up the ramp into the street no one came after them.

Cross flagged a passing black cab, shoved Charlotte in and told the man to drive; he would say where later. The cabbie started banging on about Ubers until Charlotte felt she might scream. She noticed for the first time that Cross's fingernails were bitten to the quick.

Cross had the cab take them to a bar in the docks where Charlotte watched him get silently drunk on stout chased with Jameson's whiskey. It was still early and the pub was empty. Even so, Charlotte found herself casting anxious glances. It didn't help that the jukebox was playing 'We Gotta Get Out of This Place'.

Eventually he said, 'I saw the burning man.'

She asked what that was about, but he just sat there, replaying whatever was in his head, until he said, 'Flashbacks.'

'From Afghanistan?'

He wouldn't say.

Charlotte decided the shock of seeing Parker's face must have flipped him. He wouldn't have known what to expect because she hadn't mentioned it. She could see Parker as the burning man.

She asked if Parker had been the trigger. Cross told her to stop messing with his head. He stared at her sullenly, looking lost and aggressive, which was when she realised that he numbered women among his enemies.

The man was a ticking bomb, and what was her role – victim, counsellor, hostage? Any line to Parker was blown. Like it or not, she was on the run.

13

Parker endlessly rewound the image of Charlotte with Cross's gun to her head and tried to tell himself that the man would not harm her because she was a companion for his loneliness; a disconcerting observation, as that was very much his own position.

Roberts blamed the mall debacle on Doyle's tactical backup, which he denounced as inept, despite Doyle's protests that they had been given insufficient warning and were short-staffed.

Waiting in Nando's, Parker had been called by the local officer in charge to say the operation was cancelled.

'Typical fucking fuck-up,' Roberts announced afterwards. 'Probably to do with fucking overtime. We would have had her safe if their boys hadn't fucked off, or if Cross had bothered to turn up on time.'

He also questioned Parker's ability to deliver, asking pointedly, 'Is it because you've got a thing for the woman?'

Parker switched that to say, 'I think she's safe as long as he has a thing for her.'

He didn't volunteer that it wasn't only Cross's intentions towards Charlotte he was worried about. In the car park he had seesawed between which of Cross and Roberts posed the greater threat to her.

After an intense session on the computer, he succeeded in accessing Cross's medical history and rather wished he hadn't as it revealed two spells of psychiatric observation after tours in Afghanistan. The second had included six weeks in the Ministry of Defence Hospital Unit in Frimley, Surrey, following a diagnosis of post-traumatic stress disorder. No details were given. There was a short report, with a list of medications, signing the patient out.

It turned out the doctor in question still worked there. The NHS phone system was designed to tax anyone's patience but Parker managed to book a call between appointments. He said he was Home Office and it was urgent.

Even so, he was surprised when the man rang back just before the hour and apologised for eating a sandwich while talking. He was a dry Scot.

After some prompting, he remembered Cross.

'Psychotic episodes following military trauma. In one incident he was buried alive after a building collapsed. There were others I don't recall. We get a lot of cases. I looked for his file but can't locate it.'

Parker wondered if that meant it had been removed.

'How does PTSD manifest itself?' he asked.

'Hyper-anxiety. Lassitude. Depression. Thinking you are being spied on. Seeing things others can't see. Out-of-body experiences. Believing what another person is thinking is audible. Extreme cases are convinced their mind is being controlled by an exterior force.'

I know the feeling, Parker thought, as he asked, 'Was Cross such a case?'

'If you create a killing machine and the wiring goes haywire it's hardly surprising.'

'But you signed him out.'

'Well, yes and no. I recommended further observation but I was overruled by a senior military doctor.'

'Did he say why?'

'Oh, quite breezily, telling me that a man of Cross's overwrought ability was exactly what the intelligence services needed in its war against terror.'

Cross had to be living somewhere in Belfast and he might even have Charlotte there. He could be with family, except there appeared not to be any. Parker remembered that the mother's only sister had died some years before.

He rang letting agencies and reverted to his role of probate genealogist. He had to decide whether Cross would be registered as O'Grady. He went with that and the third agency he called gave him an address, and a mobile number. He was surprised by how casually it was given but the boisterous young woman he spoke to bought into the story of good fortune, asking if he could look up her name when he had the chance. She was flirting. Parker could be a persuasive voice when his appearance was not an issue.

The mobile number was discontinued. Google Maps showed the address as a small road running off an avenue of tall trees near the university.

His breaking and entering skills were limited. A search warrant would take forever, so he told Roberts, who clapped him on the shoulder and said, 'What are we waiting for?'

The man's Range Rover left Parker wondering if Roberts was taking the piss. On the back was a Christian fish symbol and on the dashboard stood a tiny, garish statue of a black Madonna, hands joined in prayer, eyes cast upwards, reminiscent of Father Jerome's departing look.

'What's that?' he asked, gesturing at the statue.

'Souvenir from Guadalajara,' said Roberts, setting the satnav. 'Are you a believer?' he asked as he pulled out.

Parker had no answer to that. He had never understood organised religion any more than he'd got the hang of women; or anyone else, come to that. Roberts was probably one of those militant Christians who viewed the world according to what had to be contested. Parker decided his belligerence was that of a man who was angry at God for not making him taller.

After a five-minute drive, Roberts parked on a double-yellow line and produced a disabled badge. He handed Parker a jacket out of the back bearing the logo of a leading pest control company. Roberts had one for himself.

O'Grady was flat C. No answer. A woman in B buzzed them in after Roberts announced he was Rentokil.

He winked at Parker as they went in.

The common areas of the building were functional, with the usual junk mail lying in the hall.

The flat was on the top floor. Roberts knocked twice, got no answer and set to. His lock-picking skills were as Parker expected. Before opening the door, Roberts produced a handgun, different from the one used at the range. He motioned Parker to stay back as he went through his moves – testing the handle, pushing the door open as he stood aside then stepping smartly in to sweep the room with the gun. Parker thought if it were him on the other side, he would just wait until Roberts appeared in the open doorway and blast him.

Roberts padded around the interior with the stealth of a professional thief, opening and closing drawers in silent unhurried haste.

The place gave little impression of being lived in. The fridge had milk well past its use-by date. Parker went to the bedroom and felt under the mattress. He was hoping for at least a computer. In the standing wardrobe he found a few clothes, all high-street brands.

In the bedside drawer, nothing. Above the drawer and beneath the top was a recessed space. He felt around. There was something. He pulled out a sheet of first-class stamps. Several had been used. There was also a pad of Basildon Bond writing paper and envelopes to match. Who writes letters these days? he thought.

He showed Roberts the top page, which bore a faint imprint of what had been written on the sheet above.

Parker's subsequent effort with a pencil wasn't particularly successful. The pressure of the original writing was too variable and much of it was indecipherable; what little he could read included – 'Well, mum', 'sending stuff' and 'keep safe'.

Parker couldn't remember the last time he had bought a stamp or posted a letter. It was obvious, though he had not considered it before, that in an age of hacking the postal service was probably as secure a form of communication as any.

Roberts said Cross must be using his mother in Liverpool as a safe address. He argued aloud with himself over whether to turn her place over or wait, then decided.

'We'll get a watch put on the biddy's house; meanwhile, we keep looking.'

14

Over the next three days Charlotte found out what being on the run entailed: sitting in a cellar with no natural light, surrounded by beer barrels, while Cross and his mate, who ran the pub upstairs, got drunk.

She had no idea of her location, other than it being a thirty-minute drive from the bar where Cross had arranged for them to be picked up by a man with a van, in the back of which she was locked while he rode up front. It was at least more comfortable than the one that had taken her to the Chinese stakeout. Its floor was covered by a large mattress with dubious stains.

Their destination turned out to be a rundown pub in a rural hamlet. They were there to give Cross time to organise, Charlotte was told. She gathered that the landlord, who looked like he was drinking the proceeds, had been in the army with Cross. She was told she would have to spend the time waiting in the cellar. She couldn't think why but it wasn't an argument she was going to win.

Whenever Cross came down he stank of drink but was not aggressive. He promised to make her comfortable and was as good as his word. He made up a camp bed, brought down a chair with a padded back and seat. An old beer crate served as a bedside table, with a reading lamp provided. He showed her a toilet and basin down a corridor. Worried that she would get cold, he brought an electric radiator. He found her a couple of books, both SAS fiction adventures. She asked if there was anything else. He came back with a Rosamunde Pilcher. She struggled with all three until she decided to rotate them, a chapter at a time.

Most of the time she slept. Otherwise she lay in bed, her mind stalled by what she supposed was delayed shock.

Sometimes she sensed Cross knew what she was going through and sympathised. Temporarily domesticated, he asked after her wellbeing and cooked regular meals. Despite being drunk, he was proficient at fry-ups, curry and bolognese. He even offered wine, brought in a china carafe, like on French holidays.

Now she was in his domain he no longer consulted her, and whenever she tried to raise the matter of what they should do he turned away.

The next time he came he brought clothing: all new wet-weather gear, still in its wrapping, including walking boots.

He had checked her shoe size, he said. He must have done it while she was asleep, she realised, spooked.

'I added a size,' he said, 'and bought extra-thick socks.'

Charlotte asked, 'Are we walking?'

'They're shutting everything down from the day after tomorrow.'

Her news was days out of date. It all seemed very remote. Life in Belfast had amounted to its own form of quarantine.

Cross said they couldn't use public transport or risk a car as Roberts would be looking for them. He told her to get dressed in the gear then made her go upstairs ahead of him. She was very aware of him having the gun.

It was after 11pm and the pub was closed. Rain was lashing against the window. Charlotte was surprised. She'd had no idea of the weather since going down to the cellar. Cross picked up a heavy rucksack that made him look like he was on military manoeuvres. They went out with the landlord and got into a battered old Ford. Cross told her to sit in front. The landlord drove for about ten minutes then stopped with the headlights illuminating a metal gate.

Cross said, 'We get out.'

'What for?' Charlotte asked. It was not obvious as they were in the middle of nowhere. Cross's silence told her she had no choice, so she pulled up her hood and felt the rain beat against it as she opened the door. Cross followed. Nothing was said between him and the driver. Then the car was gone, leaving them in the dark.

He told her to climb over the gate. Its bars were wet, slippery and cold. She found herself in a field. She feared he was about to shoot her. Prodded forward, she walked fifty yards or so, waiting for the bullet, until she saw a light winking, blurred by the rain. She mistook it for a torch at first but it turned out to belong to a small waiting aircraft. How insubstantial it looked was her first impression, and she asked Cross if it was safe to fly in such wretched weather.

Cross told her to get in. The door was flimsier than on any car. The pilot nodded her towards the back of the cramped cockpit. The aircraft was so basic it felt no safer than a tin can.

The pilot fired the engine once Cross was in. With him and his bulky rucksack there was hardly space for them and she was disconcerted by his leg pressed against hers. The plane moved forward, gathered speed and Charlotte was aware of the release as they left the ground.

They seemed hardly to climb before the pilot set a course. No one said anything. Charlotte could see nothing and supposed they were in cloud. After twenty minutes it cleared enough to show lights below. The pilot spoke for the only time to say it was the Isle of Man. The lights soon disappeared. Charlotte presumed Cross had a plan but he had said nothing to her since the shopping mall about Roberts or Parker or what his own intentions were. She wondered if she were his hostage now and whether he would use her as as a bargaining tool. She thought it likely that when Roberts found them he would just kill them both. If he was the one who had already tried once to remove Cross, he didn't seem the type to change his mind.

After another twenty minutes the plane began its descent and soon after they landed on what turned out to be a golf course. It was still raining hard.

The pilot kept his engine running and as soon as they were out he turned around and was gone. Charlotte listened to the plane pull away, thinking its disappearance marked the severance of her world.

Cross had a map, a torch and a compass. He told Charlotte in which direction to walk. She asked where to and how far, feeling both stroppy and scared. She had spent the landing in a state of mute terror, thinking they were bound to crash because it was like they were flying blind.

Cross was in no mood to share anything. She cursed him under her breath, loud enough for him to ask what she had said.

'Nothing,' she replied, and set off into the driving rain, muttering to herself: Don't think, walk.

The flat, open countryside was not difficult to navigate. When the rain at last stopped and the cloud cleared she saw they were in a wide valley between silhouetted hills. She walked on, concentrating on putting one foot in front of the other. They stopped for ten minutes every hour. The second time, Charlotte said her heels were starting to blister. Cross produced plasters and she took off her boots and socks. Her feet looked spectral in the dark. After that, walking became easier but her reserves were ebbing. She supposed he must have somewhere in mind but there was no sign of lights or civilisation.

She didn't know how many hours had passed. She realised she had mislaid her watch and supposed she must have left it in the cellar, though she didn't remember taking it off. It was a good one, bought as a present for herself after her last promotion when everything could still be calculated in terms of advance. Its loss depressed her. It was her last personal possession that connected her to the life she had once had.

She lost count of the number of times they stopped. The darkness gradually receded and the landscape took on the translucent greys of a developing negative. She could make out low stone walls. The valley became narrower, the hills closer, with no buildings and few trees.

Cross said they would rest up for the day and move on when it got dark.

They walked by a stream. A sudden hailstorm stung Charlotte's face and drove away the last of the shock that had seized her since the farm, to be replaced by utter physical exhaustion. Never having had a gun pointed at her, and never expecting to, she had had it happen twice within two days. She could find no connection between the woman who had sat watching the Chinese takeaway and the one limping through the grubby dawn, or between the man with her and the one to whom she had once so recklessly given herself.

Cross found them a small stone barn to rest in, about half a mile across fields, in the lee of a low hill, with mountains behind. Part of the roof had collapsed and been repaired with corrugated iron. Cloud had come down and a damp mist hung.

Charlotte's hope of hay to burrow into was dashed by a space full of rusted machinery, oil drums and agricultural detritus. It was gloomy inside and colder. The place felt unvisited in a long time.

Until then they had managed on energy bars. Cross produced a small Primus stove and heated water. They drank black tea and ate canned meat with the tiniest key for peeling back the lid. Charlotte scooped out the last of the jellied fat with her finger. Rarely had anything tasted so good.

She asked if Cross had toilet paper. He had thought of that too. Outside she squatted by a stone wall. Cross was in his element, she could see. He knew how to read the land, unlike Charlotte, whose sense of direction would have had them walking in circles.

There was nothing to use as bedding. Charlotte lay on the ground and, despite her aching muscles and the hard floor, fell into a dreamless, deathlike sleep until shaken awake by Cross. At first she had no idea where she was.

Darkness was falling as they walked on. Cross made Charlotte go first, as though he expected her to make a break across the fields. She was depressed to realise that she would be lost without him.

Charlotte was aware of a large stretch of water to their right, with the crescent of the moon reflected in its slick black surface. They stopped as usual for ten minutes, ate more energy bars and she had to change her plasters.

The lake seemed to go on forever. Despite its length, it was narrow and she could make out a steep fall of scree on the other side. Her legs ached. She was starting to turn numb with cold. She told Cross she wasn't sure how much longer she could carry on.

'Not far now,' he said.

It started to rain again. Then, just when she thought she would be left to stagger on endlessly through a gone world, she saw pinpricks of light.

They walked towards them until a large inn was revealed, standing alone at the head of the lake. She wondered if there were such a thing as a nocturnal mirage.

'Did you know it was here?'

Cross said it was on the map.

There was a car park. The place didn't appear busy. She was still adjusting to the fact of its existence; perhaps Cross had had it in mind all along.

'Can't we at least go in and dry off?' she asked, disliking her whiny tone.

Cross deliberated. He seemed to be checking out the few parked cars. She wondered if he was going to try and steal one.

Exasperated, she said, 'Can we please go inside for a bit. Nobody has a clue where we are.'

He eventually led the way.

Stepping into the light, Charlotte felt as though she had embarked onto an old ocean liner making its way through still, nocturnal seas. They passed through a generous reception area into a comfortable lounge bar with wood panelling, log fires, atmospheric lighting and a sense of space not apparent from outside. Yet there was an air of abandonment, as though it were waiting for guests who never would arrive.

She and Cross sat at the bar. He got a lager for himself. She asked for the same and when he ordered a half she said, 'A pint.' She inspected the puddle forming on the floor from her wet clothes and experienced the feeling of her life being turned inside out.

Less than a dozen people were in. The mood seemed

both alert and subdued. From the way Cross kept glancing around she gathered he was expecting someone. She supposed it was another of his army mates and hoped he would be more together than the one running the bar.

She asked if they were waiting for anyone but he refused to say. When it became obvious to her that no one would come she asked again, thinking: A pissed army mate, a plane that could barely fly and now this.

'Is there anyone you can call?' she asked.

He looked at her as though she were trying to trap him, and said, 'They've got technology now where you can locate anyone through the ethernet.'

She supposed he meant the internet. 'It's called tracking,' she said.

'Not that. It's a form of control. The plan is in five years most people's brains will have degenerated to a point where their functioning will cease.'

She thought: Oh, for fuck's sake, where do you get this stuff from! Instead she said, 'Knowing the people I do, I would say that's happened already.'

He was immediately demanding, 'Are you talking about me?'

She supposed the nonsense he was spouting was from embarrassment because whatever plan he'd had wasn't going to materialise.

'I'm not that stupid,' she said. 'I need to eat.'

The kitchen was shut and all that was on offer was sandwiches. She said she didn't mind what, so long as it was edible. Like everything else about the place, the staff looked like they didn't really belong, being posh kids rather than local.

The prospect of being banished again into the night was too much for her and she asked the waitress if they had rooms. On the way in she had seen a sign for a residents' bar. The waitress said she would have to ask. Charlotte saw Cross wasn't pleased by this.

She said, 'The world is looking the other way. Nobody gives a shit about whether we treat ourselves to a comfortable night. We won't be able to tomorrow.'

An older woman with a helmet of permed hair came and asked if they were the ones enquiring about rooms. She said she was unable to help because she had to cease trading at midnight according to government regulations.

Charlotte told a pack of lies about being on a walking holiday and needing to get home before everything shut down to make arrangements for her friend's mother who was ill, so could they please stay the night to organise themselves? She managed to sound quite tearful.

Cross surprised her by offering to pay cash, implying the woman could pocket it. After haggling, she agreed to give them a self-catering flat, cash upfront.

They were shown to a small upstairs apartment. The woman told them to leave it tidy. Cross said they would be gone early.

They were left alone. Charlotte sensed Cross didn't trust her, and he was right. She had formulated a plan while going to the toilet when she had noticed an old-fashioned telephone booth in the reception area. She considered calling Parker and immediately ringing off, hoping he would be able to trace the number. She trusted him no more than she did Cross but at least the contact would leave her with the faintest hope that Parker might know what to do.

As it was, the telephone had a sign saying 'Out of Order'.

The apartment had a living and cooking area, with two bedrooms and a bathroom in between. Cross kept the key to the front door. The bedrooms had old-fashioned locks and when he threatened to shut her in her room she protested it was hardly practical if she needed the bathroom. She said her period was due, hoping it would discourage any thought of physical advances.

Charlotte said she was going to take a bath. He asked if she wanted her back washing. She said, 'Ha-ha,' desperate to make light of it, and made a point of noisily locking the bathroom door.

When she came out into the living room she found Cross had set up a makeshift bed for himself on the floor.

She asked what his plans were now. 'We can't stay here. Where were we supposed to go after this?'

'Liverpool,' he said. 'But not now.'

She thought about that and said, 'There must be empty places around here where we can stay for a while without being seen.'

As usual he didn't like her giving advice and ignored her. She gave up, went to her room and fell asleep in front of an old episode of *Starsky and Hutch*. She woke up wondering if she wanted to be found. She thought she could relate to the life of a fugitive. She was even secretly pleased the country was shutting down.

Someone had left behind a pair of scissors that looked like the sort used to groom a dog. She stood in front of the mirror, snipping at her fringe, rather attracted to the idea of a transformation. She started slowly and found she couldn't stop. By the end she looked like Joan of Arc awaiting the stake and doubted if even her father would recognise her.

Cross knocked on her door at 7am, as arranged. Charlotte got up and stared at Parker's fading number on her wrist. She remembered crayons in a jug and a child's drawing pad in the main room. She retrieved them while Cross was in the bathroom and went back to her room and wrote a short note for the cleaner with Parker's number. She left it on the bed, covered by the duvet. It would probably come to nothing but at least she had tried. She went out and joined Cross, who was impatient to get going.

'What do you think of my hair?'

'What did you do that for?' he asked, showing no curiosity.

'And now?' she asked.

'We carry on,' he said.

They walked down a valley and up a ridge, which after a steep climb gave them wide views on a rare sunny day. Charlotte was surprised by the emptiness in all directions. In the undulating distance was either a river or a road; she wasn't sure which until she spotted a solitary vehicle crawling along it like an insect.

She was starting to think it could be an ordinary walk on a normal day when she was shoved and sent sprawling, and Cross landed on top of her. She struggled, thinking he was attacking her, until he hissed, 'Helicopter!'

She lay still and picked up the almost imperceptible sound of a distant engine, coming closer until it clattered overhead, low enough for her to see its shadow.

Cross waited to see if it would come back. Once it was gone, he declared it unsafe to carry on and they would have to lie low for the rest of the day. Charlotte tried to reason that it was just a helicopter. Cross blamed her for wasting time staying at the inn. She asked what difference that made. Time was out of the window from what she could see.

They left the high ground and climbed down into a dark valley of dense trees, with no sign of spring, apart from a few snowdrops. As they made their slippery descent, Charlotte's mood deteriorated, seeing in the twisted branches and strangling ivy a mirror to her own anger and confusion.

At the bottom, their valley gave on to a broader one along whose edge they walked until, in a field surrounded by trees, they found a tall barn made of corrugated iron with no fourth wall, stacked full of hay.

They crouched among the bales. Cross seemed relieved at not having to go on. His ear was cocked, still listening for the helicopter, or whatever the voices in his head were telling him. He started to twitch and seemed to recede before Charlotte's eyes, in the way he did before one of his episodes.

He struggled to speak until he managed to say in a strangled voice, 'My life is a mess.'

This sounded more like self-pity rather than any wish to confide.

'Mine too,' she said flatly, not adding: Thanks to you.

'I don't know when I realised things weren't going so well. It didn't matter much to me but I could no longer deny I was in a bad way.'

She listened, fascinated by his weird delivery, as if the words were lines badly learned in front of the mirror.

He shrugged, suddenly normal again, and said, 'Come on, I'll make you a den, up in the roof.'

Charlotte looked up. The roof was twenty feet high. Cross shrugged off his rucksack and set to, moving bales. She could see, watching him, that he was a master of improvised accommodation. He grew boyish and lighthearted, encouraging her to join in. It was hot, sweaty work that took most of the morning and she was relieved not to think about anything. They even laughed, the higher they got, sending bales tumbling down to make space.

When they were finished, Charlotte's den was big enough

to stand up and lie down in. Access was by a stairway of bales, constructed to be invisible from below, leading to a tunnel of six feet or so through which she had to crawl to reach the space, which was unroofed so natural light could penetrate.

Once they were done, Cross stood back, proud. They sat in the den and ate tinned meat in silence. Charlotte felt secure. Cross said she should rest.

She lay down and grew comfortable, listening to the start of rain on the tin roof, thinking how nobody knew where she was, her mind suffused with a childish sense of adventure. Perhaps she could persuade Cross to let them stay. It was warm there. The hay acted as insulation. It seemed miraculously free of rats, though her observation was followed by an unseen scuttling. She pictured tumbling streams with icy water running down from the hills. Perhaps they could forage and live there for ever.

15

It was the first time Parker had flown in a helicopter. An AW109SP, said Roberts, as though that were important. Many commercial flights were cancelled. It had taken Roberts an hour of 'can do' on the telephone before he announced that they were hitching a ride from RAF Aldergrove to its camp at Woodvale, near Liverpool. During the taxi ride to the base he boasted how much he enjoyed fucking with red tape.

The big helicopter's engines were idling and Parker instinctively ducked as he passed under the rotors and climbed the short flight of steps into a well-appointed interior with plump beige leather recliners. Two other passengers were on board, senior men in plain clothes. They appeared affronted by Parker's appearance. One glanced at his watch because they had been made to wait.

Parker suspected the flight was to distract from a general lack of progress. Lafferty's Mercedes had been found vandalised in a side street. A nearby mobile home in a shut caravan park showed signs of recent occupation. When neither produced leads, Roberts decided they needed to know what Cross had been sending home from Belfast. Parker suspected he was being pressured from above.

He couldn't help notice that Roberts was carrying his rifle case, which perhaps explained why he was keen to avoid the commercial airport's security.

*

Normally you get a run at it before leaving the ground, thought Parker, unsettled by the sudden uplift. It seemed quite wrong that the blades keeping them aloft should be overhead rather at the front or on the wings, and where were the wings? The two men looked blasé, as though they did it all the time.

It was a clear day over the Irish Sea. Parker reviewed more messages from FOE, which he read with mounting dismay, with Roberts sitting only a few feet away.

FOE texted:

– Special Reconnaissance Regiment in which Roberts served, the only regiment with women on operational duties. SRR camera-shy but off-duty show-offs. This image posted on veterans' site, hard to say where it was taken as these guys operated off-grid, mainly on non-intervention ops.

A snapshot showed seven men and a woman standing with bottles of beer in front of two rugged four-wheel drives. The photograph looked like it had been taken as part of a post-op celebration. They all wore boots and practical workwear, none of it military, and were pointing handguns Wild West style at the camera. A grinning Roberts was giving a thumbs-up, holding his beer bottle by the neck. The woman had her hair tied back and looked pleased about being the only female in a gang of boys.

Parker didn't make the connection at first because she wore no make-up and her hair wasn't blonde then, but when he looked again he recognised a younger Hopkins.

He deliberated on whether or not to show Roberts. Impulse got the better of him and he did, asking if it had been taken in the Balkans.

Parker studied Roberts's reaction. Not a flicker. If anything, he appeared amused.

'Montenegro. Moffat said you were good at digging. I can see I am going to have to keep an eye on you.'

It was offered as a joke that wasn't. Parker decided not to bring up the matter of the Russian wife.

Cross's mother lived in one of the poorer areas of Liverpool, near the Everton football ground, in a row of Victorian terrace houses, like millions of others, not unlike the one Parker had grown up in. The Polish store on the corner had closed down. However modest people's means, they had not stinted on their cars, many of which matched the size of the RAF Police Land Rover that Roberts had wangled after landing at Woodvale. The vehicle had been in the motor pool awaiting service. Roberts boasted afterwards, 'The thing about the military is someone always knows someone you know.' Parker had watched him slip a roll of notes to the mechanic in charge, what Roberts later described as mates' rates, fifty quid a day to a so-called 'charity of choice'.

After the hectic improvisation of the journey, Parker felt it only fitting that Cross's mother wasn't at home. He was tired of Roberts's hustling. The man always seemed to be proving a point by throwing his weight around and being obnoxious.

Cross's mother turned up after half an hour, a tough little woman who asked why she should be letting them in.

Roberts said, 'We were in the forces with your John. He's asked us to fetch the stuff he sent from Belfast.'

She asked sharply, 'Where in the army?'

'Peshawar,' said Roberts.

Parker picked up on that. None of FOE's texts had made that connection. Did that mean Cross and Roberts went back that far?

'You'll be wasting your time,' she told Roberts.

Turning to examine Parker with unflinching curiosity,

she said, 'You need to get some cream for that skin, son. And who are you when you are at home?'

He could see the woman was thinking the last thing he looked like was army.

He said, 'I was in Frimley Hospital with John.'

'That was a terrible time for him,' the woman said. She regarded Parker with suspicion. 'Do you call him John?'

'We called him Criss after the cross hairs on the rifle sight.'

She sighed and said, 'That boy never could make up his mind what he was called. You had better come in, though you're not supposed to, rather than standing on the doorstep. If you're here to rob me you'll find nothing.'

Every psychopath has a mother, Parker thought. She pointed them into a small front room, with a three-piece suite, a gas fire, a magazine rack with a copy of the *TV Times* and a disproportionately large flat-screen television.

'I'll make you tea. You get milk and sugar whether you like it or not.'

She left them sitting there as polite as schoolboys on an outing. Tea came on a trolley with a plate of Wagon Wheels, which she insisted they had.

'They were always his favourite. A sweet tooth, that boy. I'm surprised he never grew fat. His father went that way.' She looked at Roberts. 'And what is it he is asking you to fetch?'

Roberts opened his mouth and nothing came out. Parker nearly laughed, thinking the man's tough training hadn't included handling such deadly hospitality. The woman was no fool.

Parker stepped in. 'He said you'd know. Criss – John – asked us to pick it up.'

The woman looked unimpressed. 'Are you police?'

She pronounced it 'polis'.

Parker said, 'We're mates. We were to meet up. He's supposed to be here by now.'

'First I've heard.'

Parker saw he would get no help from Roberts. He looked at the woman and asked, 'How is John?'

'You've a nice voice,' she said.

Parker wondered if she was drunk. Sherry bottles stood on the sideboard.

'I'm still not well since Frimley, even with the medication,' he said, struggling. 'John's not answering my calls, which makes me worry whether he's all right.'

'Maybe he's ill with this thing we're supposed to catch all over again, did you think of that?'

Parker's phone rang before he could answer. He didn't recognise the number. He made a show of excusing himself and went into the hall.

A well-spoken woman asked if he was Mr Parker. After he confirmed that he was, she said she had a message from one of her hotel guests, who had since left.

'The cleaning woman found it.'

'Where are you?' Parker asked.

She told him the Lake District and the name of the hotel.

'What does the message say?'

The woman cleared her throat and read, ' "This is important. Can you please have someone ring this number. Tell Mr Parker I am safe but say Mr Cross wasn't supposed to have left the farm." What's that supposed to mean? It's all a bit mysterious. The cleaner found a wastepaper basket full of someone's hair.'

The woman sounded caught between nosiness and thinking she might be the victim of a practical joke.

Parker told her to keep the note, wondering what the hair was about and thinking: But Cross had left the farm.

At least the call considerably reduced the scale of Charlotte's whereabouts. He supposed the hotel was only a few hours' drive. He wondered how they had got out of the country when Doyle was having all flights and ferries checked. He asked if the woman had rooms for the night. She said they were closed now, or hadn't he heard?

He said he would come anyway as he needed to talk further and would explain later.

'Suit yourself. I shan't be going anywhere,' the woman said, clearly wishing she hadn't bothered.

Parker joined the others and said to the mother, 'John's in the Lake District.'

'Was that him just now?'

He said it was, thinking that he shouldn't have, but the woman just grunted.

'Too scared to speak to his mother. Knows she would give him a piece of her mind.'

Parker shook his head at Roberts, to say it hadn't been Cross.

The woman was nodding. 'There you are, then. He likes the Lakes well enough. Ever since a school trip with the Christian Brothers and that priest of theirs they had to get shot of.' She snorted. 'Not interested in my John, on account of his being tinted.'

The woman prodded Roberts's knee.

'I wouldn't expect you to understand. Marrying as I did had its consequences, but my boy had to live with the abuse every day.' She turned to Parker. 'I'm surprised they let you join up looking like that.'

'Where did he go in the Lakes?' Parker insisted.

'He went up there a lot when he was living here.'

'Anywhere particular?'

'Oh, all over. He doesn't like being pinned down.'

A silence fell. Roberts started to fidget. Parker asked in desperation, 'Can I have another cup of tea, please?'

The woman had brought a pot. While she was pouring, he asked, 'Do you know what we're meant to collect?'

She insisted he have another Wagon Wheel.

'You mean what you're looking for?' she asked as she offered the plate, then snatched it away before Parker could take one. 'I wasn't born yesterday, whoever you are. My son has no friends.'

Roberts assured her they were there to take care of him.

The woman gave a cold smirk. 'An unfortunate turn of phrase. I know my gangster films, mister.'

She pronounced it 'fillums'.

Roberts produced one of his all-purpose laughs, waving his hands to say that wasn't what he'd meant.

'Look at you, a pair of clowns,' the woman said. 'Boys oh boys, have you got the wrong end of the stick.'

She got up and produced two small boxes from a sideboard. They were wrapped in brown paper, addressed in capital letters to Cross.

'One for you, the other for you. Open them.'

She stood watching, arms akimbo. Roberts, on opening his, looked up in disbelief.

'He collects fucking vintage comics!'

Parker had the same. The woman cackled.

'You'd know that if you knew him.'

The comic Parker was looking at was stamped 'War Picture Library'. The action cover was colour, the title: 'Cold Steel – Hot Lead'. He flipped through sixty-four pages of black and white strips, celebrating the glories of the Second World War in terse speech bubbles: 'Eat lead, Kraut!'

Parker looked up at the woman, who said, 'Collected them for years. You, come with me.' She turned to Roberts. 'You stay here.'

She led Parker into the hall and pointed upstairs, 'You first, door straight ahead on the landing.'

He found a small room with a narrow bed and a view of a back yard. Its walls were fitted with shelves for his collection.

'Only War Picture Library,' she said.

Parker reckoned there must be a thousand. He felt chastened and embarrassed at being shown the man's fantasy world.

'I don't know what John's up to and I don't want to. Unlike pally downstairs, you look like you might understand that he's a damaged boy, and I'd like someone to know that and take care of him before you all go charging in.'

'He's with a woman we know.'

Parker had said the wrong thing.

'Oh, for God's sake! Women were never his strong point. I want you to leave now but I'm entrusting you with my John's safety – he's not a bad boy at heart – and swear on your mother's life, or grave or whatever, you will telephone me to say he is alive and not lying shot to pieces.'

16

Charlotte was still asleep in the den when she was roughly shaken awake by Cross, saying they had to get out. Helicopters had been flying overhead. Charlotte wondered if they really had or he was imagining them. He was back in the same state of hyper-alertness as in the shopping mall. He had been right then and Charlotte supposed she should trust his instinct. Hers told her they could have stayed – they had two more days of rations – and no one would disturb them, but Cross was in no mood to be dissuaded. She insisted he share what he had in mind. He said there was no time for that, they had to get out. She refused to budge until he explained.

It turned out he had taken her idea seriously about finding somewhere empty to hole up, not that he would admit to it. There was a possible place about an hour's walk away.

He pointed to an isolated building on the map, surrounded by narrow contour lines that reminded her of a thumbprint. He said the cloud had come down enough to make it safe to move – she supposed he was thinking about helicopters – and there was just enough daylight to get there before dark.

She didn't ask what he would do if the place turned out to be occupied.

The house they were looking for lay in even more isolated countryside, about a mile down a rough track off a narrow country road. The valley was more like a ravine, its steep slopes covered with tall pines, which cut out most of the sky, which added to a general oppressiveness. After half a mile or so of track, the trees on the right gave way to a high, broken rock face. At the first sign of habitation – a dry-stone wall in a state of frequent collapse – Cross insisted they leave the track and move up into the trees on their left. The slope wasn't so steep that they couldn't walk upright but sometimes Charlotte had to hold on to a trunk for balance because the dead pine needles underfoot could be treacherous. Many lower branches were stripped of vegetation and in the fading light appeared the colour of burnt rust.

As they worked their way along the valley the planting became less dense and Charlotte was able to make out the house fifty yards below. Her first thought was: Who on earth would want to build there? The back was up against the rock face, and such a plain house too, with the single addition of a plastic sentry box of a porch. A small stone outbuilding stood immediately to the right. Apart from a pocket of lawn at the front and a long narrow field beyond the outbuilding there was no open ground. A sinister stillness hung over everything.

Although no lights were on, no car stood outside and no smoke was coming from the chimney, Cross insisted on waiting, at first where they were then moving down to the foot of the valley where they continued to watch from among the trees.

Charlotte, cold and impatient, found the place dispiriting and wished she was back in the barn. Damp penetrated her bones. Lichen and moss grew where it could. The base of the house's dirty render was covered in an aggressive grey mould that reminded her of her grandmother's abandoned sandwich, pressed between the pages of her book; it was rather how she felt.

After more pointless watching, Cross at last told her to take a look.

She approached with caution, thinking how she found Cross less threatening outdoors than in. She patrolled the exterior. Between the rock face and the back of the house she found a narrow alley not much wider than her. This took her to the outhouse, whose door was locked. She went to the front and peered through windows. From what she could see in the near darkness there was no evidence of recent habitation. She wondered if they would break in. She supposed Cross would know about such things.

Remembering that her father's house had a spare key hidden outside, she looked in the obvious places. It took five minutes to find it, an old-fashioned mortice key, tucked in the eaves of the porch. It opened a side door into the kitchen and she slid inside. The room had been knocked through to make a single cooking and living area, with a large inglenook fireplace at the far end. Charlotte noted a wire basket with winter vegetables, starting to turn, showing it wasn't that long since someone had been there.

She inspected the cold downstairs, feeling as though the space was intruding on her rather than the other way round. She wouldn't like the owners, she decided, with their chintz and wildlife prints. A narrow archway from the living area led to a small hall, off which was a front room, which appeared little used, and a bathroom at the back. A brief look upstairs revealed a landing and a single and a double bedroom facing the front. Her impression was of a second home, possibly used as a holiday let. The place had none of the usual knick-knacks or photographs.

She saw no internet router, no telephone or television,

just a radio in the kitchen, beneath a board for keys, helpfully labelled. She tried the one marked 'Outhouse' on the stone building outside, and in it found stacked logs and a huge chest freezer with a hinged lid. She peered inside. Far from full but enough ready-made meals to be getting on with.

She went back and said at least they would be able to eat. She looked forward to making a fire. Cross wouldn't allow her to light one, even after she pointed out that no one would see the smoke in the dark. She supposed it was about becoming too comfortable and off-guard. She went around turning on electric heaters.

They started bickering. Charlotte quite fancied cooking, even if it was only to chuck a ready-meal in the microwave. But Cross regarded the provision of food as his preserve and set about preparing soup, using the vegetables from the wire basket: leeks, carrots, potatoes and onions, which had started to grow green shoots. They could have done it together, Charlotte wanted to say as she switched on the radio, which he told her to turn off.

'Shouldn't we know what's going on?' she asked, and watched him not answer as he carried on scraping with methodical intensity. She saw the evening ahead as a minefield: one wrong move and detonation.

Cross retreated into himself. He refused to be drawn on the subject of Belfast or what plans he might have.

'A smoking gun, you said.'

He shrugged that off and went back to preparing his soup.

'It is delicious, by the way,' she said later, hoping flattery might work.

'What's "by the way" about it?' he asked.

Afterwards Charlotte dutifully cleared the plates,

washed them up and left them on the draining board. Cross insisted she put them back where they had come from.

She said, 'I'll need to find a store tomorrow.'

He shook his head and said, 'You shouldn't have cut your hair. You stand right out, so no store.'

She said there were hats in the hall.

Cross's response was to produce a sheath knife, which he started to stick repeatedly into the tabletop between his splayed fingers until the blade became a blur. Fearing he would harm himself, she shouted at him to stop and was grateful when he did.

He gave her one of his blank looks and she left him to it, fearing another episode.

She took the room with the single bed and jammed an upright chair against the door handle. It wouldn't stop him getting in but it would at least alert her if he tried.

She concluded they were both quite mad and blamed the house for turning them that way in the space of a few hours.

17

Parker and Roberts reached the lakeside hotel after driving the last part without seeing a single vehicle. The car park was deserted, the buildings mostly dark.

The woman who ran the place had sounded posh on the telephone, so Parker was surprised by her Kappa tracksuit, for which she was too old by several decades.

She greeted them warily, saying, 'I've got enough trouble as it is with the regs.'

Roberts introduced himself as Home Office, without saying which bit, and invited himself in without being asked. When Parker stepped into the light he saw the woman recoil with a familiar spasm of disgust.

Roberts made a beeline for the bar and inspected the beer. The woman said the taps were off. Roberts pointed out it still came in bottles.

'We're officially closed.'

Roberts put a ten-pound note on the counter and said, 'Keep the change.'

The woman reluctantly opened two bottles without offering them a choice and made a point of not giving them glasses.

'Cheers,' said Roberts. 'Are you not joining us?'

He started to question her. She confirmed that a man and a woman had stayed the night before they closed.

'I need to see the registration cards.'

The woman was forced to admit they hadn't filled in any. 'They turned up late and everyone was distracted by having to close down,' she said. 'They were rather stranded so I took pity on them. It was just the one night. There were a couple of other guests. Providing they had checked in the night before, regulations stated they could leave in the morning, just that they couldn't be served breakfast.'

Parker saw that the woman was afraid of Roberts, hence her over-explaining.

'How did they seem?' he asked.

She avoided looking at him as she said, 'Quite normal. Well.'

That was at least something, he thought.

Roberts asked her if they had said where they were going. The woman remembered Charlotte mentioning about having to care for a sick mother, without saying where that was.

Parker wondered if this was a reference to Cross's mother in Liverpool. Were they in touch after all? Had the mother subsequently told them of a visit by two so-called army mates? He suspected Roberts was thinking along the same lines.

When Roberts went to the toilet, Parker asked the woman for Charlotte's note. He wanted to keep it from Roberts. She still avoided looking at him as she dithered around then at last found it, in time for Parker to pocket it as Roberts returned.

Roberts said, 'We'll need somewhere to organise ourselves from.'

The woman folded her arms, unimpressed. 'Organise what?'

'We're anti-terrorist. Your two clients are on the run.' He leered at her as he said, 'We'll overlook the registration business.'

Anti-terrorist was the first Parker had heard. Was this now an official angle?

'Those two?' the woman asked in disbelief. Her eyes widened as she reassessed before offering, 'The man did rather stick out, I dare say.'

Parker stared at the floor – Cross's skin colour; his own skin condition. He knew the woman found his presence offensive, which was her real reason for not wanting them there.

The woman, nosy now, asked, 'Are they on the news? I could do without any bad publicity. Anyway, I think you will find the youth hostel much more suited to your needs.'

Roberts, sensing he was being patronised, pointed out they would need more than a youth hostel.

The woman took pleasure in correcting him. 'It's quite grand really, an old country estate in its own park, better positioned than we are, being at the other end of the lake, and nearer things.'

Roberts continued to wrangle until Parker lost patience and said, 'Tell her to fuck off. I don't want to stay here.'

Cars on gravel always sounded expensive, Parker thought, as they swept up to the youth hostel, the headlights revealing a large stone mansion with half-timbering and mullioned windows.

Inside had none of the spartan air Parker associated with hostels. The large rooms more resembled a college, with a panelled library and a separate billiard room with Chesterfield sofas.

The resident female caretaker had been called by Roberts and told to open the place up for emergency government business.

She was immediately intimidated by Roberts's hyperactive

talk of a command post. Roberts asked if there was a cook. She lived out, he was told. They would need her to come in. The caretaker said she would see what she could do, without sounding pleased about it. There were vending machines in the meantime.

'Tea and coffee, soft drinks, snacks and sandwiches,' she recited.

Roberts's manner was enough to put anyone off, with his assumption of a competence not shared by anyone else.

The local police were roused. Roberts wanted drones out first thing. The police didn't have enough for his liking and he told them to get more off estate agents as they wouldn't be selling anything any time soon.

The caretaker asked how long they expected to stay.

'Until the job's done,' said Roberts, implying it was none of her business.

'Just the two of you?'

'There will be more; maybe six or a dozen, depending. We're talking about a dangerous couple. He shot a priest.'

Parker wondered how Roberts knew that for sure or if he was just saying it.

The caretaker woman said they'd had nothing like it since a taxi driver went on a rampage and shot twelve people.

Parker looked it up. Wikipedia also contained the helpful information that people in the area were among the fattest in England. Useful to know, he thought.

They fetched their bags and went to find rooms. Parker followed Roberts up the broad staircase, noting the leather case with the De Lisle rifle under his arm.

Roberts said conversationally over his shoulder as they went up, 'You know, it's a funny thing, in terms of a small world, Moffat recently said to me: "The man who taught me everything I know, his daughter has just surfaced, and what's more she's fucked the guy you're running." '

'The man who taught him everything he knew?' Parker repeated to Roberts's back.

Roberts reached the top of the stairs, stopped and turned, forcing Parker to pause. Although Roberts was seven or eight inches shorter than Parker, with him standing on the landing their heads were level.

Face to face, the man looked even stranger, with his walnut head and unblinking stare. He sounded casual as he said, 'Yes, he and Major Waites were in Northern Ireland together back in the day.'

Look to the past, Parker told himself, not for the first time.

Roberts strolled on, opening doors. He bagged himself a single room. Parker chose one with six bunks and a desk because it had a view of the still, dark waters of the lake.

He found nothing about Charlotte's father on the internet, apart from his army listing and an OBE awarded in 1983 for operational services in Northern Ireland. He wondered if the lack of record was sinister, then decided it was generational. Careers before the internet often went unremarked.

It hadn't occurred to him to talk to the man before. He supposed anyway he should at least tell him about his daughter's situation. There was always a chance that she had contacted him.

Her father's landline was on Charlotte's phone. It was still early enough to call.

A man with a slight foreign accent answered. Parker asked to speak to Major Waites.

'Colonel Waites,' the man corrected. 'He isn't well and should not be disturbed or upset. How may I help?'

Parker said, 'I was wondering if he has heard from his daughter recently.'

The man put his hand over the receiver. Parker heard muffled talk, then the man came back asking what this was about.

Parker said, 'Moffat. He knows Colonel Waites.'

They ended up in a three-way conversation, with Parker's message being relayed.

The answer came back that it was a long time ago and what was being asked.

Parker said it was also about a priest named Magee.

There was more muffled talk before the man announced now wasn't a good time.

Parker said, 'Charlotte might be in trouble because of this.'

He listened to more muttering and what sounded like a heated exchange until the father said, loudly enough for him to hear, 'Give me the bloody phone.'

Parker listened to the man's raspy breathing as he took the receiver. It sounded like he was struggling to speak.

'What is this?' he finally managed. 'I don't have long.'

Parker couldn't tell whether that meant he didn't have long to talk or long to live.

In an effort to be concise, he said, 'I think Charlotte is being manipulated by Moffat.'

'Oh, I doubt that. Moffat must be long retired.'

It was a well-modulated voice, not unlike Moffat's, almost eerily so, marked by the considered pause to eradicate anything unpremeditated.

'It's about Northern Ireland's past,' Parker said. 'It would help to know what Moffat was doing there.'

'And you are?'

Parker said he was a colleague of Charlotte. They had just been in Belfast together.

The man sounded concerned for the first time.

'Is she all right?'

'For the moment,' Parker said, sounding more certain than he felt.

'Tell her to call. I have some news for her.'

Parker said she'd gone off without her phone. He tried to make it sound like an oversight. He didn't want to alarm unnecessarily, not that the man sounded worried. He seemed to regard Parker's call as unwelcome, less for any threat posed to Charlotte than a reluctance to address the past.

Trying to steer them back on course, Parker said, 'Charlotte told me she was going to ask you about Moffat.' He finished weakly, 'I was wondering if she had been in touch.'

'She's bad at phoning.' Again the annoying pause before the accusation: 'Moffat was dirty tricks. Shoot to kill, if you remember that.'

Parker noted the patronising qualification. He answered equally deliberately, 'Magee's brother died because of it.'

'You don't have to tell me,' the man said, irritation creeping into his voice.

'Moffat said you were involved.'

'I know that too.'

Parker listened to him struggle to breathe until he came out with, 'Ask why Moffat led Magee to believe I was responsible when it was Moffat's business. Is she safe or not?'

'She's safe,' Parker lied.

'Then spare me all this melodrama. I am not in the habit of being telephoned by strangers.'

The breathing grew wetter and heavier.

'Why would Moffat be involving your daughter?' Parker asked.

The long silence went unanswered. The other man came

on and haughtily announced, 'He must rest now. I asked you not to upset him.'

Parker hung up and reflected on the strangeness of the call. In the father's voice he could hear the unspoken contradictions of Charlotte's childhood: emotional but aloof, love withheld and probably disappointment at the lack of a son. Did Charlotte know about the other man? It was pretty obvious they were living together.

Then there was the Colonel's willingness to implicate Moffat to a stranger who said he was calling on Charlotte's behalf. 'Shoot to kill,' he had said, but why mention that unless it was on his conscience?

Shoot to kill never was an official policy, Parker knew, but it was tacitly condoned. For years at the height of the conflict, police and special services had carried out ambush killings. Thinking of such targets, he wondered if there was an aspect to Father Jerome's death he was missing. He looked properly at Charlotte's note for the first time – saying Cross wasn't supposed to have left the farm.

That Cross was not supposed to have left suggested he must have *gone* there, turning up after Charlotte – as one of two assassins – and if he was supposed not to have walked away that meant the other gun – Hosseini, a known Dublin contract killer – must have fucked up.

But what exactly was Cross doing there? The man's role throughout had been so ambiguous that Parker had previously wondered if he had somehow been Dubai's man all along – enough to have checked whether he had ever gone to Dubai. He hadn't, but now Parker found himself asking if anyone else had.

He trawled through the airline passenger lists again. Cross might not have been but Roberts had, in the crucial period before Father Jerome's death.

Accompanied by Mrs Roberts, he had flown first class to Dubai from Belfast. Parker remembered the wife was rich and Russian. Roberts if challenged would no doubt claim he had been on a winter weekend break. They had flown back three days later.

Within a week of their return, Father Jerome was dead.

Parker took it that the priest's death was of mutual benefit to both Dubai and Roberts. He couldn't decide whether Cross's intended elimination was part of the package or if Roberts had privately subcontracted the job to Hosseini. Whatever the ins and outs, it looked as though Roberts had planned to remove three men, including Lafferty, all of whom threatened to compromise him.

The next question was how soon afterwards had Roberts known that Cross wasn't dead. Presumably when he didn't get a 'job done' call from Hosseini.

Parker remembered how unsurprised Moffat had appeared at the farm, almost as though he knew what to expect and Parker was drawn to the irresistible conclusion that all of them – Moffat, Roberts, perhaps even Hopkins – must be in bed with Dubai.

18

Charlotte tried to force Cross's hand the next morning, saying she needed to go to a store. He told her it was out of the question. She said she was going whether he came or not. She put on her coat and started to walk out. He restrained her. He looked more puzzled than threatening.

'No way,' he said, and tightened his grip on her arm.

She had to shout at him that she was having her period. 'Don't you listen? I told you already.'

It still took time to persuade him. No one was looking for them. Cross pointed out they didn't have masks. Charlotte said nor would a lot of people.

'So we buy them too and until then use scarves.'

The shop was about an hour away. They walked along a narrow lane and saw no one. Charlotte noted a telephone kiosk and a postbox and wondered about writing to Parker – not even about anything, just a letter. There wouldn't be much point as he was probably out looking for her, but she could remember his address, apart from the second part of the postcode. She couldn't recall the last time anyone had written her a private letter, or even a card.

The store was the only shop in a small deserted village whose plainness stood in contrast to the rugged mountains behind. Charlotte was aware of being watched from inside houses as they walked down the street, as though they were invaders from another world.

Cross didn't trust her to go into the shop alone. They went in wearing scarves, looking like bandits. It was partly a post office, run by a fussy elderly couple. No other customers were in. Four short aisles were dedicated to basic goods. Charlotte spotted a security camera and kept her hood up.

When she took the Tampax to the counter the woman asked where she was from, trying to sound conversational, but Charlotte heard only suspicion.

She said they were driving to look after her mother, who lived alone and was ill, and their car had packed up, and they were waiting for the breakdown service; it was one of those days.

Charlotte saw the woman didn't believe a word of it. She asked for masks and was told they were waiting for them to come in.

Further awkwardness followed when Charlotte had to ask Cross to pay. As he picked up the change his head started to twitch and she feared he was about to lose it. She dragged him off before he could start waving his gun.

Outside, she said, 'We don't go back along the road.'

She had seen a sign for a footpath on the edge of the village and suggested they take that.

Twenty minutes later they saw a police car driving in the direction of the village. Cross swore.

Charlotte, to distract from her flagging spirits, started composing a letter to Parker in her head: *How are you? I am as well as can be expected, given the company I keep. I live in fear of a battering. I have cut off all my hair. I am becoming quite the primitive. Sometimes I can't ever see myself returning. I exist in the hope you are my saviour, however much I kid myself all will end well when I know it won't.*

She paused, sitting on a stile, and watched Cross walk ahead, and wondered if she could go on with any of it. When he saw she wasn't following he came back. His head started twitching again and he put his hand round her throat. She could feel her racing pulse where his fingers rested. She caught his eye and held it. The twitching stopped and he undid her by smiling; not a cruel smile but apologetic. As she fell against him sobbing she was aware of his hand moving off her throat. Her breakdown had come out of nowhere but, even as it burst out of her, she knew it involved an element of calculation, hoping it would cause him to underestimate her.

Back in their valley, Cross insisted the house felt wrong as they approached. He made them move up into the trees, climbing until they reached the point where they had stood the evening before, looking down at the house. Charlotte watched Cross study the lie of the land. He settled on the outcrop of rocks above the back of the house, which he said would give the best cover and view of any approach. He kept his voice low, as though people might be listening, so she had to strain to hear.

They spent the next ten minutes moving back down the slope and manoeuvring their way round the head of the valley, between thickets of holly and brambles, then climbing again, now over boulders. The ascent wasn't as difficult as it had looked. Cross pointed Charlotte towards an old animal track among the rocks. It took them high enough to be looking down at the back of the house. Cross decided on a narrow cleft, wide enough for them to lie side by side. This gave them an overview of the area, including the approaching track.

Charlotte grew cold even though it was now a bright, sunny day with clear skies. Her hands and feet turned numb. She couldn't decide how seriously she should take

Cross's caution and presumed it was because of the police car they had seen.

'Feel my nose,' she said. 'It's freezing.'

He felt it briefly and she chalked that up as a point to her.

Time passed. Endless waiting seemed to come naturally to him.

The valley appeared less gloomy from above, being surrounded by open sky, which from below appeared little more than a gash. Charlotte passed the time watching circling crows then noticed something moving higher up that looked too precise to be a bird. It wasn't flying very fast and it wasn't very big. Cross's attention was on the house. After a while she decided it was mechanical and must be a drone.

Was it looking for them? Did that mean Parker had got her message? Keeping track of the drone's silent progress, she decided to tell Cross only when it got close enough for her to hear it. She watched it make a slow silent sweep of their valley and move on.

Still Cross refused to budge, only saying, 'They'll be checking empty houses.'

Thinking of the police car, she knew he was right.

It was late afternoon before Charlotte heard an approaching vehicle and what looked like the same police car slowly came into view, its dayglo-yellow and blue chequerboard garish in the natural surroundings. It bumped down the lane and drew up in front of the house.

Four men got out, led by two beefy cops. She hadn't reckoned on Roberts and Parker being there, though their presence seemed inevitable.

Cross tensed on seeing Parker again. Charlotte laid what she hoped was a reassuring hand on his back and felt his breathing grow less ragged.

Roberts's air of tight control was evident from a distance, as was Parker's vagueness. He looked lost and out of place.

She whispered to Cross that it must be just a routine check or they would be being more cautious. Her own surprise was the realisation that she didn't want to be found.

She watched them inspect the house. Looking through windows, they would see nothing untoward because Cross had insisted on leaving everything as they had found it. Their gear was stowed upstairs. Charlotte had grumbled, but now she was surprised and confused: surprised because she was supposed to want to be rescued; confused because she couldn't tell if she was starting to identify with her captor, or whether something more complicated was going on and she was banking on finding a way to unpick Cross rather than rely on others.

Parker, Roberts and the two other men hung around, making calls. At one point Roberts stared up at their outcrop and Charlotte froze, certain that he must see her. Cross swore under his breath.

Roberts continued to give the surrounding area a long, searching look, as if he knew they were there.

After five minutes, they all got back in the car and left. Once they were gone, Cross said they were getting out.

Any temporary alliance was over. He turned on her in spittle-flecked rage, saying she had betrayed them.

'How?'

'In the store, by giving signs and drawing attention.'

'There were no signs! You're imagining it.'

'You and your fucking woman's business; none of this would be happening without that.'

Her insides were shaking but she played along, saying, 'It's a nasty house anyway.'

*

Charlotte set off hopefully. They had looked at the map and decided on another isolated dwelling in the next valley. Cross said if it turned out to be occupied they would find somewhere temporary for the night.

She was glad it was Cross who twisted his ankle, not her. It happened at the top of a short steep climb up from the house. The going was easier and visibility not bad when he went down. She couldn't work out what had caused him to fall; no rabbit hole, from what she could see. Perhaps it was just their luck running out.

There was no question of carrying on so she had to help him back down, slinging his arm around her shoulder. She could feel his anger at himself and tried not to think about him touching her.

He wanted to watch the house again before making a move. Charlotte had had enough. She let go and said, 'Stay out here if you want. I'm going in. If anyone comes, you've got a gun, so use it.'

She was surprised when he hopped after her, looking sheepish.

They took turns to stay awake on watch. Cross was sulking about his ankle, for which she got a packet of peas from the freezer.

It remained unspoken between them that she could take herself off while he slept but both knew she wouldn't get far.

She tried anyway, after finding some loose change in a drawer. She intended to call Parker from the phone box she had seen on the way to the store.

It had turned into a mild night with a bright moon and the beginnings of a mist.

She hadn't got far when Cross appeared beside her, leaning heavily on a walking stick.

She said, 'I thought I saw someone moving around outside,' impressed by her quick thinking.

'So did I. Well, at least you had the guts to look.'

She had expected him to be angry but his tone was moderate, though he evidently didn't believe her. Perhaps he was still embarrassed about laming himself.

'Where did you get the stick?' she asked, conversationally.

'Found it in the hall.'

He seemed almost philosophical. They continued to stand there, held by something magical about the night and its softness. Cross stared at the sky.

He said, 'The weather's going to change. I reckon we will be safe for a while.'

19

Roberts was in a talkative mood. They were eating supper at the youth hostel. The cook had been brought in. Parker rather wished they had stuck to the vending machine. Either the woman was a rotten cook or deliberately bad because she and the caretaker had taken against them. Roberts was an oppressive, ungrateful presence. Police had trooped carelessly in and out of the building all day. Roberts chided them as he had in Belfast, for lack of initiative. A makeshift monitor room had been set up to observe the drone surveys. Parker found the aerial shots relaxing to the point of not paying attention. Relations with the caretaker had deteriorated further when she complained that the material on one of the Chesterfield sofas had been ripped.

While eating, masticating furiously, Roberts reminisced about Afghanistan, saying the main base in Helmand was known as Butlins because it had shops, showers and a Pizza Hut.

'Better than this,' he said, pointing to his plate of dry and overcooked minced meat. 'We used to call it BMC – Black Man's Crap.'

Parker said, 'I ought to get you a T-shirt with "Proud to be racist" printed on it.'

Roberts, thinking Parker was playing along, threw back his head and laughed.

Parker stared at his plate. He had too many questions,

none of which he could trust Roberts with. Anyway, they were irrelevant. Roberts was in manhunt mode and concentrated on the target, so Parker asked about that.

Roberts said, 'My money is on that shitty little house up the valley. I want to check it again tomorrow. This time we'll go alone.' He looked meaningfully at Parker.

'Why choose that house?'

'Less open than other places, sight lines, isolated, enough cover. I could smell him.'

Parker sighed inwardly and wanted to ask if Roberts had ever been to Dubai, but didn't; no need to alert the man that he was on his case.

'You were about to say?' asked Roberts, who sat back, inviting Parker to challenge him.

'No, nothing. Just thinking what you said about the house makes sense.'

Parker felt like he was looking at a big puzzle.

He said, 'Once when I was in hospital for my skin I spent a week doing a jigsaw of Magritte's "Empire of Light". Half the pieces were black and their positioning could be guessed only by their shape.'

It felt rather like that now. Roberts couldn't see the point of the story: if it didn't have an objective it made no sense to him. His reaction told Parker a lot. The man was unimaginative, which might yet be his undoing.

Parker now sensed a desperation to Roberts's trip to Dubai and wondered if, for all his purpose and crushing self-confidence, he was scared of losing control of whatever had been set in motion.

Upstairs, Parker googled the farm shooting and found local media reporting the slayings as an extension of the Dublin-based drugs war. Father Jerome was named as Magee, with no mention of him having been a priest or any political connections. The material, whose available information was limited and clearly being being controlled, had been planted in some of the more sensational English rags, but not in any way that drew attention, just a brief report of a man and woman wanted in connection with the killings – an unidentified male of mixed race, armed and dangerous, and a white woman in her thirties, named as Charlotte Waites; the inference was that she was his accomplice.

An online press update included the hunt switching to the North-West of England.

But only he and Roberts knew that.

Parker feared the worst. If Roberts had relayed Cross and Charlotte's whereabouts and things were starting to move then what else was going on? He again sensed Roberts's insecurity in his relentless pursuit of Cross. He suspected Roberts and Cross were enamoured of guns because they were insecure about the size of their cocks – a simplistic conclusion which nevertheless was probably the answer to a lot of excessively complicated situations involving men.

Parker searched for more on Charlotte and Cross and he wasn't even surprised when he found the start of a Twitter shitstorm, out of all proportion to the news to date. It was well beyond anything Roberts was capable of. As for who was feeding the story, Parker was aware enough to know it would have been algorithmically preprogrammed by cyber hacks using fake hashtags, acting on orders and importuning actual account holders to join in, based on their history, thus adding to the veracity. Parker didn't even have to guess its purpose: to replace whomever might have killed McCavity with a version that framed Charlotte and Cross.

Its rapid unfolding was authentically done, being messy, discursive and combative, sometimes illiterate, frequently incomprehensible, contrary and contradictory, with huge amounts of drivel, but a fierce undertow. Parker was familiar with the method. It was a classic example of a false turd: lay one then accuse others of putting a lid on it. Make it look like someone is trying to prevent the 'truth' from being told, then wait for the story to take off as the authentic nutters are attracted like suckerfish. Charlotte was soon being referred to as 'Home Office cunt' as the shooting of McCavity turned into a Muslim plot that the authorities were too scared to expose for fear of race riots and unchecked panic because the police lacked sufficient reserves to combat major civil unrest. As calls grew for vigilante action groups, Muslim communities and the police were subjected to excoriating abuse, establishing a platform for blaming them and accusing the authorities of soft-pedalling. Whatever had happened in Belfast was being scored out.

Much of the material was slurry but a line was being manipulated. Parker knew because he had steered such stories himself in his time. Key plants – Charlotte had now morphed into 'terrorist lover' – became more beguiling because of an adversarial drumbeat questioning everything being told. Parker suspected that would be being controlled by those working the material to give its core more heft. After all, only a few facts needed to stick.

The unfolding was so inevitable that he guessed the rest: Charlotte had downplayed a warning of the shooting because she was part of the plot; followed by 'Home Office woman Islamist link'. Cross was played in, under his family name of Sandhu. He was varyingly presented as having shot McCavity, after being brainwashed by Muslim extremists; as a defector to the Taliban while serving in Afghanistan; or as the brains behind the operation, with Charlotte his lover. References to Baader-Meinhof and Bonnie and Clyde – mythologising the supposed affair – was a smart move, Parker decided, because hard to undo. He sat back and thought: And X marks the fucking spot.

Someone had done a very neat job. Any IRA connection had been eradicated to be replaced by Cross and Charlotte now squarely in the frame, which ironically was of Charlotte's own making as she was the one who had come up with a Muslim shooter in the first place.

Good work, he thought objectively, while he was personally frightened by the fact that the couple were obviously not intended to live long enough for the inconvenience of any trial. Their inevitable deaths would be explained by their desperation and the romantic foolhardiness of a star-crossed love. Roberts didn't have the imagination for this, so who did?

Parker could picture Moffat saying in that drawly way of his, 'Techie kids wrote the story; it's surprisingly easy, I gather.'

Parker saw he hadn't drawn his curtains. He paused in front of the window looking at the night-time lake. A bright moon was shining then was suddenly obscured. His eyes took a moment to adjust to the wall of white fog rolling forward over the lake and across the park until it engulfed the house.

20

The next morning a strange opaque light filled Charlotte's room and she found the valley shrouded in a thick, pearly fog. It was as though the world had stopped and vanished. Even between going to the bathroom and getting dressed, time seemed to stretch and become elastic. An hour became a day. The slow tick of the kitchen clock drove her from the room. The tension that had dominated her life suddenly had no outlet.

Cross announced there was no point in keeping watch as Roberts and Parker could do nothing while they were protected by the fog.

Most of the time Cross kept to his room. She had no idea what he did, other than when she heard his awkward limp as he tried running on the spot.

She listened to the radio in the kitchen, with the sound turned down, one ear pressed to the speaker and the other cocked for any sign of movement from upstairs.

The same old voices pumped out dire warnings about the need for social vigilance, keeping distance and fines for not complying with the increasingly complicated range of health checks and controls; but at least no mention yet in news bulletins of any search for two missing people.

The radio was like white noise: men of a certain age and assumption, and the women were just as bad, all their voices trained to project modulated exasperation and weary familiarity, smeared with condescension. Each had his or her own quirks of delivery. It struck Charlotte that any such discussion was a meaningless repeat, redefining itself in ever more threatening forms to become a physical manifestation of a collective breakdown.

She considered a campaign of deliberately setting out to irritate Cross. Bickering seemed as good a weapon as any.

As for the psychodynamic of their relationship and its sexual undercurrents, would she end up letting him have sex to avoid being hit? She was being naive; the two would go together.

Her surroundings spoke of comfort and privilege that she wanted to smash. She had a vivid image of braining Cross with a household object – maybe the iron on the sideboard, its sharp end splitting open the back of his head. She started to picture him dead, wondering whether part of her really did want to kill him. The ferocity of her fantasy left her shaken. At first it had just had her bashing him over the head. The next stage involved tying him up. There was a level of sexual taunt and humiliation to some of these reveries.

Everything around her seemed to exist in a state of imminent violence. It was only a matter of when and what form it took; whether others would come or Cross would turn on her, or she on him. She was shocked by how easily the violence might turn out to be hers.

She sat down with a blanket and stared at the empty grate. She must have dozed because she woke to find Cross in the kitchen contemplating a large plastic tub with a lid. She asked what he was doing. He said, 'Rabbits don't hibernate.'

That afternoon a limping Cross took her out into the landscape where they could barely see each other. He set the trap, securing it with branches, and propping the lid open with an upside-down Y-shaped device he had fashioned with kindling from the outhouse. The lid was hinged using wire and a nail. A rubber band attached to the bottom of the bucket and the lid's outer edge was to ensure it remained shut once the rabbit had taken the bait. Charlotte watched fascinated as he prepared it.

When they went back later, there was the rabbit. Cross took it out of the bucket holding it by the ears and produced his sheath knife. The rabbit hung suspended, staring wildly. Cross told her to grab the hind legs before it started kicking. She did so without thinking and he drew the blade across its throat. Blood gushed, bled of colour by the fog to appear black. Cross told her to hang on to the legs and hold it upside down until the blood drained. As he let go she turned her head away and felt the animal buck so much that it slipped from her grasp and fell to the ground. She watched transfixed as it staggered around, coughing and twitching, rolled on its side, went into spasm and fell still. She thought she might faint. Cross looked at her as though she had passed some sort of initiation.

'It's just blood,' he said, mocking.

She pointed out quite reasonably in a voice that didn't sound like hers that there was a load of food in the freezer and Cross observed, equally reasonably, 'And it will be shit full of preservatives.'

Charlotte forced herself to watch as he skinned and gutted the rabbit in the kitchen. He was swift, economical and surgical. She told herself it was part of a natural process and it wasn't as if she didn't eat meat.

He used up the rest of the potatoes, onions and carrots to make a stew. There was no alcohol in the house apart from a bottle of pale ale in one of the cupboards which he threw in.

Cross said, 'They will be coming for us when the fog lifts. We've maybe another day. I told you they've got this technology.'

'Yes, through what you call the ethernet.'

'No, not that. If they have the actual phone – such as yours – they can link it to your brainwaves. That's why they came.'

'No one located my brainwaves when I was fifty yards from them. If you really believe that ask yourself why they didn't stick around.'

To distract herself from his pointless argument, she looked in the fridge to see what was there.

'There's some garlic,' she said. 'We could add that.'

Cross amazed her by saying he never touched it. The remark astonished her more than all his other statements together.

'Never?'

'Frog stuff.'

Charlotte decided under the circumstances it probably wasn't the right moment for culinary experiment.

She was forced to admit the stew was good, however bad she felt about the rabbit. Afterwards Cross produced his sheath knife and again began jabbing it between his fingers into the pine table.

'Put that down and talk to me,' Charlotte said. Part of him seemed to quite like being told what to do. She suspected he was more sensitive than he let on – the mixed-race kid that had got bullied and called Curry Face.

Cross paused his knife-sticking, went back to it, then stopped as suddenly as he had started, put the knife away and reached down for something she couldn't see. There was a click before he produced the gun and put it on the table.

When Charlotte saw the first head twitch and the eyes start to go she thought to herself: Just throw a question at him; then said, 'As guns are now part of the conversation, tell me about your smoking gun.'

She tried to sound flippant and he told her not to get clever.

'I wrote it down already,' he said.

'Where?'

'In a letter.'

He gave her a crafty look.

Did she believe him? Perhaps he suspected she didn't because he grabbed the gun, but instead of pointing it at her as she was expecting he pressed it against his temple and Charlotte yelped as his eyes slid off in the other direction and he pulled the trigger, followed by an empty click.

'Your turn now,' he said, levelling the gun at her face. 'How much are you betting on no bullet?'

Charlotte sat shaking, staring at the barrel, before realising it was a game intended to humiliate her.

She said, 'Take me for a fool because I am a woman, but you can't play Russian roulette with an automatic.'

He looked impressed at that. He stared at the gun as if he didn't know how it had got there, revealed the magazine in his other hand, snapped it into place, checked the safety and stuck the gun in his waistband.

'Okay, I'm ready to talk,' he said, as though nothing had happened.

'Why did you just do that, pretending to shoot yourself?'

'It's what Father Jerome once did to me.'

'Held a gun to your head?'

Cross nodded. 'He had Lafferty take me barefoot into a field and made me kneel down while Lafferty held a shooter to my head. Father Jerome said he would give me one chance between either coming clean and getting a kneecapping, or taking a bullet to the back of the head.'

She couldn't tell if he was making it up.

'When was this?' she asked.

'After McCavity was shot. Father Jerome wanted to know if I'd had anything to do with that. I said I hadn't. Lafferty pulled the trigger. Empty chamber. The priest laughed and said, "That old trick. Anyway, I believe you now. I've seen tougher men than you shit themselves over that." '

Charlotte thought Cross would shoot people for a lot less than that particular humiliation, and from that moment Lafferty and Father Jerome had signed their death warrants.

'So then you shot him instead.'

'Don't you ever listen? A change of orders, I told you.'

Charlotte supposed by then Cross would have had nothing to lose. Roberts had told him the sting operation was cancelled at short notice, which would have left him a dangling man.

However she looked at it, it always went back to Roberts.

'Let's turn to Mr Roberts, as he seems the most interested in us. When did you first meet?'

'Afghanistan while liaising with the Pakistani secret service.'

'Were you friends?'

Cross didn't appear to understand.

Charlotte rephrased the question. 'Did you stay in touch?'

'Not until he resurfaced years later and set me up doing Home Office deportations.'

Charlotte thought: A huge elision there; no mention of his time in prison. She didn't want to get sidetracked. She asked if Roberts had had him in mind for Northern Ireland all along.

Cross said, 'He wanted to know if I was interested in undercover work.'

'So you went to Belfast.'

'Went home, you could say.'

'Did anyone ask what you were doing?'

'There were plenty like me, ex-squaddies providing muscle.'

'Roberts must have had someone on the ground.'

'Connors. IRA but reporting to the Brits for years.'

The sly joker they had questioned about the takeaway fire, who had dismissed Cross as a gun-toting idiot.

'Connors recommended me for work. It wasn't difficult to move up. Most of the Micks were dead idle. You only had to pretend to be a little bit smarter. My background checked out. I could be shown to be a Left Footer – a Papist – on my Ma's side.'

'What did you think about what Roberts was asking?'

'A waste of time. Whatever the politics, Belfast was Dodge City and wide open, that's what I reckoned. Like being handed something on a plate.'

'What was Roberts telling you?'

'That part of his job was assessing what they call NIRT. Northern Ireland Related Terrorism.'

'And what did you think was going on?'

'That they were all playing cowboys and Indians.'

'How did you get on with Father Jerome?'

'Well enough at first. But he'd say to me, "The word going round is that you're agenting for the Brits." '

'Then what were you doing in Earl's Court last December, posing as a telephone engineer?'

Cross looked caught out that she knew. Charlotte sensed his anger rise, but he shrugged it off.

'It was a recon job. Father Jerome said he had it in mind to carry out an operation on the mainland.'

'Did he say what?'

'No.'

'What did you think when he asked you to go?'

'That it was a test because he didn't trust me.'

'To see if you were loyal?'

'I suppose.'

'You must have guessed what you were being asked to do.'

'I thought the man was winding me up.'

'But what did you think when you realised what was intended?'

'I still didn't think it was serious.'

'Did you tell anyone else?'

'Connors.'

'Then?'

'I didn't hear anything back.'

'Then what?'

'Father Jerome said about "that thing" in London, he'd changed his mind.'

'And you passed that on to Connors too.'

'I said I figured the priest had been wasting my time.'

'What did Connors say after it went ahead?'

'He said it made no political sense for the IRA to shoot a fucking minister.'

Which was as much as Father Jerome had said to her.

She sensed Cross starting to block her because he suspected she was close to declaring that he was the one who had pulled the trigger on McCavity.

He was still feeding her a lot of bullshit, she was sure, either deliberately or because his head was fucked.

She said, 'To be able to help, I need to know everything that really happened.'

'I might need a hand with that,' he said suggestively.

Charlotte was aghast at the implication that he expected her to go upstairs with him in exchange for talking.

'That's not going to help,' she said, and stood to clear up. As she reached for his plate he took her wrist. The man's crass attempt at playfulness only made it worse.

'We went to the shop this morning for a reason, remember?' she reminded him.

'We'll think of something,' he said, undeterred.

'Please, let go.'

She was relieved that he did. She picked up his plate and gave him a wide berth on her way to the sink. As she ran the tap waiting for the water to heat, she thought: We've done it before, just get it over with. She put too much washing-up liquid in the bowl and stared at the rising suds, aware of Cross coming up behind her. He wrapped his arms around her waist and rested his head on her shoulder. He seemed strangely docile but she wasn't taking any chances. She kicked back hard with the heel of her boot on his bad ankle and shoved him off, thinking if there was a way of getting hold of his gun she would cheerfully shoot him.

She expected him to hit her, but he stood there with a hurt expression and she saw he was afraid, not of her but something else. Perhaps his mother used to hit him when he was a kid; Charlotte wondered whether that was the source of his anger.

Her own anger took the form of a single hard slap across his face. Still he didn't react and she ran upstairs in shame.

Out of his sight her imagination ran riot. He was bound to come for her. She put the chair under the door handle. Two heavy brass bedside lamps stood on either side of the bed. She leaned down to unplug one. There was a double socket. The other was occupied by an old-fashioned phone charger.

She embarked on a frantic search for the phone that went

with the charger. The possibility of it being in the room consumed her.

She became aware of movement on the stairs. She gripped the lamp, listening to the footsteps until they were outside. She watched a piece of paper being slid under the door. She crept forward and retrieved it. On it was written a single word, 'Sorry'.

She didn't know whether to believe that or if the man even understood the meaning of the word. She removed the chair and slowly opened the door to show she wasn't afraid. Cross took a step back when he saw the lamp. Whatever she'd had in mind, she could find nothing to say and he continued to stand there, his expression unreadable, until he turned and went back downstairs. She nearly called after him but her mind was already racing ahead. The divan bed had two drawers built into the base, which she had forgotten to search.

She closed the door, put down the lamp, replaced the chair and addressed herself to the drawers. They were full of clothes – woollens, warm nightwear and thick socks – but no phone. She sat on the floor defeated.

Cross was coming upstairs again. Charlotte got up and stood behind the door with the lamp ready. He paused outside for a long time, then she heard him go to his room. Straight after that something was smashed and she stood listening to her racing heart. She put down the lamp and buried her face in a pink towelling dressing gown hanging on the back of the door and cried silently into it.

After pulling herself together, she noticed a husky waist-coat hanging under the dressing gown. It was the sort her father had taken to wearing. When she had pointed out he once wouldn't have been seen dead in one he laughed and said however horrible it was his was very practical.

Hardly daring to hope, she checked the two side pockets and there it was – a basic, old-fashioned mobile phone that was almost an antique. A simple tool for calling and texting.

The battery was flat. She plugged it in and had to wait. She was afraid of herself, as much as she was of Cross. When she had slapped him downstairs it felt as though she had been overtaken by some alien force.

When the phone was sufficiently charged, she was asked for the security code and panicked. Five digits. It could be anything. She prayed the owner, being untechnical, had left it at the factory setting, which was usually a sequence or repeat of numbers; in this case 12345, which to her relief she discovered at her fourth attempt.

It was ponderous texting, using the tiny buttons. She typed a message to Parker, deleted it, typed it again and didn't send. Instead she just wrote:

– Is secret texting wise?

The answer came back straight away.

– Certainly a surprise. In terms of what?

– Betrayal and trust.

– Will tell what I can.

– Roberts with you?

– Not in the room.

– Roberts the reason Cross shouldn't have left farm.

– Worked that out.

– What's going on?

– Roberts on hunting expedition with a rifle. You okay?

– Surviving, just. Where you?

– Can't say.

– How close?

– Close and narrowing. Once fog lifts.

– I saw you the other day.

– Where?

– Cottage in a valley. You looked lost.
– *I know what's going on not sure what to do.*
– Blow a whistle?
– *No one would hear.*
– Come on, need help here. FFS think of something!

Charlotte sat and thought for a long time. How to defuse the personal threat of Cross. Waiting for Roberts to turn up would end only badly. It sounded as though she and Cross had been written off already. Flight was out of the question. They would be hunted down. Parker's hands were tied. Roberts sounded lethal. Which left Cross, also lethal.

She knocked on his door. He was lying awake with his hands behind his head. The bedside light was on with a headscarf draped over the shade to dim the light. Whatever he had smashed had been tidied away. She wondered if he was scared of the dark and whether his aggression was a manifestation of fear.

She passed him the phone and told him to read the texts.

When he saw them he stared at her with uncontrolled fury.

'Read the fucking things!' she shouted. 'Then you can hit me.'

He read slowly then got off the bed, handed her back the phone and said, 'Maybe I should've just shot you and let that other fucker kill me.'

'And now Roberts is coming to finish the job. What's so important about you?'

Cross said nothing. He walked past her and she followed him downstairs and watched him make coffee. He didn't speak until two cups were on the table.

'What I know about him. Roberts once offered me a lot of money to kill a Belfast dealer,' he said.

'Did you?'

'No. I smelt a rat.'

'Why was Roberts getting involved in a drugs war?'

'The guy he wanted wasted was IRA.'

'Is this your smoking gun?'

'Everyone knows the Brits went around shooting people in the old days. Unofficial policy.'

'That was years ago. Isn't this just a drugs war?' she asked, knowing it probably wasn't.

'Not if Roberts is involved.'

'What do we do?'

'He will come once the weather clears, so we have until then to get ready.'

The next morning, as Cross walked Charlotte through the shrouded landscape small pockets of visibility sometimes opened up then shut down again. He said she should memorise everything, whether she could see it or not with the fog. The damp air was like being trapped inside a consumptive's lungs.

'Note how little cover there is. No ditch or stream. A lot of firs that don't hide much – you would be seen walking through the trees. Not enough undergrowth. There's that stone wall past the outhouse that's partly fallen down.'

She asked if he thought Roberts would turn up with a police convoy.

'Alone or with Parker.' He sounded quite certain.

'Parker?'

'Roberts might use him as a decoy. Now describe the house as you remember it.'

Charlotte couldn't see the point.

Cross said patiently, 'Even half a chance depends on preparation and detail.'

She talked her way round the house, which was as simple

as a child's drawing. Windows to the front, none to either side; two doors, one at the front and the other opposite the outhouse.

'No attic or cellar,' added Cross. 'So not a house of surprises. What about the back?'

'That narrow passage runs the length of the house, with the rock behind sheer to a height of about twelve or fifteen feet.' She thought about that and said, 'I can't see anyone accessing the roof that way.'

Cross appeared amused by her efforts. 'No, it's not an Outward Bound course.'

'There's the one window downstairs at the back for the bathroom,' she said. 'You could get out of that unseen.'

'Or in. Ask yourself, will Roberts approach or wait?'

'Wait.'

'Yes. Impatience is death.'

He took her up the steep hillside facing the front of the house. He was using the stick but limping less. Charlotte couldn't decide whether his foot still bothered him or he was trying to hide it.

Cross said, 'Roberts has a rifle. We have only a pistol so we have to get close.'

They walked on until he reckoned they were where they had stood before overlooking the house, which was now lost in the fog.

'We don't know when he'll come, but he'll probably take up a position around here at first light and wait for us to show ourselves.'

She stood scuffing pine needles with the toe of her boot, asking herself how it was possible to guess anyone's moves.

'He could choose anywhere,' she said.

'He won't.'

Cross then asked where she thought the best vantage point would be.

'It's hard when you can't see.'

'Work with what you've got.'

Not much: a lot of trees and hillside that offered no ground cover. She wandered around until she came to a few low rocks, just visible in the mist, and pointed them out.

'You're Roberts,' Cross said. 'What do you do next?'

Take up a position, she supposed, so she lay among the rocks facing in the direction of the house.

Cross said, 'Sufficient cover not to be seen. In normal weather, it would give him sight of the house and its surroundings, about sixty yards, which is a good distance.'

Charlotte imagined Roberts lying there, aiming between the low rocks, fixing her in his sights.

She climbed back down the hill, absurdly reminded of the children's party game of trying to pin the tail on the donkey while blindfold.

Before going inside Cross took them into the outhouse and noted its contents. He opened the chest freezer. It was about six-foot long and waist high. He rearranged the food inside so it was level and said, 'Get in.'

She looked at him as though he had taken leave of his senses. He gripped her arm and said, 'You're hiding in this shed and Roberts is outside, you've got ten seconds, what do you do?'

'Switch it off and get in.'

She did and lay on her side. Cross shut the lid. The blinding claustrophobia was immediate. She was shaking as she got out.

'No, thanks. It's like being buried alive. I'd rather take my chances with Roberts.'

'It might be the safest place you can find.'

*

Back in the house, he explained what he had in mind.

'In the field you know what you are hunting, you just don't know where the enemy is, so the job is to get him to reveal himself.'

'You make it sound easy.'

'Except he is trying to do the same. So you use distractions.'

Cross had said Roberts might use Parker as a decoy and she wondered if he meant to use her in a similar way.

'And?' she asked.

'I can prepare you so you know what to do, even when you don't know what is going on around you.'

Charlotte couldn't tell if he had any confidence in her or thought she was useless.

'We have to set up a way of luring him,' he said. 'That's your job.'

Charlotte protested she had no skills for such work.

'Don't worry. I will walk you through everything.'

He reminded her he had only a handgun, so he would have to get close to Roberts to stand a chance.

'And then?'

'Someone will probably die. If we leave anything to chance, it will be us.'

He seemed almost at ease with the possibility of death and she decided it was up to her not to let him down.

For what he had in mind, she would have to get unseen from the outhouse, across ground offering limited cover, until she reached the dry-stone wall, which he decided was the best position for what he needed her to do; a total distance of about a hundred and fifty yards.

The most dangerous stretch involved crawling across open field on her stomach where her only cover was a shallow depression. He talked her through it. 'Move too near the top of the slope and you break its line. Go too far down and you are no longer hidden.'

He made her crawl that stretch over and over – shouting, 'Bang, you're dead!' when she strayed offline. After failing constantly, she gave up in anger and frustration, and yelled back at him that she hadn't volunteered for boot camp.

'Let's try and make it easier,' he said.

He found enough twine and kindling in the outhouse to mark out a line on the most exposed section that she mustn't cross.

He made her go over it again until he was satisfied.

'You'll be okay,' he finally said. Coming from him she took this for high praise. Walking back to the house, she felt both proud and despairing at the thought of the unlikelihood of her survival.

'Now we need to catch another rabbit,' he said.

That evening, unable to face more rabbit, Charlotte offered to cook as Cross remained busy with his plans, calculating angles. He had drawn her a simple plan of action: outhouse, thicket one, field, thicket two, stone wall, destination. Then the quicker return because there would be no time to go back the other way. When she asked why she couldn't just use the shorter route he explained that it was too exposed because of stretches of collapsed wall, but if she was fast enough going back she would be all right as Roberts would be distracted by then.

She found pasta and a tin of tomatoes. The onions were finished. She said she could use garlic instead.

'A first time for everything.'

She was surprised he agreed, and even more when he ate it and admitted it was not bad.

'Different,' he said.

They went over everything again, until Cross was satisfied. However afraid she was, she felt reassured by his calmness. She had never seen him less agitated or nervous. She decided to press her luck and said, 'You've been walking me around all day getting me to describe things I can't see, so maybe you can fill in a few blanks in return.'

'It depends,' he said.

'So here's the question,' she said. 'Why did the shooter use a Rimfire?'

Cross said he didn't know what she was on about, but she could see he did.

'A Rimfire is not a professional's gun so either the shooter was an amateur who got lucky or a master of his craft.'

Cross liked that. In some ways he was easy to please.

'I watched you today,' she went on. 'Focused, methodical, nothing left to chance. I can see you doing it.'

Curiosity got the better of him and he asked, 'What are you saying?'

'I'm thinking if you can do that you can get us out of this. Call it a vote of confidence.'

He didn't answer, saying instead, 'I sleep okay here. Usually I don't.'

'What about your flashbacks?'

'Sometimes they come in clusters. Weeks can pass, then they come out of nowhere like someone's worked a switch.'

'If we're going to our graves tomorrow I might go more willingly if I knew who the shooter was.'

Cross took his time answering, then playing along, said, 'I heard it was a fellow by the name of O'Grady.'

'So you're saying O'Grady did the job?'

Cross nodded, seeming relieved to be asked and able to share.

'Does he have any regrets, do you think?'

'No, but what should he say if anyone else asks?'

She noticed a change; usually he didn't ask her.

'Say he was trapped into it, is probably his best bet. But I suspect when the opportunity presented itself he couldn't come up with a single reason not to.'

Cross gave a shy smile. 'It's what I do. Shoot people. The job.'

Charlotte noted the shift to the first person.

'And that's it?' She found it hard to keep the surprise out of her voice.

'It's what I do,' he repeated, seemingly content to talk about himself. 'What I did,' he corrected. 'Shoot people from a distance, in exchange for the Queen's shilling.'

'Why a Rimfire?'

'Sporting chance. Margin of error. Calibration. Distance. It was a hell of a shot. I had allowed myself two. A second if necessary to the body. As it was, the first was perfect, or so I thought.'

'For the sport?' she said. 'No other motive?'

'Like I said, it's what I do best.'

'This was very different from the battlefield.'

'True. Usually you don't get to select the target. You can stalk him for days but you have no idea who he is. In that sense, you are always hunting yourself.'

He paused before going on. 'No one complained when Clint Eastwood shot people.'

'That was in the movies!'

'Yes, but they tell us that violent death is central to everything we live by. Only a few get to practise it, fewer still under the authorisation of law. But there's no rule book.'

'What if?' she asked. The idea had only just occurred to her.

'What if what?'

'What if you don't kill Roberts when he comes.'

He looked at her as though the question was stupid. 'What else would I do?'

'Shoot him, just don't kill him. Think about it. He's more valuable to us alive. You're a trained interrogator. After the Heathrow exercise you said you'd stuck it to the fuckers. Stick it to Roberts. You must have questions for the man.'

Cross still couldn't see it.

Charlotte insisted. 'It's your best chance. Our best chance. I can't think how I will explain myself otherwise. Give me something I can take to get you your immunity deal, otherwise you will be on the run for the rest of your life.'

She considered her props for when Roberts came – a cardboard cut-out of a man's head and a bottle of rabbit's blood – and wondered: What chance, really?

'Anyway,' she said, 'we don't know for sure he will come tomorrow.'

Cross didn't like her taking control and she feared he was about to lose it.

'But at least I can tell Parker I am here on my own. Would that help?'

Cross waited for her to go on.

'I can text and say I'm contagious and as sick as a dog and you have abandoned me as a result, so I want him to come and fetch me.'

As usual with anything suggested by her, he took his time.

She prompted, saying, 'Roberts won't completely fall for it, but it might at least create uncertainty in his mind.'

Cross decided. 'Do it now.'

After she had, Charlotte noticed the fog was lifting. She went and stood outside. As she watched the world return she thought about Cross, his uneasy combination of discipline and detonation, and decided she was no longer afraid of him. She couldn't afford to be now her life depended on him.

Back inside, she found him sitting in front of an array of items he'd laid out on the table. He was making a tube out of cardboard. Charlotte noted weedkiller, plastic plant pots, twine, household matches, a key ring and children's wax crayons.

She asked what they were for.

'A surprise. Get some rest. Big day tomorrow.'

Being told that didn't make her feel any better.

He said, 'No worries. You'll be around to watch the sun go down. Roberts isn't as good as he thinks and he'll end up squealing.'

Charlotte went upstairs and, through nervous exhaustion rather than ordinary tiredness, fell into a shallow, fretful sleep.

21

It was bright daylight when Charlotte woke late in a panic before remembering she was supposed to be sick. She put a blanket around her shoulders and opened the curtains. Cross had told her not to keep still for too long. Despite that, she remained in the window, as if daring Roberts to shoot.

Downstairs Cross had left a fire lit, for the first time; smoke coming out of the chimney would give the appearance of a normal day. He was already out to take up his first position on the rock face behind the house in anticipation of Roberts's arrival. Charlotte kept the curtains drawn. Part of her wanted just to sit in front of the fire and let whatever the day might bring take its course. She waited for the kettle to boil, made her tea, went back up to bed and sat warming her hands on the mug, feeling foolish and apprehensive. During all the crawling around the previous day, she had not pictured herself sitting waiting.

She found Parker hardest to calculate. After texting him to say she was ill and on her own, he'd answered with a terse 'okay'. She had tried him a couple of times after that and got no answer. She hoped he would turn up alone and they could go off, leaving Roberts and Cross to their games. Although she had developed a dependence of sorts on Cross, she asked herself what was the point of her being there when her position was at best one of collateral damage.

Then she remembered Parker didn't drive, so he could not be coming alone.

Parker came with an ambulance. Like any ambulance, its presence seemed reassuring, plausible and alarming. Alerted by the sound of a vehicle, Charlotte had taken up a position to one side of the window. She was surprised Parker had gone to such lengths and supposed he had taken her seriously, but when she looked again at the ambulance it appeared sinister in the manner of Parker's postman: subterfuge, perhaps, masquerading as normality. She noted the driver on the nearside – a tough butch woman in a medical tunic and wearing a mask.

Parker got out. He also had a mask on and appeared nervous as he approached and knocked. Charlotte took her time answering. She opened the door, wrapped in the blanket. Parker was visibly taken aback by the sight of her hacked-off hair. Charlotte couldn't decide whether he looked furtive too. He said rather uselessly, 'We're here to take you away. You'll have to travel in the back, then we'll need to isolate you.'

Charlotte, still thrown by the manner of his turning up, realised she had a choice between leaving and staying, between him and Cross.

She said she needed time to get herself together. Parker made a move to come inside and she reminded him he could get sick. She shut the door, saying she would be as quick as she could.

Her outdoor clothes were waiting in the bathroom. She hurriedly chucked them on top of what she was wearing – a pair of borrowed pyjamas she had found in the bedroom – put on her boots and anorak and left through the bathroom window.

*

After waiting ten minutes, Parker went inside, nervous now, thinking Charlotte must have thrown in her hand with Cross and the two of them were waiting for him upstairs.

He called out before going into each bedroom. Nothing. The last room he checked was the downstairs bathroom. On the floor lay the blanket Charlotte had been using. The window latch was up.

It was a casement window, easy enough to get in and out of. Perhaps she was running away because she was afraid, though Parker couldn't see why until he saw his arrival through her eyes, as a possible abduction. He doubted if she would come voluntarily now. He had been shocked by her savage appearance.

It was Roberts who had said take an ambulance. Parker had voiced his concern that a hostage situation might develop. Roberts dismissed that, saying Cross would have fucked off because he'd had enough of the woman.

Parker was sure Roberts no more believed that than he did. No doubt the man had his own separate plans for Cross, involving his precious De Lisle. The best of a bad job would be to make sure Charlotte was removed to safety, though he suspected Roberts might also have an ulterior motive: for her to be taken to a confined place where she could be dealt with later.

Parker climbed out of the bathroom window, checked the outhouse and found nothing. He had no choice but to leave empty-handed If Roberts was already watching that presented another problem. Leaving without her would alert Roberts that she was still there, making her a possible second target. However, if he could be led to believe she had left, he would, with luck, not go hunting her.

The ambulancewoman cracked the window when she saw Parker. Whatever was going on, she wasn't bothered.

He said Charlotte was in a bad way and he would need the wheelchair. The woman pressed a switch that unlocked the rear doors. Parker got the wheelchair out, leaving the doors open. He wheeled it into the house and hastily gathered enough bedding to make it look as though someone might be sitting in it. He wrapped the lot up in Charlotte's blanket. As he had taken the wheelchair in forwards it wasn't that unnatural to come out backwards, using his body to obscure it from view. He waited until he was covered by the ambulance doors before turning, at which point his plan threatened to fall apart because he had forgotten to set the wheelchair ramp. That took some fiddling as he had to position the wheelchair between the doors, hoping it remained out of sight. With the chair at last in the back he told the driver they could go.

The ambulance's bumpy progress down the lane jolted his conscience, telling him he was taking the easy way out and abandoning Charlotte.

Cross had previously bagged up the contents of the deep freeze and chucked them in the rubbish bin, switched the freezer off and thrown in a duvet and a couple of pillows.

Charlotte hadn't been expecting to use it so soon to hide from Parker. It was as tomblike as she had feared.

She could hear Parker moving around outside then held her breath as she listened to him come into the outhouse, look around and leave. She risked cracking open the lid to let in some light. Sometime later she heard the ambulance depart and hauled herself out.

The outhouse elevation protected her in the short distance to the first bramble thicket at the top of the field. Cross had shown her how any standing shape could be spotted in the varying density of the bush so he had made her crawl on hands and knees. Doing it for real was much slower and more tiring because she now saw only danger in her every move. The sudden dart of a startled rabbit nearly made her cry out. She prayed its dash across the field hadn't alerted Roberts. She remained paralysed, doubting if she had the courage to carry on. Summoning the last of her reserves, she set off again.

Reaching the end of the thicket, what confronted her looked frighteningly flat compared to the ground she had gone over with Cross – the depression now seemed barely more than a furrow. She looked around in panic until she finally located the peg ahead, marking the start of the twine laid by Cross. Using that she was able to work out the line of the slope and set off feeling horribly exposed. She inched forward, using spread elbows and splayed knees, taking extra care not to lift her head, which meant she could only see sideways with her cheek pressed against the ground.

After ten yards she felt like she was swimming uphill. What seemed like an age passed before she reached the twine. She became increasingly aware of how difficult it was to crawl on her stomach in a straight line and kept wanting to look up. When she saw she was lying on the twine she froze, expecting the shot she might never hear, knowing that the report would come after the bullet had done its job. She prayed that Roberts's attention was elsewhere as she slowly shifted right until she was back inside the line. She lay in a funk, giddy to the point of fainting, as though she were suffering a strange horizontal form of vertigo, like clinging to a ladder, too high to turn back or to carry on.

She moved on only because it was easier to crawl forwards than backwards, her head twisted awkwardly to keep the twine in view, fearing that if Roberts were as good a reader of the land as Cross was it left her route as obvious as if it had been drawn on a map.

She pressed on, the ground dragging against her cheek. Only when the brambles scratched her head was she aware of her arrival at the second thicket. She manoeuvred herself under full cover, rolled on her back and lay in a cold sweat, aware of the sky's indifference. She was nothing but a trapped animal.

The next section involved a crawl through a low tunnel that Cross had hacked through the brambles. The passage was safe but unpleasant with thorns tearing at her face and scratching her knees and hands, making her wish she had worn gloves.

At the tunnel's end she reached the stone wall, which stood a couple of feet high until two gaps further down. These were obscured by a straggling hawthorn whose lattice of branches Cross had pointed out could serve as an observation post to look across the valley.

'Good cover but not full cover. If you can see out, others can see in.'

A calculated movement could draw an opponent to fire.

Charlotte passed the first gap, keeping down behind the hawthorn. She got to the second where the cut-out was waiting – a pathetic piece of cardboard shaped like a head and shoulders on a stick. She did as Cross had shown her, lying on her back, holding the stick at arm's length, lifting it up and down very slowly. She did it until her arm ached. Either she hadn't been spotted or Roberts was biding his time.

Taking the cut-out with her, she returned to the first gap and repeated the action, once then twice. She was about to lower it when a dull smack punched out the centre of the cardboard.

She heard nothing of the shot. She thought she must have

screamed. The sight of the drilled cutout unnerved her as much as if she had been the target.

Parker was still some way short of the house when he heard what he thought might have been a shot, but couldn't be sure. Roberts had boasted the De Lisle was virtually inaudible beyond a range of fifty yards.

At the end of the lane he had told the ambulance woman to let him out, wondering what she would make of her eventual discovery of a wheelchair full of bedding. He had no plan apart from trying to extricate Charlotte.

To his left, about a hundred yards ahead, he saw a figure coming down the side of the valley, moving from tree to tree. Parker cautiously lowered himself to the ground, careful to make no sudden movement, and saw it was Roberts. At the edge of the trees he stopped and assessed, then sprinted across the track and rolled over the wall in a fluid movement that left him on one knee with the De Lisle aiming up the valley.

Parker found this exercise both impressive and absurd as performed by a grown man. He watched Roberts stand and advance, rifle ready, then stop and bend down to inspect something. After that he disappeared below the wall. Parker glimpsed him further down, in one of the gaps, moving fast towards the house.

He considered telephoning for help, then realised that whatever happened would be over before anyone arrived.

After the shot Charlotte had almost forgotten what to do next. She shoved the cutout deep into the hawthorn until it was hidden. The plastic bottle of rabbit's blood stood propped against the wall. With shaking hands she splashed some on the ground. Scuttling back, hidden by the wall, she spilled more blood every seven or eight yards. The exposed parts of the wall she rolled across as Cross had shown her how to do.

She reached the outhouse and hurried down the gulch behind the house, splashing the last of the blood, past where Cross was now supposed to be positioned in the bathroom, waiting for Roberts to pass. That was the plan.

Expecting Roberts to appear any second, she ran back to the outhouse where she clambered into the deep freeze and surrendered herself to its black space. Adrenalin kept fear at bay but it soon felt as though the darkness was eating into her. She waited for something to happen and nothing did. She imagined Cross waiting crouched in the bathroom, ready to make his move. She tried to picture Roberts making his unsuspecting way down the gulch into the trap.

Instead she was hit by a stab of light as the freezer lid was lifted. She was too scared to scream when she saw Roberts. She had heard nothing of his approach. He looked just as surprised because he was clearly expecting to find Cross there.

After losing sight of Roberts, Parker had taken up a position in the trees opposite the house, in time to see Charlotte emerge from the outhouse, followed by Roberts, looking thunderous as he shoved her forward. He now had a pistol as well as the De Lisle. They disappeared into the house. At least he hadn't shot her.

He supposed he could walk in, trying to pretend everything was normal, or go round the back and enter by the bathroom window, but whichever of those he tried Roberts would probably shoot first and ask later. If, on the other hand, Roberts saw him wandering around outside, he might think twice.

Parker moved into the open, trying desperately to appear normal. A brief scream from Charlotte came from inside the house. Feeling he now had no choice, he went and knocked on the door, tested the handle, and entered.

For all the fear coursing through her, as she lay on the floor, Charlotte reasoned that Roberts hitting her was a sign of his desperation. She was wondering where on earth Cross was when Parker walked in. She assumed he was there to join Roberts until Roberts made him lie down next to her. He told her to keep her face pressed to the ground but by swivelling her eyes she was able to follow his boots back to the end of the kitchen. Parker's face she couldn't see because his arms were in the way. To her right was the fire. Ahead of her was a carpet runner in front of the narrow arch into the hall. She concentrated on its horrible pattern in a futile effort to distract herself. Of all irrelevant things, she found herself thinking about her father's infidelity and supposed she would never know what lay behind it. She was still angry with him, except she saw now she had been mad at him for most of her life, though it was a bit late to realise that.

She was aware of a strange fizzing sound, seconds before an object came flying through the archway and landed on the runner in front of her – a cardboard tube about two-foot long, hissing and billowing a cloud of thick orange smoke. Roberts was racing across the room to take up a position against the narrow partition wall between the fireplace and archway, pistol in hand. The belching smoke was like an indoors version of the fog, toxic enough to make Charlotte cough and her eyes smart. Within moments all she could see was a narrow space above the floor.

From what she worked out later, Cross must have moved

into the room at speed to be stopped by Roberts swinging out his arm and smacking him hard enough to send him staggering back. The shot that followed she thought was Roberts firing into the hall, before resuming his position where she could just make him out, crouched down to avoid the worst of the smoke.

Cross stormed in, firing high in the direction of Roberts, who threw himself forward, knocking Cross down.

Charlotte, half-blinded, made out Roberts's legs standing on the runner. She leapt up, screaming like a banshee as she grabbed the end of the rug and pulled. Roberts lurched but didn't fall. Charlotte was surprised that Parker was thinking with her, grabbing the rug, and together they gave another tug. As Roberts's feet went from under him he was jumped on by Cross. From what little she could see of the men's blurred grappling on the floor, it looked neither efficient nor effective, involving a lot of grunting, with desperate efforts to deflect the aim of the opponent's gun while kicking out. Charlotte blundered her way through the smoke across the room, banging into furniture, desperately feeling her way along the countertop for the iron she remembered being there. As she stumbled back with it she saw Cross's gun skitter across the carpet. She threw herself in their direction, swung the iron at what she hoped was Roberts's head and felt it make contact, enough to knock him sideways.

Cross was scrabbling for his gun. Charlotte could just make out Roberts sprawled on the floor, stunned but hesitating apparently only over who to shoot first. Charlotte threw the iron with all her force, hitting him in the face. Roberts's gun went off, simultaneously with another shot and Parker saying, 'Fuck me,' as Roberts fell back clutching his stomach, his pistol clattering on the floor.

Parker was staring at Cross's gun in his hand in stunned amazement.

Charlotte was surprised by her fury as she turned on him and shouted, 'Let's hope you haven't killed him.' He didn't understand what she meant. 'We need him to talk,' she told Parker, disconcerted by how hard she sounded.

Parker looked at her mystified. Charlotte turned to Cross to say get on with it.

Roberts was groaning, his eyes squeezed shut from the pain, furious with himself for how things had turned out. Cross slapped him across the face to get his attention.

Roberts turned away with a look of contempt and said he wanted a priest.

Cross jabbed his finger in Roberts's wound, making him cry out. Charlotte was thinking why couldn't Parker have just shot the man in the leg. Roberts was saying nothing. Cross jabbed again. Roberts screamed and coughed up a lot of blood. His face was sweating and deathly pale. Parker looked appalled.

Charlotte told Roberts to explain about the shootings at the farm.

Roberts remained silent. Cross jabbed again. This time Roberts didn't cry out and glared at her, refusing to say anything other than, 'Fuck off, bitch.'

Charlotte shocked herself by kicking Roberts in the side, more out of frustration than aggression, but even so. Roberts was muttering to himself, what Charlotte realised was a Hail Mary: 'Now and at the hour of our death.'

Cross looked at Charlotte and said, 'Give me five minutes alone with him.'

Charlotte said she doubted if Roberts had that long. Cross slapped Roberts again in the face.

Parker, aghast, said, 'You should see yourselves.'

Charlotte told Cross to stop; it was too late. She watched Roberts struggle to say his last prayers, until they became swallowed by a gurgling in his throat, and he coughed, belching more blood down his front, and fell back dead.

Any relief Charlotte experienced at her survival was overtaken by confusion and anger. She was coming down fast, overtaken by a sense of hollow victory. Roberts's death solved nothing and someone still had a lot of explaining to do.

They covered Roberts's body with the runner that had been his undoing. Charlotte started to giggle inappropriately at the thought of leaving him for the owners to find. She managed to stop herself and wondered if she would ever laugh again.

She asked Parker if he had his phone. Parker felt around, as if not quite sure, until he found it. Charlotte said, 'Use it.'

He did but not in the way she was expecting. He handed it to Cross and said, 'I told your mother I would let her know you're alive.'

Cross went outside to make the call, leaving Charlotte and Parker standing in silence, avoiding looking at each other. She busied herself opening windows.

Cross came back in and returned the phone to Parker.

He said to Charlotte his mother had a letter he'd written. 'I told her to give it you. It tells what I know.' He prodded Roberts's foot with his boot. 'A pity he took his dirty secrets with him. I'm out of here.'

He took Roberts's De Lisle from the countertop at the other end of the room, and went off to fetch his rucksack.

Parker was on the phone to Hopkins when Cross came back.

'You're his responsibility now,' he said, gesturing at Parker.

Charlotte said as she followed him outside, 'I can look after myself.'

'You did well, considering.'

'Considering what?'

'Considering nothing. You did well, full stop.'

After that they grew tongue-tied. As an afterthought, he gave her his handgun, saying, 'Not that you need it, more as a souvenir. You deserve it and anyway I have got the rifle now.'

She took the pistol, wondering what she would do with it.

'Where will you go?'

'Lie low, disappear. You?'

'Go home.'

'Home?'

'To my father at least. I'm thinking if I am going to get arrested it should be to his discomfort because what happened to me in Belfast wouldn't have occurred without him.'

How stilted she sounded. She realised she had volunteered next to nothing about herself in all the time they had been together.

He replied, equally awkward, 'Tell me about it some day.'

She didn't point out it was unlikely they would ever see each other again.

He gave her a casual salute and wished her good luck. She watched him limp up the hill. She was both surprised and touched when he turned to wave before he disappeared from view.

Back inside, Parker was still on the phone to Hopkins, saying it was her job to make everything go away, given all the other shit they could bring up if she didn't.

He said, 'Roberts told us everything.'

Not true, Charlotte thought, but it wouldn't hurt for Hopkins to think he had.

Parker hung up. Charlotte felt like she had hit a wall. Parker behaved like he was making a point of ignoring her. Perhaps he considered her too much of a handful. She didn't know how to deal with him after Cross.

'We can't stay here,' she said.

Parker explained about the RAF Police Land Rover Roberts had borrowed.

'It's probably parked somewhere down on the road. We can take that.'

There was the unpleasant procedure of retrieving the keys from Roberts's jacket. Roberts looked so dead that he might never have been alive and Charlotte wondered how this shrunken little man could ever have been seen as a threat.

Liverpool was about three hours away. Charlotte argued for going there, wanting to know what Cross had written. After that she would drive through the night to her father's house.

She asked Parker what his plans were.

He said he would think of something, without sounding happy about it.

He rummaged around in his pockets and returned her phone and purse. He said her other belongings were where he was staying. Grateful for getting back her essentials, she said she wasn't bothered about the rest and someone could send them on.

She left the house without a backward glance, in no mood for any discussion, and walked ahead of Parker.

They found the Land Rover parked off the road among trees, a couple of hundred yards from the track.

She made a point of driving with the radio on loud after

finding some mindless music. Parker appeared to sleep, leaving her thinking how after everything she had gone through you would expect things to change, but they hadn't. Half an hour earlier she had feared for her life; now it was back to the same old shit.

22

Cross's mother had an air of bitter amusement, as though to say however bad things were she could show they were a whole lot worse. In that discrepancy lay a source of much black humour, Charlotte suspected. Cross must have grown up terrified of her.

They weren't invited in. The woman handed Parker a regular envelope. 'It's what you were looking for when you were last here.' She gave him a mirthless grin. 'Where's your pal?'

'Indisposed,' said Parker.

'No loss there. Is missy here the one you were talking about?'

Parker nodded, looking embarrassed.

'He always was a romantic boy,' she said. 'A bit half-baked.' She nodded at the letter. 'That nonsense about confession; in my book you never discuss anything with a priest apart from the local tombola.'

She insisted on giving Parker a packet of Wagon Wheels for the journey. Charlotte tried one later and swore never again.

She didn't want Parker reading the letter aloud while she drove. Everything seemed an effort of negotiation. She said she couldn't concentrate while driving in town. Some miles later she pulled into a lay-by on a dual carriageway and they read it, tilted at an angle so the paper turned yellow in the reflection of the street lamp.

Dear Mum,

I am writing this to make sense of myself though there is not much chance of that and I don't know who else to tell. This won't mean much in terms of names, though you know of Lafferty. I have been in Belfast some while now doing James Bond stuff but a lot messier. I had to go to London for a few days and I was shitting myself when I came back because Lafferty said he had been received back into the Church by Father Jerome after making 'a full Confession'!! So I was left thinking does that mean Lafferty 'confessed' that he and I were assets? I doubt if he came clean with Father Jerome about how he was running around secretly shooting people for the Brits, but that's another matter, nothing to do with me, Scout's honour, but what had he told? Lafferty was a mess.

I'm a mess too, Mum. Father Jerome was the 'enemy', one of the bad guys, and I had to pretend to work for him. His being a priest complicated everything. I know you still go to church but I haven't thought about it for years, let alone stepped inside one.

Father Jerome asked if I might also have anything to confess. Because of the sanctity of the confessional he said I would be talking directly to God through him and anything I said was between God and me. There was a lot of cat and mouse between us in terms of what Lafferty had told him but Father Jerome insisted he couldn't say and the same would go for me. The Church's rules were strict and he took his vows seriously. So I took the risk.

The way I saw it, I had no choice except to come clean and confess I was working for the Brits, which he probably knew already. Then I threw in my hand with him and suggested a way for us to shaft the Brits instead – over a sting operation they had planned that I was a big part of. Turning the tables on them would be a big 'fuck you' – excuse my French as the priest used to say – to them. A big payday that never happened, but never mind.

He was a dangerous man the priest, one of God's rattlesnakes. Maybe it was contempt he felt for me because he saw me as being weak for confessing in the first place, but his way of testing my faith was to take me into a field and have me shot, except there turned out to be no bullet in the gun. I tell you, Mum, that's not something you would wish on your worst enemy.

Afterwards he thought it all a big joke, said he was just testing.

Well, I had my revenge when the Brits decided for whatever reason of their own that they wanted Father Jerome out of the picture and it fell to me because I couldn't let on to them I had switched sides, so I had to swap back.

The thing is in the old days out in the field it was just you, the ground and the target, not this constant shifting. I never would have guessed it was going to turn out like this. It gets pretty lonely in my head which is messed up enough already. Well, I can hear you saying what a bad boy I have been. I try not to see it like that and I am writing in the hope you will forgive me if any of this gets out and I am not around to stand up for myself.

Your loving son

They hadn't said much after reading the letter, apart from Charlotte declaring it made more sense of Cross than anything else she had heard, until Parker surprised her by asking what she knew about her father. He said he had talked to him.

'And his friend who is looking after him. He's not well.'

'Friend?'

'Not English.'

'Greek?'

'That sounds like him.'

'How unwell?'

'He has trouble breathing.'

'He told me he was in remission. Is this more spying by you? That's what it feels like.'

'I wanted to know if you had contacted him. I was concerned. We talked about Moffat.'

'About?'

'From what I can see two things have been going on in Belfast, overlapping but separate: one to do with Hopkins, the other with Moffat. Roberts was working for both. Moffat and Hopkins probably have the answers between them and your father will be able to tell you more about Moffat than I can.'

Charlotte was going to ask about the Greek but didn't as it suddenly all fell into place. Whatever shadows she had grown up under she blamed on the secret nature of her father's work and what he could not tell, which became an excuse for everything else that could be covered up. It explained the false extroversion and charm, the absence of photographs in the house, the conventional front that gave nothing away. And there was her mother's role, which now looked more like one of hostage than unwilling partner; had she been privy to his secret?

Perhaps she was completely wrong but it made sense in the way of Cross's letter in terms of the deals people make with themselves. The adulteries her father had mentioned weren't with women, which she had had trouble picturing anyway. He had set out to mislead because the issue was, and probably always had been, men.

The realisation had an extraordinary effect, not of liberation exactly, more like a cold wind that brought clarity. Her immediate reaction was anger at having been cheated on as much as her mother. Even after her death her father had admitted nothing. The Greek had been introduced as a professional friend. She wondered how long that had been going on. A whole side of her father's life had remained occluded, which she now saw as blindingly obvious. It was rather like having something explained at the end of a mystery story. While she had been caught up with events in Belfast, her father's secret life – which perhaps underpinned everything – had been unfolding all the time on a private level.

Charlotte felt bad about dumping Parker but decided she had little choice. She wasn't his responsibility, as Cross had suggested. For what she needed to do she didn't want anyone tagging along. She left him at a service station after asking him to get her a sandwich.

Charlotte had whole stretches of the motorway to herself as she pushed on through the night. She was still dressed in the wet-weather gear she had been wearing for days. She felt grubby in more ways than one and found it hard to see herself returning to a normal life. Absence of traffic made it difficult to stay awake. At some point she must have drifted off for a second, snapping awake to find the car driving at speed towards the central barrier. She swerved in time to miss it and drove on as frightened as when Cross had held a gun to her head: to have survived all that then to die from carelessness. After that she kept under the speed limit, hands clamped to the wheel, working her jaw to ease the tension.

The motorway around Birmingham was deserted. She peeled off onto the M5, which was disrupted by roadworks and miles of cones. A police car parked on a ramp paid her no attention; no alert out yet for an errant RAF Police Land Rover. She missed her turning at Worcester South and had to take the next exit for the M50 and loop round, crossing the river at Upton.

After the enforced company and intense confinement of her life since going to Belfast the isolation of the drive made her see how lonely she was.

The familiar cluster of shops at the foot of the Malvern Hills where her father lived looked both the same and like they belonged to another life. Rather than park in his drive she left the car in the street, not knowing why until she realised she had no wish to announce her arrival.

It was a clear night, much warmer than it had been. She found herself reverting to procedure: approaching the house with wariness, assessing everything as though it were hostile. She let herself in through the gate in the high garden wall, avoiding the gravel path overgrown with weeds. She patrolled the house, which was in darkness. The burglar alarm light was winking. She was dog-tired. Daylight wouldn't come for a couple of hours. A lean-to woodshed full of logs stood in the corner of the garden about thirty yards from the house. She cleared a space for herself in the corner, lay down and fell into a deep sleep.

She was woken by the sound of footsteps on the gravel. It was bright daylight. She crouched down, hidden by the stacked wood. She heard logs being chucked in a basket. As the footsteps departed she raised her head and saw her father's Greek friend.

A period of what she could only later describe as temporary insanity followed. She found herself incapable of walking up to the door and announcing herself. Instead she slipped out of the side gate and went to the local supermarket as though everything were normal. She had to buy a mask in a pack of three for an exorbitant price. She looked for the tinned meat she and Cross had eaten and couldn't find any. A lot of shelves were half-empty. She bought a horrible fizzy drink and a selection of meat pies. The few shoppers that were in avoided each other. The checkout girl wore transparent blue gloves that made her hands look diseased. Again, as though everything were normal, Charlotte returned surreptitiously to the house, took up her position in the woodshed and gorged herself until she felt sick.

It was a beautiful day, warm and springlike. She moved from the woodshed to an exposed sunny spot among the high thickets of holly and brambles, thinking she just wanted to stay there and rest, with the pale sun on her. She slept again, dreaming she was safe in the barn den Cross had forced her to abandon.

In the afternoon she watched the back of the house. Compared to the Lake District, the overgrown garden offered nothing but cover. She held conversations in her head about what she thought she was doing and decided she wasn't ready to rejoin the world, which had shut down again anyway. She could stay there for as long as the weather held.

Sometimes she saw her father moving around in the living room and was struck by how frail he had become. The Greek seemed to be a constant presence. Smoke was coming out of the chimney. At dusk they drew the living room curtains. Later on, lights went on upstairs only in one bedroom. Charlotte told herself it was none of her business what they got up to, really. She was content with her isolation. She felt secure. When her phone ran out of charge it was a relief. Nobody had tried to contact her, neither Hopkins, nor Moffat, nor Parker. With Parker she hoped it was because he had the sense to leave her alone. She gazed contentedly at nature. Everything was good, she told herself, which was when she decided she would probably grow quite as mad as her grandmother. She slept in the woodshed again that night.

It could have gone on indefinitely, except she was seen the next morning coming back from the shops, walking up the drive carrying a black bin liner she had found dumped outside one of the closed charity shops, hoping she might find something in it she could wear.

The Greek also had a black rubbish bag, which he was putting in a bin kept next to the garage. Charlotte adjusted, trying to make it appear as though she had just arrived, thinking she must look like a refugee. She saw the Greek had no idea who she was, given her appearance and the state of her hair.

She asked, 'Is my father in?'

Charlotte played the daughter coming home. The Greek assumed the role of carer. And her father, as sick as he was, pretended everything was normal. He didn't even remark on her appearance – her shorn hair, the bramble scratches on her face, the bruised cheek where Roberts had hit her – as though she had grown invisible to a point where she wondered if he had ever really seen her. She overcompensated by being too eager to please, thinking perhaps her father knew she was in trouble and was waiting to see what she said.

They sat in the eating area of the kitchen, a room she had never liked for no reason she could think of.

She wanted to say, 'I expect you are wondering why I am here,' except before she could her father asked, 'Should you be travelling?'

She took that to mean that her intrusion was not welcome. She had been fairly cheerful during her sojourn in the garden and was depressed by how quickly he could reduce her to sullenness.

What did any of it matter, after all? The man clearly didn't have long to live. So what if she had known nothing of his private life?

It wasn't even ten o'clock and she wondered how she would get through the day. The Greek – she refused to use his name – showed no sign of leaving and loitered, fussily tidying.

They could talk about death or she could play the fool. She reverted to her usual role of filling in her father's silences by prattling on about the weird familiarity of everything shutting down again. She knew there was no point in asking him anything because he would only deflect it. She in turn ignored his question about not travelling and said she had lost her luggage and was stuck for clothes. She explained about the bin liner, saying she was hoping to find something in it to wear, make an appropriate donation and return the bag.

The only item that fitted her was a novelty Christmas sweater, which she put on and promptly burst into tears, to the evident embarrassment of the men.

The Greek brightly asked what anyone might want for lunch. He could go and fetch something.

Charlotte apologised and said she had been under a lot of pressure. It had been a mistake to come.

Her father surprised her by asking, 'What is it you want to know?'

'Everything,' she said.

The Greek slunk off. Charlotte pictured him standing on the other side of the door, eavesdropping, as she went on.

'I want to know about you and him. My mother. How long you've got and how you feel about that. And about Moffat.'

'Moffat?'

'Everything,' she repeated.

He took off his glasses, playing for time, cleaning them with a dirty silk handkerchief. His hands shook.

He held her eye, when he usually never did, and said, 'My mind has grown clouded. I am becoming senile. I repeat myself. I need looking after, which I resent. I am falling apart physically. I have become incontinent. I have weeks, maybe months left. Eight weeks ago I was in remission. Now they tell me I have various cancers and they don't know which to treat. And because of the shutdown they are cancelling appointments so I will probably find myself dead before anyone gets around to seeing me.'

'Are you afraid?'

'What do you think? When one lives a life of secrecy and avoidance one always is. Most of the time one manages not to get found out, but not by death. A cliché but, like most, unfortunately true.'

Some sort of personal alarm beeped and Charlotte watched her father take a cheap plastic container out of his jacket pocket. It was full of pills, each in its own separate tray. He carefully laid three on the tablecloth, asked her to fetch him a glass of water and took each pill with a high tilt of the head that showed the swallowing motion of his Adam's apple. He had nicked his throat shaving that morning.

Charlotte saw nothing of herself in the man.

He announced that he wanted ice cream. There was some in the freezer. He said the pills gave him cravings.

Charlotte got up and rummaged through the freezer trays, thinking how she would never look at a deep freeze in the same way again.

'Butterscotch or pistachio?'

He said pistachio, then changed his mind.

'There's one of those scoops in the drawer next to the sink.'

She put the ice cream in a bowl and gave it to him.

'Aren't you having any?' he asked as he carefully cut slivers from the side of his scoop with a spoon.

'I should have had pistachio,' he said, and fell to his own thoughts.

'Were I to weep I would weep for you,' he finally said.

Charlotte sensed he might crack but he composed himself as though he had said nothing.

'Have you had enough to eat?' he asked.

She didn't point out that he had just asked if she wasn't having any.

He returned to the ice cream and repeated that he should have had the green one, except he couldn't now remember its name.

'I always preferred sex with men,' he said, and then carried on as though still discussing something as mundane as an ice cream flavour.

'You know where you are with them. It was legal by then – I'm talking about the late 1960s – but not really, if you were a security risk. One married, as one did. For years I didn't stray. There were special pubs. I went sometimes, like a man who has given up smoking, buying a packet of cigarettes and not opening it. When I reverted it was as easy as falling off a log. I picked up a sailor. We agreed to meet in a hotel. He asked for money to pay for the room, which I stupidly gave him, so of course he never showed up. Others were more accommodating. I appreciated the generosity of such encounters. I was anyway used to and enjoyed work's clandestine assignments.'

'And my mother?'

'She could be cold.'

Twist the knife, Charlotte thought.

'Did she guess?'

'She said she hadn't when I told her. I was afraid of AIDS by then.'

Charlotte tried to picture him kissing her goodnight.

'Would you have behaved any differently given a second chance?'

'Probably not. I did a terrible thing telling her. She had nowhere to go with it. She should have left me. Instead it became a burden for both of us. She represented the lie I had chosen to live with but neither of us was able to break free of that.'

'So she became your hostage.'

'Oh, yes. And you never tell the whole truth, do you? Where's Dimitrios?'

'Gone to the shops.'

'He takes for ever. I suspect he goes cruising on the common for men.'

'But he looks after you.'

'I never told your mother about him, if we're talking about being partial with the truth.'

'You met when she was still alive?'

'Yes. I had renounced my other life for good, so I thought. I met him on a train and knew he was the one I wanted to spend the rest of my life with. I once saw him off to Athens from Heathrow, standing there with tears streaming down my face, and realised I was lost without him.'

It had never occurred to Charlotte before that her father was a dependent man.

'What's in it for him?' she asked bluntly.

'My money probably, such as it is. You'll get the house, which is worth more than whatever else I have. I've yet to make a will. He is considerate and decent, too attentive perhaps, and insecure.'

'Yet you stayed in the closet after my mother died.'

'Force of habit, I suppose. Besides, you've not exactly shared your life with me.'

'You never showed any sign of being interested.'

'Touché. A cold fish stumbling across feelings late in life is not a pretty sight. I'm probably only telling you now because the censoring mechanism which served me so well in a lifetime of secrecy has been fucked every which way by the medication I'm on.'

Charlotte stared at the tablecloth and asked, 'What did you do in Northern Ireland?'

Her father looked at her carefully and said, 'I plead memory loss.'

'I met a priest who said you were responsible for killing his brother.'

'Magee?'

'I knew him as Father Jerome. He said he knew you.'

'It was a small theatre.'

'In an ambush,' she said.

'You will have to ask Moffat about that.'

'I was wondering when we were going to get to Moffat. What exactly did you do there?'

'Deep interrogation, mostly. They later tried to claim

it was torture but the European Court of Human Rights would have none of that.'

'Did you know Captain Nairac? Father Jerome said you did.'

'Like I said, it wasn't a big theatre. '

' "Mostly", you said. Was there any operational work?'

'Some training as far as I recall.'

'Of Loyalist gangs?'

'You have to remember the IRA was a deadly enemy, with the advantage of home turf.'

'How undercover were you?'

'As deep as it got.'

'For instance?'

'Oh, you can find it written up in books. Pretty much all of it. I am tired now. Will you be staying for lunch?'

The Greek returned carrying shopping bags.

'Here's Dimitrios!' announced Charlotte's father unnecessarily.

The man's demonstrative show of concern, putting an arm around her father, sensing he was upset, left Charlotte uncomfortable. Her father blew his nose, laughed loudly and said, 'Bloody pills.'

Dimitrios sat down and gripped her father's hand. 'How have you been getting on?' he asked Charlotte.

'No one's run away from the table in tears. He's probably given no thought to the fact that it remains all about him.'

She said it to provoke her father, who laughed again and said, 'We're not so different after all.'

After that he sat silently content as Dimitrios went about preparing lunch. She could imagine them all endlessly discussing her father's situation. Dimitrios, able at last to exploit his companion's weakened state, and tired of being consigned to the shadows, would no doubt want the world to know about them. Charlotte sensed he had been just as corralled as her mother. She suspected her father was capable of almost feminine levels of intuition and advanced passive aggression that made Hopkins look like she was still in the paddling pool. She supposed Dimitrios had the upper hand now her father needed to be looked after. As for any broadcasting of their relationship, she suspected her father was a reluctant party and only the fear of being abandoned would override the instincts of a lifetime of secrecy.

She was impatient to be gone and leave them to it. It wasn't as if she understood what her father saw in the man. As her mother might once have said, he was nothing to write home about.

'About Moffat,' her father suddenly announced, 'come with me. I will show you something.'

He'd had a stairlift put in since Christmas, which he used with childish delight.

'Such a boon,' he said.

He took her into the spare third bedroom and started rummaging around in a tallboy, which was stacked with old filing boxes and plastic bags full of papers. He grew irritable when he couldn't find what he wanted. He sat down on the bed, fists clenched in frustration, and said, 'It's not important.'

'What are we looking for?'

'A photograph.'

'You don't have any,' she said. 'None that you've ever shown me.'

'Nevertheless.'

She searched on his behalf. The boxes were stuffed with old bank statements, receipts, tax returns and instruction manuals for appliances that had long been replaced. She came across the wank magazine her mother had mentioned, with black and white photographs of naked men in tumescent poses, printed on coarse paper and quaint enough almost to be funny. She showed it to her father, who sniggered and said, 'Needs must, sweetheart.'

She could see he was starting to enjoy himself. For him it was as simple as making her an accomplice. She doubted whether it would make their relationship any easier.

'Any secrets you wish to unburden?' he asked, almost skittish, adding, 'I suffer terrible mood swings.'

'My life is an open book.'

'Oh, I doubt that.'

In the next box she found the photograph among a pile of letters, which she realised must be from the Greek. 'My darling man,' started one, and she averted her eyes.

The photograph was only half a photograph as it had been torn down the middle. Its faded colours told her it was probably older than her. It showed a young tough, with long blond hair, leaning against the bonnet of a car. He was wearing faded jeans, a tie-dye T-shirt and a zip-up blouson.

She handed her father the photograph and asked if that was the one.

He looked at it for a long time and said, 'I haven't seen this in years. The car was a Cortina with a souped-up engine. Do you recognise the man?'

He gave her back the photograph and she said, 'He looks like he belongs in a bad 1970s pop band.'

'We all did.'

'Is this Moffat?' she asked, in astonishment.

'We were undercover.'

'We?'

'I'm the other half of the photograph. Moffat has that, though he probably chucked it years ago.'

'Belfast?'

'Belfast.'

'When?'

'Nineteen seventy-one. We were barely out of our teens.'

Charlotte sat down next to her father, wondering what he had looked like then. Connecting the man in the photograph to Moffat as he was now required a huge leap of imagination. She supposed the same went for her father.

'It doesn't even look like the same person.'

'In a way it isn't. Moffat was a hard boy from the Black Country, raised in Dudley – he pronounced it "Dud-loy" – not so far from here. Rough and ready.'

'And you?'

'Posh but still hard. Moffat wanted to move up the ladder. I gave him lessons in received pronunciation while we were on stake-outs. A very willing learner.'

'And in return?'

'He gave me his rather magnificent body. I said it went with the territory if he wanted to make out he had been to public school.'

Fuck me, thought Charlotte, I should have seen that coming, as she said, 'So the man is a complete invention.'

'Totally. Made a very good job of becoming an officer and a gent. Flawless. He had served in Kenya before Ireland so knew enough to pretend he'd been brought up there when it was still a colony. If pressed, he claimed he'd gone to a Nairobi boarding school, which more or less passed muster as it was modelled on the public-school system.'

'So he was your amuse-bouche?'

'Or trifle. Educating the man proved an interesting diversion from the work. He was never particularly grateful, probably because he knew I still considered him an oik. Later on, he went out of his way to shaft me, telling an investigating commission that his dirty ops were run by me. They weren't but mud stuck. By then ops were a nightmare of under-the-table lethal initiatives hampered by official investigation, unlike in the early days, when that photograph was taken. Belfast was the Wild West then, utterly lawless.'

'Were you shoot to kill?'

'That's what Moffat went on to.'

'How did that work?'

'He liaised between the army and the Belfast police, running undercover operations that identified targets. It was never authorised but there were a lot of blind eyes, all the way to Westminster.'

'And when that photograph was taken?'

'It wasn't called shoot to kill then but it amounted to that.'

'You mean you were killers.'

'We posed as Protestant paramilitaries and shot innocent Catholics.'

'Why?'

'To stoke up conflict so they would take the war to each other – divide and rule.'

After what she had experienced in the past weeks it sounded very much like business as usual. She was growing cynical.

Her father said in a matter-of-fact way, 'Ulster was a colonial war and we used counter-insurgency tactics learned in Kenya and Malaya.'

So that was it. In that respect, her father was the author of Moffat, who in turn was indirectly responsible for everything that had happened to her. She wondered if the man had deliberately chosen to use her in an extension of the grudge held against her father.

'Where does he live?'

'Near Carshalton, or used to. He'll be in the address book

downstairs. We were polite enough to send Christmas cards until a few years ago.'

Dimitrios called up to say lunch was ready. Charlotte couldn't face it. She pocketed the photograph when her father wasn't looking. Downstairs while he was in the kitchen she looked in the address book, which was kept on the telephone table under the stairs. Moffat was listed with a dozen or so others beginning with M.

She went and told her father she couldn't stay after all. He seemed relieved. Everything reverted to as before. Their goodbye was as awkward as ever. It occurred to her that none of what had been discussed would ever be referred to again. The only slight change was when he announced, 'Come and see us again soon.' No mention of the fact that it might be only weeks before he was gone.

Dimitrios insisted on coming outside when she left, clearly wanting a moment to establish himself. He said he was sorry she had to go but quite understood.

'He is looking for redemption, you know.'

She wondered if Dimitrios was religious, while thinking that no other remark could have irritated her more.

'Wish him luck with that,' she said. 'He'll find there is no such thing.'

23

Charlotte arrived in Carshalton as the afternoon was starting to fade. She had tried to picture Moffat's house and got it wrong. She found a small jewel of Queen Anne architecture, outside town in the countryside, with extensive grounds, a high wall and a sweeping drive. She stopped outside thinking the satnav must have made a mistake. She wondered what had paid for such a pile; not a government salary.

A loud bang from over the wall startled her – a gunshot, followed by a second. Cross's handgun was in her anorak. She checked it, thinking better to be safe. There was a third shot. Perhaps the man was shooting crows. She was wrong about that too. As she drove up she saw Moffat standing on grass the size of a football pitch, using a clay pigeon trap. He wore a flat cap, had ear mufflers on, and was dressed in top-of-the-range country wear. He noted her arrival, released another clay pigeon, lazily traced its rising arc and blew it to smithereens. He broke the shotgun and strolled over as though he was doing nothing more unusual than a spot of gardening.

'I was wondering when you would come.' He sounded friendly. 'Do you shoot?'

She said she didn't.

'Give it a go,' he said. 'Never too late to start. It's fun.'

He made it sound like anything but.

She shrugged. 'What do I do?'

'Point and fire ahead of the target. Hold the stock tight to your shoulder to reduce the kick.'

He stood behind and made her do some practice moves.

'Got it?' he asked, and released the trap.

The clay disc came out so fast that she didn't even start to trace its rise. It sped away without her firing. The second she missed, and staggered from the recoil. The next she missed too. Moffat lost interest.

'It's getting dark anyway.'

She handed back the gun. Close to, she saw how pallid and tense he was, and how thrown by her arrival.

He recovered quickly, the mask back in place. 'Come and have some tea. There are crumpets, I think. I like mine with peanut butter. Rather infra dig but there you are.'

He led the way through a stone-flagged hall to an enormous range kitchen with a double Aga. He behaved as though her being there were perfectly normal, apart from reloading the shotgun on the way in. It now stood propped against the Aga while he made tea and toasted the crumpets.

He gestured at the surroundings and said, 'This was Mrs Moffat's money. I never had a bean.'

Thinking of their last meeting in London, Charlotte asked where he stayed in town.

'A shoebox in the Barbican.'

'I used to live there too.'

'Really? Such a small world, isn't it? Which house?'

'Shakespeare.'

'One of the towers. Much grander than me. I overlook Aldersgate.'

'Crumpet good?' he asked a little later.

She pulled an appreciative face. The shotgun was next to him, angled against his side of the table, all so casually done that it could have been a kitchen appliance. Meanwhile he retained the manners and appearance of a perfect host.

He persuaded her to try her second crumpet with peanut butter. Though she didn't particularly like peanut butter she went along with him.

'That's the girl. Lashings of butter first.'

It tasted better than she was expecting though she could hardly get it down, even though she hadn't eaten all day.

The whole set-up struck her as perfectly sinister: a combination of a madman's tea party and a Venus flytrap. Moffat would take his time; probably lonely and glad of an audience. Remembering Cross's warning that impatience was death she decided to stick to a skewed normality.

She said, 'I have nowhere to live at the moment.'

'How awful for you.'

'The boyfriend trouble I mentioned.' She looked around and asked, 'Where's the dog?'

Moffat pulled a sad face. 'Had to put her down. Cancer. On my own now.'

The dog hadn't looked sick when she'd last seen it. There was a strange delay to whatever Moffat said, like he was speaking on a bad line or she was a faulty receiver. Everything made superficial sense but what was really going on she couldn't say.

'Stay at my place in town if you want,' Moffat went on casually, 'until you find your feet. I can give you keys. I shan't be going up.'

He stood and reached for a set hanging on a hook on a Welsh dresser, telling her the address, while Charlotte calculated the distance between her and the shotgun. She was sure Moffat would end up using it.

He chucked the keys as though he'd known her for years. Charlotte caught them and put them on the table.

'I'll think about it,' she said, and then: 'I've just come from my father's.'

'Thought you might've.' Moffat looked cruel. 'Did he admit to being a copper-bottomed shit?'

Charlotte pretended to be amused.

'Not in so many words. He gave me a photograph.'

She got it out carefully and passed it over.

Moffat inspected his former self with what she saw was nostalgic affection.

'Look at that haircut! It was the summer of Rod Stewart. "Every Picture Tells a Story". I'll say.' He handed it back. 'Those were the days.'

'Do you have the other half?'

'Doubt it. Can have a rummage.'

He stood and took the shotgun almost as an afterthought.

She heard him moving around in the hall. He seemed to know exactly where to look because it took him less than a minute.

'There you go,' he said, resting the shotgun against his side of the table again.

'Blimey!' she said. The man who became her father had a Mexican bandit moustache, wild hair and cold, dead eyes.

She matched both parts of the photograph and thought: Two perfect killers.

Moffat gave her a flat stare as though he had read her mind.

'My father tells me you and he ran around at the start of the Troubles shooting people.'

'Shan't apologise. Rough and tumble. Classic counter-insurgency for dealing with fanatics.'

'How did you feel about doing it?'

She withered under his gaze.

'Spare me the "how did you feel" questions. This is not a television show.'

Remembering he was the host, he recovered his manners and assumed a conversational tone.

'We were professional young guns. We were trained. Your father was the protégé of a man who'd cut his teeth on what were known as low-intensity ops.'

That part her father had left out but she could see no reason to doubt it.

'Undercover and illegal but justified by the outcome.' He shrugged as though there were nothing more to it. 'The other bastard would do the same to you, given half a chance.'

'A policy recently reinstated, it seems,' Charlotte said.

That had his attention. Moffat assumed a wry expression. She gave him one in return that said she knew he was dying to tell.

'Made to look like it was part of a local drugs war.'

'I miss the dog,' he said. 'What do you know?'

'A lot of it. What I don't know is why.'

'Fair dos,' said Moffat, taking his time. 'The why of it presented me with a rather grown-up problem.'

He waited to be asked, which she politely did.

'Which was?'

'How to clean out the stables before reunification.'

'Reunification?'

'Back-channel negotiations between London and Dublin about a united Ireland. Been talk of it for years. The Yanks are broadly in favour too. The Ulster Protestants will squeal like hell but it would solve a big headache in Westminster – borders and all the rest. Then word came back that Dublin didn't want to inherit any loose ends and the problem was ours to solve.'

She thought: How obvious it all seems, spelled out.

'Did Dublin know you reinstated shoot to kill?'

Moffat stared at the ceiling.

'Um, they remained unaware, or turned a blind eye, whichever you prefer.'

'Was McCavity being shot anything to do with this?'

Moffat pondered that and eventually said, with the air of a man sharing, 'Well, there is the question of why shoot him, rather than some other politician, unless there was a good reason to. Not out of the question, I suppose, that he was the one holding secret talks with Dublin, while of course assuring the Protestant community of Northern Ireland that he was a hundred per cent behind preserving the Union.'

'And his reason for stabbing them in the back?'

'Realpolitik. Historical inevitability. Like East and West Germany. It's only a matter of time.'

It was obvious that Moffat's supposition was based on an exact knowledge of what had gone on and he was waiting for her to spot that.

'Might McCavity have discussed the matter with you, about Dublin not wanting to inherit any loose ends?'

'An interesting supposition. The man was of course a big fan of shoot to kill, said so at the time of the peace agreement, and was on record quite recently as saying the same. Shall we leave it at that?'

'But McCavity ended up getting shot.'

'It's a toss-up between the IRA learning he was behind unofficially reinstating shoot to kill and Protestant extremists finding out he was plotting to dump them into Dublin's lap. Either could be seen as enough to shoot the man.'

'But if the IRA was exposed as having shot McCavity it would blow any hope it had of reunification.'

'Quite so, but I can see someone in London thinking it

might be interesting to inform them about what McCavity was up to, to see what the reaction was.'

'Who might that someone be?'

'Let's say you're Hopkins, sitting in London and rather disappointed to learn from your intelligence that the shooting was now not supposed to go ahead after all, when it might be to your political advantage. Shooting a minister would loosen the purse strings like billy-oh.'

Moffat studied his nails, sat back and folded his arms. Charlotte could not decide whether the man was dangerously sane or completely mad or just lied for the sake of it. Perhaps he was like all the other men she'd recently encountered who were sick in the head. Even Parker wasn't altogether there.

Something was badly wrong and she knew she had to get out. She said she needed the bathroom. Moffat told her where it was, and like Father Jerome, said she might need to pull the chain more than once.

The lavatory was at the end of a short corridor. It had an old-fashioned cistern. Moffat was right. She had to pull the chain twice. She could smell the cordite on her hands as she washed them and thought: Walk out fast now. She checked Cross's gun, switched off the safety catch and put it in the right-hand pocket of her anorak where it was easily reachable.

To the right of the toilet was a large utility room, its door half-open. Charlotte looked in to see if there was an exit. There wasn't; only the remains of the dog lying on its side in a pool of blood, its head obliterated by the blast. Charlotte tasted vomit as she half ran, hurrying through the hall and out the front door.

'Ah, there you are,' Moffat said. 'Came out for a spot of fresh air.'

He was standing on the doorstep, smoking a cigarette, the shotgun under his arm.

'Are you all right? You look pale.'

'I just saw your dog.'

'Told you I had to put the old girl out of her misery. She would have felt nothing. The vet's miles away and they're not seeing anyone because of this fucking lockdown. Shall we go back in? Lots still to talk about.'

He stood on his cigarette and said, 'Filthy habit. I really must give up. After you.'

He waited for her to go first. They sat down as before, with the shotgun placed against the table.

In an effort to pretend everything was normal, Charlotte asked if she could take him up on his offer of the Barbican flat after all. 'Just for a few days.'

'As long as you like. Till you sort yourself out.'

She pocketed the keys, hoping they might act as a talisman.

Moffat picked up the shotgun, rested it across his knees and looked at her bleakly.

'I had decided to shoot myself. Out there in the garden. Three birds down and the fourth cartridge for myself. Then you showed up.'

'In that case I saved your life.'

'For the moment. Tea and a shotgun, the last companions of choice. And now you. I am enjoying our chat but it won't change anything.'

'Why shoot yourself?'

'Nothing else left.'

'We need to talk about Hopkins,' Charlotte said, hoping it might keep her alive a little longer. If Moffat was going to shoot himself then he would shoot her first. She cursed her timing. Five minutes later she would have found the man dead on his lawn.

Moffat was back to his tea-party manners, apparently still keen to share.

'There's a one-word answer to everything you are asking. What does politics come down to these days?'

'Choice, I suppose.'

Moffat waved his hand in dismissal.

'That's just stale icing on an even staler cake. There has been one major revolution in the past thirty-five years and I am not talking about technology.'

Charlotte said she didn't know what that was.

'Money! Ask any question and the answer comes back the same – money.'

'How was the recent shoot-to-kill programme about money?'

'Slush funds are not what they once were.'

'Meaning?'

'The job had to be done off the books and out of the office, which is why I had to use Roberts, who also has a Russian wife who's loaded – more money – which is what made him appealing to Hopkins. I don't know if you are aware that within the so-called intelligence community pockets operate to their own mandate, unaccountable, and almost indistinguishable from the real thing.'

'I wasn't, but why hasn't anyone exposed them?'

'Money. They are the future. The old firms will remain in name but reformed out of existence with more and more put to tender. Not even that. It will go to mates. They've been doing it to the NHS for years while pretending they're not. The security services are no different.'

Moffat's argument was one of those surprises that was no surprise when you thought about it.

'Plenty of proposed operations aren't sanctioned – cuts being the usual excuse, so it's a lottery.'

Again logical, she thought.

'The money trees come from private finance,' he continued, 'hedge funds mostly. Hopkins runs around with her collection plate, goes to the right donation dinners with the top people, and is using that to set up a private intelligence freak show, operating in the shadow of MI5, on a nod and a wink.'

Charlotte decided she very much wanted to live and use this against Hopkins.

'Really?'

'Of course. The intelligence services are a busted flush. A privatised form is more flexible.'

Like everywhere else, she thought.

'No one likes experts now and Hopkins is not expert at anything other than selling her own ambition.'

'What was Roberts doing for Hopkins?'

'Organising the money. Talking to Dubai.'

'Are you honestly trying to tell me Roberts was buying into the drugs business?'

She couldn't believe what she was asking.

'Even at the height of the Troubles there were plenty of business opportunities for the long money. Roberts and Hopkins just took it a step further.'

'Did Roberts have that in mind from the beginning?' she asked, astonished even so.

'Worked it out as he went along, I expect. It's not such a leap. Drugs is where the money is. The CIA was up to its eyeballs in the stuff in Vietnam.'

'And I am supposed to believe that Roberts was fronting for hedge funders wanting to invest in a cut of the Dubai operation?'

'They're Gatsby men. What to do with all that fucking money? It's a carousel. They like to see themselves as romantic anti-establishment bandits while buying into the establishment.'

Not unlike yourself, Charlotte thought.

'You said the recent Belfast shootings were paid for off the books.'

'Yes, and there I was naive. "Who's paying?" was Roberts's first question. It wasn't the kind of thing I could go to the firm for. Roberts came back with a budget. Far more than I could lay my hands on. Where was I going to get that kind of dosh?'

'Why only nine shootings, not including the farm?'

'Based on past experience they would achieve the first stage of tier removal. The Protestants were the more important target, seeing how they would fight any suggestion of uniting Ireland. By keeping it even, the plan was that they took the fight to each other.'

'Who paid?' she asked, suspecting she knew the answer.

'Dubai. That's what I mean about being naive.'

'So it's a sell-out.'

'More than that. Hopkins chooses not to see how her private investors shape operations, hence any lack of interest in the Russians because of the amount of their money involved.'

'In other words, Hopkins is not fussy about where the money comes from.'

'No such thing as clean money, dear heart.'

'Then you're talking about the privatisation of power.'

'Got it in one. It's the new Holy Grail. The Yanks have been doing it for years.'

'Who knows about this?'

'Not really the right question. Her Majesty's Government has condoned tax evasion, money laundering and illegal arms dealing for longer than you have been alive. In any realistic world it is only a matter of time before it moves into the drugs market. What the hell else is going to pay for anything, given the mess we're in?'

'Is that it? Really?'

'Everything gentrifies in the end. Look at me. I suppose your father told you.'

'He mentioned Dudley.'

Moffat shrugged. 'I married money. Your father said make sure to do that, though he never did. I think he wanted someone who wouldn't see him for what he was. Had he been born in Chile he probably would have ended up running Pinochet's secret police; not to disparage Chile. The point is we have reached a state where speculative and dirty money are interchangeable, the better to control the puppet show that passes for politics these days.'

She thought back to their first meeting and asked, 'Did you know I was going to be there on New Year's Day?'

'Not until I signed in downstairs and saw your name and wondered. I was curious to know if you were his daughter. Perhaps I took it for a sign.'

'Of what?'

'That our paths were meant to cross,' he said vaguely.

'That you could use me, in other words.'

'Let's say that you could unwittingly help me. Admittedly, I was able to point you in the wrong direction as it became obvious I needed to get the story rewritten in its Muslim version.'

'Have you got away with that?'

He looked at her as though he didn't understand.

'Everyone gets away with it now,' she said. 'No one is accountable except for a few mugs. And if you say it comes down to dirty washing and laundry, did you come out clean?'

He gave her a tragic look.

'Everything I aspired to was dirty from the start. There you have it, the sentimental tragedy of the perpetrator.'

He picked up the shotgun, broke the barrel to check it was loaded and rested it on the table, pointing at her.

'One for you and one for me. You won't feel a thing.'

'Are you serious?' She couldn't think of anything else to say.

She leaned back and put her hands in her pockets, trying to behave as though they might be indulging in a grim joke before Moffat came to his senses.

'You are just upset about the dog,' she said. 'You said yourself you miss her.'

'True, but I can't let you go either or I would probably dither. I never invited you. If I do you first then I have no choice.'

'Always time to change your mind. We're talking now.'

'Clock's ticking. It's the only way out. I've pulled a trigger enough times in my life, twice more won't make any difference. Nothing personal regarding you, but it would destroy your father.'

'Why would you want to do that?'

'A matter of manners.'

'Excuse me? Isn't it a bit late for that?'

'Manners matter, above all. Manners disguise hostility, intent, duplicity, the naked ape. Your father was an expert at what one might call the moment of sloth before the insult, the languid pause of a man in control of his game. I was on the receiving end of that many times, which was his way of saying I would never be as good as he was because his was the natural manner of privilege and could not be taught.'

'You could have fooled me.'

'Be that as it may. I didn't fool myself and now the time has come to stop pretending.'

As Moffat swung the shotgun at her Charlotte fired through the pocket of her jacket, hoping he was close enough not to miss. The crack of the pistol filled the room. Moffat fell backwards, taking the chair down with him, firing as he did, missing Charlotte and blasting the ceiling.

Moffat lay doubled up on the floor, clutching his shattered knee, screeching and cursing her.

Charlotte stood up and walked out fast on unsteady legs before he tried to reach for the gun again.

As she got in the car she heard a single report: Moffat's last shot.

24

Moffat's Barbican flat was, as he had said, a shoebox, with little furniture other than a sofa bed, and felt like it hadn't been stayed in for some time. Charlotte had abandoned the RAF Police Land Rover at Carshalton station and taken the train, knowing what she needed to do.

She talked it through on the phone with her father, with whom things remained as difficult as ever. She said she'd heard Moffat had shot himself – rather than that she'd heard the shot in question – and left it at that. It was her father who suggested she take everything Moffat blamed on Hopkins, throw it back on Moffat and present that as her summary of the Belfast operation.

'That way, if the woman is not a complete idiot when it comes to reading between the lines, she will know you know.'

Charlotte put it down very fast, like she was laying cards.

From what she had, she figured Hopkins – being a true-blue flyer of the Union flag – had instigated the plot against McCavity, mainly for her own self-advancement. Reckless, ambitious, clever but clueless, she pushed ahead with it, despite her uncertain grasp of history. It was her bright idea to frame the IRA – not a huge stretch with Roberts already running the operation to bring down Father Jerome in a drugs sting.

Charlotte thought it not beyond Hopkins to have planted the original intel flag, with its assassination alert, as a way of hiding in plain sight.

Cross saying he had been sent by Father Jerome on a London scouting trip would have been part of a frame, probably on Roberts's orders. Cross hadn't admitted as much to her at the time; it was pretty obvious Cross bent the truth as it suited him. A trait they all shared was that the lot of them were congenital liars.

Roberts, see-sawing between Hopkins and Moffat – hedging his bets between old and new school – probably told Moffat about the madness of Hopkins's plot, because of the lack of any proper political motive. Moffat no doubt had concurred with Father Jerome that a stop needed to be put to the whole fiasco. But Hopkins told Roberts to go ahead after persuading him that the shooting would advance their careers and, in terms of patriotic duty, the United Kingdom would be preserved.

Cross had shot McCavity because he was vain enough for the challenge, and he didn't see the job in terms of any moral complications. In the whole busted flush, Cross remained the fucked-up wild card, constantly shifting position, trying to negotiate from one tight corner to the next until he found himself so turned around that he wasn't sure whose agent he was. With all the double-dealing, shooting a politician was probably almost a relief.

When Charlotte was ready she called Hopkins, who sounded wary and aggressive, starting with, 'If we were in the office I would have you escorted from the building.'

Charlotte snapped, 'Oh, for fuck's sake, grow up.'

It was the first time she had bitten back and Hopkins didn't like that, but the woman became eager enough when Charlotte said she had something for her to read before she shared it with anyone else.

They met at the bandstand in Arnold Circus, a

thirty-minute walk from the Barbican. It was raining, so Charlotte didn't look too stupid in the wet-weather gear Cross had provided her with. Shops were closed, streets empty. Her stuff was still at Clive's but she'd had no inclination to contact him, and settled for looking as though she had just stumbled off a moor.

Hopkins turned up as smart as ever, carrying an outsize umbrella advertising Ascot races. They kept their social distance.

'I like your hair,' Hopkins said cattily. Charlotte resisted saying that Hopkins's roots were showing.

'Read this. I'll wait. It's handwritten. There's nowhere to get anything printed.' The paper was courtesy of Moffat. 'It's all quite legible.'

She couldn't remember the last time she had written by hand at such length. Hopkins propped herself against the railings while she read and Charlotte paced.

In the document Hopkins was reading her name appeared nowhere. Charlotte had done as her father had suggested and blamed the entire operation on Moffat and Roberts. Lafferty running around Belfast carrying out political assassinations was Moffat's reprise of a decades-old practice, of which he had been one of the instigators in what had been a very dirty war. Hedge funders investing in drugs cartels and the private financing of the intelligence services, Charlotte similarly blamed on Roberts and Moffat.

She could see Hopkins nodding occasionally in vigorous agreement as she read.

'The privatisation of power,' Hopkins said after finishing. 'Moffat is right. The intelligence services are short-funded and myopic. He just went about it in the wrong way.'

Hopkins handed back the pages.

'You did very well. We girls should stick together.'

Charlotte cringed.

'There's a very different version of the text with a solicitor,' she said, thinking there was a pleasing symmetry to revenge. The whole affair had started with her text being doctored.

Charlotte held Hopkins's eye, watching her calculate.

Hopkins said, 'Yes, I expect there would be.' She considered before saying, 'Come in with us. I am sure we can find you something. There are interesting spheres of influence developing – active think tanks and public relations dedicated to investing in the future, while the politicians stumble on. In the meantime, you deserve a break. Three weeks on full pay?'

Charlotte said, 'Sure,' thinking how her father had told her to keep her enemies close.

Hopkins said, 'We can't shake hands on it given current regs. Let me know if you want to be part of the new team. In your own time.'

Charlotte watched her walk away.

People got sick again and a lot died, again. Everyone had said things would never be the same after the last time but they had soon fallen back into their old ways, not bothering to pick up their dog's shit and buying stuff they didn't need.

Charlotte told herself it was over, not expecting to find herself gripped by the surreality of more lockdown, which turned the events of the past weeks into a dream within a dream. The shooting had been long forgotten with the current calamities.

McCavity's stepdaughter posted a tweet saying how much she missed weed during lockdown and she had inadvertently called her dealer 'Daddy'. Charlotte didn't laugh much now but she did at that.

She had always supposed so-called life-changing events led to reassessment, resolution and becoming a better person. They didn't. She now saw everything for what it was. None of it was worth saving and the meek stood no chance of inheriting the earth. Moffat was right. England was up for sale.

She found herself thinking about the poisoning of the Skripals back in 2018, and decided it had less to do with the long arm of Russian revenge than to show what a shitty place Salisbury was, in itself and as the price of freedom. Life came down to a crappy newish build in a cul-de-sac, a public car park, a pub, a Zizzi's restaurant and a park bench.

Of her father's secret life, had he been her age she supposed he would have come out, rather than going round the houses by getting married and having a family, which had produced her, for which she was not sure whether she was grateful.

On bad days she blamed her father for having involved her in events she had been forced to live through because of her accidental connection to their historical perpetrators. She decided that because of them she was neither likeable nor lovable. There was nothing self-pitying about the observation. People weren't lovable except in a commercial sense and the assumption of parental love was just as much of a hoax as religion.

She doubted whether she would be investing much in the future. At the same time she knew she was ripe for a Damascene conversion.

25

After finding himself abandoned by Charlotte on the motorway Parker had hitched a ride with a Tesco container lorry, thinking: Every fucking little helps. He reported sick. He gave up working.

The online accounts that had run with the Charlotte and Cross smear had been suspended, the content no longer available. A few intrepid journalists were still trying to run with the story: McCavity was now said to have been shot by an ex-Mossad agent; on whose behalf no one could decide. The usual suspects were exhumed, including the Russians and Muslim extremists. In all of this no one connected the shooting to the murder of an Irish priest.

Parker's isolated summer spared him the usual embarrassments of social encounters. He tried not to think of Charlotte but was reminded while reading a Scandinavian thriller with a carefully placed female character – an associate, pal and lover-in-waiting to the hard-drinking macho detective, celibate because of the scarred pain of an earlier book Parker had not read. The woman duly offered what he had previously seen described – by another bestselling author who should have known better – as her 'sweet love juices'.

Parker got an email from a company he had never heard of. Its website, still under construction, talked of investing in a sustainable future. The email said he had come to their attention and they wanted a Zoom meeting. Parker binned it.

Next he got an email from a company calling itself Block Investment, named after the fabulously rich American hedge funder who ran it. The little information available on Block was carefully worked over by PR speak to render it meaningless. Block was barely thirty, had a lot of charitable foundations, and made statements about 'responsible money' in terms of a sustainable future.

This time he wrote back, curious why anyone like Block would be bothered with him.

Next he received an invitation, all expenses paid, to Scotland to what was called an alpaca party, whatever that was. He found one site that referred to Block's Scottish farm dedicated to the production of alpaca wool. Parker looked it up. The 'farm' was an estate the size of a private school.

It was preferred that guests didn't fly, so a night sleeper to Edinburgh was offered, first class. Parker thought: What the hell. He accepted.

The Caledonian Sleeper departed from Euston just before midnight. Parker had taken to wearing a mask outdoors, for the simple reason that with his hat and dark glasses, it allowed him to pass for almost normal. People stared but not in the same way.

He was met at Waverley Station by a bullet-headed man holding a card with his name. They drove in silence in a black Tesla. He stared at the picturesque landscape on a perfect summer's day. The driver switched on the sound system: Bob Dylan singing 'Highlands'; as in the man's heart was in the Highlands, gentle and fair. Someone must be joking, Parker thought.

He dozed and woke to the sight of a large flock of what he thought were mutant sheep before he realised where he was. The estate's drive went on and on, until in the distance stood a huge house whose crenellations and towers suggested a fortified mansion. A whole field had been set aside for private vehicles, including helicopters. The world seemed to have switched channels. He saw marquees. He saw bouncy castles. He saw knickerbockered kids, casually dressed adults and uniformed waiters. The event more resembled a sports day. Egg-and-spoon races for the mums. Sack races for the kids. Tug of war for the dads. Pony rides. There was mixed-doubles tennis. It was rumoured that the prime minister might be putting in an informal appearance as he was holidaying in Scotland.

Easy-limbed white wives ambulated around the lawns and their even whiter rubber-jointed children scampered on climbing frames. Tarquin and Rufus and Otis and Lottie and Katrina and Daisy. Charlie was going to the Dragon.

For all their money, their world appeared even more inflexible than the one in which Parker had grown up. What he hadn't realised until then was that money brought its own insecurity. Despite the recreational mood, the atmosphere was intensely competitive. He suspected that, while their billions bought any amount of protection, fortunes still ended up being calculated in terms of insecurity, and what stood to be lost.

Richness at this level didn't have to show off, apart from wristwatches whose collective value could have paid off most national debts. The men had deceptively casual names. There was an Ollie and a Roly. No one talked politics. Parker gathered that their murmured conversations operated beyond that.

A gong was banged and a shout went up. Roasting hogs had been turning on barbecues for hours. A Scottish bagpiper played them in as they queued.

After lunch everyone stopped to watch a helicopter land and they applauded as the prime minister got out, gave a cheery wave and disappeared into the house surrounded by security men.

Later, when Parker went looking for the bathroom, he was stopped by two secret service men. The reason became clear when the prime minister emerged looking like he'd had a few. He gave Parker a shifty smirk and said, 'Good mask.' Parker wondered if the man knew anything of what had gone on in Belfast.

The helicopter disappeared back into the skies. Disappointment was expressed because he had not played in the promised charity tennis match.

Parker decided that the sour moral of the tale was that social betterment made for nastier people. Their common interests were as reliable as compass points, apart from a few artists looking for commissions, who were obvious by their shameless importuning.

Parker saw that the lack of curiosity about anything other than themselves was dedication rather than ignorance. They'd had lessons. They played well enough to be seen to be playing well. The men were educated to the highest levels. They collected. They talked fluently about areas of expertise.

The house contained an impressive library of modern first editions, no doubt bought on Block's behalf, Parker thought. But Block turned out to know what he was talking about when he found Parker in the library studying the titles.

Because Block was wearing a kilt, it took Parker a moment to recognise him from the photographs he had seen. The hair was much longer too, down to his shoulders.

He struck up a friendly conversation without introducing

himself or reacting to Parker's skin. He didn't ask who he was. No mention was made of any meeting and Parker supposed he would be approached in due course by one of the man's people. A classy act.

Block said unlike most collectors he read the books he had, though not the copies on display. After putting on white gloves, he took from the glass-covered shelves an English first edition of *A Handful of Dust*.

'Published by Chapman and Hall in 1934 and, see here, signed by Waugh. A very literate signature, don't you think?'

He said if Parker put on gloves he would let him hold it too. There was a drawer full of them. Parker tried to look reverential as he held the book.

He knew he shouldn't but he asked how much. Block said he wouldn't normally tell, then confidentially, 'Twenty-five thousand. Oh, I know! But worth it.'

Block made a point of being polite. Parker thought sourly: It's called manners. He supposed the kilt was about Scottish ancestry. He had no doubt that this pleasant young American was as ruthless in business as the rest of the basking pack. It wasn't just that they had been taught to be nice, they could afford to be nice. If they wanted to shaft you they took you behind the arras.

Everyone had politely ignored Parker's appearance. None blanched, not even the children. As such he considered himself weirdly accepted; again it was called manners. ('Don't stare at that strange man. It's rude.')

He spoke to a tall young grandee named Hugo, who looked like a Velasquez, and whose arrival had caused a flurry because he had once been a star in an upmarket reality show. He introduced himself. Parker complimented him on his shirt, which had pictures of a stoned-looking Bob Marley. Hugo said it was a Wacko Maria, bought in a sale as he wouldn't dream of paying four hundred quid for it. Everyone asked him: 'Where's Spencer?'

Parker was asked what he thought of the party. A bit Buñuel, he replied, wondering if Hugo would pick up the reference.

Of course he did.

'The one where the guests find they can't leave?'

Parker said, 'I was thinking more of *The Discreet Charm of the Bourgeoisie*.'

He could not remember the name of the show Hugo had been in. It had featured rich kids more or less playing themselves. The whole party had a similar air of being not quite real. Time to get out.

As he moved through the crowd, he was jostled by a beaming oaf with Dennis the Menace hair who apologised profusely, smiled sheepishly showing excellent teeth and said charmingly, 'I expect I'm late and a bit drunk. Spencer.'

Parker recognised him as another posh boy from the same show as Hugo. Spencer was the cad with good manners. That was years ago. Parker wondered what he did now. He couldn't decide whether someone like that would show up as an amusement to be indulged or because the amiable oaf had a keener brain than he let on and was there on his own terms.

Parker moved on, incapable now of leaving. A woman was walking towards him out of the sun.

'Hello, you masked man,' Charlotte said. 'What brings you?'

She looked relaxed, as though they were old acquaintances running into each other. It made sense now. The invitation had been from her.

'I could ask the same.'

He knew he was blushing. She was thinner. Her hair, still short, looked expensively cut. Her clothes appeared expensive too, without saying so. He found it difficult to connect her to the woman he had last seen in wet-weather gear in a motorway service station.

'You look great,' he said.

She asked why he was wearing gloves. He hadn't known he was. He still had on the ones he'd put on in the library.

'I was just leaving,' he said.

'Talk to me before you do.'

Parker had no answer to that.

'My father said if you can't beat them, join them.'

'To what end?'

'The future.'

'What future?'

'Batteries. Water.'

'Batteries!?'

She sounded serious.

'There are still all sorts of battery problems, especially for cars: weight, expense, the time they take to charge, how long they last. Top mileage for an electric car is still nothing like enough.'

Parker couldn't believe they were having this conversation.

'What's the answer?' he asked, bewildered.

'Cobalt.'

He gave up and said, 'I was approached by the American who owns this place. I'm still waiting to find out why.'

'You have to admit it is very beautiful here. They call it the Ark.'

She was starting to sound like she was part of a cult. She even had that look of dumb certainty.

'L. Ron Hubbard declared Scotland the promised land,' Parker volunteered.

'The scientologist?'

'Go on about the cobalt.'

She couldn't decide if he was pretending to be polite when he was in fact being rude.

'Since you asked,' she began, sounding defensive, 'it's a main ingredient of batteries. Cobalt was mined here in the eighteenth century. Britain is one of the largest consumers of cobalt due to aero-engine manufacture, although its exact usage is unclear due to commercial confidentially.'

Parker said, 'All I know is, if you coat a nuclear weapon with cobalt, it leaves radioactive fallout for years.'

Charlotte laughed uncertainly.

'Anyway, several large deposits have been recently been found in the Highlands,' she said.

'Are you really working for them?'

'Let's say I've seen the light.'

'I'm still stumbling in the dark.'

'It's called investing in the future.'

'Did you seriously think I would be interested?'

'I'm sorry, I'm not doing this very well. It was me that invited you. I didn't think for a minute you would come.'

Parker looked at her.

'I asked because I need you.'

'I have no place here.'

They had walked some distance from the house. They stopped and looked back.

Charlotte said, 'Remember Belfast?'

'I can hardly not.'

'Northern Ireland's fate is of no consequence. It has been examined and rejected. In that respect we weren't even a sideshow. They've written it off. They see Scotland as the future.'

'Who's "they" in this instance? That lot?' Parker pointed at the assembled gathering. 'And you're buying into it?'

'Scotland must be kept.'

Parker couldn't make her out. They walked on in silence, back to the old issue of mutual suspicion.

Charlotte eventually said, 'My father also said that if you can't beat them, join them to beat them from the inside.'

She added that she still worked for Hopkins.

'Not like you think.'

She explained about her doctored report that didn't expose Hopkins.

'Why didn't you name her?' Parker asked.

'I had no one else I could go to. I had no real evidence against her. I was compromised as it was and needed the bloody woman's protection.'

She looked back at the party and said, 'Father Jerome told me about a book by a Scottish writer where they all turn out to be dead. He couldn't recollect the title. It was *The Hothouse by the East River*. Not dead exactly – though they are – more so cushioned that they aren't alive, making them incapable of seeing beyond themselves.' She laughed and said, 'The book goes on a lot about central heating.'

'And now it's batteries,' said Parker, wondering if she still had a sense of humour.

It seemed she did when she said, 'I still owe you for the cheese sandwich you were going to buy me when I so unceremoniously dumped you.'

'Don't worry, I ate it.'

He decided he was pleased to see her after all. He pointed to the party and asked her to tell him what he was looking at. He had his own ideas but he wanted to know her version. He still couldn't tell if she thought she had made a mistake bringing him there.

'Money wants to buy into class and class wants to buy into money. Scotland is their ark.'

'The weather's not great.'

'But temperate and plenty of water. There's talk already of water wars.'

'What's this got to do with Hopkins?'

'Hopkins is their lap dog. Their vision is to create their own sustainable paradise. They take climate change seriously, as the next big investment. The rest is there for the taking. But they are paranoid about their own security. They want a say in how the intelligence services operate because they consider themselves international hitters. Hopkins concurs, so the intelligence agencies are being reconfigured to provide a bespoke service.'

'What's the alternative?' Parker asked.

'I am on the inside now. We can work against them, like before.'

He admired her resolution. He didn't know if he believed her. He was curious, but not *that* curious to expose himself to the infections of the rich. He had spent his life sitting on his own and not mixing. Perhaps he and Charlotte were in the process of crossing over to the other side, like the characters in the book she had mentioned, cushioned in the anaesthetised world in which they now found themselves. Resistance was impossible, really. They would end up being bought off, like Hopkins and all the rest. No one ever won against money.

He looked at his hands, took off the gloves and gestured towards the crowd.

'They'll be ring-fenced,' he said.

'All the more reason.'

Parker couldn't tell how desperate she really was but he

laughed for the first time in as long as he could remember and said, 'Why not?'

They walked slowly back to the house.

'There'll be fireworks later,' Charlotte said.

About the Author

Chris Petit has written a trio of 'beyond black' political thrillers covering a serial killer operating in sectarian Northern Ireland (*The Psalm Killer*); dirty money in the Second World War (*The Human Pool*); and terror, arms trading and the bombing of a civilian aircraft (*The Passenger*); as well as *The Butchers of Berlin*, *Pale Horse Riding* and *Mister Wolf*, which feature the characters Schlegel and Morgen. He is an internationally renowned filmmaker.

Mister WOLF

July 1944.

Führer Adolf Hitler miraculously survives an assassination attempt. Or does he?

What is Party Secretary Bormann hiding about that day? Why was Goebbels auditioning actors to play the Führer on the very morning of the bomb plot? And what has sparked Gestapo head Mueller's sudden interest in a decades-old scandal?

When August Schlegel, a backsliding employee of the Gestapo, starts asking questions, he finds himself caught up in a web of deadly political intrigue in which the fate of his long-lost father is inextricably linked with that of a shapeshifting Führer: the man secretly known as Herr Wolf.

'Treads the line between fact and fiction with immense aplomb'
Daily Mail

'The best of all worlds: action and art working together as one'
The Spectator

SIMON &
SCHUSTER

THE BUTCHERS OF BERLIN

Berlin 1943.

August Schlegel lives in a world full of questions with no easy answers. Why is he being called out on a homicide case when he works in financial crimes? Why did the old Jewish soldier with an Iron Cross shoot the block warden in the eye then put a bullet through his own head? Why does Schlegel persist with the case when no one cares because the Jews are all being shipped out anyway? And why should Morgen, wearing the dreaded black uniform of the SS, turn up and say he has been assigned to work with him?

'Powerful evocation of a city living in terror'
Sunday Times Crime Club

'Ambitious, darkly atmospheric'
The Times

SIMON &
SCHUSTER